THE STORYMAN

THE STORYMAN

BRYAN MACMAHON

POOLBEG

Published in 1994 by
Poolbeg Press Ltd,
Knocksedan House,
123 Baldoyle Industrial Estate,
Dublin 13, Ireland

A catalogue record for this book is available from the British Library

ISBN 1 85371 454 2

Cover design by Poolbeg Group Services Ltd
Set by Poolbeg Group Services Ltd in Garamond 10.5/14.5
Printed by Colour Books Ltd, Baldoyle Industrial Estate, Baldoyle, Dublin 13

The Publishers gratefully acknowledge the support of

The Arts Council / An Chomhairle Ealaíon.

A NOTE ON THE AUTHOR

Bryan MacMahon is one of Ireland's most distinguished writers. He has written novels, plays, ballads and collections of short stories. His best-selling autobiography *The Master* was published in 1992, and he won the 1993 American Ireland Fund Literary Award.

ALSO BY BRYAN MACMAHON

Short stories:

The Lion Tamer
The Red Petticoat
The End of the World
The Sound of Hooves
The Tallystick

Novels:

Children of the Rainbow
The Honey Spike

Autobiography:

The Master

Travel:

Here's Ireland

For children:

Jack O'Moora and the King of Ireland's Son
Patsy-O
Mascot Patsy-O
Brendan of Ireland

In translation from the Irish:

Peig – the autobiography of Peig Sayers of the Great Blasket Island

PRAISE FOR BRYAN MACMAHON

"The Sound of Hooves" – Bryan MacMahon is manipulating the craft of storytelling in surprising and risk-taking ways: fantasy, rage, humour, all have their place. It makes for exhilarating reading."

Irish Press

"MacMahon strikes a blow for all who choose to live apart from the Modern Machine."

Sunday Telegraph

"The joy of living runs through his stories like a shout in the blood."

Time

"A collection that is cause for celebration."

The Irish Times

"Definitely recommended."

Books and Bookmen

"A radiant celebration of sex, I find it at the least as convincing as DH Lawrence. From beginning to end, the book grips, thrills and fascinates. It is a crowning achievement."

Sunday Independent

"Traditionally Irish excellence you could call it."

Guardian

"Bryan MacMahon has a skilful mastery of atmosphere and a rich store of imagery."

New Statesman

"There is not one story in the collection that I did not admire and enjoy."

Spectator

"Language is a large supple animal tamed to MacMahon's disposal . . . always lending full support to the conveyance and rarely if ever distracting attention to itself.

The lasting impression is one of memorable and vivid images of human situations carefully presented."

Irish Independent

"Here is a writer who possesses the sensitivity of a poet and the rich, hearty humour of a peasant, a compassion for his fellowmen plus a rollicking remembrance of things past, a dramatist's understanding of conflict, a knowledge of the human heart, and a style as economical and exact as a theorem in geometry."

New York Herald Tribune

"You have done something that very few other writers of fiction have done – AE Coppard? Occasionally VS Pritchett? Alain-Fournier? – You have written short stories based on common life in the mood of a prose-poet . . . the wonder of it to pedestrian prose-writers like me . . . is that you have created as a result, an extra art-dimension."

Extract of a letter from Seán Ó Faoláin
to Bryan MacMahon, 27 June 1985

To the people of my home town.

"To have great poets, there must be great audiences too."
Walt Whitman.

CONTENTS

FOREWORD

THE STORYMAN

As I strolled through the streets of my native town on the afternoon of a mart day, a boy, obviously a country lad, came walking against me. At that time, my mind was occupied with finding a name for this book.

On seeing me, the boy's eyes widened. He stood still, then took a step or two to one side as if to yield me passage. He paused, then looked directly into my face.

I stopped. "You all right?" I asked. He nodded then blurted:

"Are you the Storyman?"

For a moment or two I was caught off-guard. Then, obviously confessing that I had written all kinds of stories including some for children, I said:

"Yes, I'm the Storyman." This was true. For in one form or another my whole life has been devoted to the telling of stories.

The lad said no more. He walked past me, his eyes fixed sidelong on my face.

When I had gone some distance I looked over my shoulder. He was standing on the pavement, his eyes still fixed fast on me.

Storyman? I liked the sound of the word. To me it seemed much better than storyteller, writer or author. I began to test the word and compare it with its likes; seaman, clergyman, iceman, gentleman, horseman, oarsman, footman, Batman, milkman, foreman, penman and perhaps even conman.

"That solves it," I told myself. "The book shall be called *The Storyman.*"

CHAPTER ONE

"Watch yourself now, Master; fellas like you finish up funny."

That was the odd advice of a man I met almost twenty years ago on the day I turned the key for the last time on the schoolhouse door and walked home.

To my pleasant surprise I now find myself still in circulation, albeit somewhat more muted than before.

My retiral day was also the day on which I had resolved to slough all thoughts of schemes of work, timetables, roll books and progress records. I would play truant for the rest of my days! But I would not be idle. For I was determined to confront, explore and possibly embrace or reject my other self, my alter ego, my Doppelganger with his untidy ragbag of memories, images, dreams and adventures, uncatalogued and unpredictable as they were, and dissect that part of my make-up that bound me to my other trade – that of writer. For the lust for words, the urge to still the wheel of the passing years and to set down the minor epiphanies of my passing day, had in me always lurked just under the skin of the pedagogue.

First there were two voices from the past advising me and all apprentices to the writing trade. Both voices came from Russian masters of literature. One said, "If you're born with a tarred rope in your hand, pull it." The other said, "Young man, look out of your window."

So, metaphorically speaking with a black rope in my hand, and a pane of glass before me, I begin my telling. To do so I move back in time.

I was three or four years of age when I moved with my family from a cutstone cottage in Charles Street to our just then completed new house in Market Street. The house was sited on the Market itself. I began to explore the yard; standing on a stopstone in the middle of our corrugated iron back gate I looked through the bolt square at what looked like the wonderland of the crowded place. My appetite whetted by what I spied, I raced upstairs to the top storey and looked out the window and down on the marketplace. Beyond it gleamed the river that encircled the island racecourse; to the south were the mountains of the Dingle Peninsula while to the west of my new home was a slightly downhill street of thatched houses called The Gleann or Gleann a' Phúca, to give it its full title which translated as the Glen of the Hobgoblin – an unusual member of the fairy folk.

And wonderland the Market proved to be as I haunted the place in all the impressionable years as I grew into adolescence. The place was occupied in one form or another almost every day of the week. Calf market, pig market, butter market, hay and straw market, vegetable market, day after day found it thronged with farmers and noisy with the shouting, arguing and ballad singing of men, the haranguing of fortune tellers, delph sellers, cast clothes merchants and con men; all this orchestrated by the braying, bawling, squealing, barking, neighing and bleating of farm animals, horses, cows, jennets and mules, pigs, asses and sheep. Hundreds of cabbage plants (great hundreds) of the Enfield variety were laid down in ramparts, buttressed by palisades of scollops or thatching withies – these last in great demand for the roofs of farmhouses of the barony.

There too were sellers of purple dillisc, blue-black periwinkles and orange coloured cockles; these last were sold out of a large wicker basket and measured with a fluted pint drinking glass. The vendors were Tralee women wearing dark chocolate coloured shawls. Salted ling in rolls, and sleazy mackerel and herring were on public display. Potatoes, turnips and mangolds, load after load were decanted from carts painted orange-red with the shaft tips coloured a sober black.

In those unhygienic days, meat was sold by the look of it. Eggs were sold by the great hundred. I don't expect to be believed when I say that there were dancing bears from Russia and dancing ducks from anywhere at all. When music began to play, the pair of ducks danced on a griddle, not indeed because they were rhythm conscious, but because the secret button that turned on the music also administered a slight electric shock to the undercarriage of the griddle. On experiencing the stimulus, the yellow lapeens of the ducks had to move up and down alternately in time with the tune and in a parody of the Charleston, the dance rage of that time.

Since my grandfather was Weighmaster and Boss of the Market, I grew to have a proprietary interest in the place. I often took charge of the weighbridge when the old man stole off for a drink. I recall having initial difficulties with something called tare – the weight of the cart in which the load was carried – as this had to be deducted before the final total weight was reached. But in time, I mastered this difficulty.

Potatoes bought at source by the sackful in the Market worked out considerably cheaper than if bought in the vegetable shops in the town. At an early age I was given the task of buying the spuds. This was quite a problem. If I bought a sackful of soapy spuds the family would revile me each dinner-time until the sack was empty. So I could make no mistake! *Is cuma nó muc fear gan seift.* I had a plan. The various sackfuls were ranged against the several pillars of the Market shed, the mouths of the sacks open for inspection.

I went to the first pillar. "Can I have a spud?" I asked. "Sure!" the farmer said. I dug deep down the inside of the sack and took a potato. I then took a spent match out of a pocketful of spent matches I had already picked up in the street and inserted the match deep into the potato. At the second pillar, I put two matches into the sample spud I received. So on down the line to the tenth pillar.

The final tuber with its ten matches sticking out of it looked grotesque. Racing through our back gate to the kitchen I boiled the lot of them in a large muller. Ah! Number seven was a beauty! Laughing and the proverbial ball of flour! Texture just right too! I hurried back to the Market and bought a sack of pillar seven. To borrow an expression from greyhound racing: the potatoes were winners "from trap to line". Not a bad transaction for a lad of seven or eight!

But it wasn't all fun in the marketplace. Infusing it was a throbbing undercurrent of uncertain nationalism following the Easter Rising. Before my eyes I saw Ireland in microcosm swinging toward a surer sense of identity.

Easter week 1916, at the age of six, found me each day at the railway station questioning travellers descending from the trains. I was crystal clear about the issues involved. I had worn a kilt of sorts at the Feiseanna when answering questions in Irish and had seen the Volunteers drill with hurleys while we Fianna lads drilled with stuffboard guns. Stuffboards were the boards inserted into bolts of suiting in the draper's shop to keep the material from wrinkling.

"Who's winning in Dublin?" was my boyish cry at the station.

A huge sergeant-major of the British army, returning from the Western Front, looked down at me. He stopped and said in a tone reminiscent of the parade ground. "O'Connell Street is a sheet of flame." He then added, "And I'm on the wrong side, sonny." I was filled with childish sadness.

Echoes of agrarian trouble were sporadically heard in the marketplace. Fierce mauls ensued at times. Boycott horns were blown – the horn was simply made by dipping a woollen thread in paraffin oil and tying it round a pint bottle about one third of the way from the base. A lighting match was then applied to the thread and, when it had blazed for a few moments, the bottle was plunged into cold water. The bottom third was then readily knocked off. One was then left with a crude horn through which "Boo" could be sounded at a grabber or emergency man. The war cries of that hour were "The land for the people and the road for the bullock!" and "Thousands of men need acres and thousands of acres need men".

The last dying embers of the local faction fighters "The Cooleens and The Mulvihills" were sometimes fanned to flame in the marketplace. The slogans used at the slaughter of Ballyea Strand were then recalled. Cattle houghed, freshly cut turf ploughed into mud, meadows spiked, pier gates tarred, an agrarian murder and the subsequent trial – these were the underbreath topics of conversation in the marketplace.

But good humour invariably returned. An orator on a long car is haranguing his circle of hearers on the question of the proposed partition of Ireland.

"And the day will come when this country will be . . . will be . . . "

" . . . united," from a prompter beside him.

"And the day will come when this country, all thirty two counties of it will be . . . will be . . . "

" . . . united!"

"And the day will come when this fair land from Mizen Head in Cork to Fair Head in Antrim will be . . . will be . . . "

" . . . united! – I tell you."

"Consolidated! You hoor's ghosht, that's the word I want!"

I recall the gentle Mahera woman in her green and black plaid shawl who resented my boyish staring at her. "Mahera" was the term we of the townies applied to the salmon-and-hurling area near Ballyduff at the other side of the Ferry Bridge on the Cashen river. Our own River Feale changed its name before it entered the sea south of Ballybunion.

"Is it the way I've two heads on me? That you keep lookin' at me like that?" she said.

"No, ma'am, it's only what people say!"

"What do people say?"

"That if you marry a Mahera woman you marry Mahera."

I recall her ringing laughter. "It's the way we're so clannish and interrelated in Mahera that when you're big, if you marry a woman of our country, you'll be related to us all. Out there our blood is woven like a wicker basket. Do you understand now?"

"I do," I said.

Every day a double file of carts full of turf was drawn up on each side at the main Market gates. If the weather broke the turf-sellers were anxious to go home. We who lived near the Market were then in a buyer's market so we offered a poor price for the rail of fuel. As I did so one day, and declared that a hundred weight of coal was far better value, the seller looked at me in scorn.

"Did you ever read Dean Swift?" he asked sharply.

"Bits," I said.

"Well, he advised the Irish to burn everything English except their coal."

"You win." I yielded. "I'll pay your asking price. On one condition."

"What's that?"

"That I get the tail off the hare hangin' there from the gowlogue of your rail. I'd like to tie it to a cord and play with my pusheen."

"It's a bargain," he said. "Look, I'll throw in the hide with the tail. Rail of turf, hare and tail are all yours!"

Ever afterwards I addressed this turf-seller as Dean Swift. We had many conversations together.

The Market was not wholly devoted to buying and selling. All sorts of bazaars (Stacks and Linehans are fresh in my mind) took over the place in the long summer evenings. Circuses too of course. I recall how the pretty face of one of the bazaar girls lured me into being an accomplice to cheating. "Rigging the raffle" I came to call it.

My friend and I (he was later a distinguished doctor) were nine or ten at the time. Girl singers who travelled with bazaars, together with a comedian, a musician, and a competition provided standard fare. The entertainers sometimes made references to local characters in hastily made songs and usually drew large audiences. We always saved up our meagre pocket money (two or three pence per week) to buy a ticket from one winsome lassie.

"We're broke, Martha," we said one evening as she approached the pair of us. The slyest of smiles at her mouth corners were mostly directed at my companion. "Never mind," she said glancing furtively around. "I'll let one of you win the watch just the same."

The plan was ingeniously simple. She gave me one of the two halves of the cloakroom ticket – a blue 175. The counterfoil of the same 175 she gave to my friend. Eve was handing the halved apple to a pair of Adams.

Retrieving my half, she folded it over and over until it was a slender paper spill. Drawing my index finger and middle fingers apart she concealed this counterfoil between them and then pressed the fingers together. "Hold it tight," she whispered. "Go up and stand at the right of the stage! I'll call on you to draw the ticket. Put your hand deep down into the box and work the ticket out from between your fingers. Hold it high when you take it out."

Adam-I, standing at the right of the stage quivered and shivered with fear and excitement. I looked around me at the suckers still buying tickets. Little did they realise that my friend and I had already won the wristwatch. “Haul away!” came the cry from the stage, ordering all the ticket sellers back to base. All counterfoils were now in the black box – or were they? “An honest-looking boy to do the draw,” the MC on the stage shouted. The girl nodded to me. I went on stage. “Are you married?” the bazaar master asked me. “No, sir,” I said. “Are you honest?” “I am, Sir,” I said. “Roll up your sleeve and hold your hand up high.” I obeyed. “Take one ticket, and one only from the box.”

My hand deep down, I fumbled, pretending to be engaged in drawing only one ticket while at the same time praying to heaven I could work the winner to my fingertips. At last I had it. I held it triumphantly aloft. “Number 175! A blue ticket!” the man shouted.

On the far edge of the crowd my confederate in crime held up his half ticket waving it excitedly. “Come forward, boy.” He came. I hadn’t bargained for this, as many people had seen us together. The moment of anxiety passed. We had won the watch. The girl gave my friend the slyest of glances as he and I left the stage.

Afterwards, wherever the pair of us were in the countryside or ball alley and when I asked, “What does Martha say?” my confederate would consult his watch and say, “Martha says it’s just a quarter to twelve.”

A lull in the din of the marketplace invariably indicated something was wrong. Suddenly a loud cry would burst from the people. “A runaway! A runaway!” scores of throats would shout in warning. Then a young half-trained colt, harnessed perhaps to a railful of bonnavs and terrified by the din around him, would suddenly rear up and race berserk through the crowd upsetting all before him. “A runaway!” would go the hoarse cry now frenzied in its tone of warning. But always it seemed that when this happened even in the crowded streets outside the Market, a fearless young man would leap at the runaway’s head and, swinging from the bridle and shaft tip, cling on resolutely until the animal drew to a shuddering and frothing halt. Invariably the following week a paragraph would appear in the local notes in the county newspaper extolling the man’s bravery. For weeks after wherever he went he would be complimented on his deed of courage.

I pause now to disabuse the undiscerning reader of the idea that I was wasting my time. Even at this early hour of my life I was deliberate about my intentions. I realised that I was attending the university of the ordinary people, noting everything about them, their passions and their dislikes, their subjects of conversation and the rhythm and content of the unusual dialect, then a generation or two removed from the Irish language. The clothes they wore and the food they ate, these I noted. The surnames and the names of the townlands printed on the shafts of their carts and, indeed, what the townland names meant when translated into English, these were subjects that fascinated me. Gleann na Muc Méith meant The Valley of the Fat Pigs, Garryantanavalla meant the Garden of the Old Townland and Killimeerhoe was a bowdlerised version of the Church of the Red Plain. I wasn't wasting my time at all. One old fellow who observed me observing, said loudly to his companion, "That fella never kept a cat unless it killed mice," while the assistant harnessmaker remarked to the harnessmaker, "There's a chiel amang us takin' notes and i' faith he'll prunt 'em." That was said, I believe, about the young Robbie Burns.

We kept hens in our yard. Rhode Island Reds, Wyandotte, Indian Runners and Light Sussex. I would have loved to have a bantam cock to study his strutting. A hen even? My mother said no – the eggs were too small. Our neighbours whose backyards opened on to the Market also kept hens. Why? For the simple reason that there were always horses with nosebags of oats in the Market. Some of the grain was constantly being spilled whenever the horse raised his head. The hens had rival trenchermen in flocks of sparrows: I still recall a poem by James Stephens written from the viewpoint of the horse, when the animal, suddenly raising its head, spilled out oats for the sparrow at its hooves with the implied admonition, "Eat it up, young Speckle Head."

I even learned the ignoble art of trying a hen (Eleven o'clock and not a hen in the house tried! was the local cant phrase). I prudently kept those found fruitful with eggs locked in the henhouse for fear they might lay "out" – on the side of the Market cliff. Later, in my own mind I described this operation on a fluffy and indignant hen as a "pneumatic antic": I was possibly influenced by the writer who in describing a fat lady, said she offered "promise of pneumatic bliss."

Each springtime I was given a bucket and a worn leather glove and ordered to go picking nettle-tops. These when chopped were mixed through the hen food so as to purge the blood of the poultry. Long after this I wrote a story for Radio Éireann entitled *The Man With His Wife in the Wardrobe and the Woman who Envied a Hen*.

During the First World War years my provident mother, determined that, whether it was King or Kaiser who won, her hens would not starve. So she had an Irish acre of oats sown in a field of our ancestral holding of land three miles from the town. Doffing her Manchester finery, she presided over the scythe-cutting of the crop when it was ripe: I myself had thistle thorns in my fingers for months afterwards – I had been binding the oats into sheaves and later erecting the sheaves into stooks. On threshing day in an adjoining farm my mother had her small share threshed out of neighbourliness.

Our harvest consisted of four or five fine bags of oats which lasted our hens for an entire winter and beyond it well into spring. Advised to do so by a poultry instructress, my mother heated the oats on the discarded metal base of a creamery churn. The hens had individual names – none of your anonymous battery fowl for my ma – these titles were mostly derivations or corruptions of the names of neighbours whom they resembled in demeanour or indeed that of any lady who gave her an egg or two to include in her hatchery clutch. I shall never forget my boyhood amazement on first seeing a chicken emerge from a hatched egg. Breaking off chips of shell I helped the little mite enter into a life of picking, cheeping and clucking.

Whenever a cock untimely crowed in the darkness of night my mother was seized by panic. She was certain it betokened the death of a family member. She always made a note of the event so as to proclaim her clairvoyant powers – that is if someone did die.

The self-sufficiency of the people of that day – I speak now of the twenties or so – continues even in retrospect to amaze me. The housewife's expenditure on food was meagre indeed. Cash transactions were limited; tea, sugar, flour, shoe blackening (à la Charlie Chaplin) a roll of ling and a stripe of yellow American bacon – that's if the home-produced flitches were consumed. But flitches of a home-fattened, home-killed pig glistening as they hung from the hooks on the kitchen ceiling, were the staple diet of the entire year.

Kitchen-garden, countryside, ocean, shore or river all contributed to the table. A quarter of veal from a freshly "dropped" calf could be made to last a family for a week.

Every second household fattened and killed a pig. We were no exception. A phrase sticks in my mind concerning the pigsticker as he made ready for the cutting of the pig's throat. He did so with the dignity of one of the Inca priests of Old Mexico. The description I heard was deadly accurate: "You wouldn't think there was anything hieratic about him till you saw him preparing to kill a pig." The dutiful son, who objected to the new bonnav being leg-driven into the yard for fattening, was heard to say, "Sweet adorable God, not another juvenile delinquent!"

But back to the hens! Did I fail to mention Paderewski's wife? The woman I have in mind was the wife of the great Polish pianist who was later Prime Minister of Poland. The story was told to me by an elderly returned-home Irish-American when I wormed my way past her forbidding portico and gained her confidence.

"I was companion to an elderly lady of one of the wealthiest families in New York State," she said. "We lived with others of a similar standing in an enclosed estate in Upper New York State. It even had a guardroom at its gate. As a matter of fact we hid the man who, dressed as a woman, escaped in a lifeboat from the sinking Titanic. He was not Irish as the publishers' rags of that day would have it."

She paused to control her indignation, and to return to her mainstream story. "Each year my mistress and I spent the summer in her villa on the shores of Lake Geneva in Switzerland. Mr Paderewski lived in the villa adjoining ours. I became friendly with Mrs Paderewski. She bred table fowl. There they were, beautiful birds from all parts of the world.

"Sometimes I did light work for the Paderewski family. Dusting with a feather duster – that kind of thing. One day I was doing the parlour when Mr Paderewski came in. He sat down at the grand piano and began to play. He looked over his shoulder at me. I continued at my work even dusting the piano top as he played. He got cross.

"'Little Irish girl', he said. 'Do you know how much it would cost you if I gave you a private recital all for yourself in the biggest theatre in London, Paris or New York?'

"'I don't know, Sir,' I said.

"'It would cost you a thousand sovereigns in gold. Do you believe me?'

"'I do, Sir. But will you be soon finished with the piano?'"

That was long ago. I saw something recently which set me thinking deeply on the Market and its hens.

A very old lady with her simple middle-aged daughter came slowly up our street. The mother carried a message bag. After a secret signal the daughter took something from her mother's bag and entered a small shop. The mother remained on guard at the door, her head swivelling anxiously as she surveyed the street. I looked in through the shop window. The younger woman placed three eggs on the counter. She said nothing. Nor did the shopkeeper say anything: he took the eggs then went to the till and handed out some coins. The pair resumed their slow wary passage upstreet. The word "free" in free range eggs occurred to me. Good morning, Europe!

I also recalled something I had heard or read: "There are 56 words in the Lord's Prayer, 297 words in the Decalogue, 300 words in the American Declaration of Independence and 26,911 words in a recent EEC directive on the presentation and sale of duck eggs."

Thinking back to our market-fed hens, I am impishly and impiously tempted to wonder whether or nor Mrs Paderewski, that eminent authority on table fowl, was conversant with what I have called "a pneumatic antic."

My father's health was declining so he left the seclusion of the law office and began to buy butter in the Market; this in conjunction with his brother who was a creamery manager. I got a half-day from school every Thursday as I was kept at home to help in our yard which now had its back gate thrown wide open and an office installed. Pigs and hens were banished temporarily. I came to know all about butter.

It was my task to scald the strong wooden boxes, line them with butter paper and make them ready to receive the country butter which arrived in all kinds of tubs and metal containers, loaded on all sorts of farm vehicles. I learned to drive the steel butter-taster deep into the butter taken from the carts, twist it, extract it, smell the butter, bite it, roll it round on the tongue, spit it out and pronounce a verdict on its quality prior to its being weighed, boxed and the boxes labelled for Manchester or some such English city.

Other buyers in the Market loaded their butter supplies into small barrels or firkins, the process supervised by a local cooper with a biblical beard. Between the boxes, firkins of butter and the egg crates spread out awaiting the carter's dray to transport them to the railway station, a large portion of the ground of the Market was almost covered from end to end. We lads would have a race along the firkin tops with the cooper roaring at us to stop.

Before the railways came, butter was "carred" by road over the Mullaghreirk Mountains to Cork. A huge body of folklore had grown up around the method of transport. The route along "the Corkline" was along Griffith Roads, a reference to an engineering genius which needs an extended glossary in itself, his name nowadays recalled chiefly in connection with Griffith's *Valuation and Tenements* (1852), a valuable source for genealogists. There were one or two inns along the route where the carriers stayed for the night for food and rest for man and beast. There was also a bunk-type bed or ledge on which the men could sleep.

A grand-aunt of mine was married to one such driver, a quiet man called Garret, and through him and more especially through my mother's retelling of his tales, was conveyed to me a clear-edged picture of one such rough-and-ready inn on the mountain road to Newmarket in North Cork.

A roaring turf fire, the smell of mutton pies boiling in soup in a large pot hung from the crane above the huge turf fire, the tang of frieze overcoats drying under light ill-provided by tallow candles or even splinters of bogdeal. The men were gathered round the blaze with possibly a pair in a corner whispering in semi-darkness – where perhaps one was administering the Fenian oath to the other under the cover of conversation. All this, I feel, is worthy of depiction as a powerful frieze or mural illustrative, say as a jacket cover, for such a book as Tom Flanagan's *Tenants of Time* which in fictional form conveys the powerful if secret forces in the Ireland between the Famine of 1847 and the Rising of 1916.

These crude overnight stopping places were clearing-houses for news and the exchange of ballads. O'Connell and Davitt were names often heard mentioned around the fire. Councillor Butt was spoken of for legal scholarship. Mentioned too were the Fenians of Cahirciveen. Details of local murders or the exploits of Moonlighters were common topics. By an imaginative extension, the carters who stayed there appear to me as blood brothers to the muszhiks of Czarist Russia, the peons of South America, the salt carriers of the East, or the Sherpa baggage bearers of the Himalayas. The characters may surface some day in what I write. Perhaps I shall exaggerate their importance. But then again that's the writer's business – to render the novel commonplace and the commonplace novel.

Outside the lower end of the Market, under a clay cliff with the island racecourse across the water, flowed the River Feale. About this river I shall have much to say. Into it, from an underground stream and beneath Tay Lane, flowed the raw sewage of the town, the liquefied ordure issuing in a pea-green stream from under a stone arch.

This sewer figured strongly in the adventures of my boyhood as my comrades and I explored it moving by torchlight under the streets of the town. This place too, stinking and fetid as it was, played a major part in the formative years of my teens and my confrontation with the first of manhood. It surfaces again in a recent story of mine called *Testament of a Sewer Rat.*

But first I must give fuller and more picturesque voice to the many people who clamour for their hour upon my makeshift stage and who as yet have appeared only as shadowy outlines, rimmed in firelight, or on the periphery of a crowd, which in retrospect throngs my mind. Let me now continue on my life journey by drawing on a resource I first chanced upon in the marketplace and which is called the Great Bank of Say.

I have a theory that comforts me. It may be as riddled with fallacies and inconsistencies as a sieve is with holes, but I count it mine. All art, I tell myself, comes up out of clay. Out of the cow-dung if needs be. It is refined, projected, and later imitated or developed in the city where, for a time, it blooms like a flower. The flower becomes a seed-pod which explodes and scatters its seeds. The seed can be a miniature parachute or even a canoe of sorts which leaves the parent plant to fly, glide or drift on wind or water. With luck, each seed comes to rest on a fertile plot and there renews its life-cycle once again. This theory I apply to literature.

When the devil's advocate in me begins to whine: "What about Seán O'Casey? Did he come up out of the clay or even out of a country village?" I reply as follows: the slum community in Dublin with which he was acquainted was at that time a kind of rural village. All its characters were on display and on interplay as surely as if they were in a Corkery parish in the south-west or in an O'Flaherty village in Aran or Connemara.

Still on exposition, I offer an expansion and comparison of my theory of preparation for a writing life with the method of teaching Geography as a subject.

The scheme of work begins with a prosaic cup and saucer. The pupil looks *down* upon the cup sitting on the saucer and then draws what he sees. This is simply a small circle inside a slightly larger circle with a projection for the handle. This is the *plan* of the cup and saucer. Later he draws a plan of the desk at which he sits, then moves on to a plan of the classroom, thence to a plan of the school. Now he is ready to draw a plan of the building and the playground, thence again that of the town or school area, thence perhaps to the barony. Onward to the county, province, and finally to the whole island of Ireland. Beyond it lies Europe, the Western Hemisphere, the world. All this indicates several years' work.

On the course, the pupil is introduced to scale (to put it crudely a real Ireland cannot be expected to sit on a sheet of paper) and later to the problem of elevation as posed by the representation of mountains on a flat surface. This scheme of work I apply personally to my approach to writing.

I'm glad I got that much off my chest. Fear of being misunderstood had given me pause. Now I can proceed in a livelier fashion and offer examples of the raw material of dialogue which was in the air about me, especially in the marketplace. How things are said is often a clue to the workings of the mind. Animated especially by the advice of Russian masters, I sallied forth to ask my questions, to educate myself and once and for all to discover if "popular imagination" were a myth.

There are several ways of asking "How are you?" in the Irish language. The Kerry way was/is *Conas 'taoi?* or *Conas tánn tú?* The Donegal greeting is *Goidé mar a tá tú?* and the Connemara man asks, *Cé'n chaoi in a bhfuil tú?* – this last simply means, "What way are you?" This last version I chose in its English translation for an experiment – this because it gave the old people addressed a little interval in which to think of a suitable answer. Behold me then in the marketplace idling from oldster to oldster.

"What way are you, Paddy?"

In sepulchral tones, "Perpendicular, no more."

"What way are you, Jack?"

"Keepin' the best side out like the broken bowl in the dresser."

"Jim, what way are you?"

"If I felt any better, I'd see a doctor."

Foolish replies, you might say. Ask the same question anywhere in the US and the chances are one receives the standard answer, "Pretty good, see?"

I continued with my quest.

To avoid boredom I'll now compress some of the rest of my precious replies. "I'm still the possessor of the vibrant step." "Reasonable." "My day is sound when I'm overground." "I'm not as athletic as I was." "Will you give one look down at my bockedy toes." "Doing my utmost to avoid the sepulchre." "Endeavouring to squeeze the last drop out of my endowments." "I'll shortly be making a load for four." "Shovin' closer to the timber." "An eight and a nought, what way would I be?" "That's a question which demands several considerations – mental, moral, physical and spiritual."

At this point I was pulled up short by a few percipient interviewees. The old man stood in over-solemnity against a wall. He was bleary-eyed. "What way are you, Mick?" I asked. "Pass along, friend, I'm slightly oiled," came the reply. The next old fellow was brutally blunt. "You're aisy a shit how I am," was his rude riposte. I passed on to Jacko and Minnie. "What way are you, Jacko?" But before the husband could reply, his wife said bitterly, "There a dale of fear of that fella." So I countered by asking Minnie what way she was. Being a woman, she said, "And what way would you think I am?" ("I can't win them all," I murmured to myself.)

The most exotic and even surreal answer came from an old man who had a distant stare in his eyes. "What way am I, is it?" he shouted. "I'll tell you then. I have a prolonged cough that's cryin' out for a cough bottle. I've a vindictive nerve pain in my right ankle. Every bone in my body is creakin'. An' still an' all my mind keeps turnin' to my mad uncle who spent the last of his days cogitatin' how long it would take a small farmer to set an acre of oats providin' he dibbled in each grain separately with the point of a cobbler's awl."

(At this point I find myself apprehensive that people will allege that I am straining the limits of credibility. I brace myself to pushing on regardless.)

"I'm tougher than I thought." "Livin' but not high." "Are you sure you have the leisure to wait for a comprehensive reply?" "Up to the last notch in the crane" (this metaphor was from the old time fireplace) and "Thinkin' of pullin' in to the headland" (this from old style ploughing). "I don't like to be boasting." "Fair without, foul within." "Shook for shelter, then." "Grapplin' with a crisis of prime magnitude" (this from a man who knocked at my door at three am). "Movin' up in the queue." "Dodgin' the undertaker." "Bearin' up under my burden." ("What burden?" from me. "The burden of puttin' up with stupid questions from a canister like you.") "Listen and you'll hear my belly rumblin'." "Shudderin' towards the scraw." "Sure if it isn't this, it's that; and if it isn't that, it's this." "Sweet Jesus, have I to go through all this again?" "Pedallin' away for myself." "Creeping towards the end of the tunnel." "Swimmin' against the tide." And "Me? I'm too poor to paint and too proud to whitewash."

Here's a penultimate beauty: "I'm rueful. For if I got a daub of university education, which between me an' you is squandered like axle grease on tavern keeper's sons, I'd venture to say that I'd finish my career as Governor General of Hyderabad." (A neighbour of his did become Governor General of Assam in India.)

Here are two replies which deal with prime bodily functions. "Battlin' bravely against bladder and bowel." The next man appears to have won this battle for he proclaimed, "I'm as smooth as silk and as loose as ashes."

Am I finished with my research? By no means. The final reply stopped me in my tracks.

"What way are you, Vincent?"

"Stumbling along between the immensities."

"What immensities?"

"The immensities of birth and death."

There at last I felt I had the key. The highly individual reply was each man's attempt to mute or cancel the terror of impending death. The half jocular poetic answer provided him with a moment or two of ease from this burden of fear.

And what way, I was forced to ask myself, do *you* yourself respond to such a question?

Questioned in Irish, I always reply, *"Mairim fós."* "Yet I live." My answer is of the same fabric as Galileo's reply when light-blinded on his release from prison for heresy, he looked up at the sun and said, *"Et jam movet"* – "And still it moves." So, "And still I move."

Have I grown tedious? The kernel of what I am trying to convey is this: the foregoing does not indicate my having fun, acting the fool, patronising the peasant or storing up therapy for myself. Some of it can come under the head of anecdote but a vital part of it is real, in my sense of the word. It indicates that in the last decade of the twentieth century here in Ireland, something valuable still survives in the minds and speech of what the world would call simple men and women.

It also indicates a sense of bravery and an awareness of the gentle power of instinctively used metaphor and simile. It demonstrates the beautiful rhythmic way matters of deepest personal concern are uttered. It indicates a larger philosophical pervasion, a coping with a fatalistic sense of a world beyond the grave, of meaning underlying meaning and a whimsicality that is unaccustomed to copy or conform. It adds up to the ideal seed-bed in which a writer may exercise his craft. Above all it buttresses what Synge said as he wrote on the 21st January, 1907 in his famous introduction to the printed version of *The Playboy of The Western World.*

So come in Melancholy Man, John Synge! I want to assure you that almost 90 years after you left us in Kerry to go west, the same poetic fancy still exists among us. Speak again, dear John.

"I have used one or two words only that I have not heard among the country people of Ireland . . . from herds and fishermen along the coast from Kerry to Mayo or from beggar-women and balladsingers nearer Dublin . . . I am glad to acknowledge how much I owe to the folk imagination of these fine people . . . the wildest sayings and ideas in (my) play are tame indeed compared with the fancies one may hear in any little hillside cabin. In Ireland, for a few years more, we have a popular imagination that is fiery, and magnificent, and tender; so that those of us who wish to write start with a chance that is not given to writers in places where the springtime of the local life has been forgotten, and the harvest is a memory only, and the straw has been turned into brick."

She was standing by the roadside at the gateway leading to the farm. Mary was a marketplace acquaintance of mine. She held one hand behind her back. I drove up beside her in my car and stopped to pass the time of day. After a while, noting that she still kept the hand behind her back, I asked, "Have you hurt your arm, Mary?" "No," she said in a manner that invited a further query on my part. I obliged. "I'll tell you," she blurted at last. Extending her "secret" arm she opened her clenched fingers to reveal a snow-white hen-egg.

"What's the mystery?" I asked. "Just now I did something which as a farmer's wife I never did before," she said. "A hen was clocking to show she was going to lay: I went out and spoke softly to reassure her. I put my hand behind her in the nest. She laid this egg into the palm of my hand."

"Why did you do that?" I asked.

"I did it," she said, "for the felicity of the experience."

I am leaning on the banister of the landing of one of the hospitals in Cork city. A small countryman joins me. He keeps glancing furtively over his shoulder. "Don't look now," he said, "but there's a death in the room behind us."

"How do you know there's someone dead there?" I asked.

"Ah," he said, "they're after shiftin' the Lucozade."

I sat on a *súgán* chair in the porch of a pub opening on to the Market. My companion, a countryman with whom I had held a long conversation, suddenly sighed and said, "I must be goin' now. I have the four great curses of rural Ireland upon me."

"What are they?" I asked.

"A long road, a lazy ass, a contrairy woman and a drunken driver."

The following Sunday evening I was acting as MC of a concert at a cross-roads hall in the countryside. The hall was crowded. "Well," I said, as the programme came to an end, "that ends our programme. I'm off home now for I've the four great curses of rural Ireland upon me."

"What are they?" came a voice from the hall.

"A long road, a lazy ass, a contrairy woman and a drunken driver."

Before laughter could rise from the crowd an old man stood up, waved his stick and shouted at me, "There are five great curses of rural Ireland. You left out the most important one."

"Name your five!" I shouted back.

"A long road, a lazy ass, a contrairy woman, a drunken driver and a bad ash plant!"

"Why is the ash plant the most important?"

"Because if you had a good ash plant, you'd soberise the driver, silence the woman and control the ass. All you'd be left with then is the long road."

Dialect is it? Blank verse? I wrote down the following from an old tinker/travellin' woman who often camped on the country roadside and who was also a Market friend. It takes a Kerry tongue to get around its music. She told me her tale of woe once only; as I have a good memory I brought it clean and correct. Here she goes:

What the Tinker Woman Said to Me.

Ah, may Jesus relieve you in your hardesht hoult,
My lovely man, Like myself you are
Black hair, brown eyes, yalla shkin –

That's your beauty and my beauty;
It's the trade-mark of the Wards.
Buried above here I'll be, right appusit the yew tree,
First turn to the left, first turn to the right,
Twenty, maybe thirty paces, halt, Black Bridgie Ward!
I love you, sir.
I love you for your hair, your eyes, your shkin.
It's in four of me grand sons.
I got four after meself and four after their foxy father-
(I can't shtick foxy people!)
As sure as Christ was nelt, sir, I suffered my share.
But I have my health.
Indeed I have, sir.
Over in Ballyheigue I am: I'll tell you no word of a lie.
A mother,sir!
(Genuflects) That I may be sainted to the Almighty God,
I shtarts thinkin' of my son Timothy-Thigeen we calls him
(whispers) That's in the sannytorium above here, sir,
An' the minute I shtarts thinkin' of him
A batterin' ram, sir,
Couldn't come bethune me an' my lovely boy.
I sat into my daughter's car, sir, and covered the Fourteen Irish mile o' ground.
I went in above.
"Hello,Ma!" says he, laughin'.
He's my son, sir, my lawful-got son!
The heart ruz up in me but I held it back.
"Oh yeah," says I. "isn't it full o' funnin' you are?"
"Where are ye now, Ma?" says he.
"In Ballyheigue," says I.
I had my daughter's daughter with me – a bit of a childeen barely beginnin' to walk.
"Cuckoo!" says he, gamin' for the benefit of the child.
The child was class of shy: We commenced laughin'.
"You're a godfather, Thady," says I,
"Unknownsht to yourself.

Bridgie, your sister, had two more since you left."
(That's his sister's children, sir!)
With that he fell to laughin' on account of he bein' a
godfather unknownsht to him.
I left him there, sir,
Shtandin' at the winda' advanced in his disease
And we takin' to the road.
I re'ched up my hand in his direction, sir, and I sittin'
Into my daugher's green car.
He stood there till we rounded the gateposht.
I'll tell you no word of a lie. That's a mother!
Easter Saturday that was.
At Chrussmass we were up in Newtown.
"Christmas is it," I said, "an' no Timothy."
It came to Saint Patrick's Day.
In the middle o' my carousin' I shtopped an' said:
"Patrick's Day an' no Thigeen.
Listowel Races an' no Timothy.
Puck Fair an' no Timothy."
Shtandin' at the winda he was,
Black hair,
Brown eyes,
Yalla shkin.
Buried above here, appusit the yew tree he'll be
First turn to the left
First to the right
Twenty, maybe thirty paces
Halt, BLACK THADY WARD!

"Watch the hammer and the Lord direct you! Why don't you tell me to stop?"

The cast clothes man is in full flight. An old and heavy overcoat draped across his forearm, he is haranguing a marketday throng from his open shop on the back of what appears to be a "long car" of Bianconi vintage. "Why don't ye tell me to stop?" he shouts as he slaps the garment with an open hand, "and let the poor unfortunate drapers of your town turn an honest shilling. Here it is (slap) an overcoat worn by the American Leatherjackets. Made by Miss Coxcomb the needlewoman from the Glen of Aherlow, 'twould cover an orchard and leave ne'er an apple bare (slap). Put that overcoat on your son's back, ma'am, and send him into the finest hotel in the city of Dublin and then stand back and hear the people say 'Who's the fine gentleman?' Here! Not ten pounds or seven pounds or six pounds. Here. (slap) This beautiful topcoat! (Slap) Here damn the devil and his wooden leg, I'll take five pounds for this noble garment – let 'em say what they like about their morals ma'am, but by hell it must be printed on their tombstones that the American Leatherjackets wore good overcoats. What do you say, ma'am?"

"Thirty shillin's."

The merchant looks around the Marketplace as if in exasperated disbelief. Then calmly, "Are you single or married, ma'am?" (A common query designed to discommode.)

"Single, then."

"Good, begod I've an ould lady at home that's burnin' oil. I might trade her in for a middlin' model like yourself. I might even squeeze a couple of thousand miles more out of you." As a gale of laughter sweeps the crowd, he begins to wheedle – "Four pound, miss. Four bloody pound. 'Twould be double to anyone else."

The bargaining continues until at last the coat changes hands at £2.10s.0d.

On the edge of the crowd I'm listening and noting and learning. There's the rise and fall of the man's voice, his rhetorical shifts, the rhythm and daring of what he says. The odd allusions such as Miss Coxcomb and the Leatherjackets. Above all, the way he is able to mock-insult his customers and later, riding on the tide of laughter, get clean away with it every time.

I pause in what is possibly a vain effort to define laughter, a prime ingredient of literature. Where in a lifetime of reading have I chanced upon just such a definition? It went something like this: most likely I have added or subtracted whimsies to accommodate my own unorthodox fancies.

When in conversation or otherwise, two wholly disparate planes of reference intersect at an angle there occasionally occurs a sudden coruscation which indicates the presence of a bizarre affinity between the opposites. On the sudden appreciation of this unexpected reaction, the zygomatic major muscle above the upper lip of the observer/hearer begins to fibrillate, twitch or spasm in a manner akin to the minor convulsions of an epileptic fit: coterminously or consequentially, a resonant and often raucous sound indicative of the joy of discovery instinctively fills the chamber of the head register with the consequence that both reactions merge to form the common phenomenon known as laughter.

Bizarre affinity! That is a description destined to surface in many forms in the course of my life and the work of that life.

The black doctor too had his marvellous marketplace spiel. I can see him now playing the dentist. A bloody molar is held in triumph above his head, while the paler fingertips and the similarly pale palms offer contrast to his polished ebony head. His countryman patient, from whose jaws he has with his powerful fingertips rocked and drawn the offending tooth, sits on a borrowed súgán chair with blood dribbling from his proud but laughing jaws.

The "dentist" is now claiming wider powers:

"I can cure every disease known to man and woman," he shouts. "Gonorrhoea, diarrhoea, leucorrhoea, spermatorrhoea – I can cure them all."

So attractive and mysterious was his spiel that as a boy I, a moderately useful mimic, was able to repeat it in full, holding an imaginary blood-red molar above my head as I did so. As a consequence, one of the local brothers blacksmith, the one known as "The Baptiser", gave me the nickname of "The Black Doctor."

An elderly professor in St Michael's College, the local seminary minor which I then attended, having heard of my mimetic prowess, asked me in front of the class to declaim my party piece. The poor man stopped me in mid-flight and, calling me aside, whispered, "If I were you I wouldn't repeat that in civilised society."

The fishmonger, a man originally from a fishing village in the Irish north-east, now enters the scene trundling in his handcart before him. He pauses to shout his wares in Cries o' London fashion. "Fresh fair and lovely. Jumpin' alive out of the box. I've been out all night catchin' them for yer." As a consequence of his cry he was always known as "Jumpin'".

I come now to the question of gullibility. Again in the university of the marketplace.

The little confidence-man stood behind his table. He began to mutter aloud. I was among the first to draw close, to see what he was at. He set out a selection of cheap watches each costing five shillings at the time. "I don't expect much from you good people. I know it is difficult for you to trust me." By now he had twelve cheap watches on the green baize. Then after a long harangue on honesty, "Would any gentleman trust me with a loan of a penny? I promise you, sir, your coin will not leave this table." He placed each penny received on the face of a watch. Presently the face of each of the twelve watches bore a penny. He then placed some pencils and pens and trinkets beside each watch and penny. Again the long spiel. Then came the crunch.

"Is there one brave man or woman who will place a pound note under *his own* watch and penny?" There is one man, probably a "plant", who is applauded for bravery. He does as the spieler suggested. Soon each previous contributor has placed a pound note under the watch and trinkets with his own penny as King of the Castle. After a prolonged spiel on honesty, the con man then addresses the most gullible asking him to point out where his money lies. "If I were to offer you all of that – watch, penny, valuable keepsakes and the pound for one pound note would you buy?" He would. He does. All follow suit. Gullibility! Each man really buys back his own one pound note, the almost worthless watch and the trinkets for one pound – leaving the con man with fourteen shillings profit each time – a total of eight pounds profit each time he gathers an audience.

A hush falls upon the marketplace. Drumbeats are heard. A tall soldier appears. He is dressed in scarlet; the black busby on his head makes him look eight feet tall. Beside him is a boy drummer. There is a stare in the people's eyes. The drumbeats are a call to arms. From a pub window a poster showing a moustachioed man points an accusing finger. Your King and Country Need You! is the accusatory legend.

Well, well, if it is not that boy Horatio Kitchener himself from up the Bedford Road, soon to have his breakfast in the Listowel Arms! But, according to his father's letter, not until the beasts on offer are sold.

Now another voice is heard. A ragged balladsinger with a swatch of treasonable come-all-ye's has a new song. People are already lilting it;

He whispered 'Goodbye love, Old Ireland is calling!
High over Dublin the tricolour flies
In the streets of the city the foeman is falling
And small birds are singing Old Ireland Arise.'

The Faculty of Rhetoric in the University of the People? I was just starting my education.

CHAPTER TWO

"Poor is the boyhood that hasn't had a river flowing through it."

A common enough phrase, I daresay. I think it was our own Sigerson Clifford who focused my attention on the phrase; he was a fine ballad-maker whose "Boys of Barr na Sráide" is sung and loved far beyond the borders of our county.

I had a river flowing through my boyhood; so I was not stricken by poverty in that sense. The river was the Feale; it was named for a naked lady of Irish legend named Fial. She was by no means a "stripper" except in the lawful sense of that abused word. How it came about was as follows:

Fial, wife of Lugh (the lore on Lugh of Lughnasa fame has filled volumes) was a shy lady who, on a summer's day, went bathing in a remote river. pool. She wore no clothes at all. But she felt secure. Seeing a man spying on her, she dived deeply down and, fearful to surface, remained below to drown. She did so out of needless shame. The peeper was none other than her own husband.

The river Feale curled its way around our town beneath the cliff of my beloved Market. The Fitzmaurice Castle at the ford had tales of siege and the hanging of the defenders – this in the period 1600-1601. Patrick, son of the Earl of Kerry, was an infant at the time of the surrender: daubed with clay, the baby was smuggled out of the building. Later captured, reared and educated in England, a direct descendant of his, Lord Shelbourne, became Prime Minister of England. Of a certainty, history has some odd quirks to its story.

Above the river loomed the Arms Hotel: from its stalls and stables we stole eggs and sucked 'em. The youthful adventures I have had in the context of this river were many and varied. They include drownings, Black and Tans, salmon, all the apparatus of poaching, barrel bridges, swans, kingfishers and notes in bottles. Civil War, egg-sucking and stoning cormorants, skating and a gentry bell, yellow root or spurge, water rats and sewage – all have their allotted place in my memory.

Nearby buildings remind me of workhouse records aflame, while the racing river recalls eel fry proclaiming the existence of God. There also were freshwater oysters containing mythical pearls, there was even a ghost story of the castle undermined and the castle bawn festooned with corpses dangling from trees. Add to this catalogue our makeshift rafts and leaky boats, fluke impaled on a table fork, and a blessed candle lighting on a floating raft of straw. Until this day, Mr Heron, my sentinel, is standing in a shallow ford, his eyes fast on the stream. There are swans and a few kingfishers "like rainbows on fire". (I borrow the phrase from a ballad written by my son Garry.) The shine on the river surface reminds me of the salmon it conceals and even of the forge anvil beating out gaffs from the brake rods of old Model T Fords.

That was our river and its island racecourse with the town above it. The town continues to boast an annual week-long race meeting which has all the appurtenances of gaiety. During an interval between individual races on the card, I often move into the snack bar in the enclosure to partake of a currant scone and a container of tea. There is an old ballad of mine called "The Races in Lovely Listowel" painted on a board on the wall above me. I turn at the window and look down on the now still pool below the building.

A still pool – that's all the other racegoers see. They scarcely spare it a second glance. I see more. Dear God, I see the whole of my youth. Like Dylan Thomas I am tempted to sing and sob alternately:

"Now as I was young and easy under the apple
boughs
About the lilting house and happy as the
grass was green."

The river has altered considerably since the weir was taken away and the old mill downstream pulled down. The large deep pool of dammed up water has been drained: frozen over in winter it made a fine skating rink. I once saw a motor-car driven across the strong ice. The weir spanned the river at an angle – this at a point under the thatched houses of the Gleann on the cliff above. The skew barrier diverted the water through a floodgate into a half mile of headrace to turn the great water-dripping wheel which supplied power to the mill.

The weir, headrace and tailrace had other effects which impacted hugely on the lives of those who lived on the cliff-top: it controlled and determined the course of the mighty shoals of salmon and sea-trout which perennially in spring and early summer moved upstream imbued with the lust of seeking the spawning beds in the pools where the boundaries of three counties of Limerick, Cork and Kerry meet in the Mullareirk Mountains.

There was a fish gap in the weir on the island side of the river. Erratic streams also spilled over the flood-gapped weir wall to delve deep pools filled with fish. To see the salmon hurtling upstream to surmount the barrier was like viewing a film taken in Alaska. It only lacked a brown bear, of course, leaping into the flood to emerge with a fish across his strong jaws.

We had our own brand of bears in the form of my good friends, the poachers from the cliff-top. They were gaff artists to a man. During the troubled times, much as was said of Carrick of old, there was "neither law nor order" in Ireland, my friends had a free run on the river and the weir. But on the establishment of the Free State, the Garda Síochána arrived to restore the law of the land in all the novel majesty of our indigenous state. They had a job on hands.

Aged twelve, I was among a knot of poachers and onlookers standing on the bank beside the fish-gap one day in the early twenties. A spring flood was racing and foaming in the ale-brown water. Silver salmon were leaping and frolicking just below us. Prime poacher Joe looked around. A bad egg was Poacher Joe. A garda was downstream where the race stand is now.

From behind the waistband of his trousers Joe produced a gaff head. He was a demobbed Free State soldier, I saw the bulge of a revolver in his fob pocket. Pulling up the leg of his trousers he drew a short gaff handle from his stocking. "Anyone got cord?" he asked hoarsely. Innocently I produced a hank of strong cord. I watched him assemble the weapon. The crowd drew back, ostensibly to cover the poacher, but in reality to cower.

Taking the mounted gaff the man growled at the little crowd to move a step forward to cover his movements. Reluctantly they complied. The garda – he was a friend of mine – seemed engrossed in something downstream. The poacher crouched at the river's edge, leaned forward and with a violent slash, drew upon a fish. The water boiled as the gashed fish fought back and escaped. The garda turned and shouted. Poacher Joe sped upwards and slipped into the crowd among whom I stood white-faced. He thrust the gaff handle down the waistband of his trousers and stood with his hands hanging loosely by his side, gun-fighter cowboy fashion. The garda was upon us.

"You have a gaff!" he shouted at the poacher.

"No gaff!"

"I saw you."

"Did anyone see me?" the culprit shouted at the crowd.

Silence.

"I want to search you," the garda said.

"No one'll search me." Joe's hand was now on the butt of the revolver deep in his fob pocket.

"Very well, I'll see you in court."

"I'll see you in hell."

The crowd melted. The garda looked me straight in the eye. He had taught me how to pull a drop stroke on a falling hurling ball. He did not ask the obvious question. The tension passed as the crowd drifted away.

A series of court cases began. One dark night, the accused Joe called to my house. "You know I hadn't a gaff," he growled.

"You had," I said.

"I had not. If you say that in court . . . " he tapped his fob-pocket.

"If the garda catches me, I'll swear the truth."

"By Jesus, if you do, you'll be sorry."

I went on the run. Every knock on our door sent me racing upstairs to lean out on the sill and look down over the projection of the fascia to see who was knocking below. One day I looked down and saw a garda's flat hat. Downstairs I raced quietly and scurried out the back gate. On my way to and from college I used the back roads. This procedure went on until court day, the Garda arriving at our door and I fleeing! My mother couldn't make head or tail of what was going on. In court the garda lost his case. A respectable shopkeeper present at the incident swore that the defendant had not got a gaff. (He too had been threatened.) Appeal followed appeal but the original verdict prevailed. I kept running in terror of my life. If I were caught I would have told the truth: on that I was resolved.

A strange tenet of a small minority of the poachers of that hour was this: they believed that it was no sin for a poor man to swear himself out of a difficulty but that it was the mortal and reserved sin of perjury if one swore so as to harm another man or woman. The sin of perjury was reserved in the sense that the bishop of the diocese alone could give absolution for it. The poachers adduced a theory that a poor man was prosecuted if he foul-hooked a fish but that the land-owner of the fishery rights, usually one of the so-called Ascendancy, could encircle a pool with a net and draw almost three hundred fish out of it. Salmon, the poachers said, bore no man's brand. *Ferae naturae*, I believe, is the legal term used to describe wild animals, fish and even bees, which in certain cases, fall under this heading. I too felt there was an inequity somewhere in all this. But such as it was, the law was the law.

"Water, I defy you," one bald-headed Gleann man would shout before diving from a height into a deep pool of the river. Among the breakers in Ballybunion he would give the same cry as he swam fearlessly out beyond the strongest waves, his bald head glistening amid the foam. By an irony of fate he died of dropsy, a disease characterised by an accumulation of water in the body.

I am still in reverie at the window of the snack bar of the island stand at race time. Death comes in many guises. I waded out down there one day in the long ago for my daily swim and was joined by a pair of tipsy ex-soldiers. One of the pair disappeared under my ten-year-old eyes. Later someone brought along a sheaf of oats and a blessed candle – the candle was to be set alight and placed on the sheaf. Set afloat, it was said that where it stopped would indicate the location of the man's body.

I now hear voices from the Famine days. Their cry rises from the starving thousands outside the workhouse which stood on the opposite bank of the stream. "Bread or Blood" they yell as they form up in ragged procession. I seem to see some of the children break away from the crowd and stagger down to the gravel strand of the Feale. Just over there! They stuff their mouths with weeds – poisonous weeds as it happens – and they die where they lie in agony, their mouths green with the remains of their last repast.

Meanwhile the corpses from the poorhouse move in a still grimmer procession out of the back door of the building to be shovelled underground in Teampaillín Bán. The Little White Churchyard is finger-posted just outside the town on the road to Ballybunion. For many years the Lartigue, the quaintest railway in the world, chugged its way to the seaside past the edge of this little acre of God.

On race days a beggar cry of Famine days is still echoed by travelling children up to their thighs in water under the race bridge with cardboard cartons in their hands to catch coins thrown down by the returning punters. "Throw us down somethin'" they yell in chorus. As a schoolmaster I tried to stop this practice and failed. The present race bridge replaces a plank structure laid on weighted sugar barrels which a century before had collapsed on race day at this island entry. Many of those who fell into the water were issued vouchers for new suits by the race committee.

For some reason or other I recall the name Jackety Joy and the story of his visit to the races in the long ago.

There he was, a farmer's "boy" coming down the hill into the town and jingling the thirty shillings in his pocket – this was his pay for a full quarter of the year. To himself he murmured: "God direct me whether I'll drink you or buy a pair of boots!" The pair of brogues on his feet were in sorry trim. A blackbird was singing on a roadside bush. Jackety stopped to listen. To his astonishment he found himself putting words to a phrase of the blackbird's song.

The words were "Spend! Spend! And God will send."

So Jackety Joy went into town and drank his pay. Sick, sore and sorry, his old boots leaking rainwater, and the races over (he never saw a horse), he tottered uphill out of the town.

There was the same blackbird on the same thorn bush singing in the downpour. This time the poor man found himself with different words for the songbird's melody. "Have it yourself or be without it," was what the bird now sang.

I am now high on the packed stand, race card in hand and quietly surveying the island course. Kerry, of course, is renowned for its Gaelic footballers and rightly so. I'd like to place a record that the very first soccer match in North Kerry and possibly in Kerry, was played out there in the centre of the island course. The contestants were The Black and Tans versus the Yorkshire Selection of the British Army. In view of the criticisms levelled at the robust nature of the Gaelic code, it is with a certain measure of glee that I chronicle the fact that the participants of long ago fought one another like dogs. While the scrimmage was in progress, a friend and I struck a blow for old Ireland.

The soldiers had taken possession of a fine brass bell taken from the burnt-out ruins of the Cooke Mansion half a mile or so away. (Mrs Cooke was godmother to Kitchener.) This bell summoned the demesne labourers to the fields calling them in for a nominal meal. It surfaces in a recent story of mine called *The Gentry Bell.* For me it was the Bell of Slavery.

While the scrimmage was at its height, a friend and I stole the bell. At that time there was, in mid-course, a scrub of low furze covering a few rabbit burrows. We pushed the bell far down the mouth of a burrow and covered the entrance with snapped off branches of furze. The fight over, the soldiers returned to the sideline looking for their bell. You never saw innocence until you saw us. We lied, of course. Never laid eyes on it. You had it there a while ago. Cunningly we glanced at the knot of the Black and Tans supporters on the other side of the pitch. The soldiers began to roar, implying that the Tans had stolen their bell. We almost started a war within a war by doing so.

A week later having reconnoitred the area, we returned to take possession of the bell. It was gone! Where it went to remains a mystery to this day.

The event known as "The Stop of the Wheel" was the great event of our river lives. This came about in June when the wild iris or "flagger" was in yellow bloom. For us it signalled that the white, or sea, trout were running. We had the means of knowing the exact time when the floodgate at the entrance to the millrace was being lowered to cut off the flow of water to the headrace. This had the obvious consequence that the millwheel's turning would grind to a ponderous halt.

In advance of this event we repaired to the fields around the mill and broke off sections of strong paling wire about six feet long. This each of us bent in two, and twisted the resultant hoop with the insertion of a stout cudgel into the loop until we had a serviceable weapon, its stem twisted and its ends spread to a fork, the tines an inch and a half apart. Racing helter-skelter back to the vicinity of the mill, we crouched in the bushes just downside of the point where the wheel was encased. There it was, its huge rusted bulk rumbling grumbling and tumbling much as Mark Twain had once described the sound of thunder in the sky.

A spy of ours, lurking on a bushy cliff upstream of the wheel and the wastegate, was there to tell us when the receding tidal bore was upon us. Suddenly we saw the signal handkerchief wave. The wheel, now deprived of racing water, seemed to become giant and human. It faltered as if it had been struck, gathered itself, growled indignantly in a rusted iron-and-stone voice as if asking what was wrong; then, inevitably, the last of its waters reduced to a dribble, the huge revolving drum ground to a dead halt. Below us in the shallow water of the tailrace behind the still dripping flanges of the wheel, the water was a mass of squirming, darting, chirring salmon and trout who foolishly had moved as far as the wheel but could go no further.

Wearing old studded brogues to hold purchase on the sleazy stones, we jumped down between the high walls of the enclosure. Straightaway we fell to slashing and cutting like dervishes. Cries of "That's my bloody fish!" "No, it's mine," rent the air. The ghostly and laughing faces of the millers looked down from the dusty windows – some of the slashers were their grandsons. In the midst of the piscine carnage our sentry shouted, "Bailiffs!" Grabbing as much as we could of our slippery half-killed booty we took to our heels and ran downriver to the ford which we crossed to the other side.

A law-abiding unbeliever might pertinently ask, "How could the unfortunate fish get into this blind alley? Could they not be prevented from entering this trap by placing a grille across the point where the tailrace entered the river?" There *was* a stout grille at that particular point but, much as a bible can be used to unhinge a cell door in a prison, a stout paling post could be used to prise the grille bars apart. Recall – there was no law at that time. Members of the so-called Ascendancy took part in this poaching orgy; I saw one of them even warn off the peasantry at the weir where he soon whitened the river bank with silver salmon.

As I am spilling the beans on poaching I might as well tell it all.

When the river was low, what the law called a "fixed engine" and what the poacher termed "a clown's cap" or a cage was used. This was a lattice wire trap with a narrow entrance which was weighted and submerged in the river at a very narrow point known in more precise terms as "a flash." On the principle of a lobster pot or a non-spillable inkwell, the fish which entered this trap could not again get out. Walking against the flow or stoning this pool below the trap-point often led to a fine catch.

In a legal role these friends of mine were superb anglers. They were also masters of the art of fly-tying, possessing small vices to hold the hook to be adorned and tin boxes full of feathers from birds from all part of the globe. The plumage I recall included jungle cock, teal and macaw. A smell of shellac varnish hung about these craftsmen. They could fashion lancewood rods and "whip" them too – that is, bind the rods at intervals with circles of waxed thread. These men knew the layout of the river bed as they knew the layout of their own kitchens.

About Christmastime each man would take out his tin box of lures. Seated at the head of his kitchen table, he would caress each fly by drawing the wing through his wet lips: then, holding the fly out from him, he would address it as if it were human. "Oho, you little beauty, you harnessed an eleven pounder for me below at Naughton's." And then aloud, he would chant, "And when March comes, begod, you'll kill a couple of more."

The joke of such a ceremony was this: if the fly fishing was bad with the salmon turning up their noses at every sort of a come-on, local-made minnows or prawns included, the angler would survey the area around him and then gently allow the fly to sink to the bottom of the pool. At the same time he would keep moving the top of his rod to mime the act of angling, and also to ensure that the hook did not get foul-hooked in the weeds at the bottom of the pool.

All of a sudden, after survey number two, he would whip up the rod so that the fly and its hook would speed through the water and with good fortune foul-hook a fish.

"What did you kill with, Mick?" from a friend. "Hm?" "Was it the Bulldog or the Thunder an' Lightning?" In a whisper, "No, 'twas the Makem Takem."

Of course, if the coast were guaranteed clear, he might shorten the odds of success by mounting a treble hook strokehaul and then repeating the pull. This process was known to the law as snatching and was roundly condemned from the bench. So as not to be caught in the act, the angler/poacher would often hold the open blade of a penknife or razor blade under his gripping hand and if apprised of danger while playing a foul-hooked fish, he could snip off the taut line so as to destroy the evidence.

"A beauty!" he would then say mock sorrowfully, "So big he broke my line!"

My friends had standards: they drew the line at poisoning the river with a brew of "yalla root" (yellow spurge) which they condemned roundly. But I've seen one or two of my Glensmen turned Free State soldiers blow up a pool by hurling a grenade into it. The explosion broke a gut in the fish which then floated to the surface with no injury apparent on its skin.

The miniature village on the cliff-top above the river comprising about forty-five thatched houses contained the snug homes of many, but not all, of these "anglers". This area, designated Convent Street by the authorities, was vernacularly known as Gleann a' Phúca or the Glen of the Pooka or Hobgoblin. Legend had it that a century or two before, a greater number of these thatched cottages existed in the town but were burned down as a result of a deranged girl called "Showbox" setting a cabin on fire one Sunday while the occupants were at Mass.

The story goes on to tell that the priest was called from the altar to use his priestly powers to control the conflagration but not before a baby was burned to death. The priest is said to have read out of his Mass book and the flames went out at a certain point near the entrance to the Gleann, thus saving this enclave. The burned-out cottages of the town were then replaced with two storey houses of stone and slate and that part of the street was called New Street, later Market Street.

Living as I did in Market Street, I spent the greater part of my youth and adolescence in the Gleann. The forge, where two portly brother blacksmiths worked, controlled the area. In addition to the shoeing of horses the forge was also the clearing house for all that happened in the Gleann. The elder brother dispensed nicknames, many of them ironically apt, which to this day cause members of the old stock to wince at their mention: the younger brother rebuked miscreants or informers by means of a low-pitched mocking whistle sounded on a single note, repeated in a sort of throbbing or pulsing manner. The pair were nicknamed Belly Brothers by way of retort from those whose sensibilities were wounded by the mockery from the pursed lips.

No one dared to grow angry or riled at the nightly "Rambling House" held in the smith's kitchen which adjoined the forge. If a person breached the regulation he was given what was called "the Gandhi treatment", a cold kind of welcome and in extreme cases he was denied entrance. A kind of school, it was held during the winter months.

I spent surely twenty years of nightly attendance at this odd vernacular university. This was before the radio arrived on the scene. The first lesson taught and learned was as follows: one never took offence at what was said for this was a no-holds-barred type of institution. Without compunction an adversarial member of this minor Dáil would, figuratively speaking, dig up your dead mother from her grave and slam you across the face with her corpse if he thought that it would help him score a debating point.

When the talk wasn't of salmon, the twenty to twenty-five men present discussed all sorts of subjects. The post-1916 national change from conservatism to approval of the "rebels", was implicit from the start – people of little or no property had two adventurous courses open to them – join the British Army which some of them did, or embrace nationality and look forward to the then remote possibility of Irish freedom.

The younger and fatter of the pair of blacksmiths was a nationalist from the start: Davis's paper *The Nation* had been read aloud by a literate man seated on an anvil in the forges of Munster in the preceding century and my blacksmith friends were fully conscious of the historical traditions of their trade.

From time to time one of those in the kitchen academy would be asked to sing; my attempt at offering a West End English ditty picked up from comedians in the Market Hall was shot down on the spot. "One of Moore's!" the smith would growl from his throne where he sat at the left of the fireside, his posture steadied by his grip on a leather working belt which hung by its buckle from a cuphook at the side of the timber mantelpiece.

I would then render "Believe Me If All Those Endearing Young Charms" or "Let Erin Remember", this although my callow musical soul was bursting to render the latest and to the smith the most distressing and vacuous pop songs of that hour. "Horsey keep your tail up", "Yes, We have no Bananas," or even "I'm one of the Nuts from Barcelona" to which last we often added, "I am in my poll, I'm from Listowel." Thomas Moore's father, John Moore of Keylod, Moyvane, a short distance from the town, had served his time to the licensed trade in Tralee and later (1779) bought a pub in Aungier Street, Dublin. The Kerry Moores were one of the seven septs of Laois who in 1607 under Patrick McCrossan, later called Crosbie, were granted lands in Kerry.

The men attending this "Rambling House" (I often paused to look around at them) were drawn mostly from the Gleann itself with the addition of a few shopkeepers from the adjoining streets. The members stood around the kitchen, leaned against the stairway or dresser or crouched in a corner if all the súgán seats were occupied. The place was badly lighted: an oil lamp hung from the ceiling over the table which was covered with a dark oilcloth with a Greek motif at its edges. The light barely touched the corners of the kitchen. Those present had various occupations: a miller or two, a shoemaker, a plasterer, a carter, a joiner, a harnessmaker, a gardener, a plumber, a fishmonger, a cooper, a few amateur market truckers, a postman, a dairyman, a turkey-plucker, a coffin liner, a process server, a publican or a hardware merchant, both these last of country origins. There were also old age pensioners of various trades or occupations.

To me the most interesting members were the ex-soldiers; they had been to India - and even to Jerusalem ("I'm in the land where Christ was born: I wish to Christ I was in the land where I was born"), the Andaman Islands, France and Egypt. There was one who had fought in the Boer War. "Halt the Bays, Steady the Greys and let the Lawncers pahss!" was his war cry. His nickname was Lancer.

One of these ex-soldiers told me that the cows in Greece were purple, another said that in a bazaar in the Himalayas, a beggar had plucked at his puttees (the beggar turned out to be a deserter from the Munster Fusiliers) and asked if Kerry had won the All-Ireland Football Final the previous September.

The subjects discussed were various but indigenous. Apart from one wonder tale, a rendition of which I had taken an imperfect version of from the last of the seanchaithe, the rest of the talk would come under the head of tittle-tattle, idle chat or seanchas.

Fishing, Jackie the Lantern, superstition, the Famine, famous step dancers and dancing masters, greyhounds, odd characters of all sorts, Dan O'Connell, Bulmer Hobson and Commandant Pearse (pronounced Persse as they called the Easter Week leader and indeed so named a greyhound in his memory). Faction fights were mentioned as were fairy forts, hungry grass and hidden gold. (If one spends all night digging for treasure be sure to leave before cockcrow and, if the guardian of the treasure appears in the form of a bull, one has only to stoop down and throw a clod at him and he'll run off.) Gravel pits were on the agenda as was the appearance of living men seen taking part in ghostly hurling matches, or riding ghostly horses at midnight, their deaths to be announced the following day. "The time of the Danes," or "old gods' time" were phrases often heard. "Never caught for a word," "brains to burn" or "He'd give talk to Councillor Butt" were descriptions used to praise an intelligent and scholarly man. There I learned that the Irish word *plámás* was a corruption of *blancmange* which, with coloured jellies, was the staple dessert of my childhood. I learned also that the triangular "pointer" of home-baked "pake", a bread made from maize meal at times mixed with some white flour, was so called because a ship called the "Alpaca" was one of the first vessels to bring the welcome maize to Ireland in famine days.

At times the tales told indicated the macabre and the murkier side of human nature. Here is one!

There was this middle-aged couple who lived at the foot of a mountain. They had no children. This troubled the man as he feared that, after his death, his small holding of land would "go out of his name". His wife was troubled too. She wrapped cloths around her belly and told her husband she was expectin'. The man was delighted. As months passed she increased the bulk of the cloths and later told her husband that she was nearin' her time. One day when the man was away at a fair the wife killed the cat, skinned it and laid it out in the cradle in the back room. When the husband came back she told him she had had a miscarriage. "'Twas a boy too," she told her gullible man. "Where is it?" he wanted to know. She had the cat's body dolled up for him to see by candlelight. This satisfied the man. Afterwards he told the neighbours, "What harm, but he had the sideface of my poor father."

Here's another example of the queasier side of my "Rambling House". Reference was being made to a woman of a family who lived at a distance from the town and in a boggy area. The expression that cropped up was "She's a daughter of the sheets spreader – and she couldn't be good". "Who was the sheets spreader?" I kept asking. It was then explained to me:

A good-looking, respectable girl lived a short distance from the bitter old lady who was called "the Spreader". The Spreader had a daughter of her own who was plain and bitter, so she grew jealous of the good-livin' girl. The old woman always seemed to be spreading clothes to dry on the blackthorns near her cottage but what she was really doing was watching the good-looking girl. The old witch got nothing for her trouble so at last she put out a rumour that the neighbouring girl had had a baby, that she strangled it at birth and buried it in the high mountain or virgin bog. The police got wind of it; they came out from town and questioned the innocent girl and even searched the bog for traces of a grave. The girl's reputation was destroyed: she locked herself in a back room, went into a depression and died. The old woman who caused all the havoc died soon afterwards. Those nowadays who pass that way in the dead of night see her ghost spreading white sheets on the blackthorns near her cottage. That's the punishment she'll have to keep doin' for all eternity to make up for her sin.

I liked the little story told about the first hare that came to Ireland.

"Long ago there was no hare in Ireland. Across the sea a young hare heard a story about a green island where he could be king since there were no hares at all there. So he said good-bye to his father and mother, dived into the sea and swam off to Ireland. He landed on a lovely strand and after shaking himself he stole up the grassy cliff side to see what the place was like. He met a dog: the dog looked at the hare and the hare looked at the dog. The dog dug his paws into the earth and began to chase the hare. The hare raced down the grassy cliff and, diving into the sea, got back safely to his own country.

"Years after, another young hare, son of the first hare, heard the story of his father's adventure. He said, 'I'll be king of Green Island'. Said good-bye, dived into the sea, swam and swam and landed on the yellow beach. Up the cliff side until he came upon a field. In the field was a bull. The bull looked at the hare. The hare looked at the bull. The bull stamped his hooves, lowered his head, bellowed and chased the hare. The poor little animal barely got away with his life.

"In the course of time, his son again, grandson of the first hare said, 'I'll be king of Green Island,' Did the same as his father and grandfather. Up the cliff. Came to a field. Saw a sheep. They looked at one another. The hare stamped his feet and the sheep ran away. The hare was glad. He looked around him and said, 'There's one animal here that's afraid of me, so here I'll stay and be king.' And he's remained here ever since."

Towards the turn of the last century it seemed to me that there had been a revival of interest in oratory together with a desire for self-improvement in the English language. Pride of penmanship, a command of Pitman's shorthand together with literary and debating societies, temperance societies and gymnastic societies, possibly deriving from the Young Ireland Movement, were widespread in the country. Many of these movements had halls of their own.

Like the Greek orators of old, some of the old men of my acquaintance had in their prime repaired to a rocky part of the River Feale and there, in the manner of the ancient Greeks with pebbles in their mouths, had delivered impassioned orations against the din of the roaring water. To my knowledge, the last public representatives of this oratorical genus were James Dillon of Ballaghadereen and DJ Madden of Rathkeale. The old-style Redemptorist fathers who thundered at Mass against "good honest Irish boys up to their chins in sin" were past masters of this art.

The biennial arrival of the Missioner to the parish church struck the correct note in his sermon on Hell and Eternity.

"Forever! Forever! Without end!"

"Let me give you some idea of what Eternity means. Men, Christian men, listen to me carefully. I want you to imagine a small steel ball the size of a marble. I want you now to increase the size of this imaginary ball to the size of an orange, then to the size of a football. By a great leap of the imagination I ask you to imagine a huge, polished steel ball the size of this world.

"A little wren, a bird common in every townland in Ireland, is flying through space. Once every one hundred years its wing brushes against the surface of the huge steel ball. That impact upon the steel ball would be light, you'd say. Yet I tell you that if this process went on and on into time until the steel ball was worn away by the touch of the wing, eternity would only be beginning."

As far as my memory serves the strict episcopal ban on the forgiveness of perjury was relaxed at Mission time. The Missioners were then empowered to forgive. I heard one of the old poachers say, "Next Saturday night, I'll go back to God with banners flying!"

There were others in the Gleann whose education was limited but they too sought their place in the oratorical sun.

"Make a speech, Topper," we boys would shout at an outwardly sensible, upright man who occupied the rather reprehensible occupation of process server. As we spoke, his façade of aloofness dropped like an apron from a peg. Climbing the pedestal of a low wall or cart nearest to his feet, he would begin to declaim in a stentorian tone of voice.

"Ladies and gentlemen, citizens of the august capital of North Kerry, I who address you am the most topping orator who ever topped this total town." (At this point with cheers and hurrahs we urged the speaker to further peaks of frenzied oratory.)

The accomplishment, if it was, was also in evidence in the Urban Council Chamber where Bill Fitzgerald from the Gleann, Chairman, instructed the town crier to issue a proclamation to the citizens on the theft of a wooden encased pump from the Urban Council Yard. The Crier, a huge, black-avised man with black bushy sideburns and a silver watchchain swinging from the protuberance of his stomach stood at the street corner, rang his bell and dutifully declaimed:

Lost, stolen or strayed from the Town Pits
An iron cow, with wooden tits
Whoever finds her and brings her to Fitz
Will get as reward, a mouthful of threepenny
bits.

The Bellman was a lover of poetry in his own right.
He was wont to chant:

Go forth in haste with brush and paste
Proclaim to all the nation
That men are wise who advertise
In every generation.

Or, taking his stand outside the harness maker'sshop, always a valued resort of mine, he would ring his bell and bellow in our direction:

A town seized by fire, they held consultation
Which was the best method of fortification
The mason spoke up and gave his opinion
To defend it with stone would save the dominion.

The brave skilful joiner he put in his spoke
"'Twould be better," he said "to defend it with oak."
But the currier being wiser than both put together
Said, "Believe me my friends, there is nothing like leather."

Back in the forge, on one occasion, I found a somewhat mysterious atmosphere in the place.

The pair of stout smiths always sat down on a side-seat in the intervals of shoeing a horse. (A tart neighbour commenting on their resting in the intervals of shoeing said the ceremony was like High Mass.) When the animal was shod and owner and horse gone, one of the pair looked up at me.

"Have you a cookery book by a woman called Beeton?" he asked.

"What do you want to cook?" I asked in Kerry fashion, answering question with question.

Silence, which made the query more mysterious still. "I have a bird", he said finally.

The younger brother beckoned to me to follow him. Conspiratorially he led the way to the yard closing the door behind him. He removed the cover from a barrel. I looked in. A wounded swan, one wing obviously broken, with yellow beak and gleaming eyes looked up at me. I was taken aback.

Measuring my reaction the smith said, "See is there anythin' in that book of yours about cookin' a swan." I looked the smith fully between the eyes as he continued: "It barely flew up from the river below, over the market wall, in the door of the forge, hit the roof and fell down on to the hearth."

I wanted that swan to go free so looked around as if searching for ghosts. I knew how to play on the superstitious strain in the brothers. "If I were you," I whispered, "I wouldn't kill that bird. First its flesh is oily. And then . . . "

"And then what?"

"Ten years of bad luck will follow. Ever hear of Fionnuala, Conn, Fiachra and Aodh?"

"Who the hell are they?"

"The Children of Lir," I said. "Human children changed into swans. You're an old friend of mine and I advise you not to have anything to do with that bird of legend."

The smith growled, replaced the cover on the barrel, and ponderously returned to the forge. His older brother listened to my verdict and spat on the floor.

"Bullshit," he said. "I'll gattle that swan tonight. Hang him up for a week and he'll make fine eatin'."

I knew he wouldn't. He didn't. That same night the older brother clutched the bird and bore it down through the market to the cliff side. On the way there the bird got its good wing free and knocked its bearer flat on his back. It then waddled down the clay cliffside and into the water.

The would-be swan-killer was in bed for a week. About that time too the other brother was kicked by a horse and his leg swelled as big as a pig's middle. He too was in bed for some time; a pulley and rope fixed to the rafters raised him to a sitting position.

"You both had a narrow escape," I said by way of being a Job's comforter, "Don't meddle with swans again."

The killing of a cow, its meat designed for sale in the market, took place in the kitchen of one of the smallest cottages. The actual dispatch of the beast is too gory to describe in detail but the raising up of the carcass, by means of a rope slung over a rafter, was an epic affair. The neighbours, prankish as they were, called in to uplift the dead animal, often "lid" on the rope, with the excuse that the carcass was "almighty weighty". Then, on a signal, all three men would pull together with the result that the forelegs of the beast shot out through the thatch of the roof.

The people of the Gleann looked up to the Bard of Thomond, that wilful, vituperative but talented Limerick poet. The better read among them could recite "Drunken Thady and the Bishop's Lady." They never tired of hearing about *Seán na Scuab*, the bumpkin from the Clare hills who became Lord Mayor of Limerick as a result of a tie in a mayoral election. He was then powdered, periwigged and set up as a judge to administer justice in the City Hall.

Michael Hogan, the Bard, described Seán's judicial finery in scathing terms: "Art and nature took the field, but stubborn nature would not yield." As for his poor mother who was brought before him on a charge of causing a disturbance at the courthouse door as she sought her missing son, and uttered the maternal plea of "Don't you know me Seán?" - the good lady was silenced by the filial rebuke of "Arrah, hush woman, I don't know myself."

This small huddle of cottages, scarcely worthy of being called a community, was almost completely self-sufficient and as such, in my opinion, could fairly exemplify the then Sinn Féin ideal of Ireland in microcosm.

It had its own tradesmen. Each cottage had its neat kitchen garden, some with fruit trees. Each house killed its own pig and the resultant glistening bacon flitches, hanging from the rafters, lasted the entire year. Hens clucked and cocks crew in its little haggards: the housewife fattened geese and her ducks waddled down to the river. The bog yielded turf and bog deal. Salmon and trout were a gambler's bonus but at times they paid rich dividends. It had one little shop which sold sweets to the children. The single cottage slated, as opposed to the thatch of the others, had once been a "hedge school" of a primitive sort. And for amusement it had characters galore – people who dared to be themselves.

The Gleann, as a thatched enclave or accretion to a country town, has of course vanished by now. The tricks and status and dare I say, the culture of its colourful inhabitants is but a wraith of memory. The last thatched house had its roof fall in a few years ago – take the fire on the hearth out of a thatched house and it shrinks in and down in a short time. The Gleann area is now lorded over by a huge telephone exchange: a supermarket with a doctor's surgery and a solicitor's office are among the few modest slated cottages that still manage to hold a tenacious grip on their original sites.

Its doings and misdoings continue to surface in my written work – though I keep overconsciously asking myself if these memories/ experiences, human contacts, reactions, vagaries and so forth are of the slightest help to me. Its original inhabitants also are remembered infrequently by the descendants of its forefather citizens who, for the most part, have come up in the world – largely through education. I would have wished it demolished when in its prime and the whole area redesigned by a sensitive architect. But that was not to be. It went piecemeal.

These were the people who fashioned me in my malleable youth. Their brand is on me still. My first novel *Children of the Rainbow* with its description of an archaic ghetto called Cloone is based on the happenings of my youth and adolescence in the Gleann. It's a young man's book but it still lives on. I dared to include in the narrative a highly sensitive incident concerning the refusal of the coffin of a young woman to be allowed into the local church. Conscious of being right I rode out the storm which followed. My story *The Good Death in the Green Hills,* which has to do with the death and funeral of the last seanchaí supplanted by the Atwater Kent Radio, also stemmed from the same source. I wrote trenchantly against the state and demanded that its children be educated in proper surroundings: as indicated I stood up against the Church when I felt that the virtue of charity was being breached. And I did not run away. I stood my ground and lived to tell the tale.

Even my own house, which stood on the fringe of these activities, has had to endure change. The Market is replaced by a cattle mart, which God be praised, still has the cattle cries and smells of my youth. My own home has been neatly incorporated into a supermarket. To add an odd cream topping to my dessert of memories, whenever I stand at the checkout with my wire basket of groceries dangling from my hand, I suddenly realise with a pang of recall that exactly where I stand was once the centre of the kitchen in my boyhood home.

It was at this moment of my relived adolescence that I stood still and began to take stock of myself – to determine where I stood in the mental codification of events. To some extent I had now established where I lived in terms of place as defined by Market, River and Community. These were only some of my co-ordinates. Like it or not I had now to ascertain or recognise where it was I stood in terms of wider place and elusive time. For if I were to be an Irish Thoreau, there were still more acres of my Walden to be explored.

But back to my co-ordinates. I simply had to find my bearings – where it was in my small country town I stood in terms of time and also in the context of the story of my people. My interest in what went on around me was not as yet fully concerned with a future literary exploitation or projection. Quite the contrary, I was living as my neighbours lived, my concerns were their concerns. But at times I confess to casting my mind forward into the future and then, as it were, looking back over my mental shoulder to gain unusual aspects of what took place around me. In other words I was seeking a perspective on a way of life that was doomed. At times I thought I was on a fool's errand. But there was something in me that told me that mine was the true way forward. That, with time, I would find my experiences of value.

CHAPTER THREE

"History is bunk!" As far as my memory serves me it was a most distinguished American citizen who made that statement.

Before I hasten to label it one of the most fatuous judgements ever delivered, I counsel myself to pause and analyse it more carefully. I do so as a prerequisite to finding how it was with me in the truly vital years between 1916 and 1923 and perhaps a little beyond: this was the period when I was, as it were, congealing into the shape of the manhood I would assume for the greater part of my life to follow.

I tackle this projection by changing or mixing the metaphor of co-ordinates which properly belongs to the discipline of geography and, by the alchemy of imagination, I see myself as I was then, assuming the role of an Australian aborigine, going forth into the trackless desert by invisible pathways to find what a voice in his racial memory (*pace* Bruce Chatwin) tells him are his "songlines".

"History is bunk?" As it is often presented and taught in the form of parrot-like memorisation and regurgitation of dates it is truly bunk. What is forgotten is that history is far more than the daisy-chaining of dates and the itemisation of treaties or the storming of stout walls. History – and I have often called it hi-story – has to do with people of flesh and blood, who were once truly alive and who possessed all the virtues and vices, the ambitions, faults and failures, depressions and elations which form the common heritage of mankind.

By what shift then, does one go back in thought and establish contact with the protagonists of history, to enable one to see them as they truly were? And to define oneself in the process?

One can do this only by isolating a human trait evidenced by some significant incident. The history books of themselves do not suffice. Defining one's self in the context of history is important: whether or not a person is conscious of it, history tends to shape the mind and outlook of the human being.

Laughable though it seems, I now recall an incident of my schooldays which occurred in the teaching of history and which remains clearly fixed in my mind long after the chronicling of major events has faded into mist. It concerns the negotiations leading up to the signing of one of the great treaties of middle Europe – one upon which it is fitting to say the lives of millions depended.

The plenipotentiaries had a difficult task. Argument was confronted by counter-argument until the principals were faced with the sorry prospect of an adjournment and the probability of renewed warfare.

At this point the authorities outside the council room locked the doors of the noble chamber and told the adversaries within that they would not be released until they had reached an agreement.

"We need sanitary arrangements," the deadlocked emissaries bleated. "Use what you have," was the message shouted through the keyhole of the barred door. At this point the professor telling the story said, "So all Europe, through its major negotiators (fortunately all male!), united by the common need of humanity, gathered around one large vase and urinated into it. Possibly, because of the recognition of this common bond of recurrent human need and the mild hilarity it evoked, agreement was quickly reached."

Using my odd yardstick of personalising history I asked myself how far back I could reach in an imagined time span and identify myself with the hi-story of my people, even if at times it took me far beyond the Irish shore. Folklore was a valuable resource in this regard. Presently I found that I could extend my arm as it were to the end of the eighteenth century and even touch the United States in its War of Independence in the years 1776-1777.

The early 1920s was a time of major emigration. American Wakes were numerous. My father was speaking on a favourite topic. "It's easy now to be admitted to the United States. Formality is minimal. All you have to do is go down to Monny Lyons, buy a ticket, go up to Cobh, stay overnight at Daly's and off you go in the morning. Very little fuss. It won't be always like this. The day will come when the US will be crowded with immigrants and the Government there will start to pick and choose. So entry will be difficult. You'll maybe have an interview at the Embassy. The person behind the desk will say, 'Why do you wish to enter the United States?' Stand up then and say this: 'Because a great-great-great-grand-uncle of mine fought for some years under young General Lafayette for the freedom of the United States.' After that I'll wager you won't be refused."

(I was always eager to play out this little drama in a US Consulate. However I was given an indefinite visa quite readily and the story remained untold. But seventy years after I had heard the injunction, I mentioned it in an award acceptance speech in the US Ambassador's Residence in the Phoenix Park.)

Still in the US and now a century later. That stretching and touching was still very important to me. I visited Andersonville in the southern States of the US. This area was the site of a huge concentration camp in the American Civil War and the events connected with it were the subject of a major novel. My host and old friend told me that his ancestral home had been occupied in the Civil War by Irish-speaking soldiers from the North. Conscripted almost as they left the ships!

Walking amid the almost countless markers above the dead I enquired about some twelve or so grave markers set apart from the others. "Were these officers?" came my enquiry. My host laughed grimly. "These were scoundrels who preyed on their fellow internees. They were condemned to death by a court drawn from the prisoners themselves – this with the consent of their captors." I wondered if any of these were Irish – so I checked. They were! A disproportionate number indeed.

"Bull Run" and "La Basse" were nicknames common in my home town in the old days. The latter refers to an ancestor who fought in World War I but the former has its origins in the fact that the eponymous forebear was an Irish-American soldier who served in the battle so named and who also was on duty outside the theatre on the very night that Abraham Lincoln was shot dead by the actor Wilkes Booth.

Reverting to the American War of Independence I find odd fragments of association which help me to identify with that conflict. Grown curious, I went on to read more about it. These little aids are for me like the pitons with which a mountaineer is enabled to scale mountainsides.

The 1798 rebel ballad "The Croppy Boy" contains the line "And taken was I by my Lord Cornwall." Cornwallis, as he is more generally known, was the leader of the defeated English forces in the American War of Independence. Too vainglorious to surrender in person, he sent one of his officers to fulfil the dismal duty. The victorious colonists would have none of it. He had to surrender in person and in humility! Odd that he turns up again in Wexford, his name then cropped to its basic Cornwall.

And by the way, didn't Marie Antoinette *almost* finish her days in a high house in Dingle?

Again turning the leaves of memory I come face to face with the Irish Rebellion of 1798. Again the imaginative little tag of personal identification: the sheaf of freedom upspringing from the Wexford Croppy graves where the leather satchels of grain each lad had carried with him for food, spilt in the damp shallow underground so that the germinated grain moved up out of darkness to mark the unknown grave in a gesture truly symbolic of the Irish struggle for freedom.

Another little hook-and-eye that links me with '98 is the song "The Boys of Wexford." The daughter of the yeoman captain who declared her love for the Irish insurgent and United Irishman, Tom McKenna of Monaghan, dressed herself as a man and fought side by side with him at Vinegar Hill. After the defeat and the greasing of their boots by the yeomen of Tullow with the bellyfat of Fr Murphy's body as it burned on a rack, the fugitive couple made their way to the then remote countryside of County Kerry: the girl in question, Jenny Foulkes, together with her husband Tom, lies buried in Kilsynan graveyard five or six miles from Listowel on the road to Tralee. Their descendants, the McKennas, Troys, Hegartys, O'Boyles *et al* are today numerous and honoured in this area.

(I possess a token linking me with Lord Edward Fitzgerald which I refuse to reveal. Pull off my fingernails with pincers and I'll still continue to refuse. This is unfair, I admit. Lord Edward's resting place is known: but Robert Emmet's is not. Kerry folklore mentions a carrier named McMahon who is alleged to have brought Emmet's body to Kerry; there is a perplexing clue in local folklore that it lies buried in Blennerville churchyard. This I cannot endorse as true but Emmet's mother was a Mason from outside Tralee.)

And this reminds me that Robert Emmet, Daniel O'Connell and Harman Blennerhasset were all three descended from Jenkin Conway, a planter, who in 1613 was granted castle and lands in the Killorglin area – in later years the name Conway occurs frequently among officers in the Irish Brigade in France.

It's easy for me to gain personal purchase on Daniel O'Connell – King Dan or "King of the Beggars" – take your choice of aliases, for Kerry is awash with folklore on him. I establish contact through the medium of a saucy little ballad called "Daniel O'Connell Makes Children by Steam". This song, I believe, is the *fons et origo* of the fame "The Liberator" won as a virile sire, a reputation which I suggest is greatly exaggerated.

The ditty opens with a tinkerman, his budget on his shoulder, whistling merrily as he trudges along a country road. He looks into a haggard and sees an old woman milking her cow. "Any news?" she asks him. (Julius Caesar said the Celts were forever asking one another the same question.)

"Plenty news!" the tinkerman says, with a twinkle in his gamey eye, "Daniel O'Connell has issued a proclamation that from this day forward all children are to be conceived and born by steam." (It was a time when steam was coming into general use as a motive power as indeed nuclear power seems designed to do today.)

The old woman swallows the bait. "What? Women are finished you say."

"That's right. Woman's reign is over."

Bridling up, the old lady shouts, "I'm past childbearin' age myself, but begod if I was put to it I'd make a better hand of makin' a child than either you or Big Dan of Derrynane."

But where am I off to now with my O'Connell images of Clampar

Dawley and other history bit-players? Eating sandwiches in a courthouse in Doneraile, is it? I'm establishing a sort of bridgehead or grip on events long gone. I'm collecting a squirrel hoard, a private source of glee or intimate suffering. What am I, then? An Earwigger, a Peeping Tom, a humaniser, a panner for the golden phrase, a hypersensitive but stupid mutt, a long-term policy detective, a bloodhound, a fact sifter, a screwball observer of incident, one unplugged in to the mundane and transitory, a hallucinationist, a researcher bearing a banner with the inscription, "It belongs to him who says it best."

The Act of Union, The Black Book of those who sold Ireland, and Bould Robert usher in a new century. Wasn't it a Duagh man who fired the first shot at Waterloo? And wasn't Leahy's Corner House down there in The Square built by Ned Callaghan of Coolnaleen out of severance pay received after Cape St Vincent? Privateer Paul Jones belatedly rings a bell of remembrance and shouts, "Me!" Obediently I slip back in time to recall when you, Paul, were off the Kerry Coast – kinda trapped at Tarbert-on-the-Shannon, wasn't it? Or down around coastal Iveragh where you sent some of your Irish-speaking crew ashore to ask the McCarthys to join up. Which indeed some of them did!

Ah, the foolish faction fights of the 1830s. Extraordinary when one comes to regard the phenomenon at close quarters. Faction fighting was widespread in Ireland at that time and as a means of disunity among the mere Irish it was cunningly countenanced by the landlords.

Our local battle was fought between the Cooleens and the Black Mulvihills. (My forebears belonged to the Mulvihills – or so I am informed.) On Ballyea Strand south of Ballybunion in the year 1834 a massive and quite formal affray left between twenty and forty dead and hundreds wounded. (Statistics vary!) One grim story survives.

A woman met a boy, his face streaming blood, returning from the fight. "Let me wash your head in this stream, child," the woman said. As she did so, "What side were you on?" she asked gently. Foolishly he told her. She took off her woollen stocking and slipped a round sea-stone into it. "Lower your head boy." The boy obeyed. The woman then swung the weighted stone in its stocking and crashed it down on the boy's skull killing him on the spot. And then there is the tale of the Mulvihill man who married a Cooleen woman. She brought along her father's cudgel and he his father's stout blackthorn. Every St John's Day, 24th June, the cudgels in the loft fought hot and heavy while the husband and wife stood below listening to the progress of the fray.

It was but a short step in time to the Famine.

In the teens of this century, when I was eight or nine years of age, I got this massive hang-up about the Famine period. A phrase or two set me off. I quickly realised that there must be quite a number of old people in North Kerry who, as children, had lived through the Famine and who still possessed clear memories of it.

So off I went on my bike to visit a number of old people all over eighty and living in North Kerry. After the preliminaries I ventured to ask with the directness of youth, "What do you remember about the Famine?" I heard various human stories, many of them myths. One such was of a jealous neighbour entering a house which he knew was hard hit with hunger. Approaching midday the woman of the house went out to the haggard, and later returned with a heavy covered pot which she slung by the pothooks on to the crane. She then built a good turf fire underneath. The nosy neighbour kept staring at the pot and after a time said, (and kept saying) "Try your spuds, ma'am, they'll be gone in bruscar." This went on until, in despair, the housewife with a prayer to God's mother lifted the pot (which she had previously filled with stones) and taking off the cover revealed to her own astonishment a pot full of floury potatoes.

A barefooted mother down from the hills and weak with hunger, walked ten miles and waited for six hours in a long queue at the Old Mill which then stood beside the entrance off The Square to the island racecourse. She staggered home with her hard-earned tin pan of yellow meal to receive a warm greeting from the assembled family. The meal was mixed with water and perhaps a little milk and then stirred into some sort of gruel and hung in a pot over the open fire. Just as the meal was almost cooked, a huge blob of soot fell down the chimney and dropped right into the bubbling gruel. Everyone began to cry. Soot and all was poured into the waiting wooden piggins and the tearful children did their best to pick out the fragments of soot and eat the poorest of food.

A family was pointed out to me. "In Famine days their grandfather shot a man dead who tried to steal a turnip." Another old man said, "You know the so-and-sos in town. Big shots now. Let me tell you how they began. On Gale Bridge a collector of the dead came upon the corpse of a lovely young woman curled up on the brow of the road. He turned over the body with this point of his boot. Out rolled a lovely baby. The baby was crying because it had been taken off the tit. They took away the mother's body and buried it. But the baby, reared in town, was the ancestor of those rich people I've mentioned."

Old men crossing a meadow on which the long grass had been of necessity left uncut always took off their wide black hats and clutched them on top of their walking sticks as they staggered on. If weakness overcame them they bore their weight down on the stick and hat so that standing as a signal, it would mark the spot where they were lying. This done, they slid to the ground. (A German refugee of World War II told me that when she had gathered food scraps from rubbish bins, she concealed the food under her skirt before she fainted with the hunger.)

When I attended St Michael's College in the '20s we would walk along the stone wall dividing the college grounds from the GAA Ground. From the splits between the stones we could pick out flakes of whitewash. These were remnants of the lime washed lean-tos built against the wall in famine times to shelter the fever- and hunger-stricken inmates as they shuddered to their last.

A nick of a sharp knife drawn on a cow's back and a hungry man could suck as much blood as would keep him alive for a short time. A roasted herring was hung up over the table and bread dipped in meagre gravy was pointed at the fish to add an imaginary savoury to the meal. "Bread and point", or "Potatoes and point," was on the menu on that day.

The story is told of a gentleman walking along a country road in famine days who heard the sounds of children quarrelling coming from a cabin. Stooping his head beneath the low lintel he asked what was wrong. One child spoke up and said, "We were dippin' and he was rowlin'" – this in reference to the pieces of bread being soaked in gravy by another one of the family.

In my enquiries I was puzzled by one fact: the people seemed unwilling to use the sea coast as a source of provender – if sea-angling was too laborious, shellfish off the rocks could have maintained the puff of life. I came to the conclusion that there was some superstition going back to the mythology of the Fianna which regarded the eating of shellfish as a sign of the lowest form of deprivation. The same notion surfaces in Lady Gregory's play, *The Workhouse Ward.*

I published my theory somewhere and was later flatly contradicted by an old fisherman who said the people "by the shore" *did* live on fish and shellfish. I then fell back on the defence that the generality of the population were far too weak to get as far as the sea coast: at this point I rested my case.

As a boy I stood aside and watched petrol being poured on the piled up record books of our local workhouse. The Civil War was at its height and the great building was being destroyed by the Republican forces so as to prevent it falling into the hands of the "Staters." Only for this destruction of valuable documents our locality would have figured quite prominently in books like Mrs Woodham Smith's classic, *The Great Hunger.*

Black humour? One would hardly expect this to figure in the doleful tale of millions of people dying of starvation at home or choking on cholera on coffin ships or on Grosse Isle in the St Lawrence River. Yet, here is one such countryside story which has survived.

The old man died first. He had wasted away until he was reduced to skin and bone. His thin wife wailed and caoin-ed. Laid out on the crude kitchen table with a few mourners present, an equally crude coffin was brought in to enclose the corpse. The widow ceased to cry out. "Go out, Paddy," she said to her eldest son "and bring in an armful of hay and stuff it around your father so that he won't shame us rattlin' in the box." The son went off on the errand and returned with a gábhail of hay. The widow glared at her son and, prudent to the last, said, "Bad luck to you. How well you had to pull it out of the good cock."

I got the shock of my life at one answer I received. This came from a strong farmer. "Did your family suffer greatly from hunger during the Famine?" I had asked.

The man bristled with rage. He looked at me in scorn. "We were big farmers," he said. "We had no hunger! It's only the poor who suffer in famines."

How true, I told myself, even to the present day.

On then to the Fenian times. I knew some old Fenians who were still bitter about Bishop Moriarty's condemnation of their leaders. I heard first-hand accounts of "The Fenians of Caherciveen" enshrined in a local ballad about the brave but sorry attempt at insurrection which petered out in snow and sleet. The Fenian period slides inevitably into the Land War and the foundation of both the Gaelic League and the Gaelic Athletic Association.

Davitt and Parnell figure prominently in the latter part of the nineteenth century. I have a piece of Davitt's walking stick somewhere about the house. My father was at the penultimate meeting to welcome Parnell to Listowel. The embers of the Parnell split glowed redly in my youth. One sound recurs in my memory – the sound of heads being beaten against a shop shutters as the pro- and anti-factions fought one another on the streets of the town. I see paperbags of flour flying through the air in Parnell's direction. He had slept overnight at O'Mahony's of Kilmorna – a well-know nationalist family – their main residence is in Co Wicklow. As the carriage bearing Parnell to Listowel approached the height on the Mail Road overlooking the town, cheering crowds unharnessed the horses, manned the shafts and drew the vehicle in triumph into the streets.

He spoke in The Square, probably from a window of the Arms Hotel. There is some difference of opinion as to whether or not he spoke the vibrant words, "If I were dead and gone tomorrow . . . no man has the right to set bounds to the march of a nation," here, in Cork, or in Creggs in Co Roscommon. He may have spoken them in all three places.

I had now come close to a dramatic historic event generating literature. Inevitably, I am reminded directly of Joyce's *Ivy Day in the Committee Room* and indirectly of his masterpiece, *The Dead*.

The end of the century turns over in my mind. Apart from my birth in 1909, an event with which I can empathise only faintly, the next stopping point was the outbreak of the Great War I. I was six and a half in 1916 and was quite conscious of the epic nature of the Easter Rising. My father and his friends of the Gaelic League, through the medium of Feiseanna, Aeríochta and the "bicycle men" – (itinerant teachers of Irish) – and also through the pages of the *Dublin Leader, The Catholic Bulletin* from Gills, and the Gaelic League organ, *Fáinne an Lae*, had provided an overture to the revolt. I never dare to forget that when Ireland leaped for freedom she did so from the cultural springboard of the Irish language.

Much later, in 1966, in various branches of the media, I helped to celebrate the Golden Jubilee year of the Rising. Through the medium of research I gained a clear perspective on certain human and even humorous aspects of the activities in the General Post Office and elsewhere in the Dublin of that time. Much of this from the narration of my good friend, Eamon Dore and his wife, Nora Daly, both of whom took part in the Insurrection.

Eamon had been on duty outside the door of Pearse's office in the blazing building and later took part in The O'Rahilly's bayonet charge up Moore Street, an event celebrated in verse by WB Yeats.

"Our lads had broken down the parting walls into the adjoining houses in Henry Street, " Eamon told me, "so that we had explored our neighbours' premises at a fair distance from the main building. This we did in order to guard against attack and to identify a possible route of exit.

"We came upon a miniature waxworks with various historical figures represented. One of these was Napoleon Bonaparte. One of our lads, a Volunteer, impish by nature and Napoleonic in build, shed his green uniform and donned the uniform, sword and hat of Napoleon. Putting his hand inside his jacket he struck a pose much as Napoleon is thought to have assumed after his surrender on board the *Bellerophon*. At that moment Commandant Pearse arrived on a tour of inspection. The jester held his rigid stance even though his face was smudged. For a moment Pearse looked disbelievingly into 'Napoleon's' eyes and 'Napoleon' looked sternly back. Then Nap winked and Pearse broke down in laughter. He then recovered his composure and, passing no remark, proceeded on his tour of duty."

Eamon Dore records another incident:

"My brother-in-law, Ned Daly, was in charge of the Four Courts. During a lull in the fighting, his men discovered a cache of tennis racquets but no tennis balls. They emerged into the side alleys of the district to play tennis with scraps of turf known as 'ciaráns'. It was, to say the least of it, odd to see our warriors mimicking the then aristocracy in whose province the game then belonged and crying out jeeringly 'Balls to you, Miss Postlethwaite' as they struck the knobs of hard, black turf – or peat!"

As a further exercise in the humanising and, for me, the personalising of what often can be an arid exercise called history, I uncovered the following. During the siege of the GPO a pair of Swedish sailors, somewhat soused in alcohol, kicked on the panels of one of the side doors of the GPO and demanded entrance. As the door opened they asked to be allowed take part in the defence of the building. As I understand it, they were allowed in and did take some part in the fighting. They slipped away before the final surrender. I do not vouch for the truth of this anecdote.

I then saw Ireland slowly swing to nationalism as one by one the leaders were executed.

The death of Kitchener, also in 1916, had local interest for me. On a visit to my grand-aunt's house near the railway station, I saw a sheet of newspaper and an egg lying on the kitchen table. I was seated on a chair rolling the egg a short distance along the table and also reading the news heading upside down. "Kitchener . . . died . . . in . . . dirt" I read slowly. My aunt laughed heartily. "The word is duty," she said. At this point the egg rolled off the table and smeared the floor.

Local lore also says that as a boy Horatio Kitchener was cruel to hens, whipping them until they flew in all directions. I keep wondering if he were in The Square with his cattle on the day Parnell spoke.

The years 1916-23 passed by at speed simply because they were dramatic in the extreme. Not as intense as the recent events of Northern Ireland, it is true. The outlawed flag then hung from trees, the branch to which it was nailed was half-sawn through to trap the remover. The conscription upheaval embraced an incident concerning

Cardinal Mannix being stopped by a British destroyer from landing in Ireland. Welcome fires for him were set ablaze on the coastal hills.

Later still, the great houses went up in flames and roads were trenched. On the rails of the station fog signals sounded for returning internees. On such occasions the windows of the town also carried "illuminations" – candle stubs lighting on the inside sills. On various occasions pipers' bands played laments for the dead: brass and reed instruments played "The Dead March from Saul". Evening curfew was at six o'clock; the British soldiers marched out in two files on the pavements just as the town clock struck the hour. Discharging their service rifles into the air, they sometimes brought down electric wires to curl about them. At intervals, the officer in charge halted and knocked on a doorway to check the list of occupants nailed on the inside of the front door. This he did to ensure that no one was missing from the house without an excuse.

From our first storey window I saw a curious sight one evening as the curfew ritual was in progress. To my amazement one soldier from the file of Tommys on the opposite pavement threw down his rifle with a crash and, moving to mid-road, cast off his jacket and with great aggression declared, "The bloody Shinners are roight. I'll foight 'em no more." He was placed under guard and marched off.

Locked in our houses from six o'clock on glorious summer afternoons and incarcerated until eight am or so the following morning, we told the time by the bugle calls from the Yorks Encampment in the Cows' Lawn, now the town park. The Tans had moved into the barracks; the local RIC resented their presence and mutinied to provide a still higher level of drama – this they did by making stern protest against a shoot-to-kill order. Incredible as it sounds, one of the mutineers, Constable Hughes, later became a bishop! And many years later he visited what was then a garda station. "You seem to know your way about, my Lord?" the young garda who greeted him said. "I have reason to," the bishop replied.

The Auxies based in The Square were dangerous and mysterious buckoes sporting their jaunting Glengarry caps with the saucy pompons on top. They represented an officer class and seemed to resent the presence of a detachment of Tommys in the Castle House next door. Perhaps as a mark of their superiority, the Auxies had painted the words *Sans Souci* on the circular rim above the fanlight on their front door.

The drummer boy of the Yorks was a lad of about eleven or twelve – our own age at that time – and we local lads treated him with political ecumenism. He joined us with his little pail as we picked mushrooms on the island racecourse. For some reason he kept placing his hand over his eyes and gazing into the distance looking for the succulent fungi. "Look down at your boots," we told him. He did so, and found some lovely cup mushrooms peeping up from the rich clumps of cowpat grass. As a *quid pro quo* he taught us how to dive from the island bridge into what was then fairly shallow water. "When you hit the water, turn your palms upwards" – I can still recall his injunction.

All hell broke loose when the district inspector of police was shot dead a short distance from the barracks. The Black and Tans raced through the town firing at anything that moved. In imagination I still stand before the proclamation naming the houses to be burned as an official reprisal. The ejected owners stood by, and having been given a statutory time to remove some objects, the houses, drenched with petrol, were set ablaze.

I recall my attempt to brave the flames as fire began to take root in Flavin's bookshop. A couple of us asked our beloved bookseller to be allowed to dart in and rescue some fishing flies which we knew were in a drawer at the rear end of the shop. "At your own risk," he said. The smoke drove me back but my companion did rescue some fishing gear. Further up the street I stood by as Professor Breen watched the fire crack his shop windows and heard the whiskey bottles in his bar exploding. A postman tapped his elbow and handed him a letter. Paddy Breen tore it open and laughed. "An income tax demand from His Majesty's Government," he said showing me the document. The postman – he had served in the Middle East in World War I – joined in the laughter.

Strange to say, we young lads not only enjoyed all this excitement, we revelled in it. In my capacity as a member of Fianna Éireann I did little active service. I recall being stationed at a turn in the backway with orders that, if danger threatened, I was to run like hell and give three kicks to the door of a workshop which was both a forge and a gunsmith's workshop. This I dutifully did. I also had a couple of minor escapes. One haunts me yet.

A friend and I went ferreting rabbits in the fields west of the town. When we reached the warren we found Captain Watson of the British army and his batman already engaged on the same errand. The Captain looked at us, then whispered to his companion. The batman approached us and sharply asked questions: we proudly showed him our ferret which seemed to hook his attention. As we moved off to another warren, my friend remarked, "Lucky he didn't look into my fishing bag." "Why?" I asked. There and then he produced a loaded revolver. His big brother was "out with the boys" and he had taken the weapon from his brother's dump so as to have a few potshots at rabbits. I nearly collapsed at the thought of our narrow escape.

Standing in the door of the local newsagents one rainy afternoon, I heard the sound of shots being fired in the air as a Crossley tender passed by. Attached by a rope to the rear of the vehicle was what seemed like a log or pole which rolled oddly on the watery surface of the road. When the vehicle had passed I suddenly realised that what I thought was a log was a dead body, which proved later to be that of Paddy Galvin, a young volunteer shot in an ambush outside Sir Arthur Vicar's place in Kilmorna, six miles east of Listowel. Sir Arthur, a rather feather-headed person, had been Ulster King at Arms and Keeper of the Crown Jewels in Dublin Castle. The theft of these jewels has given rise to a core of conjectural literature – *Vicious Circle*; *Jewels* and the play, *Goodnight, Mr O'Donnell* are three that come readily to mind. Sir Arthur was later dragged out and shot dead and his house set ablaze. Curious as ever, I was out there the day following; the house still smoked but I was intrigued by the pets' graveyard.

The Tans were "death down" on the green and gold elastic belts worn by us boys at that time. A friend and I swaggered down town one day, each of us wearing one of these declarations of freedom. A Tan approached. He kicked my friend in the groin: as the boy staggered to his feet the Tan made him hand over the belt. Ignominiously I fled. The following day I was nearly split open by a stone which splintered the wooden frame of a shop fanlight beside me. It was hurled by an indignant Tan who was sure I intended rubbing out the inscription "Don't write! Come out and fight" he had written on the nearby shutters of the shop window. By clutching an iron railing I had drawn myself up simply to read the time on the shop clock through the fanlight.

At this time I was an altar boy invariably serving daily Mass at about eight o'clock am. One morning early as I hurried down the rainy street, to my surprise I met the parish clerk hurrying towards me. "Tend the altar," he said in broken tones. "My son was beaten by the Tans last night and he died half an hour ago." I shall never forget the sight of his son, John, a clerical student, laid out in his black suit and Roman collar with silver coins on his eyes. Grimmer memory still, I had actually seen the Tans beating someone with the butts of their rifles against a neighbour's door the night before, but never knew it was John.

At that time he was returning from having replenished the sanctuary lamp with colza oil, the sanctuary lamp before the tabernacle in St Mary's Church.

Came the truce. We sat on stools around bonfires in the streets singing for the first time our hidden rebel songs. We sang lustily and in defiance of the Tans who sneered as they passed by, "Who Fears to Speak of Easter Week?" "The Tri-Coloured Ribbon" and "Whack fol the Diddle". This last song, written by Peadar Kearney who also wrote the National Anthem, puzzled us, for we failed to recognise sarcasm as such in the lines "God Bless England is Our Prayer".

When we were savage, fierce and wild
Whack fol the diddle fol the di do day.
She came as a mother to her child
Whack fol the diddle fol the di do day.
Gently raised us from the slime,
Kept our hands from hellish crime,
And sent us to heaven in her own good time,
Whack fol the diddle fol the di do day.

But, O dear God! The Civil War broke all this unity among our people. It tore families asunder, renewing the Parnell split in horrendous form.

Areas followed a significant leader and each area or village retains the same political hue until this day. Grim reality replaced patriotic adventure. The blowing up of Republicans tied to trees at Ballyseedy, Tralee, froze our blood: fair play demands that the previous blowing up of Free State soldiers at Knocknagoshel should also be recorded. The cliff-side was ablaze with burning tar around the entrance to the Republican hideout of Clashmealcon Cave at the mouth of the Shannon where astonishingly, an English army deserter, Reginald (Rudge) Hathaway, held out among the Anti-Treaty forces. Later we heard that Aero Lyons's body, riddled with bullets, was lying on the rocks below. Aero was a Republican leader. This tragic occurrence filled us with further dismay. Take my word for it – no war is more fiercely or more uncompromisingly fought than a War of Brothers.

Some years later the following incident indicated a revival of a sense of national confidence and unity.

After the mid-twenties cease-fire in the Civil War we in Kerry found ourselves with two senior Gaelic football teams, each team more or less claiming the official tag. One was largely composed of upholders of the new Free State; the other was formed mainly from the ranks of Republican internees recently released from the Curragh camp, a place where they had ample opportunity for developing their football skills with, rumour had it, an old rag football.

Someone on the then Kerry County Board proposed the imaginative but menacing idea of organising a challenge match between the two sets of players.

The fixture generated tension and foreboding. The match could well revive the waning embers of the Civil War and act as a fuse to blow the county to pieces. Nothing of the sort: the match proved to be a delightful sporting and skilful exhibition of our native code. As a consequence both teams came together to form a panel of more than thirty top rank players to draw upon. The composite team thus formed had some memorable games, notably with Kildare, in the decade that followed.

During these troubled times when the embers of the Civil War still sullenly burned, our local hurling team, of which I was a member, received a challenge to play Abbeyfeale, our close sporting rivals. We accepted at once. We took along our hurleys and gear. When we reached the field by the river, we were told that it was a football match our challengers had in mind. "Very well," we said, "we'll play you at football."

As we were togged out and lined up, one of the opposing mentors did a peculiar thing: fingers in mouth he uttered a piercing whistle directed at a grove of trees some distance uphill. After a time a man emerged; as he approached the field he seemed to be furtively scanning the landscape and the handful of spectators. The newcomer proved to be the referee.

The game began. First it was physical, then it was damn rough. Tony, our stalwart, shouldered an Abbeyfeale player and sent him spinning into a deep culvert on the edge of the pitch. This occasioned a general melee. When some semblance of order was restored the referee called both teams together. Digging his hand deep into his back pocket he drew forth a Webley revolver. "The next fella who fouls will get the contents of this," he growled.

The match ended in an utter and eerie peace.

Up to this time I had an internationalist outlook on all sporting codes. The bonding power and the sense of pride generated by this incident made me pause and reconsider. Thenceforward whatever allegiance I had to offer, I gave it to games of native origin.

Notable figures flit in and out of my memories of the twenties. Ernie O'Malley was there with the horseshoe marks of rifle butts on his bruised body. Countess Marcievicz too (a friend of hers told me that, labouring to the last among Dublin's poor, she would open her gold-plated cigarette case and insert a five pack of Woodbines.) Count Plunkett with his snow-white beard is there reminding me that his 1916 hero son was once a skating instructor in Cairo. WB Yeats is there with my adolescent form stalking him to see what made him tick – this last in Dublin when I was in training as a national teacher in St Patrick's, Drumcondra.

But just before this, at home in Listowel, an event on a personal and family plane – my own history to be exact, branded me for life. Its effects turned up in very many guises in what I subsequently wrote. Even in this, my eighty-sixth year it continues to control me and often provides me with a purgative of emotions in the literary sense.

One morning when I went to my grandmother's for milk, my aunt said quietly, "Grandma is dead." My grandmother kept a dairy which supplied household milk. She used to parade my brother and myself up and down the kitchen while she chanted

Bryan and Jack
Dressed in black
Silver buttons behind their back.

Somehow or other I got the idea that by saying this Grandma was indicating that she spoke English too, for she was one of the very last speakers of Irish in North Kerry with folklorists like Fionan McColum writing down "her phrases in a printed book." She and my grandfather came from Beale, a scenic place on the Shannon estuary a few miles north of Ballybunion.

The house was quiet. The front door was closed. Women came in by the yard gate with various garments and vessels of hot water. They spoke in undertones. I sat on a stool under the cavernous hearth. My dignified and stately aunt – she too came and went seemingly outwardly undisturbed by her mother's death. I would miss Grandma, for she was loving and kind.

After a time the bustle ceased. The neighbouring women went away, leaving only my aunt and the girl who looked after the cows and the dairy. My aunt went upstairs. I was left alone in the kitchen. Now and again I threw an eye on my white enamel gallon on the kitchen table and wondered if I would get any milk that morning.

After a while Aunt Mary came down the stairs. She was dressed in her black and white house best. Her jet-black hair was coiled in plaits around the top of her head. "Come with me," she said addressing me. She led the way to the wake room at the front of the house. The candles – an uneven number of them – were lighting on a linen cloth on a bedside table. Light filtered in through a cream-coloured blind, suffusing the room with a quiet brownish colour. "Let no one in," my aunt said quietly, signing to me to place my back against the room door. Grandma was laid out on the bed, her brown habit contrasting with the snow-bright linen bedclothes. The sidelong candlelight made a mystery of her features.

Aunt Mary knelt formally beside the bed at a little distance from the counterpane. For a moment or two her body remained upright, her wide eyes fixed on the corpse. Then her body began to sway backwards and forwards and her lips began to moan. I heard quiet broken words in Irish and in English pouring from her lips. At first it was merely a whisper, then came a torrent of almost musical chant with broken appellations as in litany addressed to the corpse on the bed.

I found my body stiffening. Every drop of my blood was responding to the "singing" of the caoin. I realised that, probably for the very last time in our area, I was listening to the "Irish cry." As I wrote later:

> *"Our brothers, the Scottish had forgotten it. Our brothers, the Welsh had abandoned it. Our cousins the Manx, the Cornish and the Bretons knew it no more. Alone of the Celtic edge, we had held it fast.*
>
> *If what the braggart schoolmasters had told us was true, that once we were a strong wave breaking over the civilised world, then surely this cry . . . was the last hissing of that wave spending itself here amid the stones of time."*

The lament mounted in intensity, yet stopped short of emotionally breaking the circle of its art. My aunt was now drawing on resources I could not name but which found welcome in every vein in my body. At last the chant fined down into silence. In tearless formality my aunt stood up: taking me by the hand she led me out of the wake room and into the dairy. There she poured out my milk and gave me her morning smile.

At the back of my mind, I held fast to the notion that each experience, whether humorous, doleful or exalting or, indeed, a combination of all three attributes, would prove useful in the years ahead. Although my literary cat was still a small "pusheen," who knows, I told myself, but the day might come when he would kill a mouse. It could be said that at this period of my life I was observing, closely observing. Like the school-going infant I too was "wax to receive and marble to retain." I had only begun to taste life. My native town as a whole, all Ireland and beyond, had yet to be explored and savoured. And what I found was to be stored in the secret treasure-house of the subconscious.

CHAPTER FOUR

The blacksmith had something up his nose for me. His mocking whistle pursued me as I passed the forge on my way to the convent for an afternoon music lesson. Whew, whew, whew it went, with no variation on the single note. I thought I was his white-haired boy. How had I transgressed? At last I had it . . . I had dared to write!

At this time there was an old and shaggy sheepdog called Jacko who waddled about the streets, his ownership claimed by no one and everyone. He looked as if he were put together in disparate halves; as a result the old dog moved as if he were hinged in the middle.

Children made bold with Jacko by pulling his ears. The old dog seemed to love it. Kind people fed him scraps. He slept in a nook of the streets where the winter hailstones failed to fall. His eyes grew blearier and his hearing less acute with every winter night that passed.

One morning Jacko was found dead. The town mourned. I dared to write Jacko's obituary notice in *The Kerryman*. The notice was replete with purple prose. It ended as follows;

> *And now he sleeps beneath the clay of the Market*
> *Cliff, his white teeth unclenched and the murmur of*
> *the weir below to soothe him in his everlasting rest.*

A harmless tribute, one might say. Not so the farrier-blacksmith who ruled the area. He blurted it out one night as I entered his rambling house kitchen ahead of the others. I can still see his round eyeballs cast sidelong at me.

Presently, he repeated "Jacko the Dog," in tones mounting the scale of scorn. "Fitter for you to write about the poor Christians who are dyin' every day, instead of 'Jacko the Dog'". His brother joined in the critical hunt. I felt cauterised.

I was truly in the doghouse! Was it possible that I would no longer be welcome in the sanctuary of his kitchen? No longer would I be allowed, having first ensured that the snib was on the doorlock, to prise up the sixth step of his narrow stairway, take out his Colt revolver, unwrap it from its greasy rag and clean it, my ears attuned to the noises of the street. (This weapon, a relic of the Tan war, was given to him by a participant friend then dead.) No longer would I be allowed write out his bills to slow-to-pay farmers at Christmastide or before big fair days – from his billheads I first learned the words "farrier" and "template" together with the colours roan and chestnut as applied to horses. Expulsion from the Rambling House was worst of all. I decided to test whether or not I was still on the farrier's roll book.

When, after some absences, I did enter, I found my recognisable knock on the door answered and my misdemeanour overlooked or forgotten. The smith had some anonymous boycott notes for me to write with my left hand. I was also told to lure a pedigree Kerry blue terrier dog from the house of a friend on the pretence of taking it for a walk. The real purpose of the walk was to smuggle the sire dog by the backway into the forge where it would serve the farrier's blue terrier bitch, then in heat. Both tasks I deftly avoided.

Meanwhile there was a wider world of the town to be explored. My imagination demanded that the word "town" be defined. I set out to view it as a unit of humanity with its various social strata (if any), its layers of interest, its tensions and relaxations, its hatreds and affections, its loyalties and betrayals, its tragedies and comedies, its coherencies and incoherencies and, above all, its characters.

My pair of Belly Brothers were tradesmen: perhaps there were other tradesmen to be become acquainted with, to watch their crafty hands at work and to hazard a guess as to what went on in their minds. I would find it hard to serve other masters beside the smiths: to this day when I look at the palms of each of my hands in turn I fancy I feel that each has a pleasurable and even sensual grip on an object; the left hand seems wrapped around the polished black and white horn at the end of the bellows arm of the smithy hearth; in my right palm, the tactile memory prompted by the additive of spittle adhesive, lies the handle of an ash hurley which I had once cut and shaped myself.

My peers and I had already sampled the main streets. By this time we were not completely bound up with the Market, the River and the Gleann. At that time a curious custom prevailed among the teenagers – both boys and girls. The teenage boys, in threes or fours, paraded on the pavement from the top of Church Street, for about four hundred yards, as far as Cotter's Corner. Then, turning up in hairpin fashion into William Street, they skipped for about three hundred yards and turned right about and retraced their route. The arm-linked girls did the same – in the opposite direction. There were moments when a file of boys refused to give way to a similar file of girls and a gentle skirmish took place. I now see this as a courting rite.

Pairing was established in this fashion. What is now called eye-contact was part of the game. At times one girl might convey a message to a boy on behalf of one of her girlfriends. "Mary So-and-So was asking for you," she'd venture with a skittish laugh. Emboldened, the boy might dare to say to Mary when next he met her, "Would you come for a walk?" She might answer, "I might," to be answered by, "Ah, you will," to be replied by, "Very well so." The assignation was then made.

The courtship was innocence itself. The laurel groves of Gurtenard, now the town park, were the commonest rendezvous. In winter-time the resourcefulness of teenage calf love revealed itself; I recall stately night sessions in a cab in the hotel yard just off the square. The buttoned crimson interior offered the girl the illusion of driving to church on her wedding morn. I can still see the eyes of a girlfriend ashine in the darkness as she sat beside me in the dark vehicle. Sunlight, too, had its moments. One of the boys fashioned a crude key to open the first class carriages of the train, which on Sundays lay in a quiet side track of the railway station. The carriage had an air of seclusion in its buttoned upholstery and blind-drawn luxury. On weekends, in pairs, we romped and danced on the cushioned interiors and pretended we were toffs on our way to some glittering social occasion in Dublin Castle.

Always one said to one's girlfriend at the end of such meetings,

"Thank you very much for the nice time." I daresay this compliment made the girl feel warm and happy as she skipped off home. Invariably she laughed and gave an over-the-shoulder reply as she raced away. All this was long before solemn young men and women faced a television audience and addressed their peers on the advisability of wearing neo-Malthusian and prophylactic appliances for preventing pregnancy.

The town was crammed with tradesmen – a further clear example of self-containment and coherency in a community. There were plenty of bakers (at least six bakeries in the town of just over 3,000 population) as well as pig-stickers and pork butchers. The salt for the pickle stand (from Carrickfergus?) was brought from the station in a dray filled with salt blocks. The town seemed to chime with the song of anvils, there were mantua-makers (dressmakers to you) behind the first floor windows and a tinsmith or two, his discarded chippings rusting on the Market cliff. (Of a miser it was said, 'He'd live on the clippings of tin'.) Add to this a wheelwright with his ring of fire beside the Race Bridge, a market gardener, a cow-and-horse doctor, a thatcher or two, a seller of sour milk for baking soda bread (home milk it was called), fishwomen, seagrass and dillisk sellers, butchers who called themselves victuallers if they could spell the word – and pronounce it – (fleshers they traded as in the North of Ireland). There was a toffee-maker who died when I was a child, a knowledgeable woman or two who attended childbirths (one attended mine to complement the official nurse), a dental mechanic or two, one cooper, some hackney drivers, each with a T-model Ford. Johnny the Nailer died when I was too young to appreciate the sound of his hammer ("busy as a nailer" is an old saying), but we had a pudding filler who sold tripe (she washed the entrails in the river as did the hackney driver his car) and a carriage maker. (I often paused on my way home from school to watch the left hand of the last mentioned slowly turning the wheel on its stand, the movement of the wheel tracing the neat stripe on the rim against which his right hand held the fine brush, dipped carefully in bright yellow paint. There were also grooms to handle fair day stallions and trainers to break in colts and fillies, as well as a joiner or two who made common carts and indeed coffins, if they were put to it, providing they could get the ready-made shoulder planks. There were shop apprentices of all sorts – duly indentured and proud of the trust implicit in their bond with a master.

Had we a monumental mason? I cannot recall whether or no. The young milliners in their black and white attire were delicious temptations – simply asking to be ruffled! Ordinary stone masons we had aplenty. Shops included approximately seventy pubs (we had a large hinterland!), an excellent book shop (Dan Flavin had the widest of minds), an Italian warehouse (whatever that meant), an emporium, and a six-pence ha'penny shop – a precursor of Woolworths and Crazy Prices.

I hate to see an old trade die: to me the loss of a traditional skill is like a brook running into sand. I recall an incident connected with the delightful trade of weaving. I was seven years of age at the time.

The schoolmaster had taught us a lesson on weaving, adding that all the weavers of our town had died, leaving only one old man, whose Christian name was James. And even he hadn't woven for twenty or more years. I woke up on the spot. James and his wife were old friends of mine – they lived next door to my grand-aunt: the families communicated with each other by knocking on the back of the open fireplace. I ran home as fast as I could. Breathless, I faced the white bearded man who was truly biblical in appearance.

"Are you a weaver, sir?" I blurted. The old gentleman, and gentleman he was, turned and looked at me with sad eyes. "I am," he said, then, "I was," he amended. "Have you a loom?" "I have." "Where is it?" "Out there in the shed. I haven't been in the place for a score of years." "May I see the loom?" "The lock is rusted." "I'll get paraffin oil and free it. Please," I pleaded.

The day came when the old man led me out into the yard. After a struggle I got the lock open. When we pushed inwards on the creaking door we were confronted with great grey hammocks of cobwebs. But unmistakably, beneath all that interlacement, lay the precious loom.

I cajoled, I wheedled, I coaxed, I pestered, I palavered. To see the last loom working became my obsession. James prevaricated; he said he had to send away for this and that. And then at last came the never-to-be-forgotten day when I visited the old couple and saw his dear wife with a spinning wheel by her side feeding the wool onto the spindles with the wheel whirring as in the old-time days. She nodded to me to go out to the shed where Old James was working. There before my eyes, I saw tweed take shape. I was filled with joy.

Afternoon after afternoon I helped the old man to weave. At last when the bolt of cloth was almost finished I said, "I'm glad I saw the last weaver of our town." "Wait," he said. "You take a turn now." I did as I was bidden. When my pleasant task was finished James looked at me with glistening eyes. "Remember," he said, "you are now the last weaver of Listowel." We were both happy as we left the shed.

The plasterer worked in a different medium. But he was none the less imaginative and creative for all that. Old Pat was his name. He too was bearded. He didn't work in my time but I saw him almost every day: wherever he went in the town, his creations were to be seen above his head. Pure artists may quibble but Old Pat gave us something unique of which we have grown equally fond and proud.

Picture the scene a century ago. Shopfronts and fascia boards were all the rage. A distinctive shopfront could attract business – and still does.

Shopkeepers, mainly publicans, sent for Pat McAuliffe to provide them with a shopfront. Pat looked up and down the front of the house. Said little. His few comments were monosyllabic. Nodded his acceptance – walked away. There was no knowing what he'd come up with. The publican and his wife waited in trepidation. That plasterer could put anything over their door and they'd have to live with it. The craftsman returned and began the preliminary groundwork for his masterpiece.

At last the great day arrives. Word travels round the town. "Pat's outside," the publican's wife quavers to her husband. One of the plasterer's men is now leading a common cart on which rests a huge something covered with a sheet of canvas. Pat himself arrives; he's still non-communicative. One doesn't ask. The object in the cart is concrete – that's all. At last it is uncovered. Merciful Lord, it's The Maid of Erin herself. She's seated beside a harp with a wolfhound at her feet. There's also a round tower and at her bare feet, amid a maze of Celtic interlacing (or is it Scandinavian strapwork?), is the legend, "*Erin go Bráth* – Ireland Forever." A crowd gathers. Up she goes and then –

Holy God! Did you see her breasts? Bare and big as the Paps of Killarney. What'll the parish priest say?

The parish priest of that hour was a man of wit, tact and foresight. Brought along to see the new statuary over the pub in Main Street, the people gathered round to hear the verdict. His verdict was Delphic and merry. "In the event of a Famine," he said drily, "that lady could suckle the parish." The matter was defused in a gale of wholesome laughter.

Old Pat left us a unique legacy. We treasure what is left of his work. In Oslo a unique sculptor was given an area by the municipal authorities on which his imagination could stretch itself to the very full. The result, which artistic purists view with mixed feelings and at times with a sense of lofty patronage, is an astonishing open-air display of sculpture often grotesquely resembling a can of giant worms, but which provides the city with an amazing, imaginative identity. As I strolled through the passages of this Norwegian open-air display, I thought of Pat McAuliffe. Retrospectively it makes one warm to the authorities who had the wit and foresight to authorise the existence of such displays. With our Pat – our single regret is that he didn't leave us more.

Just the same we still have eagles, parrots, bicycles and lions (a dragon or two and an angel have disappeared) and legends like Spes Mea in Deo, E pluribus Unum and Maison de Ville. A shopfront of Pat's in Abbeyfeale still has what looks like scraps of Sanskrit – to remind us of the craftsman who placed inscriptions in four languages, Latin, Irish, French and English, over one pub. His local descendants are numerous and at generational intervals indicate in different walks in life that the imaginative and resolute characteristics of the old man are still vibrantly alive and well.

I could be said to have "served my time" with two harnessmakers – "saddlers" if one wishes to be upmarket in phrasing. To me both men, though different in temperament, were ordinary and extraordinary at one and the same time. Through the common factor of the farm animal, chiefly the horse, a colourful stream of rural life was mine to ingest at first or good second-hand.

Maurice lived in mid-town with streets or lanes going in three directions from his door. Standing at the harnessmaker's counter, by glancing at the shop windows across the street, one could see the reflection of people coming and going either upstreet or downstreet, even emerging from Tay Lane. In the room overhead was his sister, Fannie, a dressmaker. Both were very close friends of mine: I spent close on twenty years in their company. Both were resourcefully witty.

If anything interesting happened in the street, the whirr of the upstairs sewing machine would cease and the tapping of a lady's shoe would be heard in the shop below. Through the doorway we would look out at our three shop window mirrors. Once it was a circus elephant which humped itself and dunged on the road outside. "That stuff could be useful for mushrooms," came the saddler's pungent comment. If the town became extra quiet, Maurice would blurt, "Go out there lads and stir up the bloody dust." By this he meant us to stir up excitement of some sort. The one crime one could commit was to "remove" a piece of gossip from the shop and by so doing cause mischief. This, Maurice called "hitting the hurdles". As a consequence the culprit got "the Gandhi treatment" and was bluntly told by the saddler, "Keep outside my territorial waters!"

I was very attached to Fannie. I always visited her on Saturday mornings when the place was empty of customer women. On the occasion of my weekly visit I always brought Fannie a new novel – one which was then at the pinnacle of the literary listing. She was a marvellously selective reader and could sum up the merits of a book as accurately as any newspaper critic. She and I could say what we liked to each other. In my unmarried days she would advise me:

"Get a woman," she'd say, "who, when things go wrong, doesn't whinge and whine. Get a woman, who when the goin' gets tough, takes down her concertina and plays you a tune."

She'd then proceed to instruct me in the wilery of women. "The smallest girl goin' the road could outfox you, you fool," she'd say. "She'd put you in a bag, sell you at the nearest fair and buy you back at a profit to herself." And when I'd protest that women weren't like that, she'd say, "Stop the shittin' chivalry! I'm one of 'em. I know. You iomparán Thady, puttin' women on a pedestal." Fannie rarely if ever went outside the door. I challenged her one day. "Why don't you go out, Fan?" I asked.

"What for?"

"For fresh air."

"Fresh air! Block the keyhole and 'twill come in under the door. Block under the door and 'twill come in by the window sashes. You can't keep that shittin' stuff out," was her reply.

I'd be fiddling with her spools of thread with their marvellous arrays of colours. Then perhaps I'd take off my jacket and ask her to tighten a button on it. Off we go then, talking about the coloured world of literature. When my old and dear friends died I changed houses and lived in a different street: I then transferred my allegiance to still another saddler. Paddy was of a temperament different to Maurice but equally a philosopher. At this time he was quite old.

This was our set-up. On summer mornings tourist coaches would stop in The Square. The tourists, looking up and down at the houses, would file up our street in two and threes. Pat's window with its array of harness brasses and mouthpieces, its plaited strapwork, bridles and little white horse figurine would cause them to stop and peer in. Paddy would be "cocked up for height" on his stool which was balanced precariously on old items of harness he had promised to repair but never got round to doing. I sat on the red stool, or form, parallel to the counter with my back to the old oats bin. Over my head was an ornate Mexican saddle. There were pictures of famous racehorses on the walls.

There was always a smell of wax, copperas and linseed. A finch or mule canary noised in the birdcage hung inside the fanlight. The faces of the tourists peered in at the pair of us. Paddy smiled.

Whatever was in his smile it drew them in. The old man was the soul of courtesy. Now began the ritual of sussing them out – finding out if they were interesting: if they were people of promise or interest he drew me into the conversation. If not, he let them go about their business. He was rarely wrong in his estimation of character.

And so our lives passed – in the summer–time especially. The winter was different. The only outing of consequence Paddy had was a single day each year when men wearing bowler hats called to his door and asked him to judge the horses at the Dingle Show.

The saddler dressed himself elegantly when leaving for the show. He stopped short of the bowler hat. In his prime he and his father had a high stepping piebald pony and a sparkling tub-trap as their entry for the local show.

There came a time when the shop was closed for two days. The shutters remained up on the mullioned windows. I was worried. After his sister's death he had been burgled. And beaten. He kept the matter very quiet. He wanted no public fuss. When on the third day his door was opened, his shutters taken down and he had resumed his perch, I questioned him.

"Were you ill, Pat?"

"No."

"Were you broken into again?"

"No."

"Where were you?"

"You won't believe me if I tell you."

"I will. Tell it out."

"I was in . . . Baghdad."

A long pause. Was he doting?

"The real Baghdad? In Iran?"

"The very place. I knew you wouldn't believe me." There was a smiling interlude. At last he said, "Very well so! I'll tell you."

He began to tell me.

"You know our friend Eddie from the hill? He keeps the best of blood horses. He stood this mare at Cahirmee and she sold at a good price. 'Take her home' he was told, 'and wait for instructions'. He did that. The other day he got this telegram tellin' him what to do. He walks in to see me.

"'Did you tell me you were never in Shannon Airport?' he asks. 'Never,' from me. 'I'll be delivering my mare at Shannon next Thursday morning at some early hour. If you'd like to come . . . ?' 'I'll be with you,' I said.

"'Very well so.' All Wednesday it rained cats and dogs. The roads were flooded. 'Come hell or high water,' says I, 'I'll see the airport.' One o'clock in the morning saw me under Collopy's balcony waiting for Eddie and his trailer. He was doubtful about advising me to travel. But I sat in. Off we went. After a terrible journey, what with floods, fallen branches of trees and diversions, we reached the airport at a quarter to four. A wicked mornin'. Only one light shinin' in the whole place. We made for it. This man came out. 'Ye're the first,' he says. 'Three more to come: wait for the plane'. Three more vehicles with trailers drew up. The man came out again.

"'Who's the buyer?' we asked. 'By the way ye don't know!' from the man. 'Devil a know,' from us. 'It's the Shah of Persia,' says he.

'The Shah of Persia!' we all said together.

"With that, this silver and blue plane nosed far over our heads. Down, down she came and perched on the runway. She blinks a lot of lights and moves up to us. The duck's tail of the plane went down and there was a ramp goin' up into a stable with horses in it. A stairway moved against the door on the side of the plane and two fellahs with turbans came down. We stood there with our horses. The other lads were from the West Clare and Ballinasloe directions.

"One of the turbanned men – I found out he was a vet – came over and walked around our horses. The second fellah was holdin' three bridles with silver mountin's like what was on the plane door. ('Monograms, Pat.' 'That's it!') We took off our own bridles: their bridles had numbers in silver on them – a different make to ours and each horse would use only the one bridle for the rest of his life. Disease, you understand. Soon we had 'em loaded. The vet signed to the groom. Your man beckoned us to follow him. Up the stairs we went and right into the plane. We sat down. The smell, the silver, the mats and carpets, the whole apparatus. Six buckoes from the Irish town and country – we were in Baghdad. They gave us strange liquor. We drank it. It hit my brain like a lightin' match thrun on petrol. They had this yoke of a pipe with tubes out of it. In turns we had to take a pull out of the mouthpiece and the smoke flummoxed us. The coloured turbans, the robes, the brown hands, the brown faces, the white teeth, the silver vessels, the badges in the turbans, the strange drinks – I didn't know whether my name was Pat or Ali Baba. Back on the ground of Ireland we watched the plane takin' our Irish horses up into the sky. I fell asleep comin' home. I slept all day yesterday. Only when I took down the shutters today did I come to my senses after my journey to Baghdad."

(I've often wondered if there's a difference in meaning between a personality and a character. Do the meanings overlap in part, much as one circle can be drawn to impinge on the area of another? If the accent is placed on the 'ac' of the word character in the vernacular Hiberno-English pronunciation, I can tell the difference at once. The dictionary definition does bear out a theory of mine; a character is an outstanding person or even an odd eccentric and unusual person while a personality indicates a remarkable person, one who by extension of the sum of his parts, adds up to the unique. I'll settle for personality simply because of the word unique in the definition.)

Brown Paddy was another important personality. He was larger than life and even larger than fiction: this latter insofar as it is difficult to pigeon-hole him or fit him into the shape or form that even fiction allows. He'd truly smash whatever frame was placed about him.

I came under his spell at a very early age. My mother – his own age – filled in the details of his youth which was eventful. By turns he was bookmaker, butcher, publican, county councillor, and public figure. Above all he was a gambler to the marrow of his bones. He'd bet on anything that raced or flew – any event whose outcome depended on the wheel of chance.

Most of my young and impressionable life was spent in Brown Paddy's kitchen. There I received an important instruction in unusual branches of education. First of all I was taught how to play poker.

The first real game I played was at the bedside of Brown Paddy who was laid up with a cold. Our other players were his two sons. God sent me hands of cards such as I have never seen since. I staked my Christmas money on the games and to my astonishment I soon won six pounds. I then looked at the clock and said my mother would kill me for being late so I vamoosed with my winnings. Brown Paddy was indignant; he said I'd never make a proper gambler if I did the likes of that. However, after a day or two he said I might make a bookmaker. My mother was the boss, I said, he could ask her. He entered our kitchen telling my mother he'd take me to race meetings as his clerk. My ma had notions of making me a University professor or a Harley Street doctor. Tears came to her eyes. She looked at Brown Paddy. Dipping her fingers in the small holy water font and sprinkling the blessed liquid on me she said, "Take him so, Paddy, in the name of the Father, Son and Holy Ghost." Brown Paddy got up with an oath. "What d'you want bringing religion into it, woman?" he shouted. He was mighty superstitious. My mother, an old friend of his, was aware of this weakness. She laughed as he went out banging the door behind him.

She added to my fund of stories about this, our most loved and greatest character. How spreading his arms wide he had soundly bussed herself and a lady teacher friend from Manchester as they paraded in Ballybunion in all their summer finery. They beat him off with their parasol. "On the razzle dazzle", as he used to say himself, he'd walk up the stairs of the best hotel in the resort, enter a man's bedroom and fall asleep to recover strength for an arduous night before him. Challenged by the irate guest now returned from the beach our hero would say he was in the wrong room. "A drop o' drink", he'd say. "Tell no one. I'm very respectable."

The stories about Brown Paddy are legion. One of his sons and I "twisted" a champion hound by giving it a false name at a local track and took him down for fifteen pounds. Paying out the notes into my hand he looked from me to the other of us. "Ye won't have luck," he said, "for takin' down yeer father." He said this with a certain sense of pride.

The traditional loaf of bread thrown at the back door on New Year's Eve with a shout of "Hunger, stay out!" was also a part of Brown Paddy's ritual. Breaking wind in a crowded railway carriage he tapped an elegant lady on the knee and loudly whispered, "Pretend 'twas me!" The innocent looking countryman in the corner of the carriage was his confederate. "Do you play cards, sir?" Paddy would ask. "An odd time," from the meek countryman. Soon a poker game was in progress with fellow travellers taking part.

He'd curtail a longwinded mission sermon by passing a tin of cough lozenges along the pew. Soon, everyone was coughing. Even the missioner in the pulpit. Undecided between singing, "Pray for the Wanderer" or "Pray for the Sinner" he'd sometimes sing "Pray for the Winner" – a fitting compromise. The long queue for Confession would wonder at the handle of the walking stick hanging at the side of the box. It was "keeping a place" for Brown Paddy. He'd confess to the three missioners in turn and thereafter advise various penitents where to go. I found myself secretary to a committee formed to bring a High Court action against the triumvirate of our UDC of which Paddy was one – this on account of a failed water scheme. He gave me a subscription to prosecute himself.

In politics, Brown Paddy was of the extreme right; as such he was elected to membership of various public bodies. Once, on the sad occasion of the execution of an Irishman in Britain on a political charge, the members of the extreme opposite wing to Brown Paddy sent out the bellman to announce that as a mark of respect, the shops of the town would be closed from one pm to two pm. The notice also requested the townspeople to attend a recitation of the Rosary at the Republican plot in the cemetery.

To my surprise Brown Paddy called at my door and asked me to accompany him to the ceremony. He was the last man in Ireland I expected to attend. Having linked arms with him to the cemetery, we found the Rosary in full swing and being said in Irish. Brown Paddy sat on a little pillar on a grave surround at the edge of the throng. The following chorus followed;

"*A Naoimh Mhuire, a Mháthair Dé, guidh orainn na peacaigh anois*," from the crowd

"Holy Mary, Mother of God . . . now and at the hour of our death, Amen," from Paddy, in his resonant racecourse voice.

After this went on for some time, a muffled outbreak of laughter seized the mourners. I knelt at Paddy's feet and stuffed my handkerchief into my mouth. Tears rolled down my face. The climax had not yet been reached.

A wasp descended from somewhere on high and attacked Brown Paddy. Paddy beat his hands frantically before his face. The intoned routine now was: . . . *"agus ar uair ár mbáis, Amen"* from the crowd, "now and at the hour of our death" intoned by Paddy followed by a roar addressed to the wasp. "Isn't the churchyard wide enough for you, you bastard?"

By this time the ceremony was in tatters. I led Brown Paddy to the churchyard gate. He raised his boot on to the lowest stone step on the side stile.

"Tie my laces, boy," he said to me.

"They're not ripped, Boss."

"Rip 'em and tie 'em," he said. He graciously saluted all the retreating mourners many of whom had difficulty keeping a straight face.

When all had gone, I asked bluntly, "What was all that about, boss?"

With a glance around him, "There's one chance in a thousand that these buggers might get into power. I always believe in having a pound on an outsider."

Arm in arm we went home. As we walked along he said with great earnestness, and with a ring of sadness and pride, "Which of those fellahs had a nephew killed fightin' in the GPO in Easter Week?" Brown Paddy had. For once his mask of levity had slipped.

Memory now plays me tricks of time.

Enter Queen Emily: she is the acknowledged queen of Charles Street where I lived as a child. A woman of great dignity and a powerful presence (and vocabulary) she stands in mid-town reviewing the last of the Massgoers and upbraiding the laggards on their way to last Mass on Sunday. Brown Paddy emerges from his shop, five minutes after the noon Mass bell has chimed. He is buttoning his flies. Queen Emily folds her arms and delivers her loud rebuke: "Brown Patrick, in the interests of public decency, kindly adjust the more intimate parts of your clothing in the privacy of your boudoir." She makes the word privacy sound like a whiplash.

On the occasion of his funeral, when priests and mourners had left the cemetery, Brown Paddy's sons emptied a bottle of whiskey on his grave. This was a family custom adhered to down the years. I was instrumental in having sculptor Séamus Murphy do a decent roadside marker for the graveyard where Paddy lies. Séamus suggested putting a hare and a horse's head on the sides of the stone: I demurred: I didn't know how the parish priest would take it. If you should pass through our town and see oldsters like myself choking laughing, we are simply telling one another stories about famous Brown Paddy.

One of his last injunctions to me was, "Put me in a book." And when I replied, "You mightn't like the result," he said, "I don't give a damn what you say about me. So long as I put Skelper's nose out of joint." Skelper was a rival coursing man who had his memoirs printed in our local paper.

In a small tightly knit community such as ours, there was no shortage of characters or personalities: these came in all sorts and sizes and of many attitudes, oddities and hues. There was the old fellow who never trusted banks to take care of his life's savings. The last thing he did each night was to steal down to The Square and by bumping his buttocks against the bank door ensured that the door was locked and his money safe. There was the almost alcoholic who had a name for each glass of whiskey in the day: the first on awakening he called the Sunriser and the post-breakfast libation was the Realiser. The pre-luncheon (dinner as it is called in the country) drink he called the Appetiser and that calculated to wash down the meal was the Digestiver. And so on, through the Terminiser and others to the final drink of the day, calculated to ensure a sound night's sleep, which he called the Somnambuliser. There was the citizen whose father had fought in foreign wars and who peppered his speech with exclamations like Shiftee feloose! (Egyptian – phonetic), Sam Fairy Ann (ditto French) and Jiggy-jig – African for copulation.

There was the man who stored the clippings of his fingernails in the sweaty band of his hat and, somewhat in the manner of Fionn Mac Cumhail and his thumb, would chew a crescent of fingernails in times of perplexity. From the outlying village I learnt of a quietly mannered butcher who, on hearing that his only son – and only child – had been drowned in a boating accident in Montreal, locked up his shop, went upstairs to his parlour and played classical music on his piano all night long. There was the newspaper correspondent returned home who, on being asked by a genteel old lady where he was going to, rudely replied: "Madame, I am off to the wood for a sylvan shit." And how about the loquacious little countryman arrested by a new big civic guard for disturbing the peace; the talker on being almost lifted up the steps to the garda station fell on his knees and, looking up into the garda's face said, "Guard, you and me are mere cogs on the great wheel of humanity."

And for no reason at all, except that I continue to be haunted by a lively vernacular, I am reminded of the aggrieved plaintiff – possibly a distant relative of mine – who made the following declaration in court almost a century ago: it appears he was assaulted by the defendant who threw a dead cat at him.

"Working in a potato garden, I was compelled to repair to a ditch-side to execute a debt of nature. While crouched in a suitable position, and in my fancied but fallacious security, I was espied by a superannuated blackguard of disreputable character who, seizing hold of the tail of a deceased grimalkin, threw the dead animal at me striking me on the shoulder blades. Were it not for the tenacity of the hide of the decomposed feline, the putrid remains would have been strewn all over me and would have contaminated my body and its apparel in their several parts."

Or – this from an old lady.

"My father, God rest him, always ate with his hat on: he said it provided protection for his fontanel."

Here's the seminal idea of a story I may yet write. I eavesdropped on a pair of chatting women:

"He couldn't bear to give away his wife's clothing after she died. So, like many a mourner before him, he locked the door of their bedroom and would let no one near it. After a while his children told him this was morbid. So one quiet morning when there was no one about, he took the big bundle of her clothing to a quiet part of a nearby wood, his nose sniffing deeply into the garments as he bore them along. There he poured paraffin on them and threw a lighting match on to the pile. As the flames rose up he lifted his two arms to the sky and offered it all up as a sacrifice of thanks for the lovely closeness of his marriage years."

The era before mine was one of pranks and practical jokes. Young, eager apprentices were sent on foolish errands: to the pub known as "The Long Bar" for a loan of a long bar, to the hardware shop for "the glass hammer", or the "wheel of the mareesha," whatever that was. A nonsense recitation greatly prized was called "The Shower of Old Hags" and was recited at turkey raffles or card nights.

I now pause to take an overview of what I am doing and what I propose to do. But first, a question or two. Am I laughing *at* these characters or *with* them? Have I the lofty attitude of patronage bestowed upon semi-peasants and exercised from a distance of time? Am I describing a second valley of the squinting windows!

I must clarify that at once by making a sweeping statement which may be flatly contradicted, but make it I will for it suits me to believe it! I shall later expand on my statement.

It is this: all art came out of the belly laugh. Art too came out of the clay or from those at a single generation removed from the clay. Above all, it came out of community. These people I delineate in their odd nodules of habitation had within themselves the total means of survival, and this, as I have shown, even in the context of food. They also had the mental stimulus with its imaginative dimensions, that quality of coherence, of belonging, that which sets loneliness – a state almost indefinable in its many manifestations – to flight, and keeps body, mind and soul together. It wasn't for nothing that some of these people described their bodies as "my Soul-case".

As a postscript, I stress that, like potatoes or apples, art too comes to flower and seed: the seeds are borne on the wind to the city where under ideal conditions they germinate to the fullness of art and where, in turn, the resultant seeds blow across the land to seek renewal in the wilder clay in which the species had its origin. A foolish theory but mine own.

CHAPTER FIVE

Simple things. Deceptively simple at times. Beneath the surface there can be complexity. And latent power. As a boy, growing up in small town Ireland, the course of the physical and political struggle in the period between the Rising of 1916 and the cease-fire of the Civil War in the mid-twenties dominated my youthful thinking.

During that time there was another struggle in progress – one it took me some time to define. Gradually I came to the realisation that this was also a clash between two cultures, the imperial and the indigenous: this conflict existed even on the level of pastimes and field games.

This divergence was recognisable in simpler musical terms. The discord symbolically presented itself to me as being one between the piano, with its drawing room and ballroom associations, and the vernacular instruments, the pipes, fiddle, melodeon and the bodhrán. This conflict also had its parallel in one between classical operatic and musical hall airs and graces on the one hand and the ballads, sets, reels and jigs of the countryside on the other.

The music of the drawing-room, to some appreciable extent the dominant musical tradition of our town, was evident in family and social gatherings where the female pianist accompanied a male singer. The man stood at the piano, his left hand clutching the lapel of his jacket, and sang sentimental ditties derived from the music hall and concert platform with now and again an essay into the operatic or classical – this latter often offered as a final flourish. Thomas Moore's melodies, since the composer was Irish and, it was claimed, of local origin, appeared as a bridge between two cultures.

All this postulated the existence of a superior establishment inhabited by gentlemen and gentlewomen as contrasted with the world of whimsical peasants. It is interesting to note the one fictional occasion where both cultures were in harmony. Viewed under a mellow light such as that pervading Joyce's famous story *The Dead* the singing of a ballad entitled "The Lass of Aughrim" in the context of a metropolitan drawing room adds up to a strange total. For me *The Dead*, the greatest short story ever written, had profound implications. Indigenous or native: that was a choice that continued to nag at me.

There was a third musical stratum which came from an unexpected source. During the First World War, individual pacifists from England came to Ireland in order to dodge conscription. Among them were stand-up comedians and a few fit-up actors. The comedians appeared on stage in the intervals of silent films in the primitive cinemas of that era. They were quite popular.

A song about a bride jilted at the altar began with "Mary Ellen at the church turned up, her Dad turned up . . . " and, after several kinds of "turn-up", the bridegroom was found "in the river with his toes turned up." The patter accompanying the ditty introduced us to Cockney humour. For my part of it, on the maternal premise that the piano was the most refined instrument, I spent years at the keyboard until after much mental agitation, I declared where my allegiance lay. I was on the side of the native, crude as it may then have been, and socially outlawed into the bargain.

"What have you got to show?" was the phrase that determined my musical future. Let me explain this reference.

When the flying boats landed at Foynes, some of the pilots rested for a few days in Ballybunion. I fell in with one of them. He kept questioning me gently with "What have you got to show?" I pressed him as to what he meant.

He explained that much of what he saw or heard in Ireland by way of musical entertainment was borrowed from, or a poor imitation of, other traditions. I led him to a spacious dance hall: the Charleston, fox-trot and waltz were the dances then in vogue. His response – "We have exactly that activity in the US only it's much better." At last I took him to a small village hall where the entertainment was reels, jigs and sets with an occasional ballad sung solo and without accompaniment, the interval designed, I believe, to allow the dancers to catch their breath.

The pilot's response to the village hall was immediate. "This is what I'm looking for. You can leave me here now."

"What have you got to show?" To this day the question keeps ringing in the caverns of my mind.

Death of a Salesman was the play in which the wire recorder first came to public notice. As soon as I reached the age of independence, I procured one at considerable trouble from the USA. I then bade farewell to the piano and set off to record the balladry of southwest Ireland and beat it into shape for a Radio Eireann programme which I scripted and, when broadcast every Saturday night, it gripped all Ireland. Its title was *The Balladmaker's Saturday Night* – a name derived from the work of Robbie Burns.

Puck Fair was a fertile source of supply of material for the programme. Some of the ballads were delightfully Rabelaisian. At times I cleaned 'em up, added and subtracted lines and finished up with a sanitised version of the original. Some of these are now attributed to ballad makers called "Anon" or "Traditional". Pirates have even put their names to some of them and claimed copyright.

Ballads could hurt on a local level. I still remember the white face of a coffinbearer as he turned his head and sternly said to me, "Forget that bloody ould ballad, will you!" I knew what he was referring to. His dad had figured in the song in a murky light. He was afraid I'd have it broadcast. I understood: and obeyed the request.

One ending to a local raffle song still remains with me;

"Comin' down th' ould road and the people goin' to
Mass
One by one in swift rotation
And the language used by the Bohareenduvs
By my oath, wasn't fit for publication."

A fire in the thatched locality of the Gleann was recorded as follows;

"Thanks be to God, the Dalker said,

The night it wasn't wild,
For if the night was wild me boys, 'twould blow fire everywhere
'Twould burn down sweet Convent Lane and lave the neighbours bare."

Not very exalted lyrics it must be conceded. Rough hewn and adze–marked. But wait! Note how pathos falls headlong into bathos in the plant of a lovesick swain:

I sat down to the table, not a bite did I ate.
For I loved my own darlin' far better than that mate.

Where did I encounter topsy-turveydom of this kind before? Surely not in literature, or was it? In the midst of my patronising howl of laughter I paused to identify a certain sympathy with the sad core of the singer's woe.

Liam O'Flaherty, that king of short story writers, has a delightful tale which evokes in my mind the same kind of mixed emotions as that evoked by the hunger-striker of love. As I recall it, it may be summarised somewhat as follows:

The parish priest of a remote western parish receives, in the small hours of a winter morning, a summons to answer a sick call from a hamlet in the hills where a young man "is dying of a strange disease." Ill-temperedly but faithfully the priest rises, throws on some clothes, mounts his horse and rides through rough weather and over rougher terrain to a cabin where he finds a young man writhing in pain on a cabin floor. A crowd of gaping neighbours hang over him in various measures of awe and fear. The priest orders all present out and demands of the young man that he confess the origin of his strange and consuming malady. After a struggle the young man at last groans, "Father, I'm in love." Whereupon the priest almost lashes him with his riding crop and stalks out into the night in the highest of dudgeon.

The same message is conveyed by both the bathetic lines of the ballad and the kernel of the literary story. And I presume that the reactions of hearer and reader are similar – if both pause to analyse.

I shall have much to say hereafter on the origins of literature, of the basic clay which the potter-writer moulds and turns on the wheel of his mind and his final firing of the vessel in the oven of his imagination.

So the ballad, even in its primitive manifestations, seeks and often wins the sympathy and interest of the hearer. I saw these simple manifestations of a prime urging to convey emotion as being capable of being transmitted and transmuted into a higher order of appeal. Further, I go so far as to repeat (and I'm not the first to say it) that all literature has its origins in the bellylaugh.

A man who realised to the full the value of the simple music of the countryside, like Dvorak before him, was Seán Ó Riada. He transmuted what those of unsure gentility would consider "base metal" into purest gold. That sudden cymbal clash in the music of *Mise Éire* follows me everywhere I go.

Ballads like "The Cliffs of Dooneen" and "The Shores of Amerikay" were songs I came upon with my wire recorder and helped to restore to life. I heard my rewritten and sanitised version of a particular song broadcast from BBC Scotland some time ago; I had rewritten a bawdy version of the ballad renaming it "Kiss in the Morning Early."

More than any other county in Ireland, Clare held the traditional music until Ireland was ready to take it back. Authorities buttress my contention that Milltownmalbay is the musical capital of Ireland. If that claim is disputed the sway may go to another Clare village not many miles away.

Few could sing a ballad like Robbie McMahon of Spancil Hill. He was also a natural showman, often keeping his audience waiting until His Majesty deigned to put in an appearance. An authentic roar of appreciation then greeted him.

I sang with Robbie until the dawn of day at a *fleadh* in Milltown; the following morning of sunlight Robbie and I swapped songs in the open street, until a benefactor in the shape of John Rynne called us into his discreet pub and gave us soup as good as wine negus which rekindled the waning flames of balladry in our breasts. The adjective discreet I deliberately apply to John, our host, for he coupled his role as publican with his devoted service as parish clerk.

Although I failed to recognise its importance at this time, I always sought and enjoyed the unexpected harmony of opposites. I experienced this odd harmony one night in the Milltown pub when John, gently urged to do so, proudly brought out his Bene Merenti medal from the Pope to be handed round to the again discreet customers in his bar. The faces of each of the countrymen as he handled the velvet lined box with its contents of winking gold was certainly a study in fleeting emotions. I have forgotten several Lucullan meals, some in the homes of wealthy Americans, but can still recall the meal John Rynne placed before Robbie and myself that morning in Sráid na Cathrach in hospitable County Clare.

That was many years ago: recently I paid a short visit to the traditional Willie Clancy Festival in the same town (it was opened by Her Excellency, President Robinson) and in the midst of a fine musical session I shook hands with another old friend, Miko Russell of Doolin. As I did so, my mind flew over land and sea to the attic of a tall house on the outskirts of Stockholm. My hostess, a musicologist, took down a tin flute from among a collection of instruments from all parts of the world and asked me to blow into it. When I did so, she said, "Go home now and tell Miko Russell that you played his flute in a high room in Stockholm." Laughingly I conveyed the message to Miko at a later date. Miko, God rest him, has since passed on.

One story follows on the heels of another. On that same occasion when I was a member of the Murnaghan Commission on Broadcasting, our researches took us to the Swedish capital. After a week's hard work we emerged at midnight from a celebrated restaurant called "The Golden Peas" – it is here the adjudicators of the Nobel Award are said to hold their meetings. When the secretary to our group stopped short and said, "I hear the pipes!" we all stood stock-still. I looked along the cobbled street to where the sentries stood at their posts at the gateway of the Royal Palace, from which building incidentally, Axel Munthe wrote letters to my neighbour and friend, bookseller Dan Flavin. I was then roused from reverie by our secretary's cry of "He's playing 'The Flax in Bloom.' And the chanter was made by . . . "

Was the secretary, a piper himself, dreaming aloud? I could hear very little as a faint wisp of music ebbed and flowed. Was I hearing anything at all? When I enquired a few days later of a knowledgeable

Swede, he told me, "Yes, there is an Irish piper here in Stockholm. By day he plays outside a great department store: by night the sound of his pipes wafts over the capital from his lodging place in Gamla Stan – the old city of Stockholm".

Not without foundation is it stated that our traditional music is Eastern in origin. I have under my hand at this moment a rare book dated 1802 entitled *Prospectus of a Dictionary of the Aire Coti or Ancient Irish, compared with the languages of the Coti or Ancient Persians and with the Hindoostanee, the Arabic and the Chaldean languages*. The book was written by Lieut-General Charles Vallencey.

I know that learned etymologists look awry at the theories of Vallancey but somehow I feel that, although details are open to question, they may have some validity in their sum.

I recall a visit to Broadcasting House, London many years ago when Louis MacNeice the well-known poet, since dead, had just brought back some recordings from abroad. "Guess what country this comes from?" he asked me as he placed the record on the machine. After listening for a while, I said, "The words are indistinct, but to me it seems to be the traditional singing from an old man in one of the Aran Islands." The poet smiled and said, "I have just returned from India; this is my recording of a muezzin calling the faithful to prayer from a balcony of a mosque in the foothills of the Himalayas."

I am aware that nowadays certain musical authorities in Ireland are engaged in an effort to prove the theory that sean-nós singing has links with Eastern music. Both have melodic decoration – an Indian friend of mine once referred to these as 'sruti' which he said were the Indian equivalent of grace notes.

The subject awaits further research. Meanwhile I recall an experiment I tried out with a few Indian friends in the US as a few of us sat on the steps of a college at midnight. Addressing a friend from Madras, I said, "Hambdi, I am going to hum-sing in as traditional manner as I can, the first line of an old Irish love song. Out of racial memory you will try to bridge two thousand and more years by improvising the second line in somewhat the same fashion." All present listened as I hummed or la-lah-ed; "*Sé fáth mo bhuartha, ná faighim cead cuarta*" and Hambdi came in with a passable attempt at la-lahing the meoldy of the second line, "*San ngleanntán uaigneach 'na mbíonn mo ghrá*."

Some years later, this time at a college party in the US Middle West, I tried the same experiment with a distinguished Indian poet: he also managed a passable version of the melody of that second line.

What all this proves, I'm not sure. I simply offer it for what it is worth.

My musical memory was a peculiar one. The first hearing of a new ballad seemed to leave no impression on me: later I would wake at four am, perhaps a month, or a year later, with a voice in the hall or pub of my mind singing the song note and word perfect from beginning to end. As a result of my *Balladmaker's Saturday Night* programme I faced an avalanche of seventy to eighty letters a week with callers by the score conveying or saying the same message: "My mother/father had the second verse different. Listen to me now and you can be sure that I have the correct version."

These different versions arose somewhat as follows: individual singers grew to love and hoard certain ballads. So much so, that with the passage of time they almost persuaded themselves they had really written these songs. They rarely gave the words as a present to a stranger. Consequently the hearer who also wished to sing the ballad had to rely on a fallible memory to reproduce the words. Quite often he altered the lines and also gave his own ornamented interpretation of the air while holding to the melodic line. As a matter of fact, each individual singer never sings any two verses the same way. With intuitive musical wisdom or intuition, he varies his interpretation so as to bring it into accord with the place, time and current mood of his audience.

At *fleadhanna* there is a protocol of entry into a group of musicians already in session. This obtains even in the timing of the opening of a newcomer's music box or case and the subsequent waiting for the barely perceptible glance or smile of welcome. The assembling of the piper's instrument can be hieratic in its solemn approach. In ballad singing there is little or no emotional interpretation, nor is there any musical direction such as crescendo or diminuendo. Deadpan almost it could be called, it depends on the hearers to supply the emotion.

My most precious memory is of a scene in the Aran Islands. A giant of a man, his eyes closed, sings a love song while at the same time he holds in his mighty palm the hand of a girl of five or six years of age. The pair are seated side by side and the girl communicates with the singer with intuitive accuracy. Sometimes she conveys confidence by gently winding the great arm as if she were using a small butter-churn. The end of the final verse is often spoken instead of sung and invariably receives a round of applause: this indicates a general measure of release from the trance induced by the song.

This reminds me of a certain pang of regret which afflicted me for many years. The late Pádraic Fallon, a Galway writer whose work I admire very much, was one of those who scripted my radio programme, *The Balladmaker* after I had opted out.

Pádraic wrote to tell me (he had a stammer) that he was averse to going around the countryside collecting songs: what he proposed doing was writing ballads of his own in such a fashion as to make it appear that they were either genuine ballads or old Irish traditional songs. Quite obtusely, I did not see the point of this and mildly conveyed my reservations to Pádraic.

Picture my abject contrition when Pádraic produced verses more authentic than the authentic, if that indeed is possible but not to be wondered at when one considers his background .

This verse I take from Pádraic's "Mary of Loughrea". It may read flatly but it sings superbly:

In her grey house by the water
My love is dwelling still
She's the moon's only daughter
She's a lamp upon a hill.
She may braid her hair at evening
While those who walk the way
They may think it's the moon that's rising
O'er the grey lake of Loughrea.

Coincidentally, another song about another Mary from Loughrea is equally restrainedly passionate. This song is by Michael Hogan of Limerick, the rather eccentric Bard of Thomond. Maybe it was another Loch Rea he had in mind but clarification on that score must await another day.

The sun will miss the glory of your glossy shining hair,
The lads will miss you from the dance on summer
evenings fair,
The grass will want your fairy steps to touch its dews
away,
But I shall miss you most of all, my Mary from Loughrea.

The late Patrick Purcell, a writer on GAA affairs, was the maker of a moving ballad on the death of PJ Duke, a fine Cavan footballer. This is a song my son, Garry, sings well;

O never more shall I walk the green sward
Of broad Croke Park but I'll see him still
His manly bearing, his brilliant fielding
His red hair flaring in the battle's thrill.
New stars will rise in the years before us
But in our eyes none shall him dethrone
The boy from Breifni and the pride of
Belfield
God rest you, PJ, in far Stradone.

For every ballad I recall, and these are many, I still maintain that there are three more out there which are waiting to be collected, mated with a singer, and again receive overdue applause. Songs like "Tipperary Hills for Me," and "The Bold Hills of Clare" still await a return to the fold. Maurice Walsh, our famous local writer, had a delightful song which he learned from his father or grandfather. "Of the Colour of Amber was my True Love's Hair" he called it, but it may be known under other titles. I often wonder where it has gone to. Or if it is lost to racial memory.

The following is the story of a ballad of mine made under unusually sorrowful circumstances.

One day there was a knock on my front door. I opened it to admit two US professors. In the course of the conversation that followed I realised that I was dealing with two unusually talented men with original and imaginative views on education.

Education, they maintained, was over-tied to the halls and walls of the University building. Their ideas were radically different: what was the purpose, they asked, of teaching Shelley's "Ode to a Skylark" to students who had never seen a countryside, not to mention a skylark? There were inner city students in the US who, as children, had never seen the stars. So, in complete practicality, if the subject to be studied was Greek, the professors took the students to Athens and from thence explored the countryside with its epic ruins. If Latin was to be studied, six months in Rome or outside it were perfectly in order. They had previously been in Greece and outside Rome.

Now that the subject was Ireland and Irish literature, they wished to lodge over a hundred students, not in a tourist district, but in an area of native integrity where the young men and women could experience the reality of life as lived close to the clay and rock of an Irish landscape and its inhabitants.

Eventually Inishboffin, off the Galway coast, was chosen largely because of its ecclesiastical history. The island had once been an internment camp (the first ever) where in Penal and "Settlement" days the Catholic clergy of Ireland had been interned – this primarily because the island offered little chance of escape. 'Boffin was also the place to which Coleman of Lindisfarne, the great Celtic ecclesiastical leader of that day, had led his defeated and dissenting monks out of the Synod of Whitby in 664: the points at stern issue at the Synod were the type of tonsure worn by the monks and the fixing of a permanent date for Easter. Wilfred, representing Canterbury, held views opposed by Coleman and was the leader of the English delegation at the Synod.

These and other interesting features and legends determined the site of their studies for the professors and students of the University of Kansas at Lawrence. In due course they arrived on the island.

Alas, and again alas – just as I was leaving for Newfoundland to talk on Peig Sayers and the Great Blasket Island, I switched on the radio and learned to my utter horror that two of the students had been drowned. On visiting the island on my return home I found students and faculty bearing up manfully under their ordeal. The islanders had buttressed them emotionally in their time of sorrow. I joined them for a while lecturing on Ireland, its literature, language and traditional music.

Some time later I wrote a little ballad on the tragedy and forwarded it to Kansas. I then received an invitation to travel there and give a lecture on the Ireland of the country town. At a prestigious tuxedo-ed gathering I was called upon to sing my ballad. The parents of the dead students were present so it was an intensely emotional experience for everyone concerned. I have no illusions about my singing capabilities: I did the best I could, wedding the words to a traditional air. For the occasion the ballad had been published on parchment.

The lark so gay at the break of day
Shall soar to the height of the sky
And the seagull glide o'er the broken tide
To utter his piercing cry.
The hare at morn shall leave his form
To race for a pleasant mile
But never more shall these young men stroll
On Boffin's so beautiful Isle.

A stained glass window in the island church perpetuates the sad memory of Richard Mathis (21) and Edward Moll (20) drowned at The Stags, Inishboffin on February 3rd, 1976.

To this day I still write a ballad or two so as to keep my hand in, and to act as a relief from other work. In spring I tend to walk uphill on a quiet byroad some miles from my town. The place is called Piper's Hill. My wife, Kitty, used to accompany me. God rest her, she loved primroses.

When the wild duck paired below the bridge
We watched, my love and I
We saw them leave the Smearla stream
And seek the heavens on high
And as they parted far above
My true love's voice grew chill

"I'll be in my tomb ere the primrose bloom
On the brow of Piper's Hill."

The ballad, as its place in musical heritage indicates, is harmless stuff, isn't it? Or is it? Why did I spend time and effort trying to probe the mystery of tradition expressed in its most simple form? Because I feel that here is a reservoir of primitive power waiting to be released, canalised and harnessed for a variety of purposes. I keep protesting that it is far more than musical pabulum for rustics. In our case it is now calling out to young people from all over Europe and they are here now in Ireland seeking a chemical deficiency missing in their blood.

There are moments of revelation which can alter one's outlook on life.

I experienced one such moment on the crowded stairway of a singing pub in Puck Fair. I was a young man at the time and as I now realise, a trembling introvert.

The house was shuddering with music and song as I battled my way upwards to what I hoped was the more genteel atmosphere of the front parlour where I could hear a piano tinkling. I wondered if all these roysterers were crazy and I was sane. Or vice versa?

At a turn in the thronged stairway, the press of people descending thrust a full-breasted country girl deep into my arms. I had to hold her fast or risk falling downwards. Her exciting inviting and laughing eyes and breasts were locked close to mine. For a moment both of us seemed alone.

Receiving no response, she thrust me from her with an exclamation of rejection and pity. "Are you the only fool here unable to enjoy himself?" was the question implicit in her final glare backwards in my direction.

The parlour was quiet and comparatively civilised. After a moment or two I thrust downstairs and joined the mob in the bar. There I joined in the merrymaking. I sang "DJ Allman," a local ballad of the War of Independence and, cold sober, in terms of liquid replenishment, shouted and laughed with the best. As morning greyed the windows I was drained and hoarse but fully alive. The timid introvert had now become a boisterous extrovert.

Again I am back in memory in a crowded and noisy pub at Puck Fair where an old countryman, his hands trembling, catches a balladsinger by the lapels of his jacket, shakes him and cries, "Another rebelly ballad, son." As the song slices the rowdy din to silence I secretly watch the tranced faces of the listeners. Above all I watch their eyes and try to interpret what goes on in the minds behind the eyes. The workings of the mouth-corners offer clues to deep emotions.

Stiff and cold his body lay
In a state of massacree
Because he was a rebel bold
And he died for liberty

There was set dancing too. I noted some of the whimsical names of the dance music, each poetic name evoking a picture in my imagination. "Haste to the Wedding," "The Maid Behind the Bar," "Saddle the Pony," "The Pigeon on the Gate," "Rolling in the Ryegrass," and most bizarre indeed, "Upstairs in a Tent."

Shadowy people now stand in the edge of my imagination. Ó Riada is there listening, his cigarillo in a holder, his profiled face a subject for reproduction on a golden coin. Also a collector-composer musician called Moeran who drowned at Kenmare pier. There too is Dermot O'Byrne, an Englishman, whose real name this is not, and who oddly, is really "Keeper of the King's Music": he wrote a poem about "some boyo whistling Ninety Eight" and releasing a broth of hate in Dublin's College Green – a poem that is far more profound than it seems at first sight.

And then there also is the great Fitzgerald who wrote a poem called "The Music Makers".

Two men with a dream at leisure
Can go forth and conquer a crown
And three with a new song's measure
Can trample a Kingdom down.

Still in the reverie of recollection, I left the Killorglin pub and went out into the starry night. On the surface of the Laune River the swans were like torches in the water. If Pete St John had at that time written "The Fields of Athenry" I would have sung it for the white birds of Irish legend.

Listening to ballads and collecting them is one thing: making them is another. In this regard let me now tell you about my adventures in the office of a small-town jobbing printer. I plead for a little latitude in doing so.

I can get drunk on the smell of printer's ink. Let me open a book just off the press to savour its virgin contents and even insert my nose into the spread leaves and I am tipsy as a lord. Let the psychologists diagnose my ailment or weakness as they wish – I do not mind.

In my teens I was drawn into the medieval atmosphere of the printer's shop. The large flatbed press was presided over by a metal cat (sometimes on a machine of a similar type it was an eagle). When the copy was laid out and set and the type later locked in the forme, this was laid on the bed and the job inked with a hand roller of rubber – a contraption just like a black roller-pin. An arm, not unlike the bellows arm of the forge, bore weight down upon the double crown of paper with its type inked. The finished poster was then plucked off.

For smaller jobs there was a platen machine into which the sheets were inserted one by one, its jaws were then made to open and close by being worked by a treadle. A third machine, referred to as the roller, was reckoned antique compared to the two other "sophisticated" machines. Trays of type and a metal topped table completed the furniture of the "jobbing" office.

(*O tempora! O mores*; how the trade of printing has altered with the passing years. Unbelievably so!)

I spent surely twenty-five years as unofficial apprentice to the trade. Put to it today, I could set a job on the setting stick, lock it in the forme with the quoin keys, lift it into the platen, work the treadle, insert the sheets of paper and proceed to print. From the books in the shelves of the printing office, I learned the art of laying-out a job, always having the chief word *DANGER* or *AUCTION* set in the optical centre of the page, one third of the distance from the top.

Robert Irvine Cuthbertson was a well-made dapper little man;

whenever he turned to greet a customer his round spectacles flashed in the daylight filtering through the mullioned window of his shop. Invariably, I recall him standing before a tray of type, a setting-stick in his hand and a cigarette in his mouth. He was something of a dandy and his hair was groomed backwards in what we called a quiff, the word obviously a corruption of the word coif. He had a hundred virtues, good humour, fine wit and religious tolerance. He was the son of Scottish Presbyterian parents both of whom had attended the local Church of Ireland. Bob was given his second Christian name because his forebears hailed from Irvine in Ayrshire. His father, also Robert, first arrived in Limerick whence, in 1884, he moved to Listowel on hearing that there was an opening for a printer in our town. His wife's name was Mathieson: Bob always maintained that she was a Gaelic speaker from the Isles or Highlands of Scotland.

On the first week of his arrival, Robert Senior walked into the local national school and said, "Dominie, gie me a bright lad to work in my office." The schoolmaster looked around his class and called a lad named John, and said, "Tell your father that I'd suggest you'd go to work for Mr Cuthbertson." That boy, his son, and grandchildren served the Scots-Irish family with loyalty beyond loyalty for the century that followed.

It was a time of land agitation and agrarian disturbance: the elder Cuthbertson equally served stern landlord and unhappy tenant in their confidential and public transactions.

If one took up the wooden letters of, say, four and a half inches in length from the special tray in the drawer beneath the type-trays one read the ordinary capital letters B, O, D, etc. But turn the letters upside down and lo! there was revealed a skull and crossbones, a coffin or some other symbol of sudden death.

Robbie the elder was at service in St John's, the Protestant church, one Sunday at the turn of the century (the building is now a little theatre and literary centre). As he knelt beside a local landlord, the latter whispered, "Thanks Mr Printer for the threatening handbill you had pushed under my door last evening." "What are you saying, mon?" "Printer! The ink was wet." There was no reply to this. This ambivalence characterised the life of the little jobbing office. A job was a job whether it came from a large Protestant church in Dublin or from

Whiteboys without a name.

In my time, Bob printed for every occasion in the life of our small town and the countryside around it – the hinterland as it is now called. He was a common factor in the manifold activities of his catchment area and sometimes far beyond it. He printed posters for dances, fit-up plays, and concerts (Mike Nono, Mark Wynne and Linton of the Little Men), *feiseanna*, *aeríochta*, country raffles, auctions, as well as for football and hurling matches. He printed the list of fairs and markets for the entire year and the timetable for the LBR – the famous Lartigue or Listowel/Ballybunion Light Railway. Appeals (We, the Poor Anglers), threatening notices, (Don't tamper with the Widow and Children, the true owners before God). He also printed advertisements for sire horses. This last, together with the raffles, were mother's milk to my imagination.

One Saturday I was standing at the setting "stone" looking out the window. A countrywoman wearing a black shawl had stolen in: she stood at the small space of open counter and whispered but not so low that I could not hear.

"A raffle, Mr Cuthbertson." Bob took up his pad and pencil to take particulars. He wrote as she spoke.

"At the cottage of Mary So-and-So, to be raffled on December 18th at ten pm, a most valuable prize. Tickets two shillings each. Of special interest to farmers. Have you that down, sir?"

"Yes. How many books of tickets will you need? And you had better specify the valuable prize." The woman hedged the issue.

"Could I do without it?" she asked.

"It's customary to specify. What's the prize?"

(My listening ears were on pointed sticks.)

"My husband," the woman said in the faintest of whispers.

"You're raffling your husband, ma'am?"

"Not himself. Just the work of him for a farmer for a full year."

"I see." Bob began to write. "First prize. The valuable services of worthy worker John So-and-So for a calendar year."

Bob looked hard at me after the lady had gone. "See what I have to put up with," his smile said. It was St Patrick's Day before I thought of asking how the raffle had turned out.

"He lasted a month with the farmer who won him," Bob said. "He was a 'sooner!' – sooner be inside than outside. He was delighted to be sacked for he had his year's wages drawn in advance through the sale of the tickets. His wife came in to me again and wanted him raffled a second time. I talked her out of it. He worked short-term with other farmers. So he was paid twice for his year's work."

At the printer's, the procedure with the sire horses was wonderful. I'm talking about the 1920s which were box-camera days.

In strutted the owner – a real horseyman – check cap, jacket and jodhpurs. A boy groom was holding the restive stallion at the door. "Take his photo first, Mr Cuthbertson. Put it on the poster."

John, now the loyal foreman, produced a shoe box painted black. It had a round hole in each end. "Trot him up and down," he ordered the owner.

The owner trotted his fine animal up and down the roadway. John put the shoe box to his eye, said "Click" and then turned away into the shop. The "camera" was shoe box only. Nothing more, nothing less.

(Let me for once project myself into the future. That little celebration of maleness on the part of sire horse and owner, with the addition of something my father once told me about a farm wife stealing into town to admire her husband and his stallion parading the street on market or fair day, was reborn in my mind, duly fertilised, and entered life as a story called *Chestnut and Jet.* The last time I saw it in print was in a US University textbook on literature in English: there it was sandwiched between a story by Guy de Maupassant and another by DH Lawrence, the three stories together illustrating different aspects of the subject of Love.)

When the sire-horse poster appeared, the black smudge of a man and horse at its top – depicted in the single block the shop possessed – pleased the owner no end. He read it aloud at the counter even while the ink was wet.

PRINCE OF OSSORY
(by Crown Prince out of Ostentatious.)

At O'Connors yard each Friday in April is a handsome black sire standing on the best of legs.
His gets are known and admired at all Southern Fairs and Shows.

Missers will be served free next season if the sire still remains the property of the present owner.

"John took that photo into the sun," Bob said pinching his lips – this was to explain the absence of detail in the "photo". The owner didn't seem to mind. His name and address stood out in bold print at the bottom of the poster.

My other duty in the little office, as I have already hinted, was the making of ballads. I was seated at the great chest in the kitchen with my ink holder of violet ink and my quill pen. Bob's initial injunction was to "make the song rowdly-owdly". I knew what he had in mind. At my last casual count I could name forty-two of these rural ditties: I feel there were more. They turn up everywhere. Passing the yeasty mouth of a village pub in western Ireland, I hear a song being chanted and then realise that it was one I made for Bob in the long ago. Many are gone into the vernacular cupboard labelled Anonymous. Some sold in hundreds of thousands. Others have been pirated. Ah, well!

As the annual races and the harvest festival approached, there was a flurry of activity in the printer's shop, much of it having to do with the printing of notices about the food available at the festival. I wrote a quatrain in praise of the mutton pie which was a local dish and another in praise of the cooked crubeen or pig's trotter which was, and still is, succulence incarnate. I recall the first few lines of the latter but the rest eludes me.

God rest the pig and may he reign forever in our hearts
To bring us meals nutritious, complete with apple tarts.

"Not very elevating literature, my boy," as the English inspector once commented on some trivial pot-boiler mentioned in our secondary school. By far the best entertainment for me in Races week was drawn from the piling up of balladry and the advent of the gypsies. Bob was ready: he had the shelves well loaded with songs. I was writing them non-stop. Each ballad bore an illustrative block on top of its broadsheet.

The representation was placed there for the benefit of the ballad-singers and tramps who, after having collected as much money as possible during the year, could stock up for the winter. Since many of the ramblers were illiterate, Bob or I would help each entertainer to identify the ballad solely by means of the illustration. "You see this ship? It's going to America. So the song is 'The Shores of Americay.' This one with the bent trees? That's 'The Wild Colonial Boy' – it's a wild day – cop?" The oddest learning aid we used consisted of an upper and lower set of dentures designed for the billhead of a local dentist. This was printed at the head of Kickham's famous ballad "She lived beside the Anner". The conjunctive clue was "Her teeth were pearls rare". Bob was not above pirating an odd popular song but was immensely indignant if one of his – sorry, mine – was stolen.

Remarks Bob passed to me remain with me yet. "Like all printers," he said, "I live in the future. At Christmas-time I'm printing for Lent and St Patrick's Day. (Lent was then the time for presenting plays as dances were forbidden by the Church – and the edict was obeyed.) On St Patrick's Day I'm printing for high summer and the seaside events. In the summer I'm printing for the autumn festival of racing and at races time I'm printing for Christmas." Then he'd add wryly, "A printer's shop – opened by the devil and closed by the sheriff."

One day as we both stood in his doorway, he called a boy who was passing. The boy had a clear glass jar with what we called a kissane (*gisiún* – pinkeen or minnow) swimming around with its nose to the glass. "There I am," he said with a smile, "a Protestant kissane swimming in a Catholic jamjar." At this time he was one of the very last Protestants in the town. No one ever commented on this fact: he seemed to merge completely, in spite of his background and traditions. His wide circle of friends mourned sincerely at his passing.

Did I mention the gypsies? They weren't really Romanies but tinker women and girls who put "a piece of cloth on their heads" – a kerchief worn gypsy fashion – and pretended to be fortune-tellers. After stuffing their pockets with ballads I coached them to recite the spiel of fortune-telling so as to have it word perfect when reading the palms of the "buffaly shams and lacks" – country boys and girls.

"There's a man (boy/girl) in a crown house who has the love of his/her heart waiting for you. You'll have children who'll wear the collar of the Holy Ghost and take news of the Great Dawloon to a land across the Northern ocean." And so forth. I spoke gammon to the younger tribes-children and urged them to keep the secret language alive.

Before they retired to their barrel caravans, lined up just inside the market gate, the fortune-tellers had to get cards printed – these were notices one foot square printed on light cardboard – proclaiming their prowess in prophecy. Before printing began it was my final duty to give them their "stage names." I had a classical dictionary handy for this purpose.

"You're Madame Cassandra," I'd say. "And you're Madame Zenia. You're Mother Aurora." ("I was that last year: I'd like a change, Master.") "All right: you're Madame Electra or Atlanta or Eusebia or even Lady Venus – take your pick."

I then laid out the card and added: "Past Present and Future an open book" or some such legend. Later as I visited the row of caravans I found that one of my "pupils" had called on the services of a rural scribe who had ruined my presentation by daubing an odd postscript to the card. It now read:

"Ireland's most famisht pamist."

Roaring laughing, and having told us of their being routed out of a parish by an irate priest, they tumbled out of the printer's shop.

Let me tell you a last story about Bob.

He had the Celtic flaw of a fondness for what the English called usquebaugh and we Irish call *uisce beatha.* The excitement of the races would often trip him up. On the eve of the meeting the shop was closed and Bob was away on a bout of revelry. Eamon Kelly and I decided to force open his shop door and sell the ballads on the one vital day when large sales could be expected. There we were, the counter piled with ballad money and the shop thronged with roaring wanderers, when Bob made a dramatic if unsteady entrance.

"How dare you, vagrants," he shouted. "Out with you! At once." We went.

At Christmas he recovered his abstemiousness. Contritely he begged pardon of his disappointed customers and requested me to apologise in verse for his neglect. I was to tell bluntly the reason for his fall.

The Christmas card was deckled-edged and the type gold dusted: these he printed and sent out in hundreds. Each card read as follows:

The Christmas news from Kerry
Continues bright and merry
No mumps, no berri-berri
And the Printer's on the tack.

I am quite convinced that at that time, each town in Ireland was stuffed with characters. What happened to them all? My only explanation is that to a man and woman they drowned in the soap tubs of television.

But a voice from within keeps telling me that, although we have lost a lot, we still have a wonderful residue. In my mind it is indeed such: for the blacksmith brothers, Old James, Old Pat; the saddlers Maurice and Pat, and Brown Paddy himself are all still alive and kicking in the community of my imagination. So is Printer Bob. He lives on in almost forgotten balladry. I had urged him to call himself "The Ballad King" and print the title on his billheads. In the lore of the Irish wanderer I daresay there are still one or two left who speak of him with pride and affection. As indeed I do, to this very day.

CHAPTER SIX

In the course of driving to the top of a boulder-strewn mountain pass – I have Conor Pass at Pedlar's Lake in mind – the traveller will come to a point where the road has been widened to form a lay-by: this is primarily designed to allow other vehicles to pass. It also gives the traveller the opportunity to leave his car, stroll to the outer fence and survey the countryside spread below.

This break also provides him with time to cast an upward glance to the point at the top of the pass and allows him to speculate as to what he will soon see on the other side. Meanwhile, the traveller inhales the mountain air, smiles as he notes the far glint of ocean water, the silver paper scrawl of a valley stream, the odd lamp of a red haybarn. In this instance the traveller may well take stock of what he is about to do and where he is to go. He examines options, shuffles alternatives, and attempts to probe the future.

I now propose to halt at a lay-by of the mind. I use the perch of age, with its erratic series of time changes, to offer an excuse for a break in the linear course of my narrative. But I feel such a digression is of immense importance if only by way of explanation.

Leaving aside the musical clamour of the public house, the din of the marketplace and the clack of the printer's office, I now evoke a far more tranquil scene – one which hopefully will come as a relief to the over-burdened senses – especially that of hearing. If I were to give this episode a title I would call it *Silence, Intimacy and the Lamp.* It will, hopefully, offer clues to the obsessive nature of the writer's mind and the writer-reader relationship. So I counsel utter patience on the part of the reader as I travel into unexpected territory.

I now evoke the picture of a person (a man or a woman) seated in a booklined study. From the appointments of the room it is clear that this is the home of a scholarly and thoughtful man who, at this moment, is rapt in enjoyment and concentration as he reads the book before him. The TV set is not turned on: perhaps he prefers to form his own images drawn from cyphers called print.

The almost total silence is broken only by the low sound of a small fire in the grate, that and the muted night noises of the winter neighbourhood outside his window. The reader is wearing house-slippers. The outside of the shade of the reading lamp is a gentle green. So total is the silence, and so absolute the reader's concentration, as to border on the intimacy indicated by a woman alone examining her face in a mirror.

The foregoing is the conventional picture: in point of fact the reader could well ply his trade even in the most inhospitable of places and circumstances.

Let me go back again to the quiet study. The outward peace and tranquillity may be deceptive. The inert book between the reader's fingers, translated into images, can assume a thousand roles imperceptible to the eyes of a watcher. Since the reader has no audience, which may not be the case in other branches of art, there is no need for him to act out a part to gain the applause or appreciation of others. He can now be truly himself.

To revert to the image of the mirror and the woman; the reader too dreams himself back and forth between his subjective self and the objective images presented by the text before him. The objective often becomes the subjective as our reader inserts himself vicariously and imaginatively into the subject matter unfolding under his eyes.

The outward peace is deceptive: this is because of the thousand roles of the book. It can be comforter, informer in the more ameliorative meaning of the word, healer, enthuser, sedative, elucidator, disturber of the peace, priest, Satan, messiah, physician of the mind and rabble-rouser. It can also be scapegoat, purgative of the imagination, acrobat, pickpocket of convictions, warmonger, peacemaker, imagemaker, and therapeutic rehearser of personal agonies.

It can be a fingerpost to areas of special beauty as well as a warning sign against dangerous cliffs ahead.

As a general rule one can choose the most amenable book as companion: the part it plays, stimulant or depressant, is constantly being stressed nowadays. Sometimes it is suggested that it can be foolish of the reader to confront the troubles of the mind when he can, through the medium of a book, dodge 'em! If one finds it difficult to get to sleep, the rabble-rouser or the cheerleader book should be avoided at bedtime. In its place the history of one of the early Chinese dynasties could be substituted: the idea being that, since the reader cannot even imaginatively be a participant in the action of the matter read, the resultant sense of stalemate will ensure a tranquil night's sleep. However, as a caveat to such advice, I mention that there are possibly among the vast host of readers, those whom the history of early China would stimulate inordinately: this indicates the presence of a notable few who demand a certain sense of stimulatory action in their reading material and who, thanking their fortunate stars that they do not live in such gory times, fall blissfully asleep wrapped in a cocoon of gratitude. All this shows the folly of generalisation.

One of the better ideas emanating from the Irish Arts Council in recent years was a scheme called "Writers in Schools". As its title indicates it involved writers and kindred artists visiting schools and talking to the children.

For some years after my retirement from teaching I took part in this activity, one which proved stimulating and gently exhausting. It revealed to me that quite extraordinary work was going on in unexpected places, in colleges and schools throughout the land, where individual teachers who possessed the priceless gift of infectious enthusiasm were resolutely at work. The pupils in such schools and colleges – many of them in quite remote areas – were fortunate indeed. However, one constant query kept popping up at the little question time at the end of each talk: somehow this question baffled me.

"Please tell us, do you ever get bored?"

"Why should I get bored?" came my reply.

"Always talking about books!"

I was hard set to explain. But I did my best. "Books are about every possible activity of the spirit, mind and body. If I were to press you to tell me what facet of living you like best, then I'd take you to a library and show you a row of books that would open up that activity for you to the fullest. A taste for reading is the finest fruit of education." Perhaps, then I would add, "Our whole lives move on words. So master words! Never pass a difficult word without looking it up in a dictionary. Now I want you all to chant the following: 'There's a doubt and there's a dictionary' – a phrase that I heard first as a student in teacher training sixty-three years ago."

Dutifully, if mockingly, the students chanted. I knew then that the phrase would remain in their minds.

Sometimes I added as a bonus, "If you wish to become a good public speaker never forget that language is learned by imitation. When you hear a good speaker, (I don't mean a posh one) say, on the television, begin to imitate him/her right on his/her heels, even as he/she speaks. (How complicated can one get!) Then you will master the 'runs' of language which will lead to fluency, the prime attribute of a good speaker who's never, as the saying goes, 'caught for a word'. Also, so as to establish a rapport with your audience, make a joke in the third sentence. Even a titter of applause will make contact and settle your nerves."

I went on to introduce the students to the hierarchy of dictionaries and alerted them to the possibilities of the Thesaurus and the Synonym Finder as tools for life. The original Roget was a masterpiece of reference, resource and correction: modern imitations I find truly disappointing. But since hope springs eternal, I rejoice on learning that there has been a reprint of the old Roget though I find it elusive when I seek to lay hands on a copy. There is a book on correct English by Quiller Couch and another by Fowler both of which I sucked dry, but the most wonderful of all, to my finding, was a book called *The Reader Over Your Shoulder* by Hodges and Graves (or Graves and Hodges). This was a winner from trap to line: it dissected passages from masterpieces of the English language and also from leading articles from newspapers and even sports reports. Without mercy it revealed flaws: I learned a great deal from its pages.

At this moment I have a retrospective picture of my dear mother watching her four children at table: a book is propped up on the lectern of mug or sugar bowl before each engrossed sibling.

After a stunned silence, she, a lover of wild flowers, dress and delph was wont to blurt. "I'd rather see pints of porter cocked up before ye, than those infernal books." She would then add, "Too much of anything is good for nothing".

But again: Silence, Intimacy and the Lamp.

The library is a most important building in any community. To get a child to walk into a library and have him walk around confidently, select a book, have it stamped, and then walk out with the book under his arm is a major step forward in his self-education. The hope is that later as an adult he will walk into a library or a bookshop anywhere in the world with the same confidence and the same sense of adventure.

I recall an incident which happened at a local funeral. The coffin of an old man was being borne into the church to be placed before the altar. His sons – all "in the buildin' line" – were home from Britain to pay their respects. As I tendered my sympathy one of the sons whispered, "Thank you for your sympathy; thanks also for giving me a love of reading."

The old man in the coffin prompts another thought in my mind. This is the influence of grandparents on children. Consider a suburban estate of a large city, where all the houses are occupied at the same time by young married couples. The children of those couples, cut off from their grandparents, in many cases grow up at the same time to experience life on a horizontal level. They never see a corpse nor experience the ritual that accompanies burial; nor is the vast range of experience born of contact with age a part of their informal education. Nor is the lore of the old theirs to inherit as a vertical experience of life.

Fortunate were those few who had grandparents to visit in the deep countryside. They had prideful tales to tell their friends on their return to the periphery of the city and quietly to boast of them in school.

Intimacy? Does the reader always establish intimacy with the text before him and indeed with his deeper self? I recognise a practice known as skimming – where a good teacher, for example, when confronted with a new text gently claws his fingers down the face of the page and, by noting the key words and, at the same time drawing on a deep storehouse of ancillary or similar knowledge, can expound and expatiate at will and indicate erudition as he does so. This is an exceptional feat born of experience: it is sometimes called speed reading.

Other more worthy examples of reading require a deeper and more mature approach. Poetry, which I define as wild beauty reduced to protocol, especially calls for one or more re-readings and the exercise of braincells rarely troubled by exertion. (There are reputed to be one hundred billion of these cells in the human brain.) The sonnets of Shakespeare yield up their treasures after four or five re-readings at the very least. The same is true of the later Yeats. Those readers who approach passages of profound meaning in a superficial manner I compare to water spiders, walking on the surface of a well and wearing, as it were, buoyant boots of air.

Another thought that remains with me concerns an experienced member of an interview board which selects candidates for posts of importance. This man once said to me, "When one is examining a panel of would-be appointees and indulges in seemingly disparate and pointless questions or remarks designed to elicit the nature or character of the applicant, the reader always sticks out a mile".

Back again we go to the reader in his study. Now we ask ourselves why he bothers his brain with fictional phantoms. We venture to reply on his behalf: "Not quite fictional phantoms since within the terms postulated, Huckleberry Finn and Sancho Panza possess as much reality as Julius Caesar or Adolf Hitler – this although the first duo may be called fictional ghosts while the second pair did actually possess a historical reality."

There was a table-top game we once played with a little brass top: graven on the facets of the top were the word *put* and *take.* If I look at the reader as one, as it were, foul-playing this game so that the word *take* always appears uppermost, I further ask myself how I can ensure that there are times when he *puts.* In other words, and why be cryptic about it, what is it that moves a reader a step higher into becoming a writer, a taker into a "putter", a comparatively passive person into one who is active. This since a prerequisite for a writer appears to be that he graduates from the ranks of readers.

(I once knew an apprentice writer who refused to read a book of any sort lest it should malform his individual style. I did not follow his subsequent career but I doubt if he made much progress in the literary world.)

Every writer of note whom I have read always counsels the would-be apprentice writer to read widely. Having finished reading a book he may, as did AJ Cronin, blurt in the presence of his wife and family, "If I put my mind to it, I'd write a better book than the one I've just finished." Whereupon AJ Cronin's good wife, hearing her husband bragging like this, took him at his word, placed a ream of virgin paper before him in a room apart, supplied him with pen and ink and told him to get on with it. To his chagrin, his children mentioned at school that their daddy was writing a book: pressurised on all sides, AJ got on with the job and, not without a struggle, succeeded.

It may now be salutary to pause for a moment, to pass from the particular to the general and ask the question bluntly. Since it is the writer, the *spiegelhalter*, who holds the mirror up to nature, why does he act as he does?

(Stay with me, dear reader. I value what follows.)

I've read many books entitled *Writer At Work*. And my response is "Hell, no. Writing is man or woman pausing to embroider life. Seeking curlicues and arabesques where they do not exist at all. Or where perhaps they are latent in the pattern of living. 'At work?' Does that mean that the man is at work only when he sits down at a desk with a pen in his hand? The truth is that the writer is at work the full twenty-four hours per day. His brain never ceases to pound. For him it's as natural as the beating of his heart."

The writer is a terrier, yes, his enquiring head tilted to one side. The breed of the terrier and the question implicit in its eyes are important.

Come clean, scribbler and mirror-holder! Why do you spend long hours in solitary confinement recalling what has been drawn in by the senses, processing it somewhere in the head to form a vision, regurgitating it – and to mix a metaphor – doling it down and out through the ball-point of a pen, at the same time expanding, refining polishing and compressing it to what is consciously called a story, a drama or a novel. The result is a kind of easi-mix which someone called a reader can take through his eyes and experience the vision anew.

The reasons a writer writes are as various as humanity itself. He writes for money. For vanity. For fame and distinction. The writer is a potter: he revels in the challenge of handling raw material in the hope that out of it he will fashion something of enduring veracity and beauty. He writes out of human blasphemy because he wishes to participate in the story of creation. "Shove over, God!" he says under his breath. "I want to muscle in on this creation business."

And even if he writes to show forth man as a creator he is quite capable of indicating that man is a cockroach. The writer writes as priest, prophet and healer. He writes out of frustration. He writes to achieve a congruence of himself and his vision and, as it were, to bridge the chasm between dream and deed. He writes to defy death as indeed Horace bragged long ago. "Non omnis moriar," – "I shall not altogether die." In other words the writer is in a state of revolt against the transience of life and sets out to affirm that he is much more than butterfly. He writes to render the familiar strange and the strange familiar. He writes himself back in time to become Scheherezade and thus become a storyteller in The Thousand and One Nights of Arabia – (Séamus Delargy the great folklorist always maintained that the world's greatest storytellers were the Arabs and the Irish.)

The writer writes out of totality – one total personality in conflict with the totality of the world and the total story of mankind. He also writes to gain oddball degrees awarded by the more informal universities of the people. He writes out of a vast egotism which implies that he has the right to act as a supreme court judge of human behaviour, and also in the belief that he himself is a pillar of fire. He writes for "a bit of gas" inferring that the world is a funnybone waiting to be tickled and by doing so to offer post-mortem proof of what John Gray had incised on his grave.

Life is a jest and all things show it.
Once I thought it, now I know it.

The writer writes amid clamour to vouch for silence: in silence he stands up and yells for clamour. In his finer projections he writes as a public affirmation that he is neither controlled, hypnotised nor manipulated by all-powerful media. He writes to indicate similarities and differences: at times he seeks to arrogate to himself the right to act as substitute for a formal creed. And a role of the writer, often dimly understood, is this; he can keep formal creeds under pressure and force them to renew themselves.

Out of the jigsaw of smithereens and potsherds of feeling, recovered like scraps of faience unearthed from the midden heap of experience and added to by the recalled flashes of imagination, which, from time to time for him, had illumined a personality, a tribe or a landscape of the mind, the writer in his role as mosaicist or montagist fashions a composite picture which has pattern, balance, beauty and the quality of indelibility.

The writer, too, by exploring and transferring an awareness of the less explored and even terrifying areas of human behaviour allows the reader to realise that he is not alone in his own more outrageous or desolate moments of thought, word and deed: the reader is comforted in some measure and is helped to rout that sense of aloneness which may well be called the dry rot of the human spirit and which often ends in suicide.

I have forewarned that the reasons for writing are legion so I crave indulgence to add a few more.

The writer writes to show man as a perpetual hunter or a perpetual prey or an alternator of both roles. He writes out of a sense of cussedness, to keep himself fully alive and, if you please, he aims to set himself up as an emperor of rectitude and coherency. He writes as fortune-teller. He writes to get rid of energy per se and because, in addition to being centrifugal and centripetal, he is also systolic like the human heart or the flowing and ebbing of the tide. He is a verbalising addict, a drunkard of words who likes to let off steam to relieve tension and create an animated scene – this with the ultimate aid of finding permanence, peace and inner harmony. Like Socrates, he indulges in question and answer and is apt to compare himself to a hornet which God has placed on a city or a people to sting it and keep it awake. (Remember: the old saddler with his, "Go out there, lads, and stir up the bloody dust!")

So there he is, the writer, convicted on evidence which I have gleaned out of his own mouth and written down in many places in a lifetime of observation, human contacts, books, seminars and so forth. Finally, I add another semi-absurd comment: this player and shaker of dice writes because he needs to transmute his almost psychosis into neurosis, his neurosis into art and his art into money to pay off his mortgage or buy more whiskey in a foolish effort to calm his trembling nerves.

After all this fulminating, I must be allowed some relief in the form of *obiter dicta.* As Stephen Leacock had it, "I beg leave to mount my horse and ride out in all directions."

In the United States, literature as such is generally (with notable exceptions, of course) reckoned to be within the sole province of the university. I shall not easily forget the face of an eminent American scholar, a friend of mine, and a Pulitzer award winner to boot, who visited me in Ireland. He was gazing as if in wonder at the façade of a grocer's shop, the owner of which had dared to write a novel. The phrase "Publish or Perish" is the common slogan among university professors in the United States. The slogan could well be compared to a monkey sitting on their shoulders.

Not so in Ireland! Things literary here tend to happen outside the university walls. Was Seán O'Casey right when he described the university as "a place where they polish pebbles and dim diamonds?"

In recent years, several significant literary contributions have come from writers denied a university education. Is there something about the higher planes of third level education that renders the graduate terrified of the self-revealment implicit in self-expression? Is there something emasculating and acidulous in university life – with the notable exceptions of those who dare to be themselves – that nourishes the critic and disembowels the creator?

But, but, but, what a wonderful experience it is to encounter a genuine critic, one who appreciates and has empathy for the labours of the literary craftsman – a critic who scorns to parade his own knowledge and who is in stark contrast to him or her who, at a loss for words, falls back on a summarisation of the plot of the piece before him, and who also has a compulsion to use handygab and in-phrases like prissy, tatty, glitz, zap, schmaltz, louch and zeitgeist.

Here I cry *mea culpa* for I once used the word zeitgeist when I was young and callow and addicted to showing off my then small store of learning. As for the words herein indicated, be not afraid that resources of neology will become exhausted: the immediate future will certainly bring a new terminology of condescension – and disdain.

Undergraduates – listen! Say "Yes" to life. Even grief, piercing to the bone, may, by its ability to hurt, indicate a crude measure of man's superiority over sticks, stones, pie dishes and lavatory bowls.

In youth and adolescence man is a carrot. Man-boy (woman-girl) carrot sends down a taproot with the finest filaments of root moving nervously before it. What he draws through these fine threads will nourish, or poison, him lifelong.

For the most part, man writes out of his roots. If he is lucky he writes in a spirit of love; he may well write out of an adolescent spirit of revolt against that which he loves. He is then testing the walls of his environment. So, dear undergraduate or sophomore of nineteen or twenty, take time out to sit for an hour before a mirror in a quiet room. It may well be the most valuable exercise of your life. Address "yourself" where you are wondrously, if transiently, imaged in mercury and ask: "You in there! What do *you* want from life?" If you are wholly sincere and patient, your reflection will offer a reply. Working towards the indicated and approved goal, inch after inch, day after day, nothing but outrageous ill-luck or ill-health can withstand your demands.

It is also salutary on occasion to rehearse one's deathbed even if it involves a sense of morose despair.

From time to time there are chinks in our consciousness which allow us the most fugitive glimpse of the reality of death but these little apertures close almost at once. My personal hope is that before the candle of life gutters out I will be able to say, "Yes, I have in some measure achieved what I have asked of life." In the case of a writer this almost always applies to his fervent hope that he has written something which will live long after he is dead. The uniqueness of the human being, and the aura of what, in the shorthand of transmission, I call the sanctity of that uniqueness, is something that, aware or unaware, continues to occupy his full attention. More of this anon.

This is the basic philosophy that works for me: it derives from the incident of an old fisherman calling my attention to the unique pattern on the back of each mackerel of the thousands which filled the bottom of his currach. Again, each writer has his own unique vision which works for him and possibly for no one else. It's a Chinese boxes kind of situation, uniqueness trying to record uniqueness in unique artistic form. And if this weren't complicated enough, he is motivated by one, two or three of the great hungers within him – the hunger of the spirit, the hunger of the mind and the hunger of the body.

All this sounds abstract and remote and appears to have little to do with the sustained but invigorating drudgery of the act of writing. To make the brew smack more of sorcery or witchcraft let me append a quotation from WB Yeats at his most mysterious. The reader turned writer may find it valuable in its holistic sense, that its impact in the sense of completeness is more important than the sum of its parts. This is the way if affects me – in its entirety:

> *A feeling for the form of life, for the graciousness of life, for the dignity of life, for all that cannot be written in codes has always been greatest among the gifts of literature to mankind. Indeed, the muses being women, all literature is but their love-cries to the manhood of the world. It is now one, now another, that cries, but the words are the same; love of my heart what matter to me that you have been quarrelsome in your cups and have slain many and have given your love here and there. It was because of the whiteness of your flesh and the mastery in your hands that I gave you my love, when all life came to me at your coming. And then, in a low voice that none may overhear: 'Alas, I*

> *am greatly afraid that the more they cry out against you, the more I love you'.*"

The quotation possibly has a tenuous application, and one tinged with special pleading. The meaning of the first sentence is transparently clear and true. After that – what have we? A hymn in praise of life or one in praise of literature? The piece as a whole does have a decided impact and I often find myself repeating it when I am alone. What it leaves me with is the task of descending from the empyrean and explaining the relevance of all this abstract evidence. I must also demonstrate its truth in the case of a writer expressing himself in the prosaic context of a small country town on the west coast of Europe. There he must forsake the caviar of fine fare and sit down at a scrubbed deal-table to a plain meal of bacon and cabbage.

What do I mean when I say bacon and cabbage? One may take this plebeian fare literally if one wishes, but what I mean is that I would note the ordinary rough and tumble of life, the unadorned comings and goings of my neighbours, no matter how unprepossessing they may appear at first sight, and examine them carefully to see if they have relevance – this in the context of the long-range aims of the reader who aims to be a writer.

I backtrack a little to remark that I reckon no exercise more futile than to offer the reader a list of what he should read when starting out on the adventure of a lamplit imaginative existence. I can only offer evidence based on my own experience. A book by a priest called Sertilange I also found of immense value in this regard.

I read omnivorously and with a sense of shifting omnipresence : *The Humours of Shanawalla* by Patrick Archer of Fingal was a prize bestowed on me for fluency in Irish at a local feis in 1915 or so. The book impressed me deeply – I was six or seven at the time. Then came *Irish Penny Readings* which my brother won in a similar competition in a slightly older bracket. Then, unexpectedly, came *Fabiola – the Church of the Catacombs* to be followed by an avalanche of Sexton Blakes, Buffalo Bills and Our Boys. These in turn were supplanted by a river of good literature when Dan Flavin, my decent neighbour, opened his famous bookshop. When we bought a new hardback at full price, he covered it carefully and told us that if we returned it in immaculate condition we could exchange it for another brand new book on payment of six pence.

The gates of imaginative glory then swung apart for me and I ran up the avenue. Ambrose Bierce, Jack London, Zane Grey, RM Ballantyne, Carleton, GKC, AE, Patrick Magill, Marcus Aurelius, Omar Khayyam, Rudyard Kipling, my neighbour Maurice Walsh of course, and a wraith-like writer who drifts in and out of my consciousness, named Marmaduke Pickthall. I also ploughed through the serried ranks of the Everyman Series published by Dent: later I imaginatively produced in the theatre of my mind, the O'Casey and Synge plays from a reading of the published texts. James Stephens's *Crock of Gold* appealed to me then just as strongly as it does today.

We young readers in our small town were not without knowledge and appreciation of the French and Russian masters especially those who were masters of the short story: Turgenev, Chekhov, Leskov, de Maupassant and, nearer home, George Moore, Corkery, O'Connor, and Ó Faoláin, this last trio my literary forefathers.

Again I return to mention Dan Flavin, the bookseller. His brother Mick, the MP for North Kerry, was a turbulent figure in the British House of Commons. He had once flung the almost sacred mace to the floor of Parliament and was then frog-marched kicking from that most august of assemblies, the while he continued to protest loudly against the wrongs of Old Ireland.

Dan was set in milder, but nevertheless in an equally revolutionary, mould – through the medium of literature. He upset all my preconceived notions of what constituted literature when he handed me one of the very earliest editions of Joyce's *Ulysses* ordered straight from Sylvia Beach's bookshop in Paris; this he did with the comment "To think that that masterpiece came out from behind the gasometer in Ringsend!"

To me at first sight it looked like a fat swatch of newsprint cut into squares holed and corded at one corner – reading for hanging up in an outhouse of a rural privy. "Guard it carefully," he said, "and return it safely. Above all, don't let your mother see it." I was about thirteen or fourteen at the time. That greatly neglected poet, Tom MacGreevy from nearby Tarbert, confidante of Joyce and later executor of his will, later fleshed out for us the physical presence of Joyce in Paris.

At this time I had been flirting with a system of memory training called Pelmanism. A friend of mine who was taking a course by post passed on the text books to me.

To my surprise and joy I found that Pelmanism had equipped me to make sense of Joyce's "Stream of Consciousness."

Somewhat the same system of mnemonics is practised by race commentators on TV and radio to this day, causing us viewers/listeners to marvel at their astonishing feats of recall.

The whole reminds one of the part: the part of the whole. Puns are of use because the intrinsic linkage of the parts can be important. Outlandish, or even barefaced rhymes, can be called on to assist. The more bizarre the connection between the units of memory the better! Much later, I pushed this to the extremity of the harmonisation of opposites or the congruence of disparates, an adventure that dominates my writing to this day. There are also binary systems and lateral thinking to be considered but with these I have only a nodding acquaintance.

So in my teenage years, working from almost basic principles, I made my own sense of *Ulysses*. In the opening lines I came up against a stumbling block in the phrase "The agenbite of inwit". This flummoxed me. Much later I inverted "outwit" to form "inwit" and for "agenbite" I read "bite again". This shed light on my textual difficulties. Molly Bloom's soliloquy tested my youthful powers of understanding to the full. But I survived, and in the act of survival, I matured and at times tended to become elated at my prowess. With a single remark, a rather top official secondary school inspector (an ex-British officer – no?) put a temporary stop to my gallop. His "Rs" were "Ws". On his asking me what book I had "wead", – I launched into a damburst of description of *Ulysses* or some similar text. Raising his hand he bade me halt. "I'm afwaid my deah boy you're vewy werbose" was the phrase that flattened me. The boy next to me, a huge country lad, had previously begged me for God's sake to give him the name of a book he was supposed to have read. When questioned, he answered, *Mabel and the Magic Teapot.* Whereupon the departmental inspector remarked, "I'm afwaid, my deah boy, that is not vewy elevated literature."

As I grew older I spread my literary wings. I subscribed to literary magazines in the US – the book sections of the *New York Times* and *The Herald Tribune* were especially welcome as was the famous magazine *Poetry of Chicago* then edited by Harriet Monroe. Libraries I subscribed to were Switzers (belated thanks to Pan Collins), and the RDS. The RDS especially were most understanding: the librarian of that day once supplied me with a box containing the whole series of Chekhov's stories. I spent a full winter analysing and devouring these. I still recall stories like *The Chemist's Wife* and *Gooseberries* as models of the craft. All the while I kept reminding myself that if books like *Spoon River Anthology* and *Winesburg Ohio* (books downgraded now but exalted then) could emerge from small American communities there was a glimmer of hope for me – that is if I served my apprenticeship and learned my trade. Books about small town life or deriving therefrom are still valid literary currency. Maurice Walsh was generous, "If I can do it from Ballydonoghue," he said, "surely you can do it from Listowel."

Here and now I place my cards on the table. With everyone urging me to be a good loyal European, I cannot feel in my blood and bones that I am really one. I do try hard – but here I dare mention, possibly in absolute idiocy, that if the whitewashed slogans on our vacant walls read "Jacques Delors" or alternatively in tar "To Hell with Jacques Delors", I would feel more at home with my latter-day identity. The trouble with me is that I see the EU being promoted in terms of trade which up to now has resulted in Alps of butter and landlocked fields of wine. But strange to say, I experience a strong feeling of identity with Europe (and most truly with Ireland North) through literature, when it emanates from the smaller nodules of living, as it does in stories such as "Pig Earth" from the Pyrenees. This seam of broad identity has been worked by my own town through events such as Writers' Week, and even through the medium of our now quaint railway, The Lartigue. So I have a ready answer for critics who accuse me of tunnel vision.

I looked about me and down at the ground at my feet – one does not search for diamonds with a telescope and as the Irish expression has it, I put "listening ears on myself" to isolate the precious core of what moved people. Men and women were on all sides about me, some of them lonely, unloved and unappreciated perhaps, others brave in heroic deeds of battling adversity, others again aspiring, defeated or successful, ambitious, sullen, rancorous, sublimated, treacherous and loyal by turns, devoted, ennobled, enslaved or, as the old quotation has it, "living lives of quiet desperation". One man said, "It takes all kinds to make a world", and in reply his cranky neighbour shouted meaningfully "And they're all there too!"

All were human; each was unique. How to convey to others these moments, or flickers, of uniqueness, these epiphanies of the passing day, tinctured by the virtues and vices this transference connotes. Much later I fell back on what Ó Faoláin crystallised, which for years I had been trying to put into words. What he said goes something like this:

"A writer goes around the world whoring after strange gods: he then returns to his own place, observes something simple that moves him profoundly; this he sets down on paper accurately, sensitively and with balance. There and then he has literature."

This was the passion that drove me – and drives me to this day. It's truly addictive and to this day gives me "a high". The body may be growing slow but the mind is as highly active as ever.

To this end and aim I pledged myself. To accepting the narrow horizon of home as a boundary to my work area. Later I would move outwards. I can't say whether or not I contemplated my image in a mirror. It was a long-term goal from which I would not be deflected. Win, lose or draw, I decided that at least one small town schoolteacher would bloody-well have a go.

Today my tenuous hope is this, (it is not easy to extinguish the schoolmaster in me) that in a proximate or faraway future some young man or woman with talent and tenacity of dedication to match will echo these lines and say, "I too will have a go!"

"Why are you always talking to yourself?" was the question pelted at a man who was often seen addressing an unseen audience.

The man replied as follows: "I like talking to an intelligent man: I like listening to an intelligent man, and above all, I like talking to a man who won't remove gossip and cause me mischief among the neighbours." Sssh! One or other of my five sons is listening outside the door of my writing room. The creak of a loose board underfoot has alerted me. "When he comes down 'twill take him a half hour to get plugged in again" whispers a young voice. "I'm in the decompression chamber", I'll say by way of explanation. When I'm dead and gone one of them will say with a smile, "He was up there year after year, his voice rising and falling in altering cadences." Like what the rabbit trapper said about old George Fitzmaurice: "Marching up and down the field, manufacturing his old dramas."

CHAPTER SEVEN

From my infancy I have had an over-heated imagination – one that does not need alcohol or black coffee to provide it with a creative stimulus – (I reserve the right to utilise one or other of these fillips when I get really old). I still react, as strongly today as in the long ago, to the great adventure presented by the wider world beyond the boundaries of my town. I'm still rummaging among my childhood memories to ascertain the forces and sources that shaped me.

As clearly as I recall yesterday, I remember the first time I saw the sea: that mysterious and restless expanse of fluid, its colour suggesting that it was a reservoir of green ink that swelled and receded in time with an unseen rhythm. And all this marvel set against the backdrop of the brown and umber cliff sides of Ballybunion! "Thalassa!" I would have cried aloud, had I known the word, as I gazed on the sea for the first time, a treat promised to me for a long time by my mother. I continued to look in awe, my hand tightening on that of my mother who asked, "Well? What do you think of it?" Then, possibly for the first time, I recall being caught for a word to describe my astonishment at having the promise of a lifetime of wonder spread before me.

Later still I realised the truth of an old man's statement: "You can look at a field for five minutes only without getting bored, but you can look at the sea or a fire forever. Both have movement. And movement fascinates."

I had travelled to the sea with my parents on the Lartigue Railway, our unique and beloved monorail designed on the system of panniers slung across the back of a beast of burden. For me the three quarter-hour journey was a journey through fairyland. As a rule, my father pointed out the historical landmarks: my mother the botanical locations, but these lines of demarcation were often crossed. The trouble was that with our kind of transport one could *not* view both sides of the track at the same time as each carriage faced outwardly without giving viewing choice to both north and south. Somewhat like the seating at a bullfight in Spain, you took your pick at the station. On a sunny day you sought the shady side. Under an overcast sky, the chances were you took one side on the way out and the other on the way home. By the time you got back to base, your conspectus on North Kerry was tolerably complete.

At last, perfect load balance achieved, a hoarse engine whistle and we were off.

We were seated on the north-facing side. My father pointed out Teampaillín Bán, the Famine Graveyard, where among a host of famine dead lies buried one Paddy the Gaisc, a famous horseman who once rode his horse around the fearsome isthmus over the Nine Daughters' Hole in the cliffs in Ballybunion. Next came the roadway leading to Coolard where one of my parents sang for me a verse of "The Maid of Sweet Coolard"; I was also told of the great dancing tradition in the area, and, with some sense of national disdain, Kitchener was mentioned as he was born some distance further to the north. At Lisselton, the half-way house, the Gaelic poets, who had a minor school of poetry there, were recalled – I learned that my maternal great-grandfather came from Glouria – just south of the hill – and that my paternal great-grandfather came from the north-west of the hill; also mentioned was the sorrowful fate of a group of people lost a century before in the Cave of Guhard. At this point someone in the carriage mentioned that the lament played by the piper over those who were asphyxiated was "Caoineadh na mBan san Ár". The word ár, meaning slaughter, prompted a dissertation on Cnoc an Óir, the name of the hill (a misnomer it was feared) for was not Cnoc an Áir, The Hill of Slaughter, mentioned in the poetry of the Fenian cycle at the dawn-time of the world? Why, their cooking pits were still there. And a daughter of the King of Greece had been in their company.

Next place pointed out to me was a townland under the shadow of Knockanore where once lived a brave blacksmith called Nolan who, when condemned to death for firing at a landlord, almost escaped the gallows by concealing a steel collar under his cravat. The Gabha Beag is still recalled on winter nights by the old storytellers like myself.

On the run-up to the little incline of the railroad leading to Ballybunion, some rascals down from the side of the hill had soaped the top rail of the track so that the spinning wheels of the locomotive of the Lartigue failed to gain purchase and the passengers had had to dismount. Jackie Reidy, the engine driver, later suspended a biscuit tin of sand directly above the track and attached it to the locomotive so that, by tugging a wire and releasing sand on the slippery rail, he negated the attempt to halt the train. And so on into Ballybunion where I got a dissertation on the O'Bannions or O'Bunyans, constables of the Fitzmaurices of Lixnaw and Kerry, who once held the castle, its landmark shaft still looming as a ruin on the green above the Shannon estuary. Before I was born, "Carty the Piper" (he lived in three centuries, he was born in 1799 and died early in the 1900's,) played during the summer season on the Castle Green. I heard that Carty's pipes had been buried with him, later to be dug up by drunken musicians and smuggled off to Australia. That was my very first lesson on local history and myth.

I gave my parents little peace until I looked down into the forbidding cavern called The Nine Daughters' Hole where a chieftain had drowned his nine beautiful daughters because they accepted advances from a Dane. An alternative version of the legend has it that the maidens were hand-linked in file to allow the eldest to draw water from a secret well; when the leader stumbled, all nine in turn fell down and were drowned. And there surrounding the abhorred hole was the narrow isthmus round which Paddy the Gaisc rode his mare.

The Grand Cave was visited by brass bands on the occasion of an ebb tide and a thunderous concert took place in its recesses.

Out there on the rim of the horizon beyond the low cliffs of Clare, an old woman once saw a South American town reflected in the sky with women spreading clothes on a line in a narrow alleyway. Another version had it that the vision was of Cill Staheen – a mirage which occurred from generation to generation and, it is alleged, is still seen from the Kerry and Clare coasts.

The homeward journey on our quaint railroad signified a further object lesson; this time we were seated on the south-facing side of the nicely balanced train. (The engine driver once stopped the train to search for my little red hat which had blown off on the outward journey. He recovered it too! To the absolute outrage of an English lady passenger.)

"Down there at Ballybunion Strand near the Cashen, where the netmen catch all the salmon, was fought the last great faction fight of Kerry between the Cooleens and the Mulvihills (otherwise Lawlors). We were Black Mulvihills – don't ever forget that," I was told by my father. By this time he had taught me the basis of Irish – beginning with coloured cards. *Tá an doras donn; tá an spéir gorm.* He was an ardent Parnellite and had attended that leader's famous meeting in Listowel. Not a drinking man, he was given to declaiming Parnell's speech which began, "If I were dead and gone tomorrow . . . " He had another recitation which ended "a traveller from New Zealand shall take his stand upon a broken arch of London Bridge to sketch the ruins of St. Paul's." His party song was "The Flower of Finea" – this I suspect was because the heroine of the ballad was called Eileen MacMahon.

My mother spoke of bog cotton called ceannavawn – she had her pupils in Clounmacon school gather it and use it to stuff cushions. Michael Ryan, Michael Walsh and Paddy Boyle were the officials who saw us all to our seats and directed the passengers to alight at the stops or at the single station on the railroad – Michael Walsh's brother Maurice was later to win international fame as the author of *The Quiet Man.*

I possessed a head stuffed with myth, legend, superstition, ballad and folktale – basic attributes for any scribbler. In passing, I object to the pejorative connotation attached to the word "myth"; the much abused phrase "sacred cows" which shallow undergraduate minds are never done deriding, must surely have had a core of salutary truth to earn such an appellation. Once upon a time there must have been a cow which saved the lives of a tribe and was thereafter revered as sacred – this reverence was then extended to special cows which bore some affinity to the eponymous (there it goes again) saviour. So a myth always has a core of important truth and as such should be respected. To dismiss it as a complete fiction is a profound mistake.

Where now? I then had a stretch of imaginative territory which I later extended and which I still hold: it runs from Kenmare (that stone circle!) all around the south-western coast with several incursions deep into the mainland: the signature tune to my journeying is Tomás Rua's "Amhrán na Leabhar" a song which has as its subject the Gaelic poet lamenting his parcel of precious books fallen into the ocean in the area around Valentia Island. My recitative backdrop is the incomparable "Lament for Art O'Leary" *(Lá dá bhfaca thú ag ceann tí an Aonaigh)*, its piercing poignancy still obtains even in an English translation. There too, in its wake room, is a Dingle man's hacked-off head hidden under a woman's smock, the head deathly cold against the skin of a woman's belly. The head was that of a man called Manning; the woman was an O'Sullivan and it concerns the most fearful Mass ever said in Western Ireland – "The Mass of the Head," a tale which pulsed in my head and demanded to be retold so that a new age Ireland would grope towards a dim understanding of the bugle call recurrent in Irish blood. *The French Cradle* is the name I have given to its fictional retelling.

Later when I crossed the Shannon estuary at its mouth, I found Clare of the Music thronged with wonders – most of them marked with the imagination and thus food calculated to nourish a writer's soul. The murdered Colleen Bawn was buried on the river's edge, there was a makeshift cabin on Loop Head in which Mass was said on the strand in penal days. And of necessity, since it must have some such, the sex stimulant of my journey is *The Midnight Court*, with women much like the daughters of Bernarda Alba crying out their man-hunger by a lakeside in Clare. As for the secret place in North Clare called Corcomroe, all I can say is that for me it is haunted: I have spent days on this "fertile rock" of the Burren: fully enchanted as was WB Yeats before me, for it was in this monastery ruin he sited his famous play *The Dreaming of the Bones.*

Dear Lord, if on occasion I champion the cause of native legend and at times grow acerbic at the mention of our former lords and masters who stunted our growth as a nation, I must not allow myself to float off on a torrent of invective. Yet I demand to be understood as something more than a *laudator temporis acti* – a praiser of time gone, and I must also be allowed pause to cast a single spit on the critic who called me to task for failing to appreciate the "philantrophic aspects of colonialism."

A learned fellow townsman of mine, Alfred O'Rahilly, reacted strongly on reading that a union branch had passed a motion of welcome for a new type of mechanical development designed to throw many workers on the scrap heap of employment. "It's like the corporation of Chicago," he commented, "congratulating the gangsters for giving work to the undertakers." There I go again, castigating the Ireland of now for its borrowed attitude to life and its aloof patronage of the small, almost undetectable values, that make life precious. As I see it, and possibly my viewpoint comes from being cross-eyed with the past, all the qualities one needs nowadays to reach the summit of popular adulation are as follows: a boundless presumption, a broad smattering of knowledge, a veneration for the foreign mass media and a false laugh. In the Ireland of my boyhood the most devastating comment on a poseur was, "Himself and his false laugh." It was a cultured and scholarly American who said of the Irish people: "They are going to a place from which we are returning."

So there I was, God love me, stuffed to my inmost gut with stories of graveyards under the sea and a priest wearing longjohns jumping a chasm or, as a revenant, entering a church during Mass and throwing his threadbare cloak across a sunbeam, then mounting the altar steps to concelebrate with the pastor. Tales too of a magic trout leaping out of a blessed well, of Horatio Kitchener flogging hens with a horse whip, of old hairy half-mad fellahs possessing the charm for shifting rats into what they saw as a hostile house, of scribes transferring their allegiance from secret shorthand Gaelic to cursive English, of ghostly tunes plucked from sea mist, of the body of a dowager crudely disinterred from her tomb and her skinny fingers hacked off so to release her gold rings. All this and stories of murderers, well-known and even secretly pointed out, but in legend and unconvicted. And so forth and so on.

I certainly had a full imaginative dimension to my young mind. And if this weren't all, at the local seminary with its classical orientation, my head was stuffed still more assiduously with Latin and Greek. There I pranced and danced with mythical Mediterranean buckos and dames, the likes of Cassandra and Ulysses and Andromeda, Caligula with his horse, androgynous pixies, and gods spurting their sperm on the foam of the sea where it would fertilise in the wombs of nymphs. All this together with centaurs and Amazons, and including the brave or stupid Spartan lad with a fox eating out his bowels under the cover of his cloak. I also walked imaginatively in parasangs and not in furlongs.

The prosaic observer might well ask, "Did this demented mass of (mis)information drive you off your head? Are you warped and diminished as a consequence of this almost incredible preparation for life? Do you recall that it even culminated in your incarceration in an examination hall on a broiling summer's day composing poetry in ancient Greek?" If so questioned, I have to answer: it was truly great. As a consequence, I possess a brain that resembles a bullbitch watchdog which puts that intruder, loneliness to flight. Loneliness . . . the supreme enemy of the individual especially when one is old as I now am old. In the light of all this who then dares call me a provincial?

Consider for a moment the geometrical allotments of the Mid-West of the United States with farmsteads set a kilometre apart. Social contact is negligible and the highest point of boyhood is fishing in a creek or swinging from a tyre hanging from a branch of a tree with a neighbouring child pushing the swing if indeed such a child is available. Consider the serried army of characters and hilarious incidents my imagination can call upon in case of emergency and especially upon the onset of depression. Even in the downgraded light of a social asset, I reckon all this knowledge is important.

But, but, but. Is that all? What does one do with all these sensations? Furthermore, with a host of other sensations gathered over a lifetime in wider Ireland moving mainly up and down its west coast and on the islands between one and the setting sun. Are they to pass through my mind like midges or coloured moths? How can I employ this beautiful mating of the native and the classical and make (poein to make) something that will endure?

Mating, harmonising, reconciliating – these words became of puzzling importance to me. Could Cleopatra in her boat of beaten gold, or Leda of the swan-mating, possibly be blood sisters to Deirdre of the Sorrows or beautiful Eimear or Niamh of our own legends? There was Leonidas before the battle of Thermopylae telling his brave Spartans "Dine heartily, for tonight you will dine with Pluto." Could he be sibling to one or other of the Sons of Usna playing chess until the moment of death? The *seanchas* and lore of the Smith's Kitchen – how was I to fit it into the mind of all my days?

I look over my shoulder and view myself at that distant hour, say at twenty-one years of age or twenty-two. After a period teaching in Dublin I was appointed to my home school. I wore plus-fours, the bank clerk's affectation of superiority, but I hasten to place on record that this type of dress was immune to the picking up of muck on the inside fold of the trousers ends – as is the case with those hideous Oxford bags worn at that time.

Everywhere I went I was accompanied by a German Shepherd dog, erroneously called an Alsatian. "Billy of Johnstown" was his pedigree name. If I stretched out my right arm fully to one side and shouted "Jump!" the dog would leap high over it: if I extended my left arm in similar manner he'd leap over the arm from the back to the front in fluent style. He guarded my clothes while I was swimming at the seaside. If I spoke to him, warning him not to stir, and left him in a car while I went to a dance he'd generally obey: woe betide anyone who tried to open the unlocked door. A courting couple unwittingly released him one summer evening and Billy roamed the town and finally nosed me out among a thousand dancers in Ballybunion's Pavilion. Those summers of 1933, 1934, or 1935 I danced each night for months on end until the muscles of the calves of my legs grew quite hard: when I wasn't dancing I was hurling on the beach or playing fifteen games of handball in the daytime.

I grew addicted to trout fishing and later to beagling on the foothills of the Stack's Mountain with a crowd of local lads. We had a twenty-couple pack of beagles trencher-fed – that is individually owned and fed. For a time trout fishing, hurling, handball and beagling so captured my imagination that I thought the hours spent in bed at night a sheer waste of good time.

My brother, Jack, was then researching the Gaelic manuscripts of our area in the Royal Irish Academy in Dublin; I complemented his studies by field work, which entailed seeking out the last remnants of the dialect of Irish spoken in North Kerry in the early 1930s. I found about one hundred and twenty old men and women with a fair knowledge of the language.

During these summers, after a satiety of fun in Ballybunion, I always spent six weeks in the Dingle Gaeltacht – possibly the happiest period of my life. There I was sun-drunk, sea-drunk, song-drunk and set-dance-drunk – this last at American wakes or what are still called "ball-nights" in Corca Dhuibhne. My mother suffering a stroke put paid to my jollification: my father was fully an invalid. My sister was a loyal nurse to both.

I began to take life seriously. Subsequently seriously meant "settling down", the phrase used for getting married: it always reminds me of a dog circling in long grass before it lies curled on the ground. Poorly paid as a school teacher I had the usual struggles in the early years of my marriage to Kitty Ryan of Cashel, a member of a long-tailed Tipperary family (a candidate needed to have some connection with a family like this with roots going in all directions before standing for public election.) So, through her one hundred and twenty first cousins alone, I found myself connected with the whole south riding of County Tipperary. I ran a bookshop in Kitty's name so as to make some additional money with which to educate our increasing family of sons. All this while in spite of my several roles – teacher, bookseller and wartime local defence soldier of sorts. I was scribbling away for myself and reading assiduously. My younger brother, Patrick, whose nickname was Bubs, short for Bubbles, since we found him blowing bubbles under the famous advertising picture used by Pears Soap, was by this time a doctor in the National Army. He is still recalled as a personality.

I have often compared Kitty at this time to a person holding down a large balloon by gripping a stout rope leading up into the sky. I was the dirigible far above, straining for the freedom of the fictional skies. Intuitively aware of my addled head, my trying to do forty things at the one time, she never intruded on my writing self – just provided a safe anchorage of understanding. She was fact; I was fiction. Her home, her children and her kinfolk – these were her world.

She was at her very best on Christmas Eve, the house decorated and shining, the Christmas tree blinking off and on, the delph gleaming – she thought holly without berries was lovely too – the turkey trussed (a beautiful bird!), the parlour fire set, the smell of sherry trifle and spices in the air, our five sons in bed and agog for the arrival of Santa Claus. She then dressed herself in her best Christmas attire prior to attending Midnight Mass, and later walked about the house with such an air of utter domestic satisfaction that even her remote-minded husband was conscious of it. We were together for a long time – over half a century. But then nothing lasts forever in this life.

At this time, fully recovered from the critical literary condemnation of my blacksmith friend, I was writing bits and pieces of articles here and there. I then started writing poetry: I had been subscribing to magazines of poetry wherever in the world I could find them. I wrote a letter to Harriet Monroe who edited *Poetry* in Chicago: she published a snatch of it. I liked to keep abreast in literary conversation with other aspirants – I could expatiate at length on the Cantos of Pound: Canto was a word that intimidated its hearers.

I noticed an odd characteristic about myself at this time: it marks me until the present day. I was taking in the details of many of the minor incidents of the passing hour and almost aloud putting them into words. Take and put! I then began describing such incidents to others – again I found myself talking to myself and laughing at my descriptive prowess, for which I earned some quizzical looks from my neighbours. I soon found that I was living in a story-telling community. Where some societies were verbally passive, to my delight I found that mine was verbally active. Thus I was always conscious of an audience waiting to be entertained. Waiting also to hear of any occurrence that was significant: whether it was hilarious or depressing, tragic or comedic, it was acceptable if it threw light on the human condition. Today I realise that I was then training myself as a communicator, and hopefully as an entertainer of some sort, whom people would begin to smile at if they saw approaching. I also began to note the technique of local narrators who were "dingers to tell a story" and some of these were brilliant. By word, grimace and gesture, they were able to hypnotise an audience. Some of them would begin a story at a point that seemed to have no relevance at all to the core of the tale, and then suddenly would come a splice to the main subject, the process done so adroitly as almost to escape detection. I began to emulate these masters of the craft and later to pit myself against them when we had a little audience of sorts. I learned to sift the material – seeking to isolate the seed of the literary story from the yarn, generally ribald, which died in value after it was told.

Roughly about this period World War II had broken out. Its most important by-product for me was that men of international literary importance were now back in Ireland. Then, for me, something quite momentous happened.

Seán Ó Faoláin, Frank O'Connor, Maurice Walsh and others began to publish a literary magazine called *The Bell* with its terse but meaningful slogan of "Let Irish Life Speak for Itself". This seemed to be exactly what I was waiting for: men of international fame willing to weigh up what one's attitude to Irish life was, and this even in the context of a small community like mine, which I had been floundering to penetrate, understand and perhaps describe. I now had a clearer definition of my goal. It didn't seem to matter that the cabins of the Gleann were of beaten clay or that the standard of living was meagre indeed – a labouring man was rich if he got a steady £1 per week, a tradesman equally so with £2.10s. per week as also was a teacher with £11 per month. But what matter, all the while human nature was at play and in interplay. And I was taking notes. But would I print 'em?

The Bell, its very name was a tocsin, a carillon of chimes, a siren tinkle, a call to arms. For me, its mention conjured up the tactile impression of the strong fibre rope going right up into the louvred loft of the steeple where there were nests of rooks and swallows and from whence at night an owl emerged to wing-rustle across the square. Up there too hung the green brown parish bell, the rope of which I, as an acolyte, had so often pulled on occasions of intense joy or piercing sadness. Begolly, says I to myself, I'll give this new Dublin bell rope a literary tug or two to see what happens and then maybe a poem or story of mine might appear in print.

Did I say story? Of course I did. It's the recalled feeling of the rope between my locked fists that's at fault – this from my days as an altar-boy. Let me be infuriating but pardonable if I pause to tell the story of the two pious old ladies, one four-and-a-half feet high, the other six feet one inch, who faithfully attended Mass each morning in our parish church. The smaller of the pair, a lovely little waddler, invariably eyed acolyte-me closely – I was standing in the porch waiting to ring the "ten-to" bell. Her lower lip dropped in speculative wonder as her eyes travelled up the rope to the hole in the loft far above us. I often clipped a minute or two off the bell time by prematurely dragging on the rope and allowing the little butter-ball of a woman to experience the deep sound and the shuddering quivering trembling, so it seemed, of the whole porch. As I did so, I was conscious of the taller of the two standing inside the church and still holding the door open for her small companion: losing patience she clucked an order to her friend not to dawdle.

One morning when neither the parish clerk nor myself was around, the little lady lagged behind her tall friend and, grasping the bell rope as high as she could manage, pulled on it with all her might. The bell growled. Down came the rope: the woman gripped it and pulled on it with all her power – this time the bell boomed in the base of the high steeple.

As the rope comes down, the little bellringer grasps it as high as she can and this time she is lifted far above the floor. Her feet barely touching the tiles again she is again borne higher than she had anticipated. Having achieved her ambition, she finds she cannot descend as her feet are now six or seven feet above the floor but she clings on to the rope with fingers made, seemingly, of steel. Her comrade, having turned back to see what can be delaying her friend, is struck speechless at the sight. "Help! Help!" the ringer yells. Fortunately at this moment the parish clerk was on the scene to rescue and scold this unusual carilloneur.

The little lady had rung her bell: it was time for me to ring mine.

I sent off to *The Bell* what I thought was the pick of the few poems I had written: one called *House Sinister.* I addressed it to *The Belfry* which was at that time edited by Frank O'Connor. The month following

I found myself in print and being welcomed as a poet of merit: Frank printed the poem in full and in his commentary on it quoted a couple of lines from my poem which he said had been in his head for days. He also rebuked me for dropping the definite article "the" and mentioned that he was thinking of establishing a society to defend it. Fair comment. Later I published another poem or two in *The Bell*. Did this make me a poet?

Much later, on a visit to Dublin, I called into the office of *The Bell*. It was situated in an unpretentious room in the top storey of a house on O'Connell Street, more or less across the road from the GPO. It was presided over by a quiet but interesting man called Paddy Farrell.

As I stood there talking to Paddy, the door behind me opened and I heard the clatter of an empty paint tin being thrown down with accompanying pungent advice to an absent Seán Ó Faoláin telling him long distance what he could do with the tin and indeed with Butt Bridge which obviously the speaker had been painting. Without turning I murmured my goodbyes to Paddy Farrell, as I did so the Dublin voice behind me shot, "I know you! You're MacMahon from Kerry." I turned to face Brendan Behan.

After a few polite words I issued my invitation. "You'll have somethin'?" making a gesture of drinking. "Sure," he said. Out on the street I dropped my bombshell. This I did with my tongue in cheek.

"Brendan," I said, "since you've been 'away' (in Borstal!) you have no idea how the ice-cream trade has developed. I'm not a drinking man, so I'd like to host your introduction to one of our finest products." Brendan looked at me in amazement but, seeming to see the humour of my invitation, accompanied me to Caffolas. The pair of us sat down, I handed him the menu and added "I'd suggest Knickerbocker Glory". Brendan's portly body shook with chuckles. I could project him into future company and hear him making a tale out of our meeting. "Le' me tell yeh about MacMahon and his 'Knickerbocker Glory'".

The impressive delicacy arrived in a tall transparent vase; Brendan was taken a little aback at the glory of the concoction: between spoonfuls he roared laughing, a ring of ice-cream round his mouth. "Tell me," he said, as finally he smacked his lips, "What's the difference between the true artist and the phoney artist?" "The true artist," I said, "is mad and has a helluva problem tryin' to appear sane while the phoney artist is sane and has a helluva time pretendin' to be mad." Whenever I met him afterwards he'd shout, "Still pretendin' to be sane."

A lovely sensitive man – when one was alone in his company. For me, his vibrations were such that I felt completely at home with him. But when others joined us, Brendan seemed suddenly to emote and he then became a performer. But all in all, a delightful and admirable person to be with.

(I have a peculiar experience in regard to this incident. At times I seem to think that it was Paddy Kavanagh who was with me in Caffolas. And this trick of the imagination leads me to imagine Paddy looking at the tall glass of Knickerbocker Glory and picture his response. I am quite capable of imagining a third personality behind the ice-cream vase just to savour the incongruity of the occasion.)

Within a short space of time I abandoned poetry. It was so condensed that it seemed to act as a nut swelling in the centre of my brain. I would wake up at night with poetic stanzas resounding in the caverns of my skull much like those in the pseudo cowboy-ese TV ads of nowadays which also tend to reverberate. "White scour in calves is mighty vexatious. But the boys got it beat." This poetry business has to stop, I told myself and then added in self defence, "Poetry is like a fashionable corset, pink, pretty and constricting. I'll have none of it." I cast around for a new medium in which to express myself. "Ah," I said, "the short story could well be to my liking."

But first, I wrote several articles for *The Bell*, some of them under pen-names. (I later solved a problem for a German scholar who had researched all the issues of *The Bell* and was puzzled by certain "authors" he failed to trace.) Ó Faoláin had said, "Let Irish life speak for itself," – didn't he? Here goes with an article on my little business venture: so first I wrote a piece called "I Own a Bookshop" and sent it off. Full of anticipatory joy I awaited a verdict. I got back a verdict straight from the shoulder. "Alas, you have been incontinent. I want length, breadth, height. I want facts not fancies. Can you bear to rewrite?" A kick in the teeth for me. I sulked. "To hell with Ó Faoláin, his bell, his book and candle," I muttered.

After a few days I changed my attitude. "He is at the writing game for a long time," I advised myself, "so he must know more than I do." I swallowed my pride, rewrote the article and received the first of his laconic typed postcards which read *"Bookshop* now fine. Will publish next month," with the written initials SO'F. After that I wrote more factually: I was learning my trade.

But Ó Faoláin wasn't above shattering his apprentice. On another occasion he wrote, "God has given you a voice, not a foghorn." That scalded me, but a prerequisite of the scribbling game is the capacity to absorb critical punishment and come up with a smile. So I began to write on a semi-regular basis for *The Bell.* Stories first – these were now part and parcel of my background and my endeavour.

The first real story I had published in *The Bell* was called *The Breadmaker.* Let me trace the graph of its conception, gestation and parturition. It began with a phrase I overheard about a recently married young woman, "God help her, marryin' in there to 'The Breadmaker'".

In the rural and small-town Ireland of my younger days a housewife often picked great pride out of her ability to bake soda bread. "She has it in her hands," was said of such a woman: it was somewhat like having green fingers. A famous breadmaker would proudly set her round Christ-crossed loaves to cool on an outside windowsill to be admired by the parish. A poor breadmaker was the subject of derision: the unrisen streak, which told its sorry tale at the bottom of the loaf, was referred to as birdlime. And the terminology and variety of home loaves ranged from the yeast bread to griddle, thence to the homeground, thence to the "pake" or yellowmeal bread so named after the ship *The Alpaca* which brought maize to Ireland in Famine days. Home bread, crumbly in texture made with sour cream, sets my mouth juices flowing even to this day.

My dear mother had a test for the lassie to whom her precious son was engaged. When my Tipperary bride-to-be stood for the first time on my parental floor I dreaded the question my mother, a champion of Home Economics, would ask her.

After the formal pleasantries Joanna MacMahon asked, "Can you turn the heel of a stocking?" For my mother this hosiery feat was the pinnacle of housewifery. There was a pause: I eyed the pair of women.

Kitty Ryan said lightly, "I can of course, ma'am," to be countered by, "And how would you go about it, girl?" And off they went into, for me, a labyrinth of purls and cast-offs – a territory which I dimly understood, though in Clounmacon school, seated as an infant amid a potential harem of nubile girls in the Senior Classes, my mother had insisted on my mastering the rudiments of knitting. "A very good girl," was my mother's later comment on her future daughter-in-law who passed the test with distinction.

I decided to write a story on the subject substituting baking as a test instead of knitting.

Noting how expert women were at this basic item of homecraft I then decided that I had to bake a loaf of bread to experience the craft at first hand.

One day when the house was empty I set to work. I got down the losset. (The Irish word "losaid" means a bread-board with outwardly slanting sides.) I had ensured that there was a good coal fire in the Stanley No. 9. I poured out some flour in a heap onto the board, mixed in bread soda, salt and sour milk (new milk allowed to go sour as opposed to buttermilk) and began to mix the ingredients so as to procure dough. The mixture stuck to my fingers and I could not manage it to my satisfaction. After a lot of pummelling, which could scarcely be called kneading, I got the lump into some semblance of loaf shape. I then cut the traditional cross on the pudge and placed it in the oven. I sat down and began to wait patiently.

Now and again I opened the oven door to see how my loaf was baking. Alas, it refused to rise. The family would be home any minute so "Hurry up loaf and bake," I said. No use. It even started to burn. When I opened the oven door a smell of toasted bread assaulted my nostrils. In despair I covered the mess with a towel and gingerly took it out of the oven. What to do with it? I had it! I'd give it to the pig. When it cooled he'd be sure to eat it. Out I went to the pigsty telling the pig to be sure to destroy the evidence by consuming the loaf. (A pig is a very intelligent and useful animal – did anyone ever see a pig on the road being killed by a car? Also, dead man no good, dead pig some good!)

To my horror, a week later my mother retrieved the loaf. (The pig, it was obvious, had refused to eat it.) She came into the kitchen from the yard, her face stamped with misgiving. "Finding good food where it has no right to be is the work of the devil," she said. "Someone wishes us evil." An egg in a hay-wynd, a red herring in the potato drills, a pig's head nailed to a tree, a loaf in a pigsty, in the pishoguey Ireland of then – all were curses directed at our family. An agony of vacillation, and then I confessed. After a dumbfounded moment or two my mother began to laugh. To my chagrin she told the story to her circle of friends.

In this, my first story, I described a young bride in a small farmhouse. She is baking her first loaf under the hawk-eye of her mother-in-law, the barony's finest breadmaker.

The girl kneads the dough on the losset, rolls it, pummels and palms the lump into shape, cuts the cross on it, knife-blades the scraps together and adds them to the whole: she lowers the loaf into the pot-oven on the open hearth, and uses the tongs to pile red coals of fire on the iron lid. Her face flushed, she steps back with a prayer to the god of fire to do the rest of the work.

Her elderly father-in-law seated on the other side of the hearth from his wife, a wry smile on his face, secretly watches the drama. (There's a faint suggestion of a metaphor – that the oven stands for the young woman's womb with the loaf as foetus.) After a protracted period of time, growing more tense by the second, the young woman finally takes the tongs and lifts the cover of the pot-oven. The old couple crane forward. The loaf has brimmed up in brown and white lightsome beauty. The smiling bride tumbles it sidelong on to a tea towel, knuckles it on its back, wraps it in the swaddling cloth of the towel and stands it on a bin beside the dresser. She leaves the kitchen in quiet triumph.

The old man who, up to this, has been wanly on the side of his new daughter-in-law is suddenly taken by old loyalty. Having ensured that the younger woman will not immediately return, he stretches out his walking stick and sends the loaf tumbling to the floor. "Shep", he calls, directing the attention of a sheep dog asleep under the table to the fact that there is food on the floor. The dog noses the tea towel, licks the hot bread, stands back from it to allow it cool and begins tentatively to lick again. As a curtain line I have the old rogue raising his voice to call his daughter-in-law, "Girlie, your fine loaf is after fallin' to the floor."

I confess to having a definite purpose in explaining the details of this, my initial story. My reasons for doing so are threefold: firstly I am making a story about the making of a story, secondly what I tell may be of some encouragement to the young emerging writer (and his name, realised and unrealised, is legion.) Thirdly, it may in some measure explain the writer's approach and thus be of assistance to the earnest and percipient reader. If one with knowledge and experience of stagecraft attends a play, he enjoys doing so not only on the primary level of an average theatregoer, but also from his background and training he may view the play on the layered level of technique. He may more fully appreciate an artistic movement on the part of a character, especially his entrances and exits; he may also find enjoyment and appreciation of the various clap-traps inserted as an integral part of the play and designed to relax the performance by means of laughter, cunningly evoked.

That was my first story. Not perfect. Not bad. I rejoiced at its appearance in *The Bell.* I learned a lot from it. First of all, I realised that there were certain valuable trigger or seminal comments to be met with in everyday life and that I had to be sharp to catch them as they came and went. "As in wild earth a Grecian vase," the poet names these tiny treasures. These phrases or comments were so natural as to appear unremarkable: at that time I concluded that I did not need details – these could be supplied by myself. Also I realised that I could transfer the essentials of the story to fit other more arresting locales or conditions or characters but in doing so I had to condense or prune.

I had to be able to distinguish between the ephemeral and the permanent in subject matter – between the transient soon-to-be-forgotten anecdote and a remark with a hard crystal-like core that could turn out to be a raw diamond fit to be cut, polished, and finally set in its literary frame.

A new world had opened before me. I had said "Open Sesame" and the rock of understanding had opened to reveal a cave of treasures.

I then took stock of my position and began to go over the evolutionary stages of my progress towards being a scribbler – not the best in the land nor indeed the worst – but one filled, not with ambition, but rather with a deeply felt sense of satisfaction of having signed a peace treaty with turbulent and rebellious forces within me. I was offering these hidden upheavals a way out, a lawful way of escape, or, as I put it to myself in terms of the publican, his wooden peg and his barrel of ale, a means of 'venting the cask'. The cask in my metaphor being the mind with its ferment of impressions which I now counted among my blessings.

I possessed a satisfactory knowledge of my town and its hinterland as a simple nodule of humanity. I now had a clear sense of being completely at home with the to-and-fro-ing of the marketplace and the fair. I had a river flowing through my childhood, had experienced the game of life and death being played out at my door with the sheer exhilaration that accompanied it, had attended the informal schoolroom of the smith's kitchen as well as the formal attendance at a classical college. I was fully conscious of the uniqueness of each human being; I had an ear for dialect and dialogue and an oddball acquaintance with secret areas of local existence. I also had a link with the past in the Irish language and another with world literature through books, and definitely including a tenuous contact through Tom MacGreevy and Dan Flavin with Joycean Paris. Ah! There the students hung up their berets and green cloaks on coat hooks and hammered the table with pewter mugs to accentuate a point of debate. I had glimpsed them once in Montmartre and ever after recalled their camaraderie and chatter with a deep sense of envy.

The seminal phrase – that was one discovery I would hug to my bosom. Each phrase opened up the possibility of portraying, even in minor measure, an aspect of the human condition. I was as yet only on the brink of the fullness of awareness. I glimpsed that there was a discipline known to the initiated as technique but perhaps that was a mathematical exercise and it could be mastered.

The intuitive sides of the writer's trade I had yet to explore through "the shorthand of the nerves" – to use a phrase borrowed from Pádraic Fallon. I was resolved to explore this aspect of my craft in quiet reflection. Certain other things I needed to know, to experience at first hand. A few more clues and I would feel moderately equipped for the story trade insofar as one ever feels ready for such an exacting profession.

The voices of Russian masters were ever loud in my ears. "Young man, look out of your window," and, "If you're born with a tarred rope in your hand, pull it."

And then, unforeseen by me, major clues presented themselves in quick succession. They were simple yet complex but they turned my small-town pedagogic existence topsy-turvy. This could turn out to be a landmark event, much like that experienced by me as I embraced the young woman on the stairway at Puck Fair.

This time, I told myself, I wouldn't be remiss in reading the signals of welcome. But then, even as I realised that I was short of a few more details or features of knowledge, it dawned on me that my quest should, and would, be open-ended. I then came intuitively to a second decision, that I would, as the saying goes, "take things as they came." That I was now close to a breakthrough – of this I was tolerably convinced. I looked forward to the future with a mounting sense of eagerness. "One more clue," I told myself, "and a pinch of luck." But where to search, that was the question.

CHAPTER EIGHT

From the known to the unknown – that's a well-known maxim of education. With a reasonable knowledge of my hinterland – street, town and barony in its several layers, para-historical, historical, social, religious and superstitious, its pastimes, dialect, and its patriotism (if it's permissible to use that now despised attribute – this since our small nation-frog insists on blowing itself up to pretend that it is Europa the Bull) – I decided further to explore my native county, and subsequently my country, with the accent firmly on its western coast. What was I looking for? Where would I find the missing piece of the jigsaw I felt I sorely needed? These were questions I asked myself.

To hear Irish spoken widely, naturally and picturesquely in Corca Dhuibhne in the Dingle Peninsula, even to the delightful extent of hearing children quarrelling in angry Gaelic *(Ná bí ar an mbóthar romham, a deirim leat),* was for me both a surprise and a treat. One old fellow – an exception be it admitted – was chasing his grandchildren and threatening them with his blackthorn stick as he urged them to turn from Irish to English ("If you go across the Maam into Dingle, you'll be a right fool if you can't speak English") was his cry. But the arrival of scholars from Britain, Germany and the Scandinavian countries altered that kind of attitude.

Needless to say there were always individuals who clearly understood, despite jibes and jeers, that they were custodians of something of prime national value: these won the day, else the Irish language, nowadays threatened by radio, television and mass media of all kinds, would have long since perished.

There was also an intrinsic advantage in the fact that the Irish language proved to be a means of promoting a rare type of linguistic tourism. The Gaeltacht people were naturally a most welcoming people, this too was a factor in language preservation. The translation of the Blasket Island books into English and other European languages won widespread appreciation: it was a depiction of a rarefied way of life that once existed to a lesser or greater extent throughout Europe. The then powerful influence of the Gaelic League helped enormously. The identification of Pearse of the Rising with the Connemara dialect of Irish was also a component of the Gaeltacht's attitude to itself. That "to itself" was important.

So there we were as young men in the Gaeltacht of sixty-five years or more ago "coorting" girls through the medium. And very shy and reserved those young women were. We were also climbing to Martello Towers, identifying the field which held the mass graves of the Spanish-Italian expeditionary force butchered by Walter Raleigh and company in the 1580s, attending American Wakes, gathering mushrooms and being chased by parish priests for dancing at "ball nights", as they are still called. Attending Dingle races on our side-car was a signal event: when we weren't swimming until our bodies were pickled in brine, we were out all night mackerel fishing or listening to old men at firesides. (*Ciacu a b'fhearr leat scéal fada bog binn nó scéal gairid greannmhar?* – "Which would you prefer, a long gentle sweet story or a short funny one?") For dinner we consumed chicken, salmon and various types of fish straight from the overnight catch of the currachs. Our table fare was laced with jugs of cream, and graced with laughing floury potatoes.

I got the task of soaping the black back of a canoe (otherwise called the naomhóg or currach) before the annual currach races so that the beetle-like vessel would move more fluently through the sea. No radio! No television! An odd gramophone or two but plenty of fiddlers, box players, traditional singers and above all, voluble talkers.

Every simple activity was endowed with ceremony, whether it was the coming of the postman or the attendance at Sunday Mass where once I fell back into the trough of holy water inside the main doorway. The placing of the panniers on the donkey's back before setting out for a load of turf from the hill was a major event.

All our outdoor activities were shot through with the most delectable smells of sea air, (the next landfall was the Americas) and the smell of sea marsh flowers of which pinks are the most memorable. If today I pause on a west coast beach and eye the sky I seem to hear again the elemental pulse-beat of life; if I look down at my bare feet it is as if, by the alchemy of memory, the sand-dust of the roadway has entered through the openings in thin sandals and filmed-over my bare toes and instep. And all the while from just over the sandhills came the never ceasing Sssssh of the sea, mesmeric and evocative.

The recalled murmur is forever counselling me to stop, listen and experience, as if for the first time the faint far grumbling of the mill-wheel of creation and the dripping of water from its blades.

At this time I was contributing a story or an article under my own name, or indeed under a pen-name, almost on a monthly basis to *The Bell*. I seemed always to be looking out for the postman to deliver me the laconic cards signed SOF. I discovered something else about myself – that I liked writing for an individual; I could not bear to have my 'prentice efforts submitted to someone I did not know – or trust. This weakness or strength has remained with me for the rest of my life and stamps me even to this hour.

But now for the major revelation of my passing day. I confess to a twinge of anxiety that my precious secret will be laughed at or ignored or proven to be false or, worst fate of all, deemed of no importance whatsoever. That's a risk that must be taken on many levels of experience. So tell it out I will.

I angled for a chat with Ó Faoláin. Possibly the initiative came from him. At this period of my life I was quite often in Dublin. At last I got the welcome card saying he would be in a teashop in Anne Street – that's somewhere near Nassau Street – on Saturday at eleven o'clock and that he would be glad to see me if I were there. It was an appointment I was eager to keep.

Frank O'Connor was with him: there were others. If I recall the incident clearly, they were indignant about someone of their coterie being refused a visa to visit the United States, so that for a while they paid me scant attention. Finally I was addressed directly. After a few introductory sentences I ventured to put the one question I had come determined to put. Whether it was of Ó Faoláin or O'Connor I asked this question, I am not now sure but the answer was shatteringly effective and changed my outlook to literature and to life. Assuming the post of an ingenuous Kerry boy, and with all the mock meekness I could muster, I asked one of the two men:

"How does one write a short story? Mr Ó Faoláin (O'Connor)"

The man questioned looked penetratingly into my eyes. The look clearly conveyed, "You're not fooling me, cute Kerryman. But I'll answer you just the same." Was the gleam in his eye touched with mockery as he answered? "You get a male idea and a female idea and you couple them. The children are short stories."

I retreated into my shell. I was puzzled. Had I been rebuked or most valuably instructed? What was this? A crazy coition of ideas? A mad match-making of opposites? I was certainly taken aback, but I had asked for it with my forwardness. And yet, and yet, as I continued to mull over this cockeyed theory I stumbled forward towards some measure of understanding, if not, as yet, of comprehension.

I recalled the "yin and yang" of ancient Chinese philosophy. Yin was the passive female principle of the universe, Yang the active male principle. These were believed to be complementary – Yin was negative, dark and feminine; Yang was positive, bright and masculine (Watch your step, I now counsel myself, else the feminists will pour scorn on your now disingenuous head). However, I forestall such an attack and, with special pleading for the purpose of my theory, concede that the roles of male and female together with the given attributes may be reversed without doing violence to my hypothesis.

Yin and Yang, male and female I told myself – the intrinsic complementary aspects of their nature may be paralleled to include phenomena on many levels – many of which were right under my nose without, until then, winning a clear recognition from me. What I was trying to identify, to utilise, in the literary sense, was the reconciliation of disparates, the harmonisation of opposites which, to revert to my prime reference, man and woman can achieve in the ecstasy of coition at its best and thus reach heights of congruence indelible in the mind of each partner, no matter how basely vernacular it may be expressed thereafter.

Examples abound even on the culinary level – pork and apple sauce, sweet and sour preparations of all sorts exist even on the level of cartoonery. Today I ask myself why Miss Piggy of *The Muppet Show* is such an acceptable and indelible character? Because she is the superimposition of the image of a smelly piglet or bonnav on the delectable image of a debutante on the morning of her presentation at court – truly the reconciliation of disparates. On the level of fable? Beauty and The Beast and The Frog Prince are two examples that spring readily to mind. Examples of stories of this genre are legion – is there not a tale in classical lore of a person falling in love with a donkey: there are also centaurs and mermaids aplenty which achieve memorability by suggesting the mating of the human and animal worlds.

How to bring this welter of impressions to clear recognition and, by processing the result in the brain or imagination, to achieve something worthwhile in terms of literature? In other words to achieve indelibility. I began a life-long hunt with this goal in mind. Much time elapsed until, in the writings of George Moore, I came upon a statement: "The woof of life is merely a tangle and our imagination deceives us when we think we perceive any design in it." Was it not the writer's duty flatly to contradict this? I asked myself. And to offer examples in proof of his contradiction.

Many years later when I was explicating my theory to students in the US I asked them to call up the image of a billiards table. Euclidean is the most accurate word I can find to describe a billiards table. Flat in surface, its ends are rounded, its pockets accurate circles or rough cylinders, the balls perfect spheres. To offer an example of my possibly mythical and even bizarre harmony and its consequent indelibility, I place an image of a live lobster on the surface of such a table. The lobster in its whole bodily structure is the complete opposite of the table. And then I ventured to employ a soupçon of voodoo-ism. I would say to the students, "I shall place a spell upon you that henceforward whenever you pass a poolroom you will take three backward steps on the pavement outside and peer in to see if my lobster is crawling across the emerald coloured baize."

Or, taking another example, I would continue: "I want you to imagine an old canon dozing in a confession box. His biretta with its red tassel is somewhere beside him. Overhead hangs a paper Chinese lantern in which a candle is lighting. There is a rustling noise: this is made by a live elver which I have dropped into the lantern. The fry is going around in a circle as if bewildered by its incongruous presence therein. The movement of the elver is causing the rustling sound. This conjoined image has elements of the indelible harmony I am pursuing on a lifelong basis."

From the moment of recognition and illumination, I kept seeing people, events, inanimate objects even, animals, in a novel way. (I hoped the prognosis of my intense thought wouldn't prove barren as are jennet or mule or some such progeny of mismating.) Events, football jerseys, fashion, sentences – the positive and negative of every aspect of the world about me, I now examined in a new light.

Switching on a bedroom light I was conscious of the felicitous result of the fusion of positive and negative forces lighting up the room. I began to chat with a variety of women to determine, even in an attenuated fashion, how their thought patterns differed from mine. The conclusion I came to, and I expressed rather facetiously and in language with a whiff of a schoolroom to its composition, was: "Women don't do the sums like men: they simply cog the answers at the back of the book." As a sop thrown to bristling men students I would then whisper in a mock stage aside: "Sometimes they get hold of the wrong answer book."

Back to the teashop in Anne Street. Belatedly I came to the conclusion that what was said to me on that occasion was the distillation of wisdom. So there and then I resolved and almost declared my resolution aloud: "I shall sally forth and search all Ireland if needs be, to seek seminal phrases. Each idea I shall mate with its opposite, and then hopefully write even one story of literary merit."

Speaking of women, fashion and the colour-wheel of harmony. I once heard a man say "A woman, when she tires of wearing all the colours in the spectrum, returns to the most elegant colour ensemble of all – black and white." These two primary colours I told myself, are the mating of opposites, of day and night, of crows and snow to bind as magpies or to form the more austere and impressive effect of black print on white paper.

There were subtle side issues to be explored to employ the full use of the opposite hues on the colour-wheel. In my harmony there are exclusions to be explained. Male and female in the ecstasy of congress mutually agreeing as it were to suspend almost totally four of the senses, leaving only the sense of touch and thereafter finding harmony in the delirium of tactility. I became so obsessed with my theory and its extensions that I looked for proof in the casual happenings of the humdrum day. I sought it in the pages of books and newspapers, in every aspect of my life as I then lived it, and rejoiced on chancing upon an incident or union that buttressed my obsession. So extreme did my mind fixation become that at times I almost became convinced that, if I could pursue this theory of reconciliation to its inmost atomic unit, I could then solve the central riddle of the universe. And prove George Moore wrong into the bargain!

Lecturing on this theory in the US it was pointed out to me that, despite my attribution of its origin to Ó Faoláin or O'Connor, neither the former in his book *The Short Story* nor the latter in *The Lonely Voice* made the slightest mention of it. Where then had it come from? In heaven's name, I asked myself, was it something like a Pauline revelation or was I the reincarnation of the Dublin mathematician, Hamilton Rowan, scribbling the details of his famous formula on the sidewalk of a bridge?

Undeterred I ploughed ahead. By now I had conceived the formation of a short story as follows: a powerful male idea thrusts forward from a point in the form of an arc of trajectory moving upwards at an angle of 45 degrees. At the highest point of its flight, where the arc loses its momentum and begins to fall, out of space comes a second or female idea which couples/mates with it occasioning what I term an inevitable coruscation; then bound together, the two as a unit fall to the ground together.

As I say, I don't quibble if the first idea as it takes to the air is called the female idea and the second idea which couples and causes the coruscation is called the male idea. In my opinion, this may not matter. Above all I stress that the notion can have a far wider application than that of sex. I may at this point be trying to forestall female indignation as regards priority but that remains my formula for the story.

Let me give a simple example from my own work; one with which very many people in Ireland may be familiar since the story was for many years on the programme of the Intermediate Certificate Examination, a test now superseded by the Junior Certificate, the name by which the test was known in my days in secondary school seventy years ago. The name of my story is *The Windows of Wonder*: as far as memory serves me, it first appeared in the pages of *The Bell*.

I recall the moment of my recognition that I had a little story.

Imaginatively I place myself standing on a hill pass in the Irish west. Below me in the valley, among the black turf banks of an extensive bogland, is a whitewashed school. (White on black; extremities.) To this scene I apply a phrase I have once heard. Speaking of the husband-and-wife teaching team of a school similarly situated, an observer said, "No good! The pair of teachers down there! Never stirred our imaginations. Never told the children a story. Always we were stuffed with facts and more facts."

I pondered this scene and these words for months, possibly years. To me they conveyed the male idea of a story – the valley that had let the imagination die! Then it occurred to me: how about introducing a young woman – a storyteller or storywoman – as substitute teacher for the mistress and let's see what happens. Fine! But there was still something missing. I already had scores of these unfertilised beginnings. I almost despaired of this one.

One day a woman teacher came into our bookshop.

She started to speak of our new inspector. "He's a topper," she said. "Let me tell you why. On his first visit to our shanty of a school he came in, winked at me, and stretched out his two clenched fists to the children saying, *Tabhair tombas cad tá agam im dhá dhorn*. So the children started to guess what he held in his fists. *Mirlíní* . . . marbles, sweets, nuts, they answered in turn. All were incorrect! At last he opened his fists and there clinging to each palm was a highly coloured butterfly. He took each butterfly from its palm with two fingers of the opposite hand and then cast the pair into a dusty shaft of sunlight that slanted across the room. As the butterflies fluttered in and out of the light, the children went mad with excitement."

Hearing this I too got excited. This was exactly what I wanted.

"Thank you!" I told my fellow teacher. "For what?" "For providing a bride for my waiting bridegroom." She looked oddly at me, then left the shop. Good! By this time I realised that I had become a literary matchmaker.

Let me return in imagination to the hill pass where I now place my young imaginative woman teacher standing beside her bicycle. Her substitute teaching term is ended and she looks down for the last time on the school in the valley where she had met with surly opposition to her story teaching methods. She is ending her teaching stint just at the point where she felt she was on the edge of success. Her stories and attitudes had opened "windows of wonder" for the children. Their imagination was fully alive! A new spirit moved in the dark valley. A few more months and she could have succeeded. Now it seems that her work has been in vain. Her eyes smoulder. Did anyone in this valley understand? And then . . .

"It was then that she noticed the old russet-faced man. He was standing inside a rough timber gate. . . his fists were securely clenched. She had her right foot on the pedal and was hopping with her left foot when he addressed her. 'Wait! Wait! I heard the children talkin' about yeh . . . with no one to say goodbye to yeh only me. An' they have me down for bein' half cracked . . . if I was fifty years younger, I'd chance me luck with yeh, my lovely woman . . . because I know your mind the same as I know me own mind . . . A present for yeh an' yeh goin'.

". . . She watched the gnarled fists unlock . . . clinging to the coarse palms were two butterflies . . . carefully, he removed the butterflies from each palm . . . The old man tossed them into the air . . . at last they began to entwine their flights as they climbed higher and higher into the dark heavens.

"The old man turned away . . . the young woman began to pedal down into the town valley."

I have mated many disparates in this story. Dark bogland: white school. Imaginative young teacher: surly principal. Dark eyes: blue eyes. Town: country. Dusty school: coloured butterflies. Gloom: sunshaft. Turf ricks: white shirts. Solid mountains: glittering sea. Old man: young woman.

Bare toes: stout soled boots. Dark sky: coloured butterflies. Clean gulls: livid clouds. There are more.

These disparates were placed there deliberately. Each coupling adding up to the totality of my story called *The Windows of Wonder.*

At this period of my life I began to wander aimlessly here and there in Ireland, chiefly up and down the west coast, sometimes with a travelling companion, sometimes without. I spoke to a variety of people, not with the avowed intention of picking their brains, but rather for the gentle relish of speaking to another human being and with luck, learning what his or her unique vision of life was. There was a part of my brain always on the alert for the seminal phrase – this I readily concede. But I went haphazardly about my task, letting the cards fall where they would. I was also noting the inanimate appointments of locality; personality in literature responds to place, time, fauna and flora and a host of imponderables, many of them so subtle as to escape attention. To some extent I was the inert instrument which certain forces would use as a clean film on which they would cast an image.

I kept seeing myself seated on a rock beside a pool at the foot of a waterfall. The waterfall is caused by a stream (of consciousness?) flowing down from the hills: it passes through defiles, races beside villages and towns, moves under bridges and on to the falls itself; the pool below at which I, the watcher, am seated is at a point where the physical matter, or debris, the stream bears swirls and is subject to examination.

The objects a real stream regurgitates at the pool of observation are many and various. Tin cans, bottles, a branch of fuchsia, a dead fish or a timber box, all these objects may show up under the gaze of the observer as impersonated by the matchstick seated figure. So it is with me. I pause at evening and, seated at the still or quietly swirling pool of the day's events, I file for later reference those diurnal happenings, conversations or comments that go round and round in my brain. I am trying to recycle the flotsam and jetsam of the day and isolate, note and perhaps set aside for use, something of literary value. One clue letter or symbol at the back of my jotter, prefaced with the cipher ST for story or CON or D for dialogue, dialect or conversation, will serve to identify what I wish to recall. The single word or phrase I note resembles a prompter slingwhispering a cue on stage by uttering the key word the actor needs so as to continue.

There are possibly fifty other factors that go into the making of a story and I hesitate to mention even some of them. Angle of narration, light, general mood, temperature, character, smell, pace, balance, rhythm (this last works for me) and variance. Above all the senses must be most subtly appealed to and the story-line seen as unforseeable before reading and inevitable after. The first draft, done hurriedly, must be allowed to cool. Then I proceed to behead it. I do so by asking myself if I can do without the first paragraph, or even reduce it to a single phrase. Perhaps the second paragraph can be similarly treated, or compressed with the first? This in order to reduce exposition which can be dreary. After all this is a *short* story. Again, my opening sentence is of extreme importance. Can I use direct speech? Make a little mystery to arouse the curiosity of the reader?

All this may sound cold-bloodedly mathematical and even devious; to me it is as natural as day and night – if it is incoherent, it's my effort to reduce a mental process to coherency that is at fault. I do not set out to measure and assess every minute of every day but I recognise that an attitude, a word, an odd but memorable item of clothing, a quirk of character, a mannerism I have observed – all are grist to the writer's mill. These are my raw materials; to change the metaphor, they resemble small squares or cubes somewhat like tesserae, which later may form part of the pattern of a story mosaic.

I am glad to have the foregoing off my conscience. I have qualms that sometimes I find myself trying to make a story about making a story and at a further remove I endeavour to add a third dimension to my effort – tell a story about a story about a story. In the mind of a reader it may conjure up a vision of Chinese boxes, one inside the other and result in what as kids we used call "a right ball of wax", somewhat like what an eel makes of the last yard or two of an overnight spilliard – a mess of eel-goo with hooks, worms, fishing line and sinker all balled together in a tangled mess that defies unravelling. (An Icelandic writer has written a memorable short story about a can of worms.)

Behold me then, like the man in the aforementioned phrase, "mounting my horse and riding out in all directions." Perhaps I did not know what I was looking for, but begod, to use an Irish bull, I felt I could recognise it when I found it! And in another corner of my convolute brain, among its X-hundred billion cells, lurked the flimsy notion that a reader might possibly draw double or treble enjoyment from a piece of literature if he understood how it came into being. All this in the context of the vapourings of a small town schoolmaster. Nothing like aiming high even in the pursuit of an elusive goal. For I am never done reconciling the sublime with the ridiculous, the bestial with the human, the material with the ethereal, the physical with the metaphysical, the transient with the permanent. And so on and so forth chiefly in talking, talking, talking. Learning to distinguish between the anecdotal and the potentially valuable. Communicating with the most outwardly unprepossessing people and finding them of great value. Finding the reverse also true.

All this happened to me during the period of what was called The Phoney War. The nations of Europe and, indeed of the world, seemed to be engaged in shadow boxing. But it ended with the carnage of Coventry, Dresden and the atomic bombs falling on Japan.

The War! The old lady grocer a few doors from me kept sending her tea customers to me to learn how many ounces per week out of the tea-chest they were entitled to. But since I had no idea how much they had already taken, and they had no coupons to indicate their entitlement, I either estimated a reasonable weight or sent them off with a mysterious statement that even I myself could not understand. In the Local Defence Force, I was intelligence officer; this involved communicating by signal lamp from the hill above the town with other unit officers on hilltops within a radius of approximately twenty miles. My fellow patrol soldier on duty in the countryside in the early hours kept telling me interminable stories about the hospitality accorded him in various places. All his tales ended with the refrain "and the bottle was produced." A holy lady, whose son had joined the Irish army, was heard nightly to pray aloud in the church: "And Dear Lord, I entrust to your care Private Jonathan So-and-So, Regimental Number 56859," each number clearly articulated lest the Good Lord should fail to get the message. There were repeated warnings against tampering with mines that had drifted ashore. Also, sealed packets of foreign bank notes drifted into beaches in Kerry. There was a rumour of their being passed at fairs as lawful currency in Ireland.

I was married a few years prior to the declaration of World War II. My eldest son was on his feet and my second son, as the saying goes, "on the way," or, as a delicate rural expression has it, "and another goin' to Mass." In addition to the nocturnal and weekend writing of short stories I had finished a novel with the ominous title of *Let it Be Forgotten.* This I took from a verse by Sarah Teasdale, an American poet:

> *Let it be forgotten as a flower is forgotten*
> *Forgotten as a fire that once was singing gold.*
> *Let it be forgotten forever and forever*
> *Time is a kind friend – he will make us old.*

The novel is completely different from the story. Almost anything can be strung on the storyline of the novel which allows for greater elbow room on the part of the writer. But it can be a long, hard pull.

My title proved prophetic indeed! Aiming high, I sent it off to an American agent and it was never again heard of; perhaps it went down with some ship torpedoed in mid-Atlantic. Search as I might, I failed to find a copy. Maurice Walsh, the author, comforted me by saying, "It may have been a 'prentice effort. You will profit by the experience of having completed a full length work. Back to your stories."

I had previously sent a copy of the novel to an Irish publisher – he had returned it with a comment that inadvertently hurt me but I sloughed it off. Being patriotic I sent it to a second Irish publisher – he locked it up in his safe ("It's perfectly safe in my safe") for over a year and I had difficulty securing its release. My next book, finished towards the end of the Second World War, was a collection of my short stories taken from *The Bell* and entitled *The Lion Tamer.* I sent it to an English publisher: ("Start at the top" was the advice of an old literary friend) – this time I despatched it to Macmillan of London where to my high delight I got a gracious welcome and acceptance from the then literary editor, Lovat Dickson. I was familiar with, and was indeed a subscriber to, another of his productions, *Lovat Dickson's Magazine* so I could communicate with him on his level of interest. As far as I can recall, the war had just ended.

First book published! An epic occasion in the life of a would-be writer. Commercial confirmation of his inner belief that he has something! The opening of the parcel containing the author's advance copies. Hmmm! The cover depicting a lion-tamer in all his glory. Not quite what . . . I had a different idea of what the cover would or should be like. That infernal publishing superstition that circus stories do not sell . . . (I did not find it so, but then again, *The Lion Tamer* was only one story of the collection.) Now to take the book aside and handle it reverently. It contains my dreams. Most carefully to open it so as not to crack the glue of the spine. There is a correct way to do this with a new book. Hold the book spine flat down against the surface of a table, open the hard covers one, two, left and right, and smooth gently with the hand. Next steal open groups of pages, alternately coaxing and smoothing left and right, until the book lies flat open more or less about its middle pages.

Ah! Now lift it up and dip the nose into the fragrant book inhaling deeply at the same time. Finally, re-read the stories and experience two warring responses. First, one's eyes and moving lips race ahead of the printed text which one knows almost by rote: the other impression is that the stories have been written by a complete stranger.

During my afternoon siesta in bed I stand the book on the dressing-table and admire it from a distance. "Mine!" I gloat. Then with a sigh of satisfaction I close my eyes and murmur, *Rud éigin déanta!* – Something done. Always before I go to sleep at night I examine my literary conscience and ask myself aloud, *Bhfuil rud éigin fiúntach déanta agat inniu?* – Have you done something worthwhile today? If the answer is *Tá* I am truly satisfied.

As already mentioned – a first son born! That too was an epic event. He proved to be the first of five sons. After No. 4 I said, "Four to carry my coffin." God forgive me, with black humour I quoted Macbeth to Kitty, "Bring forth men children only!" She took it as a compliment. A daughter would be nice. I had been given superstitious recipes to change the sex. If a man tossed a penny five times surely it couldn't come down heads, five times. It did. Dr Toddy, my friend, knocked on my door at six am. I put my head out the window. "What is it?" went my question. "This fellah – the fifth – will carry the priest's hat!", he shouted with a laugh. Before anyone has time to offer misguided sympathy I say, "With five fine daughters-in-law and nine 'grand-girls', as I call them, I now have a considerable feminine presence in my extended family". So, no pity please.

I recall the following sequence of events. On the celebration of Macmillan's 100th anniversary of publishing I was invited to London for the occasion. I flew over in some kind of a pioneer plane, whether from Shannon or Dublin I do not recall, and presently we nosed down over the shattered and jagged skyline of post-war London. From the plane, the scene below made quite a change from unscathed Ireland. The following afternoon I found myself being ushered into an extensive upstairs hall in Macmillan's. A scarlet-coated flunkey silenced the crowded room with his announcement of "Mr Bry-an Macmawn!"

There I was right in the heart of literary London: Macmillan had summoned its writers from the ends of the earth to celebrate the happy occasion. The first man I met was Paddy Kavanagh. He was in fine fettle. And a fine poet he was.

"Come with me," he said threading his way through the throng. He approached what seemed to be a sacred and secret circle of four people standing in a clear space in mid-floor, the group consisting of three men and a woman. "The Sitwells," Paddy said extending his hand to what I presumed was Sacheverell "You're the only bloody people worth meeting in this place!" Paddy declared in a loud voice. This drew smiles of appreciation from the literary core of four. Someone touched Paddy's coat – a man called Jack (I found out afterwards that he was Sir John Squire) who said, "Paddy, I want to introduce you to somebody here." Paddy was not to be weaned off the Sitwells. "For Christ's sake," he exploded, "don't introduce me to nonentities." No one seemed to take umbrage – everything was urbane. Sir John Squire called me aside – I think he was the reader who accepted my manuscript – and encouraged me to keep on writing stories.

A man stood aloof from the crowd. A stalwart man stood in silence on each side of him. I engaged the central figure in conversation. The minders kept glaring at me. I believe the aloof man was General Alexander.

I met Frank O'Connor. He was the soul of kindness. "Where's Paddy Kavanagh?" he wanted to know. "He's here, but he's dodging you," I said. "Why is he dodging me?" "Because of Coloured Balloons," I said – a reference to a *Bell* review in which Paddy said O'Connor's stories were coloured balloons. "Oh, that!" – Frank laughed. "If you find him, tell him I'd like to see him," he said, "I have a BBC appointment and must go soon." I found Paddy. "All is fine," I said. "Come and chat with Frank O'Connor." "It's not fine," Paddy said. "I know he hasn't forgiven me. I wouldn't have forgiven him if he wrote about me like that." Back with Frank, he laughed still more and went off to his appointment. I stayed in the company of Paddy and a scholarly lady called Nancy Orgel from Trinity College, Dublin – she had written a book on Racine.

The function thinned out so Paddy and I went off for a meal. The first restaurant was a disaster – the soup was made from a meat cube. Paddy insisted we leave and go to Bartarellis in Soho. There we had a good meal served by a Tipperary girl. After this Paddy insisted that we visit Terry Ward, the *Irish Press* editor, at his office in The Strand. We spent a long time there.

By this time, having drunk barrels of lemonade, I was growing weary so I wondered how to get back to my hotel. Out in the street – it was now one am – Paddy and I had a mild argument as to what direction we should take. Along came a bus. I leaped on board: Paddy followed. "Garage!" the conductor shouted as the bus paused, then moved on. I turned, advising Paddy not to board: he faltered then fell sidelong. I helped him to the wall of a huge store. Paddy sat at ease, his back to the wall. I sat down beside him, to sort of normalise events. A huge Rolls Royce drew up at the kerb. Members of the Macmillan clan – Daniel, Maurice and young Dan – looked out at their recumbent Irish authors. "You all right, gentlemen?" came the civil query. "Perfectly all right," I said in as blasé a tone as I could muster. The Rolls Royce drifted off. Paddy spoke up and scratched his head. Then we parted.

After this colourful but somewhat unusual harmonisation of opposites in London the reception of *The Lion Tamer* in the US came as a welcome surprise. It got the cover review in the important *Saturday Review of Literature* and was reprinted, I think, five times in the months that followed. (Another reprint is due this year – thirty-five years later). The reviews were excellent. The literary editor of EP Dutton, my New York publisher, was Nick Wreden (Nicholai Redensky) a 'White' Russian trained under Maxwell Perkins, the greatest editor ever, and the man who found Wolfe, Fitzgerald and a host of other major US writers; Nick paid me a visit in Listowel and became a firm friend. Also the great MacRae himself, who owned the firm, visited Listowel bearing gifts. He told me a story that remained with me. With me it was always a story.

"My father was a clerk in a large bookshop in the US," Mr MacRae said. "A gentle old man called Dutton would come in each week to select a book. My father attended him. Over a number of years the two became friends. One evening a car drew up and a chauffeur asked my father to bring a selected book to the brownstone mansion of the old gentleman customer, who at this stage was gravely ill. My father went along to the building and chatted with the old man, sitting at his bedside. The old man stopped talking, looked keenly at my dad, then rang a bell. Miss Dutton, his daughter, entered the bedroom. The old man looked from the young man to the young woman. 'Would you like to own a publishing firm?' he asked my father – the young clerk. My father suddenly realised that the old man was head of the famous publishing firm of that name. The answer was obvious. My dad plucked up his courage and went over to kiss the daughter. The bargain was sealed."

My comment on the story was, "MacRae, Macmillan, MacMahon – three Celts."

"Well said!" he exclaimed with a ringing laugh.

I had made a beginning but that was all. My publishers, Macmillan in Britain, and EP Dutton in New York, were urging me to undertake the writing of a novel. This was about 1950 or so. To me this seemed a huge undertaking. A different kettle of fish completely from the vignette – the very significant vignette – presented by the short story.

Then. "Have a go Joe; your mother won't know and I won't tell her," I told myself.

Mindful of what the Russian masters of literature had advised, and which advice we lads had in turn tendered to the drummer boy of the army of occupation, I began to look more closely at the world around me. The comment of the saddler's assistant, "There's a chiel among ye takin' notes," referring to myself, was recurrent in my mind. Life in general was moving on, accelerated by the slaughter of two great wars. The society about me, though still coherent, was growing more quaint and folksy by the minute and by my reckoning was doomed. I asked myself if the archaic nature of its structure could possibly be of interest to generations as yet unborn. Why not set down in fiction what I knew of it before it was too late? Since it smacked of obsolescence, it called for treatment in kind – a kind of rhythmic approach which would establish its own standards of treatment and rectitude such as poetry does on occasion. If I did so, I felt I would be misunderstood by many, but possibly vindicated by the future. A risk it certainly was. With realism calcified or even thrown out the window, how could my novel succeed? But if I did not write from my own conviction and certitude, what other way could I write? Borrowed plumes would make me appear ridiculous.

And once again I repeated, wasn't the real goal of the writer to make the commonplace novel and the novel commonplace? And, repeating myself ad-nauseam, might not the passing years endow the production with the patina of *social* interest born of age – how once upon a time a small nodule of people had acted, responded, feuded, relaxed, had ideas of nationality, broke laws and made laws, poached fish, raced hounds, mated, given birth and died whether by galloping consumption, the hangman's rope or as mercenaries clad in Imperial khaki without knowing clearly on what shore they lay breathing their last.

So I addressed myself to the writing of a novel which I would call *Children of the Rainbow* – a title from which even the superficially percipient could deduce that I intended my characters to strut their fictional stage with their outlines rimmed with prismatic hues. Ah well, I was young then and the eyes I cast on life were those of a young man. Soon enough ("Time is a kind friend") I would be old.

My mind rolled back once again to *I am a Camera*, a play at the Gate Theatre. In this production, mention was made of a new machine called a wire recorder which could record the human voice. The contraption was as yet unavailable on my side of the Atlantic so I moved quickly to procure one from the US. When it arrived – (Micheál Mac Liammóir confessed to me at a Drama Festival at Killarney that he had never seen one before) I first set about using it to record ballads but quickly realised that I could use it for a wider purpose. Working from a few notes I proceeded, to use my own term, "to spit a novel into it." Night after night I continued to dictate the novel on to the wire and when the hour-long stint of wire was full I lugged the heavy machine to the house of one Daniel P, a brilliant and accurate law clerk who working late, chapter after chapter, won through to a typewritten draft of the whole undertaking.

The harsh part of the work was now to begin: I had to hack my way through the text page after page like an African slave wielding a machete, and, as it were, cut a pathway through virgin jungle so as to reach something like unity and coherency.

EP Dutton accepted the manuscript as it stood but Macmillan wanted it reduced by 10,000 words. To please my British publisher was the hardest task I have ever undertaken – if one tries pulling a character or an incident out of a novel one finds loose ends or odd references all through the work. Harsh was no name for it. But I did it!

EP Dutton told me to keep my fingers crossed, adding that I had a chance of *Children* becoming *Book of the Month*. I did as I was told, knowing that the prize was well over 100,000 dollars – a sizeable sum in those far off days. I wasn't unduly fazed when informed that I had been pipped at the post by another title but that I had come first in the extra book choices available. "What beat us?" I asked on the transatlantic phone and was told that *Children* was 10,000 words too long. "Dear Lord," I answered, "the English edition was that much shorter." "We didn't know," came the sad message.

The book was made an Irish Book Choice and a Book Find Choice in the US. It was well reviewed on this side and on the other – except by one or two critics, among them my maestro, Seán Ó Faoláin. However, I made some money out of it. For income tax purposes I was assessed on the year of payment for a book that took me five years to write. So I had to pay supertax. In effect this meant that the tax was deducted from my pay as a teacher. So . . . for one month every quarter, four months in the year, out of a pay cheque of say £75.3s.4d , I received £3s.4d. In other words, I was paid ten pence per week for each week in the dreaded month. And I with a growing family of sons to educate. If the song had been made at that time I would have sung it:

The Scots have their thistle
The Welsh have their leek
Their poets are paid about tenpence a week
Providing no evil of England they speak
O Lord, what a price for devotion.

I didn't cash any of the attenuated salary forms. Officially queried about it, I said I was keeping the four pay sheets as souvenirs. The Department of Education continued to query. I said I was framing the forms and hanging them on the wall. At the year's end, events gathered momentum. Did I know I was upsetting their accounts? No budge from me. At last, in the January of the year immediately following, I got a normal salary pay order which included the arrears of 13s.4d. from the year before.

This was before Charles Haughey, may God grant him a silver bed in heaven, came to the rescue of Ireland's scribblers.

CHAPTER NINE

Stories and the impact of stories. The source of stories in the writer's mind. Stories and the seeking of stories. Where to hunt but by the margin of the sea – the sea with its flux of fertility. With me it is always the sea – even though I stay on land!

I walked on a clifftop pathway, revelling in the boisterous but far below clamour of the sea, the waves gathering, rolling inexorably forward to smash upward in the blossoming glory of spray against the ochre and black brown cliff side. This on a winter evening above a beach in the Irish south west.

At the deepest point of my reverie and my communion with the tide, a middle-aged woman came walking against me. She was formally dressed, complete with hat and coat, but since it was off-season at the resort, her appearance was normal. Drawn level with me, she stopped and in a cultured voice said, "I have a story for you, Bryan MacMahon. And you are a big part of the story. But it's my story too. This is a story you must hug to your heart."

"Hug to my heart?" The phrase gripped me. I nodded my willingness to listen.

"I was a young student at this time," she began, "had just begun attending University in Dublin. Crazy for literature. Mad about poetry. Crazy for stories. And for the young men and women who felt as I did.

"There was this young man in my class, a powerful fellow and a bit of a poet. I fell for him. To this day I'm not sure whether it was his poetry or himself that attracted me. I had tea or coffee with him a few times in Bewley's. Then one day he said to me, 'Will you come to my flat this evening and I'll give you a little treat?' 'Humph', I said to myself, 'I know the treat you have in mind.' However I kept a fair face and asked, 'Where's your flat?'. 'In Ballsbridge.' 'Upstairs or down?' 'It's the basement flat, the door is under the steps going up to the main door.' 'All right,' I said, thinking to myself that if I went, I wouldn't be deep into the house. He opened the door on a neat little flat. Bookshelves laden down with books. A broad sofa – I kept well away from that and sat near the door. I had a drop of sherry and nibbled a biscuit. I was doing fine until he said 'Don't be alarmed.' He then quenched the lights.

"I gripped the edge of my chair. Eyed where I thought the door was. Solemnly the man lighted two ornamental candles, took down a book from a shelf and squatting on the floor before me, his eyes shining, he began to read. It was a story about a dying wife asking her useless and drunken husband, a noted singer, to sing a song for her at her wake. As the young man read, I found my terror being enfolded in his elation." The woman on the clifftop pathway now began to chant.

"In Teerla, gentle and simple can tell you how Milo Burke kept his word to his dead wife. The night of the wake was still and windless – such a night for singing had never been before. The wakehouse was thronged. About half past ten Milo came into the wakeroom and began to sing.

> *The song called the dead woman jewel, darling,*
> *treasure, calf, secret, share and bright white love . . .*
> *It told the people how to be beautiful though ugly, how to be*
> *rich though poor, how to be happy though sad, how to be*
> *young though old.*

"When the song was finished, Milo retreated into a corner of the room and remained there for the rest of the night, quite silent.

"There you are," the woman said telling me what I already knew. It was in fact my own story. "Sing, Milo, Sing." "So hug it to your heart," she added. And off she went smiling quietly.

This incident on the cliff-walk, slight though it was, offered me a new perspective on myself. And on the impact of what I had written had had upon persons unknown. I shall not descend to the absurdity of a diagram but, if I did so, it would go somewhat as follows.

I visualise a small circle with three dots, A, B and C equidistant from each other on its circumference. A represents myself as a Storyman, B represents the student poet who reads the story. C stands for the woman who retells the telling of the story back to A. And on this page of print I retell the telling of my story and now it's about a man telling my little tale to a woman who later retells the story back to me standing still but receptive at point A on my circle!

Clockwise and circuitous – eh? I realise that I'm being complicated and even perplexing. But I stick my neck out further and ask: does movement finish with Me at A or has it a further dimension? I think it has that further dimension: it has a tangential spin-off outwards into the unknown from point A. Into an unimaginable world of D or X Y Z.

For the writer, the incident illustrates something important. He now has a sounding board, an echo and a whole range of possibilities. A new perspective on himself. He is charged with an emergency that urges him to go forth and hunt for further tiny but significant incidents among the peaceful or turbulent world of women and men. And in my search today I am bound by the picket fence of peace. I shall explain that reference later.

Again a cliff walk on a day in summer. A tranquil sea. A circle of cork net floats just below me. The tide of ideas flowing and ebbing in my mind.

I am now in Ardmore in the County Waterford; it's a seaside resort of character on the south east Irish coast – a place with a round tower, and a foreshore boulder beneath which pattern day devotees of St Declan crawl to be rid of various physical and mental ailments. Above all, Ardmore has more than a whiff of the old Gaelic world with its still living memory of the Irish language and its summer college.

In Ardmore, I felt completely at home, staying at Melrose or the Cliff Hotel with now and again an excursion to Ring Irish College (God be good to you, *Fear Mór*!) or searching for the tomb of a lady buried in a field. I was also wondering what went on in the minds of the winkle-pickers reaping their shelly harvest at the north end of the lovely beach. In retrospect, life was happy and carefree.

But here I plead guilty to the charge of being digressive.

Academics have engaged in furious debate as to the admissibility or occlusion of digressions in what is generally called an autobiography. I come down on the side of digression. Life as lived by any human being cannot be called linear. Nor is it a stretch of catgut on which a series of similar beads representing typical incidents may be strung. To change the metaphor, life does not run on rails: it sometimes takes the form of a crazy locomotive which, rocketing off its iron road, wander-thunders through a terrified countryside, climbs trees to pick crab-apples or calls at rural inns to order caviar and wine.

And then with good fortune dutifully returns to its beloved rails.

My mind had already fully turned on short stories. That morning, from behind a sand dune, I heard a woman urging a young girl, probably her niece, to sing over and over the chorus of a song then popular – "Che Sera Sera". No sooner had the plaintive-voiced singer finished than the older woman's voice urged her to begin again. I peeped over the little sandhill. Ah, the woman was a nun. That shed a new light on the incident! Had the chorus, with its lines, "Whatever will be, will be. The future's not ours to see," evoked some resonance of solace or comfort from the memory of the older woman? I went back to the hotel brooding on the possibilities.

Back at the hotel, "There's a message for you," my wife said. "Phone home at once." I did so. At my request, one of my sons opened and read out for me the contents of a letter from the BBC. It asked if I could write five short stories to indicate that peaceful areas of Ireland still existed. (This was in the early '70s when the Northern troubles were gathering momentum.) I phoned and accepted at once: the editor stressed that the stories were needed urgently. Since the offer was a good one, I agreed that within a short time I would submit five scripts of a series called *Stories from a Peaceful Ireland.* "I'll be back in a week," I told my good wife. "I'm going hunting." "Hunting what?" "Stories," I replied.

I drove off. "Che Sera" was still ringing in my ears. "I'll hold it in reserve," I told myself, jotting it down in a small notebook I keep in the inside pocket of my jacket. I was now aiming to travel by the coast from Waterford as far as Sligo. I would talk, casually I hoped, to everyone I met – this with the aim of finding and exploring five separate seminal ideas which I could expand into stories.

I stress that there is a difference between a radio story and a literary story set down in print. On the occasions I have read one of my own stories aloud on radio either here in Ireland or in the US, Britain or Germany, I have had to skip portions that drag. The printed story admits of the reader's turning back to elucidate or clarify: for obvious reasons the story on the air does not countenance this. I drove west. "Find! Find!" I cried, evicting the sand dune chorus from my head.

It is now early evening. I've spent a day peering, stopping, asking, searching. Fruitlessly. I am on a mountain pass. Not an immensely lofty one, but one with a splendid view towards the great plain of the west. I leave the car and walk to a point of vantage. Far to the west behind a forest of pine trees the sun is about to set in a mighty conflagration. The yellow-scarlet light splinters and twinkles through the ranked tree trunks. The world is silent.

I continue to stand by the fence imbibing the evening world. I watch the house lights come on in a village below. Suddenly I am conscious that someone is standing behind me.

I turn and find an old man regarding me closely. His figure seems touched by the scarlet and yellow hues of the setting sun. I greet him gently, engage him in conversation and gradually win his confidence. He lives nearby. He comes to this spot each fine evening to enjoy the view. The talk grows more confidential. "'Twas here too . . . " he begins, then breaks off. I sense something deeper. I probe. The term "tidy lady" occurs again and again in his talk. Slowly I tease out the origin of the phrase. "This tidy lady . . .?" I venture. He tells.

Standing there one evening at sunset he first met her. She rode up on her horse, talked to him, remained talking to him for some time, then rode away. "Oh, she was a tidy lady. An ascendancy lady." In the gentlest of tones he conveys to me how well she sat a saddle, how her young-womanly buttocks rose and fell with the movement of the horse. He saw her once after this; he goes on, "At the fair of Cahirmee. She might come back here again. One never knows."

I then learned that his first encounter with the young woman had happened sixty years before.

All this time he held a small rolled magazine in his hand. He gestured with it as the sun sank below the horizon to leave a broad swathe of lemon light along the skyline.

As cautiously as I could, I asked to see the magazine. Reluctantly he handed it to me. It was old, dirty and handsoiled. It was rolled open about a page in the middle. I held up the page to catch the rays of the dying light. The article was boldly headed – "How the English Make Love."

Story No. 1. *The Tidy Lady.*

I slept in a B & B in the village that night. I had scribbled out the bones of the *Lady* story before I slept. The following morning I was on the road. Instinctively I rode in the direction of the sea.

In the afternoon I came on a small seaside village about which – something quite rare in Ireland – beech trees grew down to the cove's edge. I stopped beside the little post office, with its "green boxeen" of post-box inset in its window. I peered in through the glass. A gentle old lady was paying out what was obviously pension money to an old man. I withdrew my head.

There was something about the office that puzzled me. What was it? I walked over to the low sea wall and sat upon it. A boy was fishing with a feather-jig, casting it out from the small pier. I was fishing in my brain. From time to time I glanced back at the green post-box. Come on subconscious, I said, almost aloud, spit out whatever it is. You have it there, hidden in one of your brain cells.

Almost at once the machinery of my brain clicked into gear. I seemed to be transported to a large mansion somewhere in the Southern States of the US. A man was speaking in low tones telling me a story he heard in Ireland. By the hokey, I had it! I could see it all happening between me and the swirling sea below the wall.

"A post office inspector enters a village post office. He calls the old postmistress aside. He talks at length, obviously telling her something not quite pleasant. The old lady's face drains. The man places a form before her. She must fill the form and give an accurate account of all monetary transactions. The old lady draws back, points to the safe. 'It's all there. Every penny,' she says. The man taps the form. 'I realise that you are honest,' he says in a low voice. 'As were your mother and grandmother before you who were postmistresses here. But this form must be filled . . . auditors . . . given plenty notice . . . final chance . . . avoid dismissal. I'll be back in an hour.'

"The inspector, (as I visualise it), walks to the pier. He watches as a hooked mackerel swings through the air. Drums his finger on a bollard. Lights a cigarette. Idles. Returns to the post office when the hour is up. As a pensioner leaves, the inspector stands in foreboding silence. The postmistress calmly completes her business then turns and pushes the form across the counter to the inquisitor. He takes it. Scanning it, his face registers puzzlement. The man takes the form to the window, reads what is written diagonally in spidery writing across the official paper. The stern look ebbs from his face. His lips curl about the words on the form. 'The veil that hides the future was woven by the Angel of Mercy.' A long pause. The inspector's face softens; he says to the old woman, 'As long as I am in my present post I'll see that you are not bothered again.'"

In quiet glee I murmur, Story No. 2. *The Veil That Hides the Future.*

That night I stayed with a retired and scholarly schoolmaster. We talk until the morning hours. At day-break I am off. I'll keep to the sea coast, I tell myself. For me the beloved flux of the sea is fertile. I have travelled this way before and now experience recurrent excitement. For me water is a valuable medium of communication and movement.

I come to a pier with a huddle of fishing trawlers beside it. Big arc lamps on high posts for night unloading. "Was it here?" I ask myself. Yes, yes. It was right here. Surely, thirty years before. From here we set out on an excursion to visit the island where the Algerian pirates had taken refuge after they had sacked the coastal town. On that occasion there were fifty or more of us on board the trawler – a large number of them young continentals from the local youth hostel. The trawler captain recognised me: he nodded in the direction of a young man with olive features and closely cut dark hair, seated apart from the others. "Draw him out," he whispered. He drew deep on his cigarette and scanned the sea before him.

I stalked the young man. Carefully. After a while he and I talked on Ireland. On the locality. On furze and fuchsia. On geography and history. Our island destination drew near. We had a drink in the island pub. He told me his story.

"I come from Madrid. My family are in the wine trade for generations. We have an office in London. My grandfather served in it at the turn of the century. So did his son, my father. I now follow in their footsteps. In my grandfather's time, a young Irish girl with red hair kept house for him in the flat above the office. They fell in love. There was a good deal of trouble from my grandfather's family. 'Who is this penniless Irish nobody?' they asked. My grandfather brought her to Spain. Yes, the family all fell in love with her too. The pair married."

The Spaniard paused and looked out on the sea.

"I am camping on my grandmother's land – my grand-uncle, his hair was once red – gives me milk and potatoes. His son and wife and their family, my cousins, do not know me: they call me The Spaniard. The children play about my tent. We gather mushrooms. These are the fields among which my grandmother grew up. I have been here now for two weeks."

"Do they know who you are?" I asked.

"No," he said.

"Do you intend telling them?"

"I'm not sure."

"Why are you not sure?"

"Because I'm the kind of person who likes a mystery."

Story No. 3 – *The Spaniard.*

That evening and as indeed I did every night, I sat down and faced and challenged myself in a feverish mood. "Stop the lights!" I said, "What are you up to? Isn't all this somewhat ghoulish and predatory? Chasing people in vulnerable moods, pretending to sympathise with them and then callously moving off to write about them in altered attire and circumstances. What excuse can you possibly have for such conduct?"

This is a charge which requires refutation or, at the very least, explanation. The writer is on the defence and his protestations sound wan when he ventures to explain.

My motives and the motives of other writers of literary history have not been ignoble I daresay I'm an ordinary run-of-the-mill scribbler with the compulsion of attempting to explain the foibles, the adventures and bizarre attitudes of my fellow human beings). The writer hopes to establish a sense of identification between reader and characters as portrayed in stories, novels or plays. By vicariously identifying with stressful, oddball, winsome, romantic or even brutal aspects of human behaviour, the reader is enabled to rehearse and thereby understand, partially or wholly, circumstances of his own life pattern. In simple terms, since to understand all is to forgive all, the reader is emotionally enriched and enabled to cope with the unforeseen. He becomes possessed of an attitude of tolerance and forbearance which is the hallmark of wisdom.

If this is seen as being too noble by half, I cannot explain further without embarking on a long treatise on the nature of literature itself. All I can vouch for is that this attitude works for me. Nor am I always predatory and eager to exploit. But even in ordinary life I possess the resource of being able to recognise, on most occasions with a start, that which is important to myself as well as potentially of service to others.

I push on regardful to keep close to the sea. I come to a seaside village which in the autumn holds a memorable pattern – or patron-day – much like the "patrons" of north west France. I am now in the Irish west. My memory is awake.

Here the great brown sails of the hookers came ponderously in to dwarf the small boats already in the harbour. I recall the little festival in every detail. A choir is practising to sing a Mass in Irish: a tipsy bearded man is moving through the throng, his hat proffered in lieu of begging bowl. He sings in grace-noted Irish. But now, as I muse, it is not pattern day and for me the place is empty. I am floundering. I push on for a mile or two. I am conscious that there is something of value quite close to me. Then, with an inlet of the sea just below the road I come upon a strange sight.

Two girls in medieval costume are walking against me. I leave the car and greet them. Below us, on a self-contained little peninsula, stands a castle: I recognise it at once for I have scripted the entertainment for a comrade castle some miles inland. Here each season is held a medieval dinner with a show to follow – the show is literary. I squat on the kerb: one of the girls knows me – she probably has taken part in a pageant of mine.

Soon we are deep in vivid banter and conversation – I seated on the kerb, each of them on a clean grass tussock, one on each side of me. We resuscitate old memories. Along come a pair of American hitchhikers – both women. "Why not join us?" I say. "It's just a roadside chat." They do so. One reveals herself as an ordained priest working in New York; the other is a student. We talk – the five of us.

Along comes an old countrywoman wearing a short shawl which she draws about her face and allows recurrently to fall to her shoulders. She is chattering to herself in some agitation and obviously, in retrospect, abusing a shopkeeper with whom she has had a quarrel. In her basket the old lady has a dozen sticks of rhubarb. The end of one of the sticks is hanging by a thread of fibre. It swings daftly. "Sit down, woman," I say. "Tell us your story." The art of engaging a total stranger in conversation is one in which the Irish excel. It depends on a voice inflection and a certain kind of smile.

We are now six. The newcomer launches into a further tirade as she does so. The shopkeeper refused to buy her rhubarb. As the saying goes, she "reads" him.

I cannot help noticing that ten eyes, my pair as well as the eyes of the medievalists and the hikers, are firmly fixed on the piece of rhubarb dangling by its thin thread from one of the sticks protruding from the old woman's basket. The piece comes from the white and red portion near the root of the plant, the white groove being the part into which one slides one's thumb before gripping the stick and dragging it properly upwards from its parent stool.

The odd swinging piece seems to have a life of its own. It is the seventh member of our assorted group. It glistens. It forms itself into a claw which moves menacingly with every stir and resonance of the old woman's recital of personal outrage. Vaguely but pleasantly I realise that our conversation has become superficial: it is now uttered merely to conceal our inner absorption with the movement of an odd hypnotic pendulum. I claim myself as master of the situation, since I alone have surfaced subjectively and identified the source of trance. On goes the rhetoric of abuse: the old woman characterises as a hungry bastard the shopkeeper who refused to buy her dozen of rhubarb. The vehemence of the charge almost breaks the spell but not quite, for the pendulum resumes, casting its rhythmic spell over all of us.

This cannot go on forever, I tell myself. *Ex nihilo nihil fit.* Out of nothing, nothing comes. I decide to act the part of the intruder, the solvent – this in order to evoke a finish for my story, and by so doing perhaps to transform an anecdote into a literary tale. I lean forward, mutter, "Excuse me," snap off the pendulous piece of rhubarb and, lodging it securely in my fingertips, its flatter end safe in the tip of my right index finger, I stand up and sling it out into the inlet of sea below the road. I am aiming it vaguely in the direction of a serene pair of sailing swans. The splash alarms the birds: at first they strain away. Then the cob turns back, stretches out his looping neck, and catches the scrap of rhubarb in his beak.

He tests it, drops it and, still regardant of where it came from, sails quizzically back to join his pen. The group around me, medieval, transatlantic, ecclesiastical, local, frantic, hypnotic and anecdotal, dissolves.

Solvitor scribendo – "Yes, it would come out in the writing," I tell myself. I'll call it Story No. 4 – *Rhubarb and Hypnosis.* Which I did.

I spent the night in the Burren – an old haunt of mine. One last story to go! Where now? I asked myself after breakfast. The Aran Islands? If I went out there 'twould take me a week to leave my dear friends the Conneelys of Inisheer. After Mass at Doolin, and a word with Gus O'Connor of the famous musical pub, I scampered off to Galway city. There I said "Hello" to the winsome statue of that picaresque writer and Storyman, ex-civil servant, Paddy Conroy, better known in Gaelic of course as Pádraic Ó Conaire. I then sauntered down the street towards the Cathedral. I came upon a bridge over the Corrib. Hundreds of onlookers were leaning over the parapet watching the serried ranks of salmon below, the size of the fish slightly diminished when seen through water. A marvellous sight in the middle of the city.

It was a beautiful sunny day – a Sunday too with a clock chiming the noon hour from a nearby steeple. I joined the salmon watchers. Cries of "Look, Look!" rose from eager tourists and hikers. Fingers pointed downward. God forgive me, I couldn't help remembering my being reared in a nest of salmon poachers. To those, the friends of my youth, this place would seem like Heaven.

Presently I noticed that something odd was afoot. It was now eight minutes past twelve, midday. A narrow plank stretched from one end of the bridge to a kind of limestone quay-island high above the hurrying water. A young man, wearing what were called winkle-picker pointed shoes, walked carefully across the narrow plank. On the island he sat on a bollard of sorts. He lit a cigarette; from time to time he surveyed the world fore and aft through cigarette smoke. His eyes lifted to check the clock in the steeple: they then enfiladed the rank of watchers behind and slightly above him. As he gave some sort of signal, a similar young man left the file of people on the bridge and swayed across the plank. This man squatted beside his friend, the winkle-picker, and inevitably lit a cigarette and blew smoke upwards to the sun.

Both men were suddenly on their feet, their movements now action bright. Indolence was cast aside. A short stick appeared in the hand of one of the pair. A long line caught the sunlight. As did a small lead sinker, a tiny torpedo-shaped weight. Was that a treble hook known as a strokehaul – three hooks back to back on a single stem – at the end of the line? Surely not here in mid-city.

A glance at the clock on the part of one of the pair suggested that the bailiffs (nowadays called water keepers) were attending last Mass, and that the coast was clear. The shamrock of hooks and the little torpedo were lowered to the torrent. A pause. A low-struck but swift haul on the line yielded nothing. A second pull proved equally fruitless. The third pull was a success. The water below began boiling and swirling. Hand over hand, the pair, one screening the other, drew a heavy protesting salmon up out of the water. On the stones the pair pounced on the fish. Thuds were heard; then the winkle-picker, himself erect and even defiantly noble, with the fish clutched to his breast, scurried towards the plank above the torrent. Like a circus acrobat he raced over the narrow passageway. In mid-career, the salmon came to life; the crowd reacted with a great "Oh!" of horror. The picker, now followed by his chum, as by a miracle, recovered his balance and flung himself to safety on the bridgehead.

As he did so, the fish slithered out of his grasp, fell over the bridge wall, thudded onto the pavement, squirmed and thumped onto the road, and stopped right in front of a tourist coach which had squealed to an abrupt halt. The crowd gathered around the vehicle on the realisation that the salmon was now under the coach. The tourists emerged.

It was at this point that a most accurate Japanese gentleman materialised from somewhere, most accurately placed an unfolded handkerchief on the roadway, knelt on it and, with the crook of his umbrella, tried to retrieve the kicking fish. All this was too much for me: I had already noted the distant pub into which the poaching pair had vanished. After a short time I entered it. The pair were as cool as cucumber. They watched me closely and covertly. As I did them. They had half empty pint glasses of beer before them. The half glass was significant, for they had been there only a few minutes. An alibi, if questioned?

My quest was ended. Now I had Story No. 5. For the first time in a week I could draw a sigh of relief. I also realised that the craft of poaching was not confined to a huddle of lads in a smith's kitchen in a lane in a country town. So I would call my last story – *City Poachers*, which on the face of it, seemed to contain a contradiction in terms. With the Jap gent to provide the oddest of reconciliations. I confess to have gloated over my little store of stories. I whispered their names over and over in my mind as a patron of the track or turf would gloat over the names of his string of hounds or horses. *Tidy Lady, The Veil, The Spaniard, Rhubarb and Hypnosis,* and *City Poachers.* Now to return to Ardmore to flesh out, and trim my quintet of tales.

But, but, but . . . it was at this point that my personal Jack Heckler voiced his query of dissent. "How about your precious theory of the reconciliation of opposites? Have you dumped that?"

I recovered quickly, if somewhat wanly.

Each little story contains elements of my polarities, I squeaked. *Tidy Lady?* Old and young. Peasant and Ascendancy, English love and a naive Irish brand of obsessive affection. *The Veil?* Cold officialdom confronted with what looks like a relevant and consoling quotation from Gospel or Psalm. *The Spaniard?* Red-haired maid from Ireland and dignified Madrelino family. Spuds versus grapes. *Rhubarb and Hypnosis?* Polarity implicit in the title plus a novel alternative to rhubarb crumble. *City Poachers?* The winkle-pickers (not those at

Ardmore!) and the Japanese gentleman on his knees with the futile movements of the brolly handle. The stories stink with polarities. Harnessed, foreshortened and procrusteaned, they would serve. I am allowed use the last term (I hope) for the purpose of communication and the projection of tiny but significant incidents from Irish life as I have experienced it, and because of the medium on which I find myself, is compressed within a short period of time.

Broadcast later on BBC World Service, a friend wrote from Paris that he had heard *The Spaniard.* Turn and turn about, I hoped (and feared) the sound waves would, or would not, be heard in Madrid.

These five stories of mine are of their nature superficial, even "instant" in the odd comparison of say, instant tea or instant soup. But for me the basic theory of a story being grounded on a single phrase remains valid. And the polarities exist.

Turning over the pages of short story collections of mine I can identify with great clarifty the initial seminal phrase and the moment that each story originated. The story, *The Lion Tamer*, had its *fons et origo* when the only Irish lion-tamer walked into the local printer's office for the purpose of ordering some handbills for a little circus. *The Ring* grew from a sentence a neighbour uttered about his mother's refusal to allow haymaking to continue until she had recovered her wedding ring, lost in the aromatic fodder benches of the hay barn. At the end of a public reading of the tale in Siamsa Rural Theatre outside Listowel, a dear friend of mine stood up in the audience and holding aloft a gold ring taken from her finger declared, "This is The Ring my grandmother lost and found in the long ago, and which is the subject of Bryan's story."

The audience applause warmed my heart.

A Woman's Hair is the story of a motherless girl who saved the beautiful hair of a tramp's woman from being cut off and in doing so, revived the far memory of her own dead mother. Most clearly I recall the whispering woman who gave me the Open Sesame sentence of that story.

Whenever I meet a certain young woman returned from Canada she greets me by a filming over of her eyes and by clutching a trinket suspended from a chain about her neck. Set in silver is a pebble: the pebble about which I wrote in *Stories for Young Adults.* It tells of a young woman reading a book as she lies in summer grass on a high bank above a little river falls. A young man, stark naked, she realises from her sentry post, is swimming down river through a gap in the falling water: he stops to tread water in the pool just below her. "Hey, you up there," the boy calls out, "why don't you come in for a swim?" The girl hides deeper in the grass. "We're young, it's summer," he shouts. "Come in and enjoy the water. You!" As he continues to heckle, the girl raises her head, "I've no costume," she bleats. "Neither have I. I won't harm you."

"We're not married. I don't know you!" she says.

"I'll marry you," he counters, then dives deep into the pool surfacing in a moment with a fistful of pebbles. He selects one. Flicks it up. The girl catches it. "Your engagement token," he shouts.

Eventually having disrobed under the trailing branches of a beech tree, the girl enters the water – as indeed did Fial of old, the legendary queen for whom the river is named. (Fial drowned of shame when a man she did not recognise as her husband came on her bathing place.) The pebble did prove an engagement ring: years later, the young man presented it, mounted in silver, to his bride on the morning of their wedding. When she sees me the girl returned from Canada clutches it close. She knows I have written her story. And is proud.

I could keep on till morning talking in this strain. *Exile's Return, Chicken-Licken, King of the Bees, Testament of a Sewer Rat, The Tallystick, Chestnut and Jet* – for this last I can hear my father's voice telling with pride of a forebear who paraded a stallion through the streets of the fairday town while the people came out to admire man and animal. When *The Red Petticoat* comes to mind, I leave a butcher's kitchen in my own town and a magic carpet wafts me through the air to a crowded and cherub-ceilinged music room in a German city on the Rhine. There a Swiss scholar reads my story translated into German. In the story I tell how I have stolen an old lady's petticoat to cut up and sell as rags to take a girl to the cinema. The old lady's manner of protesting the loss of her petticoat is to keep shouting *"Hoch den Rebellen!"* "Up the Rebels"

The German audience rewards the narration with appreciative roars of glee. The following day in Hohe Strasse in Cologne, a solemn burger and his wife pause to look me up and down. The man raises his hat and with one voice the pair chant "Hoch den Rebellen." I reply with a loud "Up the Rebels!"

So it goes. The story of the origin of the stories. For the writer there is the love-glint of recognition of a phrase, the conception, the gestation, the pains, as of childbirth, when the story takes shape. When it appears in print there is a pang of parental pride as the infant story takes its first step into a friendly or hostile world.

Again I pause to ask myself what goal I have in mind in these pages. I'd like the reader to look behind the curtain and see how the writer goes about his work. It may well transfer to the discerning reader the faculty of watching the affairs of men and women with a sharper eye. He may thereby vicariously experience the imaginative joy of the recognition of some valuable incident in his own life which may heighten his sense of being truly alive. It might also tempt him to say "I can write as good as another". Or even, "I can orally tell that story in attractive form or include it in a letter to Paddy in Adelaide, Mick in Camden or Josephine in El Cajon, California."

There is another aim of mine which I hesitate to reveal. I have a distant goal of viewing my country as a last haven of the imagination, a place where the materialistic inhabitants of much of the globe, their variegated appetites sapped by materialism and consumerism and blunted by countless distractions, may find sustenance, and provender of mind together with peace and harmony within themselves. If I am right in this, the Irish world we inhabit could be a resource of great international value. ("Our greatest resource is our people.") This aim should manifest itself in our literature. Being unexpectedly coy, the ultimate aim should more or less be concealed lest those who tend to package everything might assess human life in the unit of the "bed night" and by doing so twist the concept out of shape and destroy it.

Excelsior! Onward to the final outpost of true humanity. I have thrown down the gauntlet: I now bare my breast for the pointed spears of the bilious and shrivelled.

Meanwhile with me it's stories, stories, all the way. I read novels and biographies, of course, but my passion is the short story. Somehow I manage to procure collections from all parts of the globe.

When I stay with my son who holds a European post and lives in

Matthew Arnold's Cumnor Hill over Oxford, I play the part of a scholar gypsy browsing in the bookshops of that glorious city. Blackwell's, Dillons and other speciality bookshops are places where I can buy collections of short stories in translation from many parts of the world. *Ex-Africa semper aliquid novi,* I find to be true comment. In these latter years there is always something new finding its way into print from the emerging post-colonial nations of that enormous continent. Some have already appeared in English while others are in translation from the French or from whatever language was that of their European once exploiters.

I've encountered a few wonderful storytellers from Egypt. One story tells of a blind mullah who marries one of three spinster sisters. At nightfall each of the three wears the single wedding ring in turn and sleeps with the communal husband. The holy man, even if he "sees" through the deception, never upbraids the impostors.

Across the globe, South America is suddenly finding a voice. Columbia despite its ill-reputation in the drug underworld has produced some excellent storytellers. From South America I cherish one story in particular – that of a slave being pursued who falls in love, physically, with the Virgin Mary and cries out his love in agony. For many this must be close to blasphemy but for me it is much more than that. The West Indies have always been a fertile hunting ground of mine; there was also a time when I was familiar with the literature of the Philippines. But, of course, literary attitudes in various countries are changing all the time. The old classical tales of India and China are, to our western minds, tedious, age-frozen and mannered. But certain celebrated cases of recent date indicate that even the literary mountains are in labour in these immense lands. In Britain, our own William Trevor is up there with the best, following in the footsteps of Coppard and Bates. But for me, my man in Britain will always be a quiet writer from the Orkneys called George MacKay Brown whose prose I find is as clean as a bone in sand, and who succeeds, in small but beautiful compass, in portraying those fleeting moments that generally elude capture in mere words. Jules Renard of France is for me a writer's writer. I wish I had more of him in translation.

And now I possess the outlandish naiveté or innocence or ignorance to mention the literature of the United States – so various, so vast, so different in the climates of its different component regions.

We Irish always have had an intuitive affinity with the writers of the Southern States. We like to brag that through the medium of literature we both took a subtle revenge on our former masters. I have the audacity to make one general comment – a stupid thing to do – the US story writers as a whole take great trouble with detail. This prompts me to say that in Ireland we tend to flick open a story-oyster with the quick insertion of a knife blade which we then twist to open the succulent bivalve. Others like the German, Thomas Mann, a writer greatly admired in the US seek to do so by bashing the shell with a hammer. But this is a harsh generalisation which I may live to regret having made. The emergence of black African-American writers, as they are now known, is a modern phenomenon: I like ethnic stories – for me it's the joy of finding my own level in other cultures. Malamud writes against the backdrop of Jewish culture and at times, in one of his tales, I find myself completely at home.

The perspicacious will have noted that, apart from Malamud, I have mentioned no names: I must be believed when I declare that I could pour out names in a torrent. Welty, Gaines, Baldwin, O'Connor, Faulkner, et al. To do so would, I reckon, be the refinement of pedantry.

I read more and more stories, not indeed to copy slavishly, but rather to be familiar with new approaches to what is essentially a new medium. I like especially those welling up from the soil culture of peoples come fresh to literature.

I am now reminded of what Micheál File, son of Peig Sayers, said as he set about writing down what his mother had to say about her life on the mainland and on the Blasket Island. "Slow laborious work it was for the likes of us for we had no exact knowledge of the business of literature." But then again as Paddy Kavanagh had it, "The gods make their own importance."

Will Ireland run out of subjects to provide the switch-on for literature? As far as poetry is concerned, I have already prophesied what the future holds. There will be changes of course, but I hold that for literature in general there are certain basics that will not change; I have set down this prophecy elsewhere and as follows:

Mass media have made us far more impatient of superfluous stage directions and truly more ripe to respond to apt allusions world wide in range and stretching from the beginning of man's story until this moment. Poetry, which is intense experience reduced to protocol, must always struggle with a series of foes from the sham folksy to the computerised, but always it will return to constants based on the emotions of man. Erect grief, intuitive courtesy, stoic acceptance of exaltation and decay, ephemeral beauty captured, the pang of parting, the hilarity of greeting, flowers, fine food and wine, the series of webs that bind man to woman and woman to man, the pride and sorrow engendered by the hearing anew of the fate of the Sons of Usna, hazel trees in springtime, sandpipers over a tidelip at dusk, the waves breaking at the foot of the cliff on which Dun Aonghus hangs, the smell of engine oil and herring, hunger, pride, covetousness and all their black comrades, self-sacrifice too and what Seán Lucy calls the 'hard-boiled eggs' of uncracked mystery – these are the renewers and the replenishers of man. And essentially, the emotions they summon will tend to retain a certain constancy.

I call as my final witness the great Isaac Bashevic Singer: "Progress can never kill literature any more than it can kill religion," he begins, and goes on to say that the pervasiveness of technology will drive humans ever more towards literature.

"The more technology, the more people will be interested in what the human mind can produce without the help of electronics . . . if we have people with the power to tell a story, there will always be readers."

But maybe the electronic engineer, the artist and the Storyman will yet team up to renew the ancient art of telling stories – that is if they haven't done so already?

"Knock-knock – who's there? Why, if it isn't Aladdin all the way from Arabia. Wearing a brand new electronic costume! Come in my lovely immortal son and don't forget to bring along your lamp."

PS And then again, Christ was a Storyman. He called them parables.

CHAPTER TEN

The play's the thing – or is it?

I begin this episode in morning sunlight. I shall then continue in darkness looking up at a three-sided room shot through with brilliant light.

I had landed on the western island off the Galway coast late the night before. I had gone there for the purpose of examining some interesting ruins. Early next morning – a bright sunny morning – long before breakfast, I was out of bed and down to view the ruins of the Castle beside the little harbour pub.

There was no one about except one old man. He was seated on a low stone wall scribbling with the point of his walking stick on the dust at his feet. He raised his head, offered me a slow shrewd glance, and then quickly transferred his attention to his blackboard of dust. I knew by the passing glint in his eyes that the old fellow had recognised me. I had been on the *Late Late Show* on RTE a week or so previously.

Silence between us. I was looking up at a window-gape in the ruin and thinking of Pirate Queen Grace O'Malley – she who had travelled to London and outfaced Queen Elizabeth herself. Was it through the high aperture in the broken wall that the cord tied to Grace's big toe had stretched, its other end tied her to her pirate ship in the harbour below?

Suddenly I heard a voice saying "Psst."

It came from the old man on the wall. He looked at me, his eyes then transferred my gaze upwards to a pathway descending from the top of a clay cliff. A second old man was descending the pathway, his eyes fixed on the pair of us below. At the point where the pathway came to a hairpin turn, and the newcomer had to pick his steps more carefully, there came a second "Psst." The man on the wall had dared to look at me; "Salmon," he whisper-called, shaping his lips fully about the word. I hadn't the faintest idea what this antic meant: I had not long to wait.

Presently the two old fellows were glaring at each other. I interpreted this as indicating that the pair were old adversaries – in a friendly and bantering kind of way. For a time, there was no move on the part of any of the three of us. My eyes were cast sidelong on the boats bobbing in the harbour; the newcomer stood watching us, his lips slightly apart. Meanwhile Old "Psst" on the wall, his lips pursed, was engaged in some solemn calculation in the dust.

Psst then raised his head. Addressing the Cliffman he said;

"His name is Mr MacMahon from the County Kerry," at the same time vaguely pointing at me with his stick. Pausing for effect he then added, "He has the gift." Cliffman spat on the ground. "What gift?" he said with the voice of Gruff Enough.

"The gift of looking into your two eyes and being able to read your name."

The newcomer moved a few steps towards me. He made a scoffing snort as he did so. There was a pause of appraisal. Then, "Hey, Mr MacMahon from the County Kerry, look into my two eyes and tell me my name."

I looked up. Narrowed my eyes. Looked intently into his. "Salmon," I said. Slowly, as if grudgingly. "Good! Damn good!" came his reply. Then, "Were you ever here before?"

"Never. I came in last night."

The man on the wall said, "Tck-tck."

Both men looked up. A third old fellow was descending the path. When I got the chance, I read the name O'Toole on the moving lips of the scribbler in the dust.

The man who had been duped faced the third of the old trio. It was his turn to assume the role of know-all. The routine began with the duped man taking the lead.

"You see him?" Etcetera. The now newcomer peered into my face, drew close and challenged me to read his name. "O'Toole," I answered. "That bate the blast," was the meed of praise accorded me.

Two duped in a little drama. The pub door opened. A youngish man came out. He began briskly to brush the pebbles from the flagstone before the door. The pair who had fallen for the bait called out to the man of the pub. They spoke almost at the same time telling him of my extraordinary powers of clairvoyance. Barman came closer. He examined me. "He was never here before," he said. "Tell my name," Barman said, somewhat truculently.

Three men faced me now. This was the supreme test. If I won this I would go down in legend as the champion Mind Reader of the Western World. The snag was that the line of sight to my prime prompter was cut off – then suddenly like a shaft of sunlight I got through to him for one fleeting moment. Behind the backs of the others his lips were working furiously. The slimmest of slim clues came through. I was certain I had the first syllable of the Barman's name.

I furrowed my brow. "This business is heavy on the mind," I said. "Give me a moment." Again I looked deep into the barman's eyes. "Let me see. It begins with a 'Co' . . . it's either Corscadden, Corcoran or Colcannon."

"Colcannon it is!" the three said with one breath. All three drew a communal breath of amazement.

At this point Old Rogue o' Bones seated on the wall, who had initiated this little drama, got up, grasped his walking stick, hawked his throat, spat on the dust at his feet, and said scornfully, "I couldn't listen to any more of this nonsense."

The remaining three glared after him as he stalked away. "Take no notice of him, Mr MacMahon," one said. "He's an ignorant man."

I have used the word drama deliberately, for that was exactly what it was. The three constituents for the formation of a very simple play were present. The constituents were The Playwright, The People and the Producer. It brought me back with a bang to the Stone Age – that is if Frank O'Connor is to be believed. Drama/art as he mentioned in his book on the short story, *The Lonely Voice,* had its beginning as follows. I paraphrase and condense.

A group of Stone Age men squat on stones around an evening fire.

They have now finished their meal having hunted all day. All are dressed in crude fleeces. One of those present is a playboy: he makes an excuse and goes out into the darkness indicating with a gesture that he is off to answer a call of nature. On his return he seems agitated. Looking back fearfully into the night, he tells a story to amuse his companions. "Out there in the darkness," he says, "I met a lion. He spread his jaws to eat me. I thrust my hand down his throat, caught him by the tail and turned him inside out. You'd laugh if you saw him trying to run away." As he speaks he mimes the incident. His laughing audience are aware that he is lying but they suspend their disbelief. This playboy was the first playwright or storyteller.

I now make a leap of narration that requires adjustment on the part of the observer. I refer to a book by Arthur Koestler called *The Act of Creation*. This is a book which influenced me greatly on the theory of writing. In it is a parallel theory that bears an affinity to the stone age incident and somewhat more remotely to my Rogue-o'-Bones incident on the western isle. Koestler develops the genesis of art as follows:

It begins with the belly laugh occasioned by an antic answer or pose of a Jester. After the laughter has died away the Sage enters the scene: he begins to analyse the laughter, muses on its therapeutic possibilities or recreational content, and identifies resonances hitherto unrecognised. He voices his thoughts. Enter the Artist, who, building on the foundation already laid by Jester and Sage, refines the prime incident, enshrines it in words (or on canvas), perpetuates and adorns it in an orderly fashion so that it becomes a codal resource by which the original glee, profit or sensitivity can be drawn upon and reproduced in varied conditions of time and place.

I have personally reduced the process to my own culinary terms of reference, a Jester's wine becoming vinegar in the mind of the Sage and eventually by the addition of other ingredients becoming some kind of celebratory confection like trifle, complex salad or wedding cake in the mind of the Artist-Confectioner.

I may be accused of special pleading in widening the theories put forward by Koestler in the title already mentioned and also in a less translucent book named *Janus*. But of the basic validity of the interpretation I stand convinced: whenever a resounding belly-laugh is heard, I try to move from the guffaw to the thoughtful smile of recognition on the part of my wiser or more thoughtful self and thence, if I'm lucky, to the abiding sensitivity that lies at the heart or nerve ends of the writer.

Wine? Did I mention wine? Also bread or cake. Is it by mere chance on my part that I realise that the greatest story writer of all founded his most sacred mystery on these central items of food and drink?

We had a genuine playwright in our area in the old days. His name was George Fitzmaurice. He was a parson's son from Duagh, a village about five miles from Listowel. HIs mother was a Catholic. We thought very highly of him but he seemed to have been side-tracked by the powers-that-were in the critical circles of his hour. All sorts of stories were told about him – especially those concerning his being downgraded by the critics of the metropolis!

George Fitzmaurice's dialogue is an extraordinary mixture of languages. The North Kerry dialect of English is its dominant feature but there are intrusions of all sorts, many of these derived from the phonetic use of words from the Irish. For example, "Cullagriffeen" is used for "pins and needles" but there is a host of other transpositions. There also occur variants and intrusions from Cockney slang, French and Latin, added to which a music hall atmosphere prevails to form, in sum, a mish-mash of what appears to be gibberish, but for those of us who understand the dialect the total makes sense in its holistic impact.

I give an example from *The King of the Barna Men* first produced at the Abbey Theatre as late as September 1965.

"Here speaks Aeneas Canty self-styled factotum-in-chief to Conacher the High King. A murmuring I hear and a gaping I espy, and I do hear it and I do espy it. But let not the surprise be taking away the seven senses, petrifying the perceptions or coagulating the mentality or bamboozling the conceptions, for marvels will happen and marvels will be, though a golden crown will be the victor see. And we continue; brooks run and rivers too; grass grows and so do trees, 'chip' from the cricket and buzz from the bee. (Loudly, waving his hand.) Silence! Aeneas has said it and 'tis said: folde rol, folde rol folde drum, folde dee folde dido."

His genius was expendable. All that was needed to raise him to acknowledged greatness was a word of welcome and the services of an understanding play doctor. With his extraordinary concoction of communication is it too much to say that he could have enriched in some small manner the entire tone and resource of the English language?

The story mentioned most often about George was that certain dramatists, or their cronies, grew jealous of the fine critical reception of Fitzmaurice's work in London. This occurred early this century on the notable occasion of an official programme of Irish plays being presented in the British capital. "Only for the begrudgers" our plaint ran, "George Fitzmaurice would have out-sung Synge." Later, possibly as a result of feeling deeply hurt by a review (he was before his time), George as the local saying goes "went into himself" and became a recluse of sorts.

I first heard of him in circumstances, and in language, worthy of the occasion. I had been chatting with "Clara" Leahy, an old rabbit-trapping friend of mine who played handball with me until he was well into his seventies.

"I was ferreting in Kilcara, Duagh," Clara told me, "and the bloody ferret lid up deep in a burrow. Couldn't get him to come out – he probably had killed a rabbit, ate it and gone to sleep. I bent down, put my ear to the mouth of the hole and heard the most marvellous chanting comin' up from under the ground. It was telling of kings and queens, magic glasses and pookas, quack doctors and omadhauns. 'What in the name of God is this?' I asked myself.

"I ruz my head and peeped through a hole in the hedge. Who was there but Parson Fitzmaurice's son, marchin' up and down the field manufacturin' his dramas."

Many people think ecumenism is a modern development in church matters. Not so.

George's father, Parson Fitzmaurice, drove to Listowel each Sunday to conduct service in St John's Protestant church, now a Little Theatre and Heritage Centre in mid-square. His Catholic wife accompanied him on the gig or back-to-back. As also did their son, then young George. Reaching The Square, the wife alighted and moved off to attend Mass in St Mary's Catholic church which was a mere 100 yards away. Father and son moved into St John's.

I have heard a tale, derived from local folklore, that an ancestor of the parson's had been evicted from Bedford House, a stone cut building which lay a few miles north of Listowel: one local rumour also had it that after Sabbath service the parson often drove his gig north and stopped for a few minutes outside the embrasure of the old home so as to keep the Fitzmaurice claim alive. If this were so, it was most unusual for a Protestant to lose his home in this fashion.

The Anglo-Norman Fitzmaurices counted for a great deal in Kerry; the family tree is littered with Earldoms, Lordships, Viscounts and Barons. The ancient seat of the family was the Old Court in Lixnaw. Within a further hundred yards of the church where George worshipped, stood the ruins of Listowel Castle, also a Fitzmaurice/Lord Kerry seat; it was taken in 1600 by the English under Sir Charles Wilmot. He undermined the castle and, on the surrender, hanged eighteen of the defenders in what is now the Square.

Because of his dual religious parentage I always saw George Fitzmaurice as a man standing on a fence with a broad field on either side of him – the Catholic experience of the ordinary people was one, and the Protestant experience the other. Polarities both, their reconciliation in the form of his plays was objective and amazing. George knew every nuance of the English dialect spoken around his childhood home – this also indicated polarities, for Duagh parish had patches of Gaelic speakers up to the turn of this century. I still experience great difficulty explaining the meaning of certain phrases to American scholars researching the Fitzmaurice plays. I almost gave up trying to make clear the subtleties of the expression "by the way" and the adjective "fine".

By the time I was grown up I had never met George: I did indeed once hold a surreal conversation with him through the bedroom window of his house in Kilcara, Duagh. Though long resident in some part of Dublin, where he lived retired from the civil service, probably from the Land Commission, he occasionally paid a visit home. But if anyone mentioned plays in his presence he was off like a redshanks. I wrote to him once on behalf of the Listowel Drama Group asking him to give permission for a production of one of his plays in his native town, adding that we would host a ceremonial dinner to honour him on the occasion and make him a presentation. He never replied. I was anxious for our group to produce one of his plays – either *The Magic Glasses* or *The Piedish*. I secured my objective by dubious means.

I knew his publisher at Talbot Press. One day I remarked idly to Mr. Lyons that we would send him the fees for production of *The Magic Glasses*. This we did in advance. In due course, with our Drama Group production of this play, we won the All-Ireland One-Act Drama Competition in Athlone. Lennox Robinson had attended our production of the play in Scarriff, Co. Clare. We heard no murmur of protest from George. Then came my personal meeting with him which had all the elements of drama in it.

Visiting Dublin with my wife we invariably stayed at the Edenvale Hotel in Lower Harcourt Street. That's a historic area: Seamus O'Kelly who wrote that wonderful story *The Weaver's Grave* died in No. 6 – now Connradh na Gaeilge Headquarters – after having been beaten by Crown forces. Carson also lived in this area.

One evening in Dublin I opted to see a play, *I am a Camera* by Van Druten at the Gate Theatre while my wife said she was keen to see a film in the Grafton cinema. Most amicably we parted with an appointment to meet outside the cinema at ten-thirty pm. The play overshot my estimate of its time run and to my regret I had to leave before the beginning of the third act. In Grafton Street, I found I had half-an-hour to spare before the film ended. I entered a café and above all beverages I ordered a glass of Horlick's Malted Milk. As I reached for my hip pocket to pay the bill I realised that I had left a conscience debt unpaid.

Some years previously a countryman had tendered me a £5 note to be given to "George Fitzmaurice the playwright." It was money for meadowing due for a considerable time. I told the man that I found it difficult to meet George but he replied, "By giving it to you it's off my conscience and off the soul of my father who owed the money. You'll meet George some day." For years I had carried the old rumpled treasury note in an envelope in my wallet. In the café as I reached for payment, I took out the old envelope with George's name on it.

I suddenly had the feeling that George Fitzmaurice was near me. I looked around. Having paid my bill I went to the door. Grafton Street was thronged. "Where are you, George?" I asked the remote sky. Oblivious to my question crowds hurried past. Quite close to me moved an old bent figure in a stained trench coat. He looked like an elderly newsvendor. The man was almost doubled over with age. I went back into the cab and sat on a seat by the doorway waiting for the film to end. The hunch again assailed me. "Where are you, George?" my mind shouted. I walked out onto the street. That old newsvendor? Where was he? There was something about him. I threaded upstreet almost pushing people out of my way. Newsvendor? Newsvendor? Where are you? No trace of him. I turned into Chatham Street. At last I came on the old fellow. He was standing in the deep doorway of a building, his face turned inward to the closed door. There he was, more bent over than before. Statuesque. He did not turn as I came behind him. In the direction of his ear, I whispered, "Excuse me. Would you be George Fitzmaurice?"

After a long pause, the old head swivelled, and a barely audible voice croaked up at me, "I am."

"We're very proud of you in Kerry," I ventured.

"Why so?"

"Because of Jaymony Shanaham in the Loft. And Morgan Quille the quack doctor. And Leam O'Donoghue with his pie-dish. And Aeneas Canty . . . "

The bent body did not swivel. But his face was still upturned to mine.

"That's something anyway," he said. There was a hint of deep emotion in his voice.

I told him of the conscience money, at the same time explaining the circumstances of the debt which, by my estimation, was then fifty years overdue. Handing him the money and hastily scribbling a receipt, I asked him to sign for it.

"Well, well!" he said, as he signed in the dark. "Aren't there honest people in the world, after all?"

Suddenly he seemed to be in a time warp. He asked about people in our town who were long since dead. He asked me if the railroad had been continued from Newcastlewest to Listowel. This was a last century happening. He then asked me my name. When I told him: "Why didn't you say that before?" he said in a pettish tone. "I've read about you."

"I'll leave you now," I said when we were back in Grafton Street.

"You'll leave me now?"

"You're a man who likes to be independent," I said. "That doesn't count with you," he said. "Walk with me to Harcourt Street." As I did so, I said as if it didn't matter, "We did your *Magic Glasses* with our drama group in Listowel. And won the All-Ireland One-Act Competition with it." "Did ye now?" he said mildly. "Mr. Lyons of Talbot Press has your royalties safe and sound," I added. He made no fuss. As we parted and the light came on in the first storey front room I realised that he lived in the house next door to my hotel. All these years I had been seeking him, a foot of brickwork had divided my room from his.

Sometime later I attended the opening night of an Abbey play of mine at the Queen's Theatre, Dublin.

As I was leaving the Edenvale Hotel by car, I glanced up at the window of the house next door. At that very moment, who should I see moving up the steps and pushing in the front door of the building but the bould George himself.

I gave him time to settle in his room above. I went quickly up the old staircase and knocked once, twice, on his door. He came out, a milk jug in hand. He said something like, "Put it into that" – possibly a reversion to his boyhood days in Duagh when he took a jug to the cross-roads to be filled with "loose" milk.

I mentioned my name. He admitted me and asked me to sit down in his untidy room. I recall a heap of books in the corner. He was just settling down for a long chat when I broke in upon him.

"George," I said, "a play of mine is opening at the Abbey, playing at the Queen's, in just twenty-five minutes. I have a car at the door and am about to leave. Why don't you sit in just as you are and come with us? If you please, I have a box in the theatre and no one will see you. But if you do wish to be known, you'll create a sensation, whatever about me or my play."

"The Abbey Theatre," he mused aloud, his wise old eyes upon me. "They can't do plays at all down there."

I had to leave him be. I had mixed thoughts as I left him.

One final word on a kindred spirit of this forgotten dramatist.

Francis Carlin – does anyone now recall that name? No one except perhaps my dear and omniscient friend, Ben Kiely. Carlin too during his later lifetime seemed a forgotten poet. Not completely forgotten because at the end of his days an inquisitive reporter found him in an Old Man's Home in New York City. He was winkled out to receive honours at a great dinner organised by the American Irish Community.

I feel sure that at that dinner someone stood up and recited Carlin's "Ballad of Douglas Bridge" which commemmorates a man who rode with the outlawed and dispossessed Redmond O'Hanlon. The final lines continue to haunt me.

On Douglas Bridge we parted, but
The Gap o' Dreams is never shut
To one whose saddled soul tonight
Rides out with Count O'Hanlon.

There were only a few people at the burial service of George Fitzmaurice. He had written to a cousin expressing a wish to return to Listowel. He mentioned my name and that of John B Keane. But it wasn't to be. My name appears on the list of the handful present at his burial – but it was really my son who, at my request, represented me. His cousin Minnie Mulcaire of Ballybunion brought me back his well-smoked pipe as a souvenir.

When some of the one-act plays were later revived at the Peacock Theatre in Dublin they sent for some of our members in Listowel Drama Group to play parts. John O'Flaherty and Bill Kearney, both now dead, did so with great distinction. Another Listowel actor, the late Eamon Keane, also interpreted the pieces in masterly style. Recently we celebrated the 50th anniversary of the founding of our local group. My youngest son, Owen, was the producer of Brian Friel's beautiful and splendid play *Dancing at Lughnasa.* The little theatre (once the Church of Ireland where Fitzmaurice worshipped) was crowded night after night. We were reaping a harvest of which the seeds were sown by George Fitzmaurice.

I have written plays. As I'm in a confessional mood, I'll mention some of my divergent attitudes to the stage. In a word or two, I'm not enamoured of it. And why not, you may say, if your work was on the Abbey stage on four separate occasions?

My distaste? I believe the rejection or ignoring of brilliant work by

Fitzmaurice (we Kerry people understand it in our nerves, blood and bones) set my younger self aflame with indignation. Also, the first person I met on entering the Abbey Theatre after the rehearsal of my first Abbey play *The Bugle in the Blood* was the late Earnán de Blaghd. His handshake was as cold as if he had proffered me a frozen mackerel. For me his vibrations were as wrong as Moll Bell – whoever Moll Bell was.

I tend to write at certain people – at single persons at times: the players of the Abbey were splendid, as indeed the women artistic directors: Ria Mooney, Lelia Doolan and latterly, Garry Hynes, were people I could talk to straight from the shoulder. Beyond that I am not prepared to go. Speaking in the most general terms, and of wider issues, I found in my experience of the metropolitan milieu that the number of mediocre people in high places was for me a recurrent cause of perplexity and irritation. And again, speaking in general and on many public activities, I abhor intrigue. And finally, very little is achieved by committee supervising committee. Success, as I see it, is dependent on one brave artistic spirit. Otherwise it is a case of forming a commission to design a horse. The result is a dromedary – the camel with the two humps. And in my few forays into the artistic world, I realise that if there is the art of politics, there is also the politics of art.

Shall I mention something that quite recently caused me much satisfaction: it was the unusual Abbey production of my play *The Honey Spike* by a distinguished international producer, Francesca Zambello of New York. I'd prefer her uncompromising treatment to a pretty-pretty showing forth, for Zambello mercilessly and uncompromisingly probed the core resources of the play.

Above all, *The Spike* drew a thousand travellers, itinerants or tinkers, whichever name you wish to call them, who flew in in droves from the edges of the great cities of Britain, to plant their bottoms on the sacred seats of the Abbey Theatre. Aye, and to see some of their own folk take part in a production in the Theatre of the Nation. That caused me immense satisfaction and kept me chuckling for some time. It provided me with the polarity to the clammy handshake of Earnán, to whom, however belatedly, credit must be given for his tenacity in the building of the New Abbey. And undoubtedly he possessed a pawky sense of humour as witness his description in his autobiography *Treasna na*

Bóinne of curiosity driving him – a man from the deepest Orange North – into asking a Catholic friend to take him to see the service of Benediction in the Dublin Pro-Cathedral. And of his falling head over heels across the body of his guide who unexpectedly went down on both knees to genuflect to the exposed Host. I found him otherwise than humorous.

Conscious that, although I wrote further plays (and still pen 'em), and that I was welcomed by the amateur movement, I still harbour the resentment, childish though it may seem, that I could perhaps have written a play a year if I had taken the major professional route. But then, I have to ask myself if I could have lived with myself in a type of servility, as betokened by the bould Earnán shouting at players and producers in rehearsal as he passed through the stalls. Was every one afeard of him?

The professional theatre puzzles me with its element of superficiality and gloss. I recall productions of my plays by amateur country and country town groups which, though lacking stage appointments, transferred the heart of my plays to appreciative audiences. Carrick-on-Suir, Navan, Carrigallen, Abbeydorney and Birr are cases I have in mind. And it is people like Ted O'Riordan of north Cork, and the late Brendan O'Brien of Athlone, who really kept drama alive in Ireland.

But I place on record that I found little problem in the writing of plays, and my passion for observing people and the ancillary passion of being able to interpret the motives for their actions, could have stood me in good stead. But then, what would I do with the memory of a dead fish in my paw?

What I know about the technicalities of a play as produced could fit into an eggcup – the rest is intuition. Challenged to place my meagre knowledge on the table, confused as it may be, I set down the following;

Above all, the playwright is at the mercy of his interpreters, particularly the producer who should be a creator in his own right. The initial moments of a play should be taken very slowly – this is exposition! It should be recalled that now the audience is rapt with the novelty of the opening scenes and is taking in the layout of the stage, and its odds and ends of properties – verbal and otherwise. The arc of the play's progress has been whimsically summed up as follows; Act

One – There is no God; Act Two – There may be a God; Act Three – There is a God. This formula can be filled in *ad infinitum.*

God help the playwright who sets out to be cerebral. I did it once in a play called *The Golden Folk* which my own drama group first produced and later, when Abbey-produced, was called *The Song of the Anvil.* I shall never forget the agony that particular play occasioned me. It lacked some chemical, as I later found out to my cost, when reading a book called *Act One* by Harte. This omission could have been rectified in rehearsals, perhaps by the introduction of a few lines of broad comedy, this is often the practice with upstate productions in New York. I must admit that, even to me, it still reads well. I've decided to cut my losses with regard to this my histrionic plea for the enthronement of the imagination, and to seek my goal in other ways.

In an audience, it must never be forgotten that the intelligence quotient falls. Those present as a unit become a human amalgam and that amalgam seems to possess an adolescent or pre-adolescent mentality. As a whole the audience seems to be about fourteen years of age. (The plays of Shaw I've seen seem to negate this theory.) The biggest laugh I've ever heard in the theatre was in a little sketch of mine which introduced the phrase "an elephant of a bird flew in the winda'". This intelligence quotient is still more markedly ponderous on the occasion of pageantry as I have proved before audiences of eighty thousand in Croke Park and elsewhere. I am sure that this theory has some parallel veracity in the matter of the readership of a newspaper, conditioned as its readers are to react in a particular manner by long-time editorial manipulation. Ah, pity poor me, forever doomed to be a loner ("an intelligent minority of one") with no national newspaper to represent his possibly archaic views. I sometimes sigh for the vanished independent periodicals of my younger manhood which laid the foundations of our truncated state. Does anyone now recall the name of Séamus Upton? Or that of Dublinensis in the quite revolutionary *Catholic Bulletin* of Gills Publishers? None? Good begor!

The soldier's word, swearing and other expletives, are effective on the stage only if sparingly used. These words are intrinsically interesting and tend to call a halt to the thrust of the play: overuse spoils their theatrical effect. I have used the prime four-letter word once only and on that occasion it proved very effective. The most famous stage usage of a word, then reckoned outré on a stage presentation, was the phrase, "Not bloody likely". At that time it hit the audience like a bomb. The word "bloody" (By Our Lady), its former image and superscription now deleted by overusage, hardly occasions a yawn when used nowadays. On the communicative level – the most commonly used four-letter word is intrinsically interesting: from my training as a teacher I know that two oranges and two oranges make four oranges but two juicy oranges and two juicy oranges add up to water in the teeth.

With complete irrelevance I mention the fact that if the beam of say, a blue spotlight, is criss-crossed with that of a red spotlight, each colour is retained by its own beam after the passage.

From Michael Farrell – he wrote one beautiful book, *Thy Tears Might Cease* – I learned that an actress on stage ironing clothes can express a whole range of emotions simply by the way she moves the iron – angrily, pensively, humorously and so forth – and this without uttering a syllable. I forget where I learned, or intuitively understand that there are scores of ways in which, for example, the words "Women! Women! Women!" can be uttered to ring the changes on emotion and produce audience effect. Allocating various notes of the diatonic scale to the word repeated is a rewarding and illuminating exercise. A further variance is indicated if the speaker is a man or a woman.

From producer Ria Mooney, I learned that the actor on stage should transfer a series of pictorial images into the mind of each member of the audience. She illustrated this by making a rectangle formed with two fingers from each hand to frame the image – as it were: she then moved the framework suddenly forward as if slinging an image into the audience mind. The actor, watching its passage, should learn by experience when to intervene at the critical point of the fading laughter with the formation and the outcasting of a new picture. Accurate timing is necessary for this. The actor, about to speak, should by some almost imperceptible movement of his eyes, or even by a gesture in miniature, take, or appear to take, the attention centre of the stage.

As already said, the first five minutes of a play is exposition time and needs absolute clarity of expression to present the scene, to portray characters and, by implication, offer the subtlest hints as regards plot. This is also true of a lecture or classwork by a teacher. I stand convinced that readers of detective stories, bamboozled by premature action, haven't a clue about 50% of what happens subsequently. Dorothy Sayers I have always found opaque.

The ancient Celtic craftsmen had an occupational disease called *horror vacui* – horror of leaving a vacant spot. This led them to decorate even the bases of sacred vessels with ornamentation. A mistake? Debatable. But in the writing of a play the playwright should aim for a tight text and, most importantly, leave room for the actor to express his personal creativity in delineating a character. I once made the mistake of over-writing in this context and have no appetite to repeat my mistake.

As opposed to many of my theories already mentioned, a man of the amateur stage for whose opinions I have great respect, tells me that nowadays, due to the impact of television, audiences are far better equipped to pick up clues than were audiences of say forty years ago. This seems to rock my adolescent theory of the childish audience mentality but I still remain to be wholly convinced of this development.

Finally, each phrase or sentence or verbal image in a well-seasoned play (read Synge's introduction to *The Playboy of the Western World*), apart from being as he indicates, should do one, two or all of three things; it should promote the plot, shed light on character or raise a laugh.

I am fully aware that I have become overly didactic – something I wish to avoid. Let me step aside to lighten the proceedings somewhat.

I have also written several pageants (the practice had fallen into disuse and was reckoned obsolescent, so I was tempted to revive it) for major mainly historical occasions – commemoration of the 50th Anniversary of the 1916 Rising is a case in point. Again it intrigued me that, if one knew how, the suspension of disbelief could be achieved and maintained even for quite extended periods and with huge crowds. Pondering this matter led me into all kinds of contemplation, especially as regards the exercise of hypnosis of a mild type by a writer. In this context I call to mind my mishap in the Rocky Mountains where I almost lost my life. (I fell of the highway into a snowdrift!)

At a convention of representatives of the American Teachers of

English, where I was the keynote speaker, several writers were secretly observed by psychiatrists who watched us as we spoke on far out topics, one of which was Hypnosis and the Writer's World. How can the writer, on the written page, exercise a hypnotic or semi-hypnotic control over his readers?

After I had spoken, one of those "observers" called me aside and, to my astonishment, told me that I was the raw material of a hypnotist. Yes, he could teach me with very little trouble – there was no mystery about it, he declared. I was tempted but did not fall. The memory of seeing a subject of Paul Goldin's hypnosis, a most respectable citizen indeed, kneeling at midnight in front of a local shop and calling on his leprechaun to emerge, bade me to look before I leaped.

Still discussing the pageant and mild hypnosis, my experience has shown me at first hand how properties and atmosphere can exercise a profound effect on an audience, especially on one drawn from the United States.

The place is Knappogue Castle at night. Outside there are stars in a clear sky; there is even a crescent moon. Americans pronounce the word "castle" in a tone of voice that indicates mystery and reverence. Within the castle are medieval costume, old world tables, even bibs for the diners together with candlelight and harp music. The stone walls, hung with tapestry and flags, compound the sense of timelessness. I sense the breaking down of barriers people have taken a lifetime to erect. Mead and claret come into their own. As my post-prandial pageant of Irish history begins, I watch row after row of people in trance. The pseudo-omniscient may sneer, but it works.

I recall a humorous incident in this connection.

The audience consisted of my friends from the State of Iowa where I had built up a following consequent on my teaching at the State University and my radio programme on WSUI. On their annual visit to Ireland, the Iowans always persuaded me to be with them. Invariably I spoke to the audience from the dais when the meal had ended. It was a nostalgic occasion where I mentioned the small towns and the friends I had made in that State. On one occasion there were two elderly couples present, both American, but not of our group. I could sense their glowering up at me as like Kerry, Iowa is the butt of many jokes. Later, out in the cobbled courtyard under torchlight, as I was taking leave of my friends, a loud voice broke in on our farewells. "Do you think there's any place in the US except goddamn Iowa?". It came from a man, one of the four who had glowered. It was a moment of tension for all of us. "I do," I said, then rashly added, "I know every part of the US (Billy Liar was taking a huge chance but it had worked in Germany and on Granuaile's island). So name your city and I'll praise it!" "How about a fine city in Indiana called Hobart?" the man countered.

I caught my breath. I had been there three weeks before. Now for some of my island-recalled magic. I closed my eyes, held up my hands, spread my fingers and chanted, "Close your eyes. Walk down the main drag of your city in your mind and I'll read your thoughts."

Curiously enough he did so. The onlookers waited. The torchlight flickered on my face. "You're on Grand Boulevard," I chanted. "You now stop before a large building. It's a hospital."

"Jeez! Uncanny!"

I tightened my eyes in mock patience. "St Brigid's Hospital. Two young nurses coming down the steps. Your name is Florence? . . . Yes! Half Irish and half Croatian. I see."

"Incredible. Go on!"

I opened my eyes. Looked at him as if in pain. "You've broken the thread. I can't go on now."

"Know who I am?"

"If you had allowed me to continue . . . "

"I'm the resident medical superintendent of that hospital. The girl with Florence is my daughter."

I gestured weariness. Said fond farewell to my friends.

(When he went back to Hobart he discovered the truth. Some day I'll get caught out at that game and be shown up for the chancer I am.)

The Honey Spike, possibly my best known play, and one which leads a separate existence as a novel, sprang from a single seminal sentence. A word of background explanation is needed since the "Our Father" is recited in travellers' gammon in the play.

At one period of my life I had close association with the travelling people. I learned what was left of their language from Arthur McDonagh whose ancestors were a prime source of linguistic lore for

McAllister, whose *Secret Languages of Ireland* was, at its time, the standard work on the subject. It may come as a surprise to many people to learn that these "cants" or "slang" or "argots" existed at all but they certainly did. Apart from Shelta, the tinkers' argot is derived mainly from backgammon Gaelic: other sub-tongues were "Béarlagar na Saor", the secret language of the stone masons, and "Bog Latin", possibly once a depraved form of Latin deriving from dispossessed monks on the Irish roads (the word 'panis' for bread is also common in Shelta but not used as frequently as 'durra'). I found traces of two other gammons, the broad gammon and the narrow. Which of these was the cant of the circus folk *(niente parlari)* and derives from Italian and vaguer sources is debatable but various books on different kinds of English thieves' gammon exist. The name Eric Partridge occurs to me in this context.

Back to basics and the seminal incident which engendered my play. Walking along the road outside my town, three tinker carts caught up with me, all moving south. The leading cart stopped: in it was the grandfather of the tribe, who greeted me. I had often held his children's allowance book and, in minor respects, acted as his banker. "Where are you off to?" I asked. "Ach," he said, "we were up north and this one (indicating his granddaughter, a girl obviously heavily pregnant) made us travel day and night to get to what she calls a lucky spike to have her *gahaire*. No place else would do her. She's on her time so we have to hurry." "Drive on so," I said as I waved my good-bye.

It flashed across my mind. Mating, birth, death and a race against time. Out of this little incident came *The Honey Spike*.

Cry hold! Enough! Turn up the lights! Let me out of the dark claustrophobic and stale atmosphere of the theatre (cleansed by Jeyes Fluid as they used to brag on the old programmes of The Abbey) to enjoy the open air, to experience again the smell of mown meadows or the salty brine of the ocean, or at best the swung thurible of the woodbine. In some unconfined surroundings I may find again a story or an open air presentation such as I have described at the start of this episode.

CHAPTER ELEVEN

But I wouldn't have anyone entertain the impression that writing is all moonlight and roses or, for that matter, all sunlight and sunflowers.

It is an exacting and exhausting trade which can engage the utmost intensity of mind and body. There are times, especially as the writer approaches the end of a sustained piece of fiction, when to him or her, so total is absorption that the unreal is more real than the real.

At such moments the writer has the sensation of walking on a crumbling cliff edge or of rolling a wheelbarrow on a taut steel wire above the outfall of Niagara. His mental stability can even be in question as he gropes for the requisite brake power to enable him to slow down. For him each night can truly be a nightmare; he sometimes suffers from the delusion that all his outer skin has been pincered off to leave his body red and raw: as often as not he has a dull headache as if he has been struck on the poll by a mallet. It is by a supreme effort he goes out of doors to face the world of reality.

In such moods, when he shows his face in public, there is too fine a point on his sensitivity; he imagines he has been insulted where no insult is intended. He apologises, in retrospect, when he thinks he has offended friends, only to discover that no offence whatsoever has been taken. He is liable to utter the most out-of-context comments which haunt him later: these comments often come from imaginary characters who populate his brain. He sometimes conjures up a hostile world leagued in intrigue against him: he can even experience a trembling of his limbs which he cannot control. At such times he is truly vulnerable.

To use a metaphor drawn from electricity – he simply is not plugged in to the world of matter that surrounds him. Or again, it may be that he is broadcasting on a wave-length that exists for no one but himself.

But also, at such times, so acutely heightened is the awareness of his senses, that he seems endowed with the gift of prophecy: he then enters into something of a clairvoyant state. He can experience, in advance, vibrations both friendly and hostile. In essence he is an explorer or adventurer, a surrogate victim who enters the caves, mazes and labyrinths at the extremities of living, places where others dare not venture. By so doing, and by artistically conveying his later impressions to others, he enables less adventurous folk to experience the trials, tribulations and horrors of such experiences. But like the explorer, he also can return with beautiful botanical specimens of human love, valour and dedication.

Either way, he enriches the reader by leading him to rehearse odd roles he might be forced to adopt in the reality of living. He comforts the reader by telling the lonely one that he is not alone in his moments of despair or elation. This, of course, is special pleading for the artist or writer in the role of test pilot, or as it were, a guinea pig of sorts testing the untried drugs of living and who all too often becomes the victim of his own foolhardiness.

In a long life of reading, perhaps the best apologia for the somewhat inner bizarre life of a writer I have found, is taken from a book I have read and re-read over the years. Its name is *Two Flamboyant Fathers* by Nicolette (Macnamara) Devas.

Ennistymon is a town I like very much to visit, especially on a fair or market day when the houses, with their traditional shopfronts, and the road edge itself with its old time "standings", are crowded. There I was likely to meet old friends like Micho Russell of Doolin, that great traditional musician with a reputation known far and wide in Europe. Alas, my friend Micho died in a car accident in March 1994.

If one goes into an archway off the Main Street in Ennistymon to watch the river in spate, one sees a different facet of this country town. Above the river and beside the falls stands the Falls Hotel, once the residence of Francis Macnamara, a man of the landlord class. He was a most unusual character to say the least of it. The book I have mentioned was written by Nicolette, one of his daughters. Francis had other daughters too: all these girls lived life to the bohemian full. The story of the Macnamaras, their literary and artistic friends, illustrates the important role played by such families in testing unprobed patterns of human behaviour. Important also is their reporting back to prosaic mortals to tell how they fared under the most unusual conditions.

Caitlín, one of the Macnamara girls, married Dylan Thomas which event multiplied and intensified the bohemian impact of their lives.

I focus on Nicolette, who married artist Frank Devas. Deserted by her natural father, Francis ("Fireball" was the nickname applied to members of the Macnamara clan whom I number among my antecedents), she adopted the artist Augustus John as a father figure. Nicolette has much to say on the effect of writing on the writer.

She most accurately describes the approach to writing of each fresh morning, the blind gradually descending on the window of the mind after two or three hours of work – this to be followed by the "physical trembling and the feeling that someone has gripped her head and shaken it violently". She stops – by now she is "an empty jug." She goes on to describe the various therapies by which the body is enabled to recover from the agitation and turmoil of brain and emotion. "A yawning inner vacuum" is experienced, the empty jug has to be refilled if normalcy is to be restored. How is this to be achieved? By various types of physical work? By a compelling distraction? Or indeed otherwise . . .

"Otherwise" for some, is a blanket word involving the traditional remedies of the artist: wild parties, alcohol and sex. All designed to achieve replenishment and the filling of the empty jug. Rather patronisingly, the author refers to those outside the sacred circle of art as "the yokel type"; these she implies are more likely to succumb to sudden severe shock than artists, who, having already vicariously experienced stress on a daily basis, are enabled to cope with unexpected shock and violence. I offer the theory for what it is worth – no more no less. At its core it is a plea for some kind of understanding of the wear and tear in the artist's life.

But whatever way he approaches the problem of recovery, each scribbler – if he is lucky – has his own idiosyncratic way of crawling "home" and regaining some semblance of balance and poise. I once did a tour of Germany in the company of my then translator – an eminent novelist and travel writer who made the whole world his subject. Though not a Catholic he unwound in this fashion. He might drive for thirty or forty miles without saying a word or indicating our destination. Arrived at a monastery, he'd enter the quiet chapel: I would follow and smell the, to me, familiar tang of incense in the air. My friend would sit in a pew and, as I saw it, deliberately relax. Some pews to the rear I would do the same. No sound then except the rustle of a monk's habit, and once the faint rattle of a rosary bead. We would remain there for about an hour. Peace did come dropping slow.

For the writer, a hostile review has the power to wound him grievously; he is quite capable of forgetting a review that is 99% praise and concentrating on one or two items of which the reviewer has disapproved, which indeed is the reviewer's right – if he is competent. "The bloody literary editor gave it to that fella purposely, knowing that he'd savage me," is a common reaction on the part of writers I have known. But back to the healing process as I experience it, which for me could be a full day spent in the ruined abbey of Corcomroe in the Burren, or more generally through conversation with a friend as we walk the streets of our town.

Tom is returned from voyaging the seven seas of the globe. For me he bears a cargo of reminiscences and stories; I am a stevedore more than willing to help him unload. He arrived home just as I was recovering from the death of a dear friend called Ned. Ned was Ireland-wise. Of Tom, it may be said that he is world-wise. As a radio operator on various ships large and small, rusty tramps, enormous tankers, elegant yachts and almost every other conceivable type of floating vessel, Tom was there, dressed in the uniform of universal "Sparks" and thus has tales to tell of almost every port in the world. And into the bargain, Tom, son of classical Professor Tim who taught the classics in our local college, is a scholar in his own right.

Spin the globe and place your finger on it at random and so stop its spinning. Tom has a tale to tell of where your finger rests. Fernando Po, the Piraeus, Archangel, Dubrovnik (Pearl of the Adriatic), Brindisi (a plaque there to Virgil), the Persian Gulf, boiling hot Abadan (124° F in the shade) – with Basra (arsehole of the world). New Orleans (Pat O'Brien's complex of pubs with students singing after a football game), Orinoco (a cargo of iron ore), the Balearic Islands (Phoenicians had slingshooters from these?), Nicaragua (the menacing clatter of the cantina parrots is proven prophetic when the room heaves and bucks in an earthquake), Los Angeles, another earthquake as a long tall brick wall does a Mexican wave before Tom's eyes, Odessa (dinner on St. Patrick's Day), Bombay (what was suspected to be smallpox turned out to be chickenpox), Bulawayo (having a drink in the Bowling Club), stories pour from the lips of world-wise Tom. For Tom too, is a Storyman.

Today it's chasing a "cooker". In Tahiti.

"What's a cooker?" I ask.

Tom laughs.

"A wild pig in the mountains. Two thousand feet up there, you're on a shelf a foot wide. You have a gun. You get advice 'If a pig comes jump to one side! They're savage beasts, then fire? (Jump to one side!)' Captain Cook brought pigs to the islands to supply the natives with protein instead of human flesh. French brandy is dirt cheap there too."

"Jump to one side." I echo the jocose life-saving advice.

Another day it's Cartagena in Columbia (Captain Morgan the pirate from the Caribbean, sacked a convent there. The nuns jumped over a cliff to avoid being raped.)

"Captain Morgan?" I comment, "that name rings a bell."

"Three kinds of rum: Captain Morgan, Three Daggers and Old Seadog. When first I went to sea I got my daily ration of rum."

Today Tom gives me a lecture on bananas. I learn that it was a priest who brought the banana (*musa sapientum*) to Central and South America. While still green, the "stems" are placed in ripening sheds and ripened overnight by gas. He then gives me a talk on plantain, yam and breadfruit. He goes on to mention locusts. One morning on the Red Sea, the deck of the ship was blackened with these – they crackled when anyone walked on their bodies. The ship's cat turned them over and ate and ate until her body got as tight as a small football. She died then.

But Tom's best card has yet to be played. Leaving aside his

comments on Aztec and Maya civilisations – he has visited the sites in South America – he comes to a didactic peak when he tells stories of ancient Greece. Torrents of classical Greek fall from his lips, he paints a picture for me of his sitting in the gathering dusk beneath the age-eaten caryatids of the Acropolis in Athens; he then tracks the steps of a man whom he calls War Correspondent Xenophon. Later Tom is off to the Gulf to tell the story of Darius, that noble satrap of Persia. The Gulf he knows as well as he knows his native Coolard where his Kerry blue terrier is still housed. As I blunder in his conversational and classical wake, the pair of us establishing a classical cocoon in a busy town as we go on trading Odes of Horace for Greek irregular verbs, with occasional shouts of *"Non omnis moriar!"* – (I shall not altogether die) – or crooning pop songs of seventy years ago which I then translated into pidgin Greek, I modestly claim one small victory. This I do by singing for Tom the local traditional ballad written over a hundred years ago by a blind poet: its subject is the beauty of Tom's grandmother; this ballad I have already referred to but, in the sense that I chant it for a grandson of the dead beauty, it now has a new dimension in my mind.

Adown beside the gentle Gale
Should you at leisure roam
Below you in that smiling vale
You'll view her lovely home.
And if you there should chance to stray
Your heart be sure to guard
Against the charms of Gentle Kate
The Maid of Sweet Collard.

That's a song that would silence a pub if it was sung by the right man and with the right "nyaa".

Wednesday, and more so Thursday, are notable days in our small town. Those are mart or market days: on those occasions I meet all my country cronies and hear the news of the barony. Invariably we start with standard gambits of "Fierce weather." "Ach, there's no asking after it." "It rained the world last night." "What way are cattle?" "They're doin' fairly well." "The country is swimming." And then, the opening rubrics of conversation having been observed, we're off on other topics.

Mikie is a water-diviner, a self-taught historian and the tradition-bearer of our area. I meet him on Thursdays. We stand aside in the Small Square, perhaps under a shop canopy if it rains, and beside the little barrow of my friend the periwinkle seller. Mikie reads the numbers of the cars passing by. Any number between 1 and 1994 is of quizzical interest to him.

"There!" he shouts. "1315! What does that remind you of?"

"Give me a chance," I parry.

"No chance! 'Twas the Bruce invasion. Here comes another car – 1651," he shouts. "Ireton died," I say – "Where?" "In Limerick". "What of?" "It was called the plague but it could be anything." "What month?" "November". "What date of the month?" "I don't know." He then turns to the knot of passers-by, halted to watch the joust, and from behind the blade of his hand set to his lips, Mikie mutters, "He's not much good for dates." Recovering, he adds a footnote on Cromwell's sons, Robert, Oliver, Henry and Tumbledown Dick. Our audience applauds Mikie.

Sometimes Mikie wins: at other times I retrieve the honour of the pedagogue. "Knocking the schoolmaster off his perch" is my name for Mikie's practice.

The window cleaner casts his squeegee into his bucket and joins in the fray. He recites an old Tex Williams song called "Life gets tedious." A series of calamities befalls the subject of the song: in the end he gets dandruff. We applaud the singer's efforts. He came to me (he's an ex-pupil of mine) one day and said, "Tourists gettin' off the coaches pester me about the castle in The Square – tell me what I'll say." So I told him about Sir Charles Wilmot, Carew and Mountjoy. Beseiged in 1600 the castle was the last to surrender in the Elizabethan Wars. The hanging of the defenders followed. I tutored him well. Then I added, "If they express surprise at a window cleaner's knowledge of history say 'Ma'am (or Sir) you can't bate an articulate proletariat'". This he did later to great effect. He now insists that he made up all the spiel himself.

There's a characteristic of the country people which I note and like. They're addicted, like myself, to jingles. A good jingle, timely used, can amuse, confuse, abuse and, if necessary, enlighten the wisest of men. "Hey!" a man shouts at me from across the road:

I had a wife and she was a Quaker
She went to bed and the devil wouldn't wake her.

or it might be

Two things empty since the Lord knows when,
The pockets of a gambler and the gizzard of a hen.

I reply with:

The Temple of Fame is open wide
Its halls are always full
Many get through by the door marked PUSH
And the most by the door marked PULL.

Some jingles have an anti-war bias and echo that famous ballad "Johnny I Hardly Knew Ye."

Tommy my son, war isn't fun,
It's a terrible thing, once it's begun
For high and for low, war is much more
Than comin' and drummin' for glory my son.

or one which may well be of English origin;

You may go and get a bayonet
An' stick a feller through
Government ain't to answer for it
God'll send the bill to you.

Another old friend has returned from abroad to retire. He stops, strikes a mock heroic attitude, and declaims a quatrain which from pungent internal evidence dates back to the rebellion of 1798. It refers to the fact that, of the forces confronting the French at Castlebar, many were drawn from fencibles and yeomen raised in the Irish south west.

The Tarbert yeomen call for arms
And all they get are horn spoons
But when they hear the French have landed
They beshit their pantaloons.

As we argue I realise that history is omnipresent. The corner house across the road was built from the severance pay of an officer who fought under Nelson at Cape St Vincent. Of the room over my head, an old man informed me that his grandfather once saw Lieutenant Scanlon drinking tea with the girl called The Colleen Bawn whom he later had murdered. The tale generated a novel and an opera.

At this point a gentlemanly figure passing by pauses to render in the mock-heroic voice of his old schoolmaster:

Boy, you come of noble blood,
Though now of low degree
Where'er you go, may God the good
Smile on your destiny.
Where'er your future, dark or bright
Through life's bechequered span
Go with her armed, your soul defend
And prove yourself a man.

Hurray! Yehoo! Now we're thrashing!

We're by no means finished. This is mart day, man. Cattle prices are good. The jingles are in lighter vein and taken together form a rather demented anthology. Someone chants

The smell of paint would make me faint
So I'll never marry a painter-o.

and another chimes in with:

There's mate on the table
And more on the shelf
And there's no one to ate it
But the old Cock himself.

Or it may be:

Are you the man who drives the train
From Farranfore to Castlemaine?
Are you the man who killed my ducks
On the lonesome road to Dingle?

The time has come for me to make my contribution. I say, "There was an old poet who wrote in Irish about one hundred and fifty years ago called Jack Breanain. He came from the Ballymacandrew-Baltovin area around O'Dorney or Ardfert. A flea kept him awake all night. Here is his poem called 'An Dreancaide – The Flea.' First in Irish. Are ye all ready?"

"We are!"

Oilithreach gan eireaball do tháinig fém shúiste
Ag eitiligh le h-element le báidh liomsa
Sé mo mhearathal nár rugas ort fé mo dhorn dúnta
Chuirfinn deire led chuid eitiligh go Lá an Bhreithiúntais.

And then in my own translation I offer:

A tailless pilgrim made his way under my couch last night
Merrily leaping from dark till day in an ecstasy of delight
O, had my fist but grasped him, he'd wish that he never
was born,
And a flattened flea would seek his soul at the trump
of the Angel's horn.

Here comes my old friend, Sir Bob (self-styled) striding through the market day throng. Each market day I set him a subject for a mildly

Rabelaisian sonnet – this to be handed up or recited for me that day week. Now I say, "Stand aside, Bob, and let me hear what you have produced."

Bob, one of the "strongest" farmers in North Kerry, adjusts his spectacles, draws himself up to his full height and begins to recite:

SONNET TO A CHAMBER POT

Loved mother of convention, old as time:
Shrine of our nightly pilgrimage ere sleep.
Our morning Mecca for an act sublime
How often have I pondered full and deep
On thee, pale urn, immobile bedroom jeep!
Chamber of commerce on the water line
Who, thy earliest potter, shall I seek?
Thou hast been found in King Tut's ancient tomb.
This mummied monarch, too, should have his leak
And dared not damp his own sepulchral room
He was before the Roman or the Greek
The Chaldeans knew thee ere they knew the moon
Old human vase, for human hemispheres
Ruth filled thee with her piss – and with her tears.

"Quite good, Bob," I say. "It keeps to the fourteen-line, ten-syllabic formula and it scans. For next week I'll suggest . . .

"Can't do one next week. I've a touch of piles."

Severely I say: "Your subject is 'Sonnet to a Pile'." (That one began with *"O vile excrescence at my southern gate"*). Beloved Sir Bob, of the scholarly Bolands who kept our barony shaking with earthen glee, I rejoice that I have lived to see your honest work collected and in print to add to the gaiety of our little nation and to remind us that we are basically human. Think of it, your natural sonnets now perpetuated in a superb de-luxe edition. And what a night we had at its launching!

This is Lady Gregory, "Spreading-The-News" stuff. Ah well, we Irish have lost a lot to what is called progress but we still have a wonderful residue. That statement breaks repetition.

Dialogue? Word weaving? I try to catch it as it flies in my local dialect. I realise clearly that I'm now in touch with a popular sense of rhythm – and the music of words – a source that can be drawn upon by the writer. I'm also in touch with what I call the Middle Ground of Irish feeling. It's there, unknown to our current crop of politicians and newspaper correspondents. And this Middle Ground which many people claim does not exist, is quite capable of moving like a mist and confounding analysts of public affairs. As a mass observationist, I try to keep in touch with this largely unrecognised force. Its face is bland and it often dons the mask of a simpleton. A searcher of the future will fail to find it. It's spontaneous and secret and is subject to a different law. As an observant friend of mine would say: "There are three law systems in Ireland: The Law of the Church, the Law of the Land, and the Law of the People. When all three are in harmony, everything is fine. But if there's a violent difference of opinion among the three 'legal systems' the Law of the People, unscripted though it is, will always prevail." As in the case of Charles Stewart Parnell who, due to the poet, is now seen as a heroic figure.

At this point of our small mart day gathering, I am on tenterhooks (a word that has something to do with the drying of blankets – Oxon?) lest someone come out with a local rhyme or clerihew (yes we have a man who makes those) that will reflect on the character of someone present and so cause mischief. At this exact point Mikie bluntly mentions that the forebears of one of the company present cut the ears off a priest during the destruction of a local abbey – an event which happened surely four hundred years before. I decide it's time to move on, lest internecine warfare break out on the streets of my native town. As the group disintegrates, I spy a farmer friend who is invariably a source of much conversational joy to me. "I can't wait," he tells me as I accost him. "I must go home and delactate the foster mothers of the human race." He's off home to milk his cows.

I walk The Square with our local raconteur – son of Queen Emily who so impressed me in my youth. He and I have a code of verbal duelling. We are silent for a while. I suddenly stop and look down at his boots which he always has "polished to the veins of nicety". I repeat the antic. I allow myself to fake a frown.

"What the hell lookin'-at-my-boots have you?" he blurts.

"Was I lookin' at your boots?"

"You bloody well were."

"They're nicely polished, that's all." He stops a passer-by. "You see him?" he says, pointing at me. "He's the village eccentric."

The man who has been addressed doesn't know how to handle this situation. He looks from one to the other of us. "I only looked at his boots," I say, "and he goes off in a huff."

"Boots?" the newcomer echoes lamely. He's completely at sea. After this start the Queen's son is happy and geared up for the telling of a story. He has a new tale. He's the best storyteller in our town. Give him a good tale in the morning and he'll visit ten houses in succession to tell his story. And embellish it more and more by each telling.

"I've a damn good one," he begins. "You never heard better than this." Leader of a family dance-band and a fine musician, trad and mod, he can truly tell the story of one hundred Ballrooms of Romance.

As we speak, an old lady gets off a cart. She is the last woman of the locality to wear a black shawl. She has one arm extended under her black shawl and has an odd gait at ninety. "Wounded crow," my friend mutters.

Do all these antics connote idiocy, feeble-mindedness, rattle-headedness, incipient asinity, and the retardation of peasantry? (Nothing like rockers of words to counter criticism). Am I engaged in rewriting Carleton's *Traits and Stories of the Irish Peasantry*? Not at all. To me these events indicate our community making restitution for a word or phrase debased by ill-usage, its image and superscription all but erased by poor treatment on the part of the insensitive. What seems like a rigmarole to outsiders, to us constitutes a seamless whole of which the love of rhythm is an essential part. The meeting of friends on the market or mart day in town is a projection of that love.

When Julius Caesar was describing the Celts in Gaul he made two comments which I suggest are pertinent even to this day. "They are mortally afraid of their Druids," he said, "and they are forever running around asking each other 'Any news?'"

The meeting of, say, two country neighbours in the context of the town has a special significance for both parties. The pair are temporarily on strange ground: they greet each other with as much glee as if they have never met for years. They have to bring back news to their homes to nourish the imagination of those who had no business in town on that day. As often as not they have a special ceremony of a drink in a pub together – stout for the men and, in the old days, wine for the women.

I now recall a passage from one of the Blasket Island books by Muiris Ó Súilleabháin, *Twenty Years a Growing*. An old woman of the island has died and her coffin is being taken by currach, accompanied by other currachs, across the sunlit sound to be buried in the mainland graveyard in Dunquin. The remaining islanders have gathered on the cliff-top above the island haven to bid a respectful farewell to the unusual cortege: all leave except one old grandfather who arrives late and now stands alone on the cliff-top. As I visualise him, he is dressed in a kind of frock coat, a stiff shirt front, an old half top hat and Sunday brogues. He is watching the bright coffin which is now close to its immediate destination – the landing place at Dunquin.

The old fellow's face twitches, he raises his hat and in a broken tone cries aloud, "My misfortune!" he says. "Once I'd be with ye, but not now. Good-bye now, Cáit, and the blessing of God on your soul." Tears stream down the old features as he adds, "You were a good comrade in a market town."

To one who understands the shorthand of rural speech the phrase means a great deal. It tells of the pair of islanders – a young man and a young woman – meeting and greeting on the streets of Dingle and their mutual cordial recognition of the fact that they are away from home. The young man then invites the young woman to have a glass of wine. First, there is her ritualistic reluctance to accept the invitation: they then enter the snug of a pub frequented by the islanders where their sense of one-ness, newness and gentle intimacy is apparent and heightened. They raise glasses in an old world toast and all the while there is that restrained frisson that lies between a young man and a young woman. This extension of the story is implicit in the phrase, "a good comrade in a market town."

The community viewed in the examples I have given will be seen to be many-faceted. Story and jingle are part of it. They bring a smile to the faces of its members. It's all about communication, the commerce of the Bank of Say and a confirmation that one is part of the human race. And also that, of his nature, man is a gregarious animal.

I live in the mid-town on the side of a busy street: sometimes I discuss with myself whether or not I should move out into a bungalow in the peaceful countryside, or into some *rus in urbe* within the town itself.

With this end in view, on two occasions I bought a site with the firm intention of building a bungalow and retiring from the busy thoroughfare where I know little peace, as peace is commonly defined. On rethinking the matter, I realised that I was born on the side of a street in a small town and that its noises were always part of the fabric of my being: I then concluded that for me the wiser part lies in living out the balance of my days in the same surroundings. Recalling an Irish proverb also had an input into my decision, *Is fearr an troid ná an t-uaigneas* – "Better the fighting than the loneliness." And I keep hearing the plaint of an aged relative of mine who lived alone in the country at the end of a boreen right in the middle of the fields. "Disease will never kill me," he complained, "but loneliness will." He even went to the extremity of leaving his house on Christmas Eve, pulling a hat down over his eyes, and stopping neighbours on the road to tell of his own death. When, later, mourners entered the kitchen he calmly walked up out of the room to wish them a Merry Christmas.

So here I sit inside a window and at a table littered with letters and drafts of stories with cars passing outside. It's where a friend can knock on the glass and tell me to forget the pen, that he has a story to tell me. I sign to him to turn the key in the front door and come in for a gossip, which indeed he does. And more often than not the story is a good one.

A final word on jingles: they make people conscious of the rhythm of words and phrases that provide the rhythm of life itself. Why, the infant in the pram, if watched carefully, will be seen to respond to the rhythm of a tune on the radio – this with the almost undetectable beating of time with its little arm. And I hold that a love of the jingle, if properly nurtured, can lead step by step to a love of poetry. There are intermediate quatrains which comment on a slightly higher level of awareness and do so pithily. And this brings me to mention my lifelong friend whose name is Mai.

Mai is the quintessential book-lover. I am fortunate in her friendship. Now retired for some years from her position as a librarian in Dublin, her life is bounded on all sides by books and art. She knows more about Dublin in the twenties than anyone alive. A relative of Austin Stack's, she met on a daily basis people like the Countess Markievicz, Maud Gonne MacBride and the Honourable Albinia Broderick – not to mention earls and lords of every political hue and attitude. For me she throws a personal light on historical events: her admiration for the Countess knows no bounds. Mai says that towards the end of her life, "The Countess devoted her energies to Dublin's poor. She could be found dressed in a smeared apron, whitewashing a latrine in the slums, pausing only to take out a gold cigarette case and from it extract her final Woodbine." The Countess, a great and noble lady, one of the great idealists of the 1916 rebellion, died in the public ward of a Dublin hospital.

I return from a stroll to find that Mai has left in some books for me. *The Genres of the Irish Literary Revival*, edited by Ronald Schlesfer. (This looks very high falutin', but I'll manage.) *An Anthology of English Poetry from Blake to Roe, Seán O'Casey* by Garry O'Connor. *Spectator's Choice* and also *The Mulberry Tree* – this last the work of Elizabeth Bowen whom I once described as "being capable of word-picturing two rival moods having each other by the throats." Mai gave me a tome on the Brontës (Prunty to the mere Irish) which I read to its very end because my good friend and ex-pupil, that brilliant actor, the late Eamon Keane, had once told me that when the fit-up rep company he was acting with broke down in Yorkshire, he took the post of caretaker-guide of Haworth Parsonage for some time. And no better man, God rest him, to fill that august position.

Today also, Mai has enclosed one of her priceless quotations which she culls from the vast world of reading: it's by Gerard Massey.

Not by appointment do we meet delight or joy
They heed not our expectancy

But round some corner in the streets of life
They greet us with a smile.

That quatrain charges my mental and imaginative battery for a full week. I keep finding new dimensions to its delightful and poignant validity. Riches are added to riches when I receive another quotation in a letter from a distant cousin living in what had been called, "The Pacific Slope." She gave the author as Hilaire Belloc.

From quiet homes and first beginnings
Out to the undiscovered ends
There's nothing worth the wear of winning
But laughter and the love of friends.

Friendship in a small community is of the essence. People with whom you feel fully at home. Who, by intuition, can sense your various mood swings (and you theirs) and make allowance therefore. This is an absolute necessity for those who live in a small town: of such a place it may be truly said that the houses have walls of glass.

Today, too, I worry about the US students who have come so far in quest of something that has hitherto eluded them. Can it be, I ask myself, that I shall end my days as a guru – a revered mentor lacking only loin cloth and sandals to complete my image? OK, I'll talk to them although I haven't done so for well over a year. I have had many such sessions in the past years. These students came from various colleges and universities in the US and sat about my feet in the foyer of the local hotel.

This group is from Minnesota, a state for which I have a certain fondness. Out there is a professor – a Benedictine nun called Sister Kirstin who knows more about me than I do myself. She was awarded a PhD mainly for her dissertation on my stories. Trained by an equally brilliant OSB Sister called Mariella Gable, who wrote the introduction to her anthology of stories called *The Many Coloured Fleece*, Sister Kristin and her students and well-wishers visit me each year.

Also in Rochester, Minnesota, at the Mayo Clinic, I was the guest of a doctor ex-pupil of mine who now fills an important executive post in that most eminent centre of medicine. Nodding his assistants from the room, and placing a microphone before me, he bids me sing a ballad about an inter-street football match in our town in the long ago. When I demur he says, "Don't forget that I was goalie on the winning team!"

Back now to the student group. There is a fine turf fire in the hotel foyer. There they are – probably my last class – (Daudet's story, *The Last Lesson,* seems to haunt me on many levels) – seated in two neat rows having a light lunch as they await me. True as heaven I make an initial blunder – after a morning of writing I address them as students from Omaha: as their erudite Professors, John Day or Graham Frear, smile I quickly recover. Of course these are from St Olaf's, in Northfield and strongly represent the great Scandinavian seam in the American North Middle West. I tell myself I must perhaps keep some of my superannuated steam for later in the year when old friends from St Ben's arrive in Ireland. They too, are very dear to me.

I break the ice by saying, "It's been raining non-stop for seven weeks – but we've no earthquakes, no bush fires, no frost, no snow, so in a way we're lucky." The students agree, for Mid-West winters can be very severe. Just as we react when rain hems us in they can experience "cabin fever" in terms of frost and snow. My visitors average nineteen to twenty years of age: each one is armed with a copy of my book, *The Master.* They are also devoting a term to studying the Irish short story. They question me on a story called *Exile's Return.* As is usually the case with groups like this, they gradually thaw out. Students from the Mid-West are invariably more sensitive to the niceties of human contact than those from the larger cities of the United States. I enjoy establishing a rapport with them. "Where are you from?" I ask: mention of home is always a lever to open up a conversation. They are from many parts of the US.

"Denver," one answers. I begin to pontificate, drawing on my Downpatrick tuition. "Denver is named for a surveyor of that name: basically it means 'De Anverre' – of Antwerp'". To a girl from Iowa I say, "You've read *The Bridges of Madison County*? I walked on the covered bridge of the story – the bridge covered so as to shed snow and so avoid a heavy load on the bridge itself – long before you were born. Upper New York State? My story *The Tallystick* takes place there in apple-growing country. In the Fall it's so beautiful near Lake George." And so on: a boy praises the forgiving ending of a story of mine. They bear gifts in the form of picture books of their state and also a pennant with St Olaf printed on it. I tell them that the Irish Norse-North Cork name McAuliffe is often pronounced McOlaf. And I tell them of a St Olaf Gaelic football team in Dublin.

I find myself quoting the Yeats prose passage – A feeling for the form of life (chap. 6) – and chant his poem *Sailing to Byzantium,* in my opinion the greatest poem I have ever read. It offers a further example of what is nowadays termed the holistic impact of a poem or a passage.

What are these young people looking for, I ask myself? Coming from the Euclidean farm-spans of the American Mid-West, with homes far apart in the vast landscape, the inhabitants may lack our colourful cloth of character ("a standing army of extras" as one critic commented on my literary resources) with all the various interplayings and shuttling of roles that animates the movement of literature. Perhaps, like so many members of the human race, the vastness and variety of a magnificent but monotonous landscape fails to supply the food needed to satisfy that hunger of the mind. This is how I expressed it on a bookmark:

There's a hunger of the spirit
For what lies beyond beyond,
And a hunger of the body
To which mankind must respond.
But beneath the gentle lamplight
With word and image twined
A book shall serve to banish
The hunger of the mind.

Ireland then as a haven of the imagination? One prosaic aspect of this poetic ideal – the touristic one – is that, in the final analysis such a resource will even sell shirts and sweaters. But first, one sincere word of caution: trumpeted abroad that Ireland is such a place will reveal a stubborn inbuilt contradiction leading to defeat, for bragging of Ireland as such will ultimately dismay the international discerning. The rare people we seek to lure to Ireland like to discover for themselves: they then revel and rejoice in what they see as a personal discovery. I encounter these people on a weekly, and in summer, a daily, basis when they phone or visit me. So beware, dear packagers – lest the very people you seek to lure to Ireland desert it if they recognise it as a populous and popular solitude – even in terms of literary presentation.

As I saw North America, and continue to see it through the lens of literature and letters – it is a vast continent with climatic differences as marked as that between say, Galway and Greece. Even within a day, or a day's drive, the American climate has almost incredible variations that react on people. This comes as a shock to our Irish bodily systems: "You must be used to this," I remarked to a US friend to whom I complained of the heat – the thermometer was hitting the low hundreds on my last visit to the States. He replied, "You never get used to sitting on a hot stove!" Again, when, after three winter months of Irish rain, I apologised for our weather to a friend home from the US on a visit he said, "I came out of Mass in New York last Sunday and the wind had a chill factor of thirty below freezing point."

So in Ireland we should, despite all that rain, be happy with our lot.

A flood of memories – "of laughter and the love of friends" – overwhelms me when I recall the United States.

Many members of my mother's large family – her sisters and brother – went to the States. Now I have exotic cousins – Croatian, Scandinavian and Jewish-Irish among them – in many parts of that vast land.

Some memories of US come more strongly than others. One I recall with a smile.

I'm seated in a lecture hall in Harvard University among men and women from every part of the world when a door opens and a truly Kerry voice silences the speaker with a shout of "Is Bryan MacMahon here?" Rather shamefacedly I come to my feet. "I won't keep ye a minute, gentlemen." Then addressing the chairman, Brother Kerryman adds in a loud voice: "I just want to ask him one question." Turning to me he says, "Did my brother's black greyhound bitch win the trial stake at Lixnaw?" Somewhat nonplussed I confessed ignorance of coursing matters. As I resume my seat, the chairman, one Henry Kissinger, queries sidelong in his deep deep voice accompanied by a broad smile, "Did she?"

(As a matter of fact Henry Kissinger did not ask this question – but the rest of my story is true. I just add "Did she?" for effect.)

Will I ever forget the waterfall? Not the "Minnie-Ha-Ha" in Minneapolis: this waterfall was about seventy feet high and was made of canvas. It rolled downwards over a series of transverse poles so as to resemble the movement of a turbulent fall of water. Children loved it. They made it look simple.

Up they scrambled in a lift, then down they rolled with shrieks of excitement and joy until they sprawled in safety on a soft landing place on the ground. The whole contraption stood right across the highway from my window in a hotel somewhere in the midwest.

"Dare I?" I asked myself; the sensible cowardy cat inside my head said "No". But I took up the dare despite the fact that I was old enough to have sense.

I shall never forget the hurtling down across those poles. Mostly I sprawled head first but also I descended pins and points, sideways and spread-eagled. I made anything but a soft landing.

Breathless, my head reeling and my stomach churning, I staggered away muttering, "I wonder am I as big an eejit as I think I am".

Not always with a smile, sometimes with a shiver of fear I recall another incident.

I almost lost my life for literature in Colorado Springs. "Take a cab," the doorman of the Broadmoor Hotel advised as I set off on a pre-seminar stroll. "The first winter snow is due this evening," he called after me. I looked up at the towering Rockies – everything seemed normal – but who was I to judge normality as regards the meteorological Mid-West? I walked for miles along quiet roads looking for downtown Colorado Springs. There was no such place. The city seemed strung out for miles.

It began to snow. The falling feathers obliterated the world. Ghostly vehicles drifted by. The door of a Kresge store closed abruptly against me as I tried to phone for a taxi. North, south, east, west were guide points unknown. Four miles from the hotel – and I was utterly lost.

I blundered on. A filling station loomed up. I asked the polka dotted attendant how to find my way back to the hotel. He gestured, shouted, pointed and then shut shop. I staggered along what I soon realised was a main highway, (the attendant must have thought I was driving a car!) – the last kind of route I wanted.

I was now in a ravine, leaping on to roadside shale and sliding down despite my best efforts to avoid death. Headlights missed me by inches in the white darkness. "Hisss" – Sweet God, that car nearly struck me. The ravine came to an end. I stepped on to a firm road edge, walked bravely along it and then fell off it and into a squelching marsh. I lay there face downwards. Snow fell on me, thicker than before. I struggled to rise – failed. Lay prone. "Is it here I am going to die?" I asked myself. "The night before last I walked the quiet square of my own town with a friend: tomorrow or a month from now my body will be found when the snow melts." Somehow I staggered to my feet, climbed back up the highway. Where was I?

For one brilliant moment the sky cleared. I saw Pike Peak, the highest point in the Rockies, against the sky ("Pike Peak or bust" was an old pioneer war cry which I recalled.) I had my bearings now. I had marked the peak on my arrival at the hotel. More dead than alive I reached my destination. Ran an almost boiling bath. Total abstainer that I was, I rang for a hot whiskey. Sipped, then drained the glass. Fell into bed. Slept like a dog. Got up to deliver my keynote address to representatives of the congress of the English Teachers of the United States.

In the US every day brings its own adventure. At least that was how I found it. Between lectures and alone in a city of say 100,000 in the Mid-West, staying at an inn like the Ramada or Holiday one wakes up on a Sunday morning to say, "I know no one at all in this city."

"Mass?" I ask at the desk after breakfast. "Catholic church, two blocks west, one block north" – the response comes pat. I enter the church long before the beginning of the service.

In cities like this roughly one-third of the population is Catholic – represented by three churches, St Patrick's or St Brigid's, then a Bohemian church, and perhaps a French church dedicated to one of the various names for the Virgin Mary in French. In University cities there is also a Newman Centre attached to a chapel.

Very few in the church as yet. Presently I have a married couple to my right, another couple enter to my left. Mass begins – there are vibrations of curiosity as the ears of my neighbours seem to sharpen as I utter the responses. I remain aloof. The priest has an Irish accent, overlaid by a seam laid down by many years as pastor in the States. The Mass goes on. At the moment of the offering each other the sign of peace the women both to my right and left readily extend their hands. The ice is broken. I retire into my false modesty.

As we leave the church one of the women asks, "You are a stranger? Irish perhaps?" I bear witness to my nationality. "A cup of coffee, in the centre?" I demur wanly. "Father O'Sullivan will be glad to meet you." In the centre I am introduced to scores of people. Father O' comes out. A major deal! I know his people. The parishioners almost quarrel for the privilege of entertaining me in the clubhouse of an elegant golf course. Presently I'm visiting gorges, canyons or wealthy Irish-American homes. The car travels so fast that, when it hits a flying pheasant, the bird is reduced to a puff of feathers. There is a sprinkle of minute drops of blood on the windscreen. I repay my hosts with stories of old Ireland.

Returning to my quiet hotel room at eleven pm I close the door on a day of epic hospitality. My phone rings. I lift the receiver. A bunch of children obviously gathered about a distant phone are singing "When Irish Eyes are Smiling". A lullaby for the Storyman.

I could multiply these story memories that have to do with many places in the United States. I almost stood on a sleeping rattlesnake in Georgia, innocently became involved in an election campaign in another state: the candidate I backed won – she had me up to greet the Governor of the State on St Patrick's Day and to be honoured by the House of Representatives. In another state capital, where I was similarly honoured as a special guest, the members, many of Irish descent, began to leave in droves as I was being introduced from the podium. I began to recite "After Aughrim", an Emily Lawless poem of the Irish Diaspora. Ireland is speaking of her scattered sons:

She said, "They gave me of their best
They lived, they gave their lives for me
I tossed them to the howling waste
And flung them to the foaming sea."
She said, "I never called them sons,
I almost ceased to breathe their name,
Then caught it echoing down the wind
Blown backwards from the lips of Fame."

The final line of the poem *Yet still their love comes home to me*, stopped the members in their tracks. They occupied the seats and stood by the doors. As I left the podium the handlers hustled me up to the Governor's office. "This guy's got an angle," they told him. "Say your piece," I was ordered. Afterwards, on his nod of approval, I was asked if I would consider taking a post as speech writer (with poetic inserts, of course) for the Governor. I shook my head. "Every guy has an angle, what dyeh want?" one of the mentors asked severely. "To go home," I said. They led me to the door. I could almost read their minds: "The guy is crazy: let him go."

Every day an adventure, every day a story of that adventure. Canada was no exception. Newfoundland, the coldest land I've visited, is also a country of the warmest hearts. I shall never forget the welcome we received in St John's University and the greeting in Irish from an old Irish family rooted there for two hundred years. Tuxedo-adorned I spoke on Peig Sayers before a distinguished gathering – almost all of them of Irish descent. Did Peig of Vicarstown and the Blasket or her son Míchéal while living, ever dream that they would be the subject of so much debate and comment, albeit in a land where the Dingle and Waterford codfishers of the 1970s were not unknown? And where they made their mark. And where they still remember their homeland.

But then it occurs to me in the forest of my memories, I have one more tryst to keep – perhaps the most important meeting of all. Sooner or later it must be faced.

CHAPTER TWELVE

To begin a story is hard: to end it is harder still. I've told the story of my story as well as I could. How now to say goodbye to the many friends I fondly, and perhaps foolishly, imagine have accompanied me on my personal journey and whom hopefully I have lured to look through my particular glass on the varied transactions of one man's story life? An old friend of mine used to say that the loveliest greeting of all began with the words "Will you come?" And the saddest of all with the words, "If only . . . "

None of this, I tell myself. No self-pity. I am reminded that the title of Stefan Zweig's famous book was *Beware of Pity.* What luxury shall I then allow myself? Standing on the pinnacle of age, I ask to be allowed to look back and find, without trying too hard, since I wish it to be a spontaneous process, what of living I recall as being significant to me and perhaps to others, if they allow themselves to indulge in the same luxury. It's going to be a ragbag of memory.

Having satisfied myself somewhat in this regard, I beg leave to take serious stock of myself and decide how I will comport myself in the matter of facing the Greatest Conundrum of all, that of life ending in death. In my story *Testament of a Sewer Rat*, and in plays such as *The Honey Spike* and *The Bugle in the Blood*, I have described death. The *caoin* was in my ears as I wrote those lines.

In the ultimate imaginative projection of all – I place faith aside for a moment – I ask myself the question – and death leading where? The old philosophers of the countryside of my youth had a sly saying barely tinged with agnosticism – "We know where we are, but we don't know where we're going." And then they would add with a sniff, "And no one ever came back to tell us." But for me, I choose to sift my memory for incidents of personal importance. Various and seemingly irrelevant, even trivial, as they come to mind I am prepared to welcome them.

Does any woman anywhere in the world of today wear a muff? Do people even know what a muff is? I look in my dictionary to see how it is defined. "Muff: Woman's fur or other covering (usu, cylindrical) into which both hands are thrust from opposite ends to keep them warm." Muffs are seen today only in photos of Victorian ladies of gentle blood, or perhaps barely discerned through the photographic sepia haze of the womenfolk of the last of the Russian Czarinas.

My mother wore a muff. In terms of time I'm referring to the teen years of this century. With other items of Lancastrian finery, she brought it back to Listowel from Todmorden where she taught for ten years, her term there bridging a century ending and the beginning of another. The muff held me in thrall. My greatest pleasure was when I was three or four years of age and beside my mother at Mass. First looking up into her face for approval, I would steal my cold hand into the warm interior of the muff where one of her hands already was. The tactile experience was lovely, secret and intimate. To this day when I am troubled I still find my hand stealing into the muff. Professors of psychology will probably explain this recession as a desire to return to the security of the womb. I'm not unduly bothered how they name it: it was mine and still is; somehow it must have conditioned my writing life.

My mother, when I look back on it, was a woman far in advance of her time. She spoke to us older children of being "near her confinement." She didn't explain the term. By some process of semantic osmosis we came to understand. Nursing one of the infants younger than I, she would say as I approached her, "If you're good I'll let you see me suckle the baby." Before she set out for the country school in which she taught, she would quite naturally drain the milk from her breasts into a glass container pressed on her nipples. After swallowing some kind of pepsin tablet, clippety clop we'd set off together, harness bells ringing, in the ass and trap.

There came a fair day. The street outside our door was thronged with farmers and beasts. My mother called me to the door. "Here comes a bull," she said, "look how it takes two strong men with a pole attached to a ring in his nose to lead him along. Hear him bellow." Then, "Here comes a cow. Look how quiet and docile she is. A child can herd her." Then she'd add, "There's a big difference between male and female, man and woman. Never forget that! They're different animals entirely. A man is not a woman: nor is a woman a man."

She had wise sayings too – blessings among them. "That your carriage wheels may blind the eyes of your foes." "As you climb the hill of success may you never meet a friend." (Riddle that out!) And the schoolmaster's toast, "Addition and multiplication to your friends, subtraction and division to your foes." Above all, the blessing for the bride and groom. "When one of you weeps may the other taste salt." Talking about success in later life she'd say, "Don't let success make you proud. Walk easy when your jug is full." Or, "Relax with the honest man: watch yourself with a rogue." And again, this very firmly: "There is no such thing as a ghost. Do you think Almighty God would let one of his souls out of heaven telling him or her to get a sheet and frighten the wits out of children? Have sense, son." She and one of her cronies are chatting: one of them says, "If you raise your head the people will lower it for you: if you lower your head the people will raise it for you." Another piece of advice against unseemly pride. As I lived onwards I learned other wise sayings: one relates to private and to public trouble and suggests an attitude one should adopt in an emergency. "Do nothing! Say nothing! If you stand on a cowdung you spread it." This is straight from the Irish, *Is leithide buailteah ach satailt air!* I happen to know that civil servants comfort each other in this way if they have given a minister faulty advice on how to answer a Dáil question.

For the following incisive memory I have to go back a full eighty-two years.

"Well, if you aren't the thundering little scut!"

That was the indignant voice of a woman who, by common acclaim, was Queen of Charles Street: it was directed at me where I lay prone on my back in the flooded channel at the pavement's edge with the muddy water washing over me.

I was four at the time. I detested, hated and abhorred that blue velvet suit with the lace collar around my neck. Strange to say it was adored by the senior and nubile country girls in Clounmacon National School where my mother taught and where she and I drove each morning in the ass and trap. But I knew from the sidelong looks the senior lads of the school cast in my direction that they had utter contempt for my sissy attire.

So on a quiet but very wet Sunday morning in one of the stonecut houses in Charles Street where we first lived, I threw what is nowadays identified as a temper-tantrum. This as a protest against being forced to wear unmanly attire.

Seething with suppressed rage, I had drifted sulkingly to the front door: there I looked out on the father and mother of a downpour which, delving in the yellowish mud of the untarred roadway and overflowing onto the channel, swirled and gurgled as it spread past the pavement at our front doorway. Its rude noise seemed to mock me and my suit: this heightened my sense of baffled rage.

Suddenly I had the solution to my problem. It was really quite simple. I glanced up and down the street then over my shoulder at the now tranquil house behind me. No witnesses! I could say I fell . . .

So coldly, calmly and with concentrated malice and relief aforethought, I went out, white shoes and all, into the mucky flooded channel and, lying down on my back, allowed the beautiful filthy waters to flow over me and over that abominable suit. Ah, bliss! I looked up at the blue-black heavens. That should settle their uppish hash!

It was then that the door of the house across the road flew open and Queen Emily, spotless and authoritative, came rushing out. First, having branded me as a scut, she crouched down, lifted me like a dishrag from the gutter, and dragging me to our doorway yelled for my mother. "Joanna! I saw him through the window. The little bastard did it deliberately!"

I've often wondered where this word-hunger of mine came from. Asked what one book I'd like to have with me on a desert island, without hesitation I'd choose a large fat Oxford dictionary. And like

Pangur Bán the old scribe-monk's cat, "huntin' words I'd spend my life."

I came across a definite clue to the source of my obsession a few days ago. The lead came from my sister Máirín who was clearing out some old papers from an ancient box. She found me a copybook of our mother's – one she had at a local convent school and dated November 1893 – at which time my mother was a girl of fifteen.

Joanna Caughlin, my mother, seemed to be in bondage to words. She appears to have gone through the dictionary and, starting with the letter A and, under an ornate heading of semi-Gothic script, listed a series of words and their meanings. First came aphaeresis, then apophthegm, argillaceous, apocrypha, asafoetida and so on. On the letter B she had noted barouche, beccafico (a fig-eating bird in Italy), benefice, bissextile (a leap year), britzska (a carriage) and bombasine. Under the C heading, among others, she had camelopard (a giraffe), canaille, cavatina (a simple song) and a few words I cannot trace in my modern dictionaries. As the copybook was full, the manuscript of the private dictionary ran out at the letter E. I felt sorry that its sequel hasn't yet shown its face. Belatedly I realise that my mother knew the etymology of all these words. At the remove of almost eighty years I hear her voice deriving some such words from Latin and Greek. While my father transferred a love of Irish to us, my mother conveyed a love of the English language. So belatedly, I confess that I am the harmonious reconciliation of linguistic polarities. A final word on my mother: on her deathbed she opened her eyes and looked about her. There was Canon White to anoint her, Nurse Gray to supply medication, and her lifelong friend Mary Frances Browne to vouch for loyalty. "White, gray and brown," my mother murmured. "I'm dying with the colours of the rainbow around me."

The words. The proverbs. The muff. The Bull and Cow. I was learning. All the while puzzling over the mystery of the opposite sex. This in my vicarious role of young bull or stallion.

Dan Flavin, our bookseller, told me of one incident which shed light on the intuitive nature of women. Would it make a story? I keep asking myself. Let Dan himself tell it.

"A farmer came into the shop today for a newspaper. We started talking on this and that. 'A man should always listen to a woman,' the farmer said. 'Why do you say that?' I asked. 'Well,' he said, 'I had this small perished little farm up there in the hills. Barely a livin' in it. But my wife and I were hardworking and prudent and we put money by. I aimed to do better. The opportunity presented itself, but there was a problem. A big problem. The flesh peeled down off my bones thinkin' of it.' 'What's troublin' you?' my woman said. 'Nothing.' I said. 'My sleep went astray, Dan Flavin. I'd get out of bed at three in the mornin' and sit in the kitchen lookin' into the dead fire. The wife got up, dressed only in her night-dress. She faced me where I was sittin' on the chair. 'Here I'll stay until you tell me,' she said. So I started to tell her.

"'McInerney's place is on the walls,' I said, 'Ninety-five lovely acres out there in the plain of North Kerry. 'Twould suit! The bank manager has promised me the balance I'm short. But . . .' 'But what?' 'You mightn't understand. It's ancient history.' 'Try me and see.' This place is boundin' a farm from which my grandfather was evicted in the bad times. Blood was spilt over it. The seed and breed of the emergency man are still there in our old farm. If I buy, the old neighbours who know their history will tell our three sons – and taunt 'em too. So 'twill likely end with crossness between the grandsons of the emergency man and our lads. It could even be back again to the rope. So, although I'm sorely tempted to buy, in the heel of all I've decided to let it go.'

"'My woman laughed. 'What are you laughin' at?' I said. She laughed again. 'This emergency man's family – are there daughters there? 'There are.' 'Then buy the farm, you fool; love is stronger than blood.'

"'I bought, Dan Flavin, I bought. The woman was right. Two of my sons are married to girls of the other family. My daughter is now married to a third so we're back in the home place after eighty years. The grandchildren, God bless 'em, are in and out to my wife and myself. That's why I always say that a man should listen to a woman.'"

I continued to gain novel angles into the female psyche from the seers of the countryside.

"Every woman is the boss but it's a fool lets her husband know it," is a saying I relish. A lady from the continent once remarked in my presence, "I am Ave and Eva: spelt backwards I'm the Virgin Mary and Eve of Eden. My mind shuttles between the sanctuary and the bedroom."

Here's a vicious one from the last century from which I disassociate myself. "A hound, a wench and a walnut tree – the more you beat them the better they be," – a walnut tree is whipped instead of being pruned. I tread down the temptation to quote WB Yeat's *Crazy Jane and the Bishop*. To do so would plunge me into a cauldron of boiling oil with the womenfolk jeering at my fate.

Two of our great personalities now flicker and steady in the centre of my mental images. Many years have passed by since Queen Emily (of my velvet suit fame) and Brown Paddy (he who tried to slap away the wasp at the graveside commemoration) met head on.

It goes without saying that women are far more biological than men: they don't quake at the sight of blood, pus or other bodily emissions. And at their best they can be far more caring and loyal than men.

A German housewife once said to me – we had been discussing the Irish reluctance to marry – "They do not marry in Ireland because they do not vork together in the harvest fields. They do not seem to realise that sveat is an aphrodisiac."

Strolling down town at eleven am when all the housewives were out doing their shopping, I have wondered why they gathered in threes and were sometimes convulsed with laughter. They fell silent as I approached. What were they laughing at? To solve the mystery I went to the cinema to see a risqué but funny film. I listened very carefully to ascertain what evoked a gale of female laughter. I had it at last. And proved it right by an experiment the following morning at eleven am. I then faced three women who were in hysterics of laughter and who shut up as I drew near. "I know what you're laughing at," I say severely. "Tell us." "You're enjoying a story about some poor man making a fool of himself – especially it if has to do with love." "Dead right!" they admitted with a gale of laughter. "Move on, Master, and let us finish our story."

Continuing with my philosophy and attitude as regards my

neighbourhood and the people therein – I refuse to name them the "material" of my stories – for this would smack of the wrong kind of patronising usage – yet I have to note certain significant social changes happening under my eyes, changes that will dramatically alter the world as I have known it. Should this be the subject of some comment on my part – this in my role as recorder and interpreter – albeit it may be in fictional form? For the fiction writer can at times borrow the mantle of the commentator.

Still more radical social changes are now "invoiced", this time by legislation. It seems to me that before these measures are legally signed, sealed and delivered it would be prudent to examine the deep social upheavals similar legislation has already occasioned in societies broadly comparable to the traditional society as we have known it in Ireland. To discover in essence if such proposed legislation will occasion individual happiness or individual hurt, family upheaval and devastation or family tranquillity and peace. And yet, in all the welter of yes and no, taunts of backwardness or progress, catch-cries of servility or freedom, not one public commentator to my awareness has asked for such an enquiry which hopefully would result in deep public discussion on its findings.

Also I'd dearly like to have a full definition of the term "pluralism" in society. I always considered myself a pluralist insofar as I tolerated and respected everyone's belief but this surely does not mean I am bound to accept his principles in their totality as my own. Nor he to accept mine. Like the frog in the fable we are now being plausibly asked to leap into the deep well of the unknown. This lack, this omission, this neglect of prudence in its most basic form, is the cause of much puzzlement to an old philosopher like myself. I feel in my bones that out there there is a huge Middle Ground as equally puzzled as I am. So dear self-styled "crusaders" who seem bent on dragging us screaming into the twenty-first century, gratuitously I offer you my wisest advice, "Don't underestimate the unsuspected power of the Middle Ground."

Returning to the psyche of women as I have experienced it, I would like to pinpoint one particular significant change which is happening right now, and this again without major public comment in our organs of mass dissemination. This is a passing of conventual life as it has been known in Ireland for centuries.

The convents are closing. Mainly for lack of postulants or novices. Abroad the story is different: the mission sisters see their sowing come to harvest, especially in Africa. Personally speaking, I find this national Diaspora truly sad. There are cynics who will say "No bloody harm," but wait, think it over, consider the task the sisters faced and finished. Consider especially their place in the life of the ordinary people of Ireland in the fields of education and nursing. To village after village these women gave identity at the cost of devotion and dedication on a lifelong level of commitment.

They had standards. Each convent was an oasis of neatness, cleanliness and grace. Each building was a house of polished floors, bells and the chiming of prayer. They taught and they nursed. As best they could, they fed the people during starvation times. As the pioneer group of sisters in my town walked back the long street of thatched houses called The Gleann, in the years just prior to the Famine, the housewives of the area, wearing their best starched white aprons, stood at their doors and bobbed and flapped their welcome. Some years later a school inspector of that time complained that when the convent girls were asked to sing "God Save the King", they couldn't utter a note. But when asked to sing a song of their own choice they joined in a rousing chorus of "A Nation Once Again." Thank you, sisters, for a century and half of dedication, caring and service. And also for providing me with a gentle polarity of existence and endeavour right under my nose.

At this point, I just wonder if it is possible if even one inquisitive person (like myself) is interested in how, in my mid-eighties, I pass my day. If so let me offer my timetable in brief outline:

I wake at six-thirty am or so. Brain too active – cannot rest. Get up, drink a glass of cold pineapple or grape juice, leave an inch or two of the liquid in the bottom of the glass, refill with hot water, sip it slowly and pensively, my brain ranging over the possibilities of the day. Then I consume boiled prunes (five) mixed with diet yoghurt. Meanwhile my mixture of oatmeal, Ready Brek, raisins and low fat milk is muttering on the electric ring. "Put a poultice to your inside first thing in the morning," an old doctor advised me. I keep the saucepan stirred; later I pour out the contents onto a deep capacious dish, shake Canderel on it and add milk to cool. I munch a soft pear and perhaps drink a mug of tea. Ponder. Then I go to my writing desk – since Kitty died I've moved some of my work from my writing room upstairs down to the dining-room, a practice formerly frowned upon.

I glance at it too idly by half; I am priming the pump of the mind. Make a few marginal notes dictated by my clear morning brain, then adjourn to the bathroom where I have a shower and shave – the shave, at times, every second day. Back to bed again goes the sluggard. Listen to the eight o'clock news and *What it Says in the Papers*. May or may not rise at this point or hang on until almost nine. Then I dress and go down to the table and begin to write. My housekeeper comes in. "Any news, Sheila? Anyone dead after the night?" "What'll you have for luncheon?" she asks later. After a while I decide. Sheila shops. I scribble on for a half hour. Sheila is back with the newspaper. Brings along my post. I glance at the headings of the paper and open my post. Slit the envelope with a paper knife. I hate a torn envelope.

My post is interesting and varied as to its point of origin. Germany (from Ingrid or Klaus), Prince Edward Island (once mooted as New Ireland). Australia (many cousins there) and inevitably most interesting US mail from Dick and Clare in Georgia, and perhaps a welcome letter from Sister Kristin in Minnesota. I sit and write for an hour or so. Down town I saunter at eleven-thirty or so, meet Gabriel or Eileen or Eleanor or any one at all for coffee, speak to at least twelve people in an hour – home for luncheon at one pm. I might fit in a half-hour of writing before the meal.

After luncheon/dinner the inevitable short snooze. Tackle post and finish my writing stint. If I have a manuscript to be typed, Christine calls (with me since she was a girl, can read my dreadful handwriting). Post manuscript typed and edited, to son Maurice and his wife Yvonne in Dublin for transference to word processor. But for Maurice my last three books would not exist. A short spasm of writing to three pm (school hours). Teacher friend calls. Saunter to The Square, thence by the castle to the Castle Inch. Sit on beach by the river. Note a wild duck with ducklings at the opposite bank, note the crane (really a heron) and with luck a pair of swans. By the Race

Bridge the heron stalks his prey. I try to see a kingfisher in flight but the colourful bird flies at speed, so I watch the antics of scarecrows. Relax. Meet one of my closer friends. Repair for coffee. Home five pm. Write until six, put match to a set fire, hear news, forty winks, read paper, visit sister up town, see old friend in hotel, return for chat show, read in bed till twelve-thirty or so. Phone or receive family phone calls. Go to sleep.

It's different in the summer. Many visitors chiefly from US or returned ex-pupil exiles. All very interesting. And always I am within calling distance of the sea. Sunday afternoons find me, transistor radio in hand, on a cliff top in Ballybunion following the fortunes of my grandsons play football in Clare.

Our town is not always tranquil. We have our local differences of opinions and an odd flare-up. But we also have our healing system and our times of amnesty and reconciliation (condoling with relatives at funerals, the sign of peace at Mass, Christmas Eve or Races time) when we present a united front to the world. Again that needs qualification.

For the first time in my life recently I had an intruder. Taking tea at six-thirty pm, I hear a strong knocking at my back door. This is followed by roars of "Open up!" From inside I switch on a yard light. Shrouded figure shouts "I have a gun." Smashes in two panes of glass in kitchen door with his fist. Time for me to work my plan. I shout that there is a Garda in the kitchen. Cheers! It worked. Gone! He left his name in the yard in the pocket of the windcheater that covered his face. Garment later found in the yard.

The shop windows of the town are a constant source of stimulation to me. I learn (from the chemist's window) a vast terminology having to do with perfumes, allergies and cures for the common cold. At times I find a window with animal mineral licks, cat flea collars and gleaming instruments for castrating young bulls. Aromatherapy, trinkets, antiques, tourist postcards and greeting cards, kitchen hardware, electronic devices and delph fascinate me. Paint colour cards offer me vistas of colour. Blue? Immaculata, Mediterranean, butcher's, cerulean and a thousand other hues of blue, their names invented by paint manufacturers. The colour-wheel indicating the reconciliation and harmony of opposites in terms of hues is there too. The window of a bookshop is obviously a place where I stop and muse and look. There's a bunch of bananas going into the fruiterers. The label on the box says it's from a city in the Canaries where stands the oldest dragon-tree in the world (cement-supported now). The supermarkets continue to reveal and present me with unusual word hoards. My brain bag full I stroll home: I smile as I spill out, stick note pads, Herbes de Provence and (hurray!) Styrofoam peanuts. These last are the small white pellets used to pack books or fragile material.

Latterly, a new planet swam into my ken. Electronic in origin. The talking book, if you please. Well, well. Ireland's finest scribe sent it along to me. Absolutely riveting and for me a welcome discovery. A relief for eyes strained from reading. This in a packet of eight tapes, sixteen sides in all – total listening time eleven and a half hours. I pop each in turn into my recorder, quench the midnight lights, recline in my armchair, close my eyes and relive history. And what a bloody history it proves to be.

The audio-book I listened to was *'Culloden'*. It tells of the defeat of the Scottish clans in 1745, when Bonnie Prince Charlie and the cream of Scottish chivalry were arrayed against the Butcher William Cumberland, son of George II of England. The flower Sweet William was (in compensation?) named after him. If ever there was a tale of savagery and barbarity wrought on the Highlanders – this the ultimate example is largely beyond words. And to think it happened only two hundred and fifty years ago.

By comparison hanging was then a decent end, but half hanging, cutting down from the gallows, disembowelling and the cutting out of the heart and casting both organs on a fire while the victim's body still quivered, was commonplace. A butcher's cleaver used to behead, and later to slash the body into quarters, was the final indignity. This book by John Prebble, superbly read by Davina Porter, comes from 55 Thomas Street, Oxford. It opened up a grisly and immense vista of interest for me. I look forward to midnight matinees with others of the same genus, possibly, *Glencoe* followed by *The Highland Clearances.*

But, hold! Aren't you indicating enmity with yourself if you praise the talking book! It may come to supplant the printed book. Adroitly I explain: the book will be printed first or at least written before it can be transferred to tape. So the writer will survive. Also, I recall my refuge of Silence, Intimacy and The Lamp.

Do I seem to be in foul mood? So be it. There's a modern departure in writing – in business too – called "the cutting edge". One is archaic if one lacks this bitter quality! Hitherto I've been bland and affable. Chasing rainbows and all that. Shall I now record the things that annoy?

At breakfast time I hear a quasi-cowboy voice saying, "White scour in calves is mighty vexatious. But the boys got it beat." I'm a calf lover but not to that extent and at that time. If the reference was made to humans instead of calves I would also protest. The misuse of the word 'simplistic' for simply nicks me – why doesn't the stupid user consult a dictionary? 'Enthusi-ism' for 'enthusi-asm' is another irritant. So does an extra intrusive 't' in longitude. The "fine" of Fine Gael does not rhyme with 'wine', nor the "Port" of Portlaoise with "sport".

But above all, as an old time constitutional nationalist, his attitudes and aspirations unrepresented in none of today's newspapers, but who reveres the memory of both Michael Collins and Eamon de Valera – I breathe a prayer for Collins whenever I pull out the knob on my front door for, as a boy, I saw his hand resting on that knob some time before his tragic death: as for Dev, I had the honour of meeting that mighty statesman on a few pleasant occasions.

There are lies, damn lies and misquotations: consider the sneer quotation levelled at Dev of his desire to see an Ireland of "comely maidens dancing at the cross-roads" – I counted misuse of the phrase quoted by three academics in a single day. Of this misquotation only the one word 'maidens' occurred in Dev's original radio address, to which I listened most carefully when it was first broadcast. "Comely" is substituted for "happy" to offer a sort of milkmaid gloss and the addition of "dancing at cross-roads" (a diversion now revived in Kerry) is a similar metropolitan invention. By the way, if the term "comely maidens" is used as a term of supercilious invective, then its opposite which I identify as "ugly hoors" must logically be a term of affectionate admiration. Try that complimentary comment for size on the father of a family of nubile daughters and experience the recoil.

I'm glad that's out of my system. It was pestering and festering inside me. 'Twas mighty vexatious!

There are times when the characters of my short stories attack me in the form of a flock of birds. Recall that in a single collection of mine like *The Sound of Hooves* or *The Tallystick* there are at least eighty characters whom I know intimately. Now and again they clamour for my attention, their wings rustling as they speed across my face. Each seems to have a sense of grievance – that I did not portray him accurately – or some such complaint. They are noisy too, and I'm afraid one of the crossest crows among them will pick out one of my eyes. There are swallows and swifts, gulls and hawks, pheasants and lapwings, cormorants and bluetits. They even shit down on me when I try to beat them off. At times a wren or a dove perches on my shoulder and chirps or coos to comfort me. "Take no notice of those blackguards," it seems to say. On a fence some distance away sit three buzzard intruders who seem to symbolise the unspeakable – cannibalism, incest and necrophilia. Suddenly, as on a signal, the flock takes flight and is gone with a diminishing clamour of wings.

When I find myself calling the name of a dead woman up the stairwell of an empty house I wonder if I am in the process of "finishing up funny." I then ask myself if the mind of man is a drunken monkey or a hypermarket, its shelves laden with goodies – and baddies? Still in simian context, there floats before my imagination the sad face of a chimpanzee and then I venture to assert that, given the order and clockwork of the vast universe the astronomer who declares that he is an atheist is a clear contradiction in terms. I finally conclude to my own tiny satisfaction that it must be that the micro of the here-and-now will become the macro of the hereafter. That here we are looking through the wrong end of the telescope and that, beyond the grave, we will turn the glass right way round and view existence in major detail. The mood passes and I am happy that I have explored it as far as is humanly possible.

But I have been devious and evasive. In a complete change of mood I now address what I have already identified as The Great Conundrum. My foregoing outburst was an attempt to avoid facing the main issue. For me it is the Final Reconciliation – that of "Time and Eternity." Bluntly, I refer to Death. And man is the one animal who is aware he must die. Life is "Box open: box shut". "When Sergeant Death in his cold arms shall embrace me". The thought of it hits me only in spots and at odd moments. There are chinks in my consciousness through which I sometimes see its face. The omnipresence and preoccupation with stories tends to beguile, distract and delude me.

Just as well. I'm a constant attender of funerals: this is an essential duty in a tightly knit community. When a neighbour is in trouble, a kind word, no great loss to the giver, is often a source of consolation to the family of the bereaved. But before confronting the issue – and I dare to say that Man – (not in all cases of course, for some folk are by nature and upbringing, obsessed by the thought and dread of death) – has an infinite capacity for assuring himself that everyone else in his community will die – except himself or herself. Death is for other people but, oh brother, not for me. I'll go on attending funerals – but not my own. My cry must be, "Press on regardless." The life force dares not say "No". Everything here is of value, even the absurd. Whatever happens one must continue to engage and withdraw. Reality fades into illusion and illusion fades back to reality.

Before I face death I must look back on life. Out of a long life what do I recall – inevitably what I name are the peaks that stick up above the horizon of my existence. And some of what springs to mind border on the vivid and others on the idiotic. I have quite a problem conquering their stubborn reluctance and dragging them out into the light of day.

I recognise what I call the surplus tessarae of my mind, surplus inasmuch as they indicate that once I wrongly identified them as being part of the mosaic of my life or of the stories implicit in that life. Perhaps unintelligible to anyone except myself, I regurgitate them now, not without trepidation.

The terrible shake hands of electricity, bum, rum and 'baccy (the sailor's fare), the healing silence of an empty church (disparates implied). "Golden stockings she had on," "finger the fob" (a tramp's plea for me "to encounter the milled edge of a silver coin") a salmon's heart beating in a saline solution in a glass jar, the haybox of the mind, people who are blunt primals, Marcus Aurelius, Nemo dat, head-lice and mange-mites, Jules Renard and George MacKay Brown (superb Storymen both), Corcomroe and a tinker holding out a lamprey impaled on a pointed stick. Burl Ives's face when I proposed teaching him "An Poc or Buile". (Christ, that my love was in my arms, and I in my bed again.)

Some encounters I have already touched upon – the *caoin* and my mother's muff. The waterfall. Some are laughable: a man stops me in the street and says solemnly, "There must be fierce money in sanitary pads; every time I turn on the yoke in the corner they're advertising 'em". As I stood pondering the spiders' webs on the railings beside the floodlights on the local hotel, a man joins me and gives me a learned lecture on the eyes of spiders.

Some events are superficially trivial: in a parlour in Lisdoonvarna away back in the thirties, a row of old ladies dressed in matronly black sat against the walls. An Indian pedlar came in, opened his old suitcase, and against the sober background of silent women, draped himself with an array of coloured scarves and cloths, then knelt in mid-floor on the duff carpet so that the room became an eastern bazaar. A shaft of sunlight, not unlike that I have described in my story, *The Windows of Wonder*, came in the window and spotlighted the pedlar's steel hair, his amber face, his sparkling trout-like eyes, his lips and shining teeth so that he paused, looked up and, fully conscious of his luminous centrality, to transfer his memorable foreign incandescence to room, women, and myself, he smiled with memorable radiance.

A similar shaft of light I see making a pig's ear resemble a red votive lamp. Typical of my work: again I tend to think in opposites – a pedlar, a votive lamp and a pig's ear. Triangular opposites at times!

Back to my mainline theme: death in a small community releases a flood of storytelling. The funeral as a social occasion is a subject rarely explored. The quiet undertones of the conversation at the old-time wakes – its former boisterous nature church-tamed – today mainly concern incidents involved with the life of the deceased. (Benevolent on the funeral day: in the days that follow the stories might turn slightly malignant as the intensity of mourning wanes.)

Depending on the stature of the deceased, the cortege could be immense yet the keen eye of the relatives could at a later date identify those failing to answer the roll call of attendance. The knots of people outside the church (or on Sundays around the door of the funeral parlour) are storytellers to a man.

The women pursue the subject in genteel fashion over tea – or coffee. I recall the incident of the bedridden sister of the deceased who staggered out of bed to watch the funeral pass by. "I'm here," she said, "to take note of them who should attend our funeral but didn't." Like Thoreau in Walden, I note even the minutest movement of animal, insect, or plant life in the microcosm of the small town. (Human is included in "animal"). But all life is transient so that for a time we stage-strut and then are heard no more. I continue to note the attitude of others to final physical disintegration.

The first man I questioned – circuitously it must be said – was a window cleaner friend and a joker. He raised his bare arms aloft and shouted: "Death? The Last Day? Women weep, children scream, dogs bark, the cow jumps over the moon, Goo' night, duckie, the show is over."

The second one was a wit. Impious and original. "We are one-agers and old friends of the long ago," he said. "So we might as well move out together. Put a black crêpe on our doors the same mornin'. Notice in the paper – both of us in the wan insert. Cheaper that way. Take our empty coffins to the church. We'll kneel side by side at the altar, to remind us of the time we were baptised together. We'll go home that night, sleep it out in the morning, put on our good suits and after the Requiem Mass we'll walk up behind the two hearses to the open graves. Let 'em take the lids off the coffins and 'Good luck, ould stock,' I'll say to you.' We'll shake hands and lie down inside, then 'Put on the lids, we're perished with cold.' Last words? 'Scuse me, Father. The rest o' ye can kiss our arses. Screw down the lids. Fill in the feckin' graves. Thump, thump, thump."

I'm not taken in by this witty and impious outburst. The man was most devotional. In its essence, it's whistling as one passes the graveyard.

The reality of death and the prelude to death present a grimmer visage. I hate to think of the withering away process, the losing control of one's bodily functions, being diurnally cleansed as when one comes into the world by wise biological women whose middle name is caring and who take everything in their stride. Worst of all are the regrets of a long life, that one didn't read or hear the love signals of this or that young woman, that one failed to answer the challenge implicit in a cryptic letter which perhaps for good or ill would have changed the course of one's life and altered one's life aim. *Tréis a chítear gach beart.* "Every issue is seen in retrospect," as the Irish proverb has it.

The writers who went before me, how have they faced death? Some Irish profligates have composed a poem of contrition: their weak plaint is *Tá an bás agam* – I have death in my bones. This was certainly the hymn of old Carolan, the harper and songmaker staggering in the doorway of the noble house of his patron McDermott, a place where he would be granted the grace of dying with dignity and buried with honour. "John Anderson my Jo" is there, and look – there is FR Higgins in the candlelit wake room of Storyman and rambler Pádraic Ó Conaire – Higgins is composing a poem – I see his lips moving and rounding the phrases.

Through a crash of waves against a great cliff side I hear the murmuring voice of Peig Sayers of the Great Blasket Island. She is dictating her story to her poet son, Mícheál.

"I'm an old woman now with one foot in the grave and the other on its edge . . . an old grey woman with hardly a tooth in my head. I did my best to give an accurate account of the people I knew so that we'd be remembered when we moved on into eternity. People will yet . . . walk into the graveyard where I'll be lying, but people like us will never again be there. We'll be stretched out quietly and the old world will have vanished."

I recall Hyde's translation of a quatrain from the Irish,

Though riders be thrown in black disgrace
Yet I mount for the race of my life with pride
May I keep to the track, may I not fall back
And judge me, O Christ, as I ride my ride.

Still relying on our own poets I recall that Dáithi Ó Bruadair, as indicated in a poem translated by James Stephens, was bitter as he stared death in the face. The Battle of Kinsale and the Fall of Limerick meant the end of the Gaelic World with its patronage of poetry, music and stories. The new planter *bodachs* who succeeded them were unimpressed by the finer arts. As death drew near Dáithi chants:

I will sing no more songs, the pride of my country, I sang
Through forty long years of good rhyme without any avail
And no one cared even as much as the half of a hang
For the song or the singer so here is an end to the tale.

Invoking the Trinity, the poet then makes the secret Sign of the Cross,

I ask of the Craftsman who fashioned the fly and the bird
Of the Champion whose passion shall lift me from death
in a time,
Of the Spirit who melts icy hearts with the wind of a word
That my people be worthy and get better singing than
mine.

Now I hear the voice of Pearse in my turning of his poem into English.

I await your coming
Old Bellman of Death
O friend of all friends
Who'll stifle my breath.

O hand in the darkness
O light Footfall
O Syllable on the wind
I await your call.

Without let or hindrance references come pelting at me from all points of the compass. Again, I hear old Horace with his war cry of *Non omnis moriar.* I hear Heraclitus and Aodhagán Ó Rathaile. Frank

O'Connor is there with his story of the lone woman living in the city of Cork who pays a jarvey in advance to take her dead body west by the long road to a little place called Umerra. There the man with the coffin on his vehicle is to stand up and cry out, "Here she is, neighbours. Batty Heigue's daughter returned to ye in the heel of all." And there's Maura's farewell to the body of her drowned son in Synge's most memorable one act play, *Riders to the Sea.* "No man at all can be livin' forever. And we must be satisfied." Her voice too is ringing in my ears. Here also are four lines that seem to be forever jingling in my mind;

I strove with none, for none was worth my strife.
Nature I loved and next to Nature, Art.
I warmed both hands before the fire of life
It sinks and I am ready to depart.

God forgive me! When delivering a graveside oration of my good friend Séamus Wilmot, I made a joke which concerned Séamus. On the occasion of the opening of the New Abbey Theatre, Dev as President of Ireland attended the opening function. Séamus, an Abbey director, was also a Registrar of the National University and closely associated with Dev who was its Chancellor. "The President," Séamus said in his speech, "had a short but brilliant career as an actor in this theatre. He came on in a small part, crossed the stage from here to there and then, great is the pity, appeared no more." He then paused and said, "Sic transit gloria Ed-mundi." My retelling of this story brought a laughing reaction from the mourners at the funeral. A tape of the incident is extant – it rather took me by an uneasy surprise to hear it at a later date.

But for me, by far the most compelling memory of an attitude to death is that of an old man I visited over seventy years ago in the Kilmoyley-O'Dorney area of North Kerry. He was one of the last who, I heard, had knowledge of a Gaelic poet called Jack Bréanain who is reputed to have made the original poem squib on "The Flea", which I have already mentioned.

As I moved through that fertile countryside, seeking information, I was directed to a dilapidated thatched cottage at the end of a rough boreen. "Hurry, if it's information you want," I was told, "the old man is in very bad shape."

A smoky smelly interior. A post holding up the sagging roof. With daylight oozing weakly through a small grimy window, I made out an old bed in the corner. On it lay a figure covered with a tattered patchwork quilt, its face turned to the wall. I discerned the shaggy grey poll of an old man and heard his laboured breathing.

"Excuse me", I ventured. There was no response from the recumbent figure. After a pause I touched his shoulder lightly and repeated my "Excuse me".

At long last the prone figure stirred, the bed covering heaved, the full body ponderously turned. Two glaring red-rimmed eyes confronted me. Most lamely I began, "Can you tell me something about Jack Bréanain, the Gaelic poet?"

The old man seemed to gather himself. One powerful hand, brown as a bear paw stole up from under the bedclothes and moved slowly across his face. The man growled and with an effort cleared his throat. "Isn't it late you've come," he said hoarsely, "askin' a man who'll be dead tomorrow?" The remark staggered me. Before I knew what I was saying my question was out. "Are you afraid of dying?" This was answered by a growl. The eyes glared at me. "I'm not," he said, each word a mighty effort. "The Almighty God put a blanket around me comin' into the world and I don't remember bein' born." After a pause, "He'll put another blanket around me again goin' out, an' I won't remember dyin' but as little." A pause. The breathing. Then as if to himself, he muttered "Comin' or goin'? One is as natural as the other."

I said no more. As quietly as I could I withdrew.

I enquired later. Yes, the old philosopher had died on the morrow.

Interesting and comforting, that's how I also found AE's poem on the same subject. AE (George Russell) was a mystic: I found his attitude quite stimulating since it carries with it a note of gentle defiance of the vastness of eternity. But I'm not sure, to say the least of it, if I could guarantee to follow his bravery or bravado all the way home. There are too many future imponderables implicit in his title.

WHEN

When mine hour is come
Let no teardrop fall
And no darkness hover
Round me where I lie
Let the vastness call
One who was its lover
Let me breathe the sky.

Where the lordly light
Walks along the world
And its silent tread
Leaves the grasses bright
Leaves the flowers uncurled
Let me to the dead
Breathe a gay goodnight.

This is as far as I choose to go. Or indeed, feel able to go. At this point the Storyman asks himself two vital questions: "What was the aim of your writing life?" And, "Have you achieved that aim?" Diffidently yet presumptuously I answer as follows:

"I set out in my own surroundings from among my own people and with limited resources to identify, isolate, and explore in some kind of literary form what Donn Byrne once called the 'elusive, almost unbearable ache that lies at the heart of humanity.'"

Whether or not I have succeeded is for others to decide.